Praise for *Grave Witch*

"Fascinating magic, a delicious heartthrob, and a fresh, inventive world."   —Chloe Neill, author of *Hard Bitten*

"A rare treat, intriguing and original. Don't miss this one."
    —#1 *New York Times* bestselling author Patricia Briggs

"A zippy pace and entrancing descriptions of 'grave-sight,' which juxtaposes a decaying spirit world on top of ours, will keep readers happily turning pages."   —*Publishers Weekly*

The Alex Craft Novels

Grave Witch
Grave Dance

Grave Dance

AN ALEX CRAFT NOVEL

KALAYNA PRICE

A ROC BOOK

ROC

Published by New American Library, a division of
Penguin Group (USA) Inc., 375 Hudson Street,
New York, New York 10014, USA
Penguin Group (Canada), 90 Eglinton Avenue East, Suite 700, Toronto,
Ontario M4P 2Y3, Canada (a division of Pearson Penguin Canada Inc.)
Penguin Books Ltd., 80 Strand, London WC2R 0RL, England
Penguin Ireland, 25 St. Stephen's Green, Dublin 2,
Ireland (a division of Penguin Books Ltd.)
Penguin Group (Australia), 250 Camberwell Road, Camberwell, Victoria 3124,
Australia (a division of Pearson Australia Group Pty. Ltd.)
Penguin Books India Pvt. Ltd., 11 Community Centre, Panchsheel Park,
New Delhi - 110 017, India
Penguin Group (NZ), 67 Apollo Drive, Rosedale, Auckland 0632,
New Zealand (a division of Pearson New Zealand Ltd.)
Penguin Books (South Africa) (Pty.) Ltd., 24 Sturdee Avenue,
Rosebank, Johannesburg 2196, South Africa

Penguin Books Ltd., Registered Offices:
80 Strand, London WC2R 0RL, England

First published by Roc, an imprint of New American Library,
a division of Penguin Group (USA) Inc.

First printing, July 2011
10 9 8 7 6 5 4 3 2

Copyright © Kalayna Price, 2011
All rights reserved

ROC REGISTERED TRADEMARK — MARCA REGISTRADA

Printed in the United States of America

To Kist,
who keeps me fed and watered, and who
is always quick with the emotional duct tape
when everything is falling apart

ACKNOWLEDGMENTS

To Jessica Wade, who believes in Alex and my story and who worked with me to make sure that story was told. There are not thanks enough for everything you've done for me through the process of getting this book out on shelves. And to the entire team at Roc, who makes this series possible.

To my fabulous agent, Lucienne Diver, for believing in my voice and getting the books out to the world.

To the Tri Mu: Christy, Nikki, Sarah, Vert, and Vikki, and to George for your encouragement and honest critiques.

To all the speakers and instructors at the Writer's Police Academy. I took great liberties with what you taught me, but you gave me a solid base from which to spring.

To my friends and family, who encourage and support me, and to the artists, authors, and musicians who inspire me.

And to the readers. This story is for you, and I hope you enjoy Alex's continuing adventure.

Thank you all. You all mean more to me than I can say.

Chapter 1

When I first straddled the chasm between the land of the dead and the world of the living, I accidentally raised the shade of our recently deceased Pekinese. The former champion dog floating around our backyard resulted in my father shipping me off to a wyrd boarding school. Seventeen years later, I still reached across that chasm, but now I got paid to do it.

"That isn't a body, John," I said, staring at the open black bag. "It's a foot." A pale, bloated, waterlogged foot.

John Matthews, personal friend and one of the best homicide detectives in Nekros City, nodded. "It's a left foot, to be precise, and I have two more back at the morgue. What can you tell me?"

I frowned and nudged the toe of my boot at a clump of grass sprouting between chunks of loose gravel. My business cards read: ALEX CRAFT, LEAD PRIVATE INVESTIGATOR AND GRAVE WITCH FOR TONGUES FOR THE DEAD. I was actually the owner and only employee of the firm, but that was beside the point. I raised shades and gave the living a chance to question the dead—for a fee. My work tended to take me to a lot of graveyards, the occasional funeral home, and to the Nekros City morgue. The parking pit for the Sionan Floodplain Nature Preserve was most definitely *not* my typical working environment. Nor was a single severed appendage my typical job.

"Sorry, John, but I need more than a foot to raise a shade."

"And I need some better news." His shoulders slumped as if he'd deflated. "We've been scouring this swamp for two days and we're turning up more questions than answers. We've got no IDs for the vics, no obvious causes of death, and no primary crime scenes. You sure you can't give me anything?" As he spoke, he shoved the flap on the body bag farther open with the butt of his pen.

The foot lay in a sea of black plastic. The sickly scent of rot filled the humid afternoon air, coating the inside of my nose, my throat. The bloodless skin had sloughed off the exposed ankle, the strips of yellowish flesh shriveling. My stomach twisted and I looked away. I'd leave the physical inspection to the medical examiner—my affinity for the dead was less for the tangible and more for the spectral. Memories hid in every cell of the body. Memories that my grave magic could unlock and give shape as a shade. Of course, that depended on having enough of the body—and thus cells—at my disposal for my magic to fill in the gaps. I didn't need to cast a magic circle and begin a ritual to know I couldn't pull a shade from the foot. I could sense that fact, the same way I could sense that the foot had belonged to a male, probably in his late sixties. I could also sense the nasty tangle of spells all but dripping from the decaying appendage.

"The foot is saturated with magic. Some pretty dark stuff from the feel of it," I said, taking a step back from the gurney and the sticky residual magic emanating from the foot. "I'm guessing you already have a team deciphering the spells?"

"Yeah, but so far the anti–black magic unit hasn't reached any conclusions. It would really help if we could question the victim."

But that wasn't going to happen with such a small percentage of the body. "You said you had a matching foot back at the morgue? Maybe if we assemble all the parts, there will be enough to—"

John shook his head. "Dancing jokes aside, unless this guy had two left feet—literally—neither of the other feet belong to him."

Three left feet? That meant at least three victims. "You're thinking serial?"

"Don't say that too loud," John said, his gaze flashing to a passing pair of crime scene technicians headed toward the dense old-growth forest. "No official determination yet, but, yeah, I'm thinking serial." His grizzly bear–sized form sagged further and his mustache twitched as he frowned. The mustache had been a thick red accent to his expressions as long as I'd known him, but in the weeks since he'd woken from a spell-induced coma, slivers of gray had joined the red. He pushed the flap of the body bag closed. "Park rangers found the first foot yesterday morning when they were checking the paths after the recent flooding. We got wardens and cadaver dogs out here, and the second foot turned up. When we found the third, I pulled some strings to hire you as a consultant."

"Do you want me to stick around? Wait and see if your guys find more of the body?"

"Actually"—John rubbed a hand over his head, wiping away the sweat glistening on his spreading bald spot—"I was hoping you'd join the search."

I hesitated. I probably even blanched. Wandering around with my shields down sensing every dead creature most definitely was *not* my idea of a good—*or safe*—time.

John didn't miss my pause. "You've located DBs before," he said. DBs as in *dead bodies*. "And the paperwork you signed covered the possibility of searching the swamp, so you'll be paid for your time."

I opened my mouth to respond—while I might have qualms about opening my psyche to whatever might be in the floodplain, we both knew I'd risk it—but I was interrupted before I could answer.

"What's wrong, Craft?" Detective Jenson, John's partner, asked as he stepped around the side of a black SUV. "Don't want to get those tight pants dirty tramping through the swamp? Got another TV appearance to run off to? Or maybe your magic eye license doesn't allow you to do any good old-fashioned legwork."

I glared at him, and I had to unclench my gritted teeth to answer. "Way to be hypocritical, Jenson, insulting me and in the same breath asking me to use magic to help." The term "magic eye" was derogatory slang for a witch PI.

"I'm not asking you for anything." He leaned back on

his heels and crossed his arms over his chest. "And I think this city has seen enough of your magic lately, what with the way they keep rebroadcasting that interview with you getting all touchy-feely with a ghost."

"What's wrong? Jealous?" I asked, cocking a hip and tossing curls out of my face. Okay, so I was goading him, but he was being an ass. A few days ago I'd participated in the first studio interview of a ghost, and to keep said ghost visible I'd had to remain in contact with him, but I'd most certainly not gotten "touchy-feely" or any such crap.

John cleared his throat. "That's enough." He glanced between us, then turned to his partner. "Get Alex some hip waders and let the wardens know we'll be joining them."

Jenson sneered at me—an expression I returned—and said, "Sure. Boots for the two-legged corpse hound. I'll get right on that." He disappeared around the side of the SUV.

I stared at the spot where he'd been standing. "What a jerk." Things hadn't always been so antagonistic between us. In fact, we'd almost been friends. Then a month ago his attitude had gone to shit. The change coincided perfectly with John's taking a spelled bullet aimed at me. Coincidence? *Doubtful.*

"I don't know what's going on between you two," John said, turning back toward me, "but let's not forget we've got three severed feet and no leads. Now, before we go in there, I suggest turning your shirt inside out."

"You what?"

John waved a tech over to take custody of the bagged foot; then he scooped my purse off the ground, where I'd set it earlier. He handed the red bag to me and nodded toward his car.

"The park rangers warned us when we started searching that the local fae delight in leading hikers astray. The unwary can end up wandering through the same patch of land for days. Pixie-led, they call it. Turning your shirt inside out is supposed to confuse their magic."

I glanced down at my tank top, the shirt clinging to me in the afternoon heat. "Are you thinking fae are involved in the murders?"

John's mustache twitched. "That's another thing you shouldn't say too loud."

"Right." I ducked inside John's car to shimmy out of the top. Not that I thought reversing it would really protect me against fae magic. The fae relied mostly on glamour—a belief magic so strong, it could reshape reality, at least temporarily.

By the time I'd re-dressed, Jenson had dropped off a pair of hip waders for me. They were a thick, waterproof one-piece with suspenders and attached boots. I stepped into them, pulling the brown material up over my clothes. They nearly reached my collarbone.

"We aren't seriously planning to wade chest-deep, are we?" I asked as I adjusted the suspender straps.

John, who'd also suited up in a pair of waders, handed me a plastic bottle of water. "Nah. With the speed the water is retreating, we'd be in danger of getting swept away. If you sense the bodies in the deep water, we'll have to send a team out. Ready?"

I nodded and followed him toward the closest path into the floodplain. John collected a couple of officers as we trekked into the forest, and I wasn't the least bit disappointed when Jenson didn't join us. The forest canopy filtered the sun, but the humidity under the trees hung heavy, making the air thick. Sweat coated my skin, and my blond curls clung to my cheeks and neck. I cracked the seal of my water bottle, but took only one long swig—no telling how long we'd be hiking.

"That is where the first foot was found," John said after we'd been walking for half an hour. He nodded ahead of him to where yellow crime tape ringed the path. "The second was found about a quarter mile farther up the path; the third a mile or more to the south. We're not sure yet if the recent flooding unearthed shallow graves or if the bodies were dumped farther upstream and floated into the floodplain, but with the speed the water is retreating, every passing minute increases the chance of our evidence washing away. We need to find those bodies."

And that was my cue.

I unclasped my silver charm bracelet. Among other charms, the bracelet carried the extra shields that helped buffer the excess of grave essence always trying to drag my psyche across the chasm to the land of the dead. Of course, that was the very chasm I now needed to traverse. As soon as the silver charms lost contact with my skin, a frigid wind lifted around me—the chill of the grave clawing at my remaining mental shields. I cracked those shields, imagining the living vines I visualized as my personal mental wall slithering apart, opening small gaps to my psyche.

The world around me lost the rich hues of life as a gray patina covered everything. My vision doubled as I saw both the land of the dead and the land of the living. In my grave-sight, the trees darkened, withering, their thick green leaves turning brown, and the officers' clothing decayed, the cloth becoming threadbare and moth-eaten. Under those mottled rags, their souls shimmered bright yellow. I looked away.

Unfortunately, opening my shields exposed me to more than just the land of the dead. The Aetheric—the plane in which raw magic existed—snapped into focus around me in swirls of brilliant red, vivid blues, and every other color imaginable. The magic twisted, tauntingly close, but I ignored the raw energy. It wasn't supposed to be visible, even with my shields open. Witches didn't physically interact with the Aetheric plane. It wasn't possible. Or at least it shouldn't have been. But I'd been able to see the Aetheric, to *reach* it, ever since the Blood Moon a month ago.

Being able to do something didn't mean I should. Or that it was safe.

I ignored the colors, forcing my eyes to focus on the decaying forest as I reached out with my senses, feeling for the grave essence leaking from the dead. And there was no shortage of dead in the floodplain.

The grave essence from a dead doe reached for me like cold wind trying to cut into my skin. *And to think I was hot a minute ago.* Her remains were no more than fifty yards from where I stood, but I pushed my senses farther, skimming over the traces of small animal bodies and not letting the grave essence sink into my being. I trekked deeper into the floodplain, my magic flowing around me.

The path washed out not far from where the first foot had been found, and the mud made squishing, sucking sounds under my boots until even that gave way to dark water. Foliage, simultaneously healthy and decaying, withered as my gaze moved over it, and I hoped my attention didn't damage the plants. I'd once crumbled a set of stairs when my powers pushed the land of the dead into reality.

"Anything?" John asked, trudging behind me.

Yeah, lots of things. Small animals mostly. Not exactly what we were looking for. I waved him off and kept walking. The water splashed up to the knees of my waterproof suit as I waded through it, my steps slow, both from the water rushing around me and because I was concentrating on feeling the grave essence while holding it at bay so I didn't accidentally raise any shades.

Something . . . I turned in a small circle, reaching with my mind, my power. Yes, there was something. My power told me it was touching a body, a human body. Male. And I felt a female too. And . . . two more males?

"This isn't good."

John stopped beside me. "You found something?"

"Bodies. And I hope I'm wrong, but I'm sensing four different essence signatures."

"A fourth victim?"

I wasn't sure, so I didn't answer. I wished I could close my eyes and concentrate just on the feel of the bodies, to get a better sense of where they were located, but it was hard enough to navigate the flooded forest with my eyes open. I waded farther in, the water lapping up to my midthighs. I slipped once, and only John's quick reflexes kept me from landing on my ass in the murky water.

"We might be getting too deep," John said as one of the officers, the shortest in our group, lost his footing and slipped forward in the current. He dug in his toes and righted himself a moment later.

I shook my head at John. "We're almost there." I could feel the bodies just ahead.

The rushing water broke around a fallen tree a couple of yards in front of us. The ancient hardwood's giant roots stretched out in every direction, dirt still covering them, so the root-ball formed a massive mound. The tree hadn't fallen in this particular flood—moss covered the mound and saplings clung to the root-packed earth. The grave essence emanated from somewhere around that tree, and not only grave essence but a dark knot of magic.

I stepped closer, searching with both my power and my eyes. Then I saw them.

"Feet."

"Where?" John asked, looking around.

I pointed. In a hollow near the base of the tree was a neatly stacked pile of bloated and decomposing feet. John's bushy eyebrows drew together, his mustache twitching downward as he frowned. He mopped sweat off his forehead before tilting his head to the side and giving me a confused look.

He doesn't see them? I pointed again, but I wasn't wearing gloves, so I didn't want to contaminate the scene. Trying to figure out the differences between what I could see and what he could see was impossible while staring over multiple planes of reality, so I closed my mental shields, blocking my psyche from the land of the dead—and whatever other planes it touched. My grave-sight faded. The gray coating of the world washed away, as did the swirls of the Aetheric. And so did the feet.

I blinked as I clasped my shield bracelet back around my wrist. Releasing my grave-sight made dark shadows crawl over my vision—I couldn't peer across planes without paying a price—but when I squinted I could make out the hollow where I'd seen the feet. An empty hollow. Or, at least, it *looked* empty, but I could still feel the grave essence and the taint of magic lifting off the dead appendages. The essence raked at my shields like icy claws, trying to sink under my skin, into my mind. I shivered. The feet were definitely there.

"John, we have a problem," I said, leaning back and trying to shove my hands in my jean pockets—which were blocked by the rubber hip waders. I dropped my hands by my side as everyone looked at me. "There's a pyramid of feet stacked in that hollow. I counted four and at a guess, they are all lefts."

One of the uniformed officers stepped forward. He lifted a long sticklike object with a glass bead on the end. *Spellchecker wand.* He waved the wand over the hollow. The bead flashed a deep crimson to indicate malicious magic, but the glow was dim, the magic only traces of residual spells.

Stepping back, the officer shook his head. "No active spells, sir."

I stared at the empty-looking hollow. "If they're not hidden behind a spell, it has to be glamour."

"Crap," John said, and turned toward the cop beside him. "Someone get the FIB on the phone. We've got a situation."

The FIB, as in the Fae Investigation Bureau. Glamour was exclusively fae magic, which meant John had just lost jurisdiction.

I slouched in the front of John's police cruiser, one foot on the dash, one hanging out the open door. I'd rather have been out of the car—or more accurately, out of the floodplain. The FIB had arrived and ruffled the cops' feathers. In turn, the cops dashed around, trying to look busy. I was just trying to stay out of the way. But being in the car made me claustrophobic. Actually, if I was honest with myself, it was more than that. Ever since the Blood Moon, being locked inside a car made me jumpy and made my skin itch. I had a sinking suspicion the sensation had something to do with the iron content in the metal. *No wonder Falin drove that hot plastic convertible.*

The thought of Falin Andrews made my gaze twitch toward the rearview mirror and the two FIB agents reflected in it. I'd met Falin a month ago when he'd been working undercover as a homicide detective on the Coleman case. In truth he was a FIB agent—and a fae—and during the course of the case he'd ended up under my covers as well. But I hadn't heard from him in several weeks. As the two FIB agents approached, I could see there was no shock of long blond hair or a towering swimmer's build among the agents who'd responded to John's call. I wasn't sure yet if I was grateful or disappointed.

"Miss Craft?" A woman in a tailored black power suit approached the car.

Here we go. I nodded, jerking my foot from the dash as I stood.

"I'm Special Agent Nori." She didn't extend her hand. "You were the one who found the remains in the hollow?"

Again I nodded, sliding my hands into my back pockets. It had been nearly an hour since I'd released my grave-sight, and my vision was returning to normal, but I still squinted as I studied Agent Nori. She was a couple of inches shorter than me in her fat-heeled pumps, but she stood completely straight, making the most of her height. She wore her dark hair slicked back like shiny black armor and her piercing eyes were set close enough that her sharp features seemed to come to a point in the front of her face. Or at least, that's what she looked like currently. Being an FIB agent meant she was probably, but not necessarily, fae. What she might look like under her glamour was anyone's guess. I could have dropped my shields and found out, but one, it would have been rude, and two, and perhaps more important, my eyes glowed when my psyche peered across planes, so she would have been able to tell. I wanted to get out of here without any trouble.

"Can you tell me how you were able to pierce the glamour?" she asked, which was exactly the question I'd feared. Luckily I hadn't been waiting idly. I'd been planning my answer.

"I was helping the police search for the remains of the . . . remains, by using my grave magic. The glamour didn't hide the grave essence emanating from the feet." I left out that I'd been able to see them. Fae didn't tend to like it when people could see through glamour. You could lose your eyes for less.

She pressed her lips together and jotted something on her notepad. "So you followed this . . . essence? Then what?"

"I tracked where the grave essence originated. I could feel that the body parts were there. That no one else was able to see the feet was a good hint we might be dealing with glamour." All true—just not all of the truth.

Agent Nori clicked her pen closed. "Miss Craft, when you realized glamour was involved, you didn't for a moment think it might have been more prudent to inform the FIB rather than let the mortals blunder around the scene?"

I bristled at the insult toward John and his team. I had a lot of friends in the Nekros City Police Department. Placing a hand on my hip, I lifted one shoulder in a shrug. "They hired me."

"Yes, well, I'm sure they appreciate your help, Miss Craft. Your services will no longer be needed." She turned, gravel crunching under her pumps as she walked away. A few feet past the car, she glanced back over her shoulder. "You realize, of course, that this means we'll have to look into the independent fae in the area." The smile that spread across her face made her brilliantly red lips stretch to flash a lot of white teeth, but it wasn't a happy smile.

I didn't balk. I'd recently learned I was feykin, but she couldn't know that. *Could she?* Plastering on my own smile, I said, "I guess so."

She left the small gravel parking lot, no doubt headed back to the place where I'd found the pyramid of feet. As I turned to slide into the car again, movement at the tree line caught my eye. While my eyesight had recovered significantly, I'd been in touch with the land of the dead and the grave quite a bit, so at first all I could see was a moving man-shaped mesh of colors. But as the figure drew closer, I quickly realized that while *male* was the right gender, he wasn't hu*man*, but fae.

He hunched, his stringy legs never fully straightening as he slunk closer. Even bent, he stood a head taller than me—and I'm not short. He had the same features as a human, but they were all slightly off. His wide eyes were dark, and overly recessed in his skull, but not from illness. His pale skin was the color of a worm's belly, as if he had never been exposed to daylight, and his hawkish nose extended nearly a hand's width from his face, almost hiding the thin lips and pointed chin.

Even now, seventy years after the Magical Awakening, it was rare to see an unglamoured fae. The fae had come out of the mushroom ring, as some put it, because they were fading from memory and thus the world. They needed human belief to anchor them to reality, but aside from the fae celebrities and politicians, a human was likely to see an unglamoured fae only in a venue that profited from showcasing the fae's differences. Most of those places were little better than tourist traps.

I glanced behind me. Across the parking pit, two officers huddled around the van that had been established as a temporary headquarters for the investigation. *Well, at least I'm not completely alone.* Of course, just because the strange fae looked creepy and was near the place where we'd found feet masked in glamour, that didn't make him guilty. It did make him a suspect, though. Or possibly a witness.

"Can I help you?" I yelled the question louder than needed, but I wanted to ensure that the officers also heard me. They would want to question the fae.

He paused, then hurried forward in a blur of movement. He crossed from the far edge of the parking lot to the front of John's car before my heart had time to crash in a loud, panicked beat. The cops yelled something I didn't catch above the blood rushing in my ears.

"Can I help you?" I asked again, not daring to look away from someone who could move as fast as this fae. I slid back a step, and then another, the movement far too slow.

"Are you daft?" he asked, his thin lips splitting with the words to reveal pointed teeth.

I blinked at him, startled, but not because of the implied insult in his words, or because of the threat in his expression. No, my shock came at the sound of his voice. The voice that emerged from that thin, awkwardly threatening body was a rich, deep baritone that made even such an angry question sound musical. He had the kind of voice that, in the old folktales, would have drawn children and young women from their beds. Unfortunately, most of those stories didn't end well.

"I don't know what you mean," I said, taking another step back. Across the parking pit, gravel crunched under the cops' running steps. Close. Maybe not close enough.

"Those feet were hidden for a reason." The fae's gaze moved over my head, and his eyes narrowed. "This is your fault, and you will regret your actions," he said. Then, as the cops neared us, he turned, dashed back to the tree line, and disappeared.

Chapter 2

"So, the cops couldn't find him?" Holly, my housemate and best friend, asked as her fork slid smoothly through the slice of triple-chocolate cheesecake sitting in the center of the table.

I nodded. "He issued his threat that I would regret leading the police to the feet, and then he ran. Once he reached the tree line, he might as well have been gone." I'd been jumpy for hours after leaving the floodplain, but today, in the afternoon sun, my tension seemed foolish. "The only thing I regret at the moment is that the FIB took over the case."

Holly shot a conspiratorial glance at the third person at the table, my other best friend, Tamara, and then leaned forward. "Did you-know-who show?"

I frowned at my fork. "You-know-who" would be Falin, the only FIB agent the three of us knew on a first-name basis. Well, actually, I knew him *a lot* better than just that. Even so, two days after we'd closed the Coleman case, he'd taken off without so much as a good-bye.

I stabbed the cheesecake with a little more force than the smooth texture required. "He's probably working some far more important case," I said, then swallowed the bite of cheesecake without tasting it. "Good riddance. He'd complicate things."

Holly pulled the cheesecake away from me. "Okay, so I

know we have to eat this before it melts—whose idea was it to meet for lunch at an outdoor café anyway?—but don't scarf it. These kinds of calories have to be savored."

Tamara murmured in agreement and brandished her fork. "Oh, I'm in calorie bliss over here," she said. "And today was Alex's location choice."

I shrugged. "I raised a shade to settle an insurance claim this morning. The family refused to believe their father had left a chunk of his estate to an illegitimate son's widow, so I spent over two hours graveside while the shade verified the will line by line. I was cold. Besides, it's not half as hot as it was a couple of weeks ago. The mid-nineties are practically a blessing in August."

"Uh-uh," Holly said, and made a production of sipping her iced latte. But though we were at an outdoor café, it was a café in the middle of the Magic Quarter—Nekros City's center for all things magical and witchy. This café boasted the very best charms available for keeping customers cool and comfortable regardless of the temperature. And despite her protests, Holly wasn't so much as breaking a sweat in her crisp courtroom-ready suit. "So, was there anyone else *interesting*?" she asked, wiggling her eyebrows suggestively.

"Hardly." I had to reach across the table to get to the cheesecake, but that didn't stop me.

"Oh, come on." Holly pushed the plate forward. "It's been a month since I've seen you pick up a guy. You've always accused me of being a workaholic, but ever since your business picked up, all you do is raise the dead." She set down her latte, pulled out her hair clip, and shook her red locks free. Then she smoothed her hair back again and twisted it effortlessly into a slick bun. She looked every inch the hotshot public prosecutor she was—less obvious was the fact that she was a witch in her own right. "I have court again this afternoon, but after that my caseload will be lighter. Let's go barhopping tonight. You need to get out."

I made a noncommittal noise and focused on my once again empty fork.

"She is out," Tamara said, though I had the feeling her coming to my defense had more to do with her new disapproval of barhopping—a stance she'd taken about the same time the large diamond engagement ring had appeared on her finger—than with my current social habits.

Holly wasn't exactly wrong. Business was good. Really good. In fact, it was better than it had ever been. But business wasn't why I'd stopped barhopping. For years I'd chased away the chill that clung to me after raising shades with a stiff drink and a warm body—preferably a guy I'd never see again after our encounter. That prospect didn't appeal to me anymore. Besides, somewhere between temporarily swapping life forces with a soul collector and discovering I was part fae a month ago, my body temperature had changed, and now most people felt blisteringly hot to the touch. There was a short list of guys who could touch me without causing us both discomfort. Actually it was a very short list. As in a list of two. That I knew of, at least. One guy had disappeared and the other ... Well, that situation was complicated. It was time to change the subject.

I turned to Tamara, who, as well as being my friend, was the chief medical examiner for Nekros City. "So did the FIB take everything out of house?"

"Not yet. So far everyone is 'cooperating.' We'll see how long that lasts. Honestly, though, I'm out of my league. I have seven left feet in the freezer, and I have no idea how they were severed from the legs. There are no tool marks, so I'm inclined to believe the dismemberment is connected to the snarl of magic clinging to the feet, but I've had no luck discerning any individual spells." She shook her head, her lips thinning as her eyes moved past us. She was one of the foremost sensitives in the state. If neither she nor the anti–black magic unit was having any success, the spells must have been rare and powerful. She shook her head again. "Maybe I'm losing my edge. I also have three bodies on the slab with no clear cause of death. All the evidence points to their hearts simply ceasing to beat, but why? I still don't know. I need to run some more tests." Her gaze fixed on the cheesecake. "I paid for a third of that slice. I expect to eat my third, so don't you hoard it."

"Take it, girlfriend," Holly said, pushing the plate across the table. "Sounds like you two need it more than me. All the cases I'm working for the DA are pretty dull."

She updated us on the case she'd be trying in court this afternoon. As she spoke, a shadow caught my eye. We were in the outdoor seating area of a café on a busy corner in the Magic Quarter, so one more passing person shouldn't have snagged my attention. Of course, this wasn't just any random stranger.

"That's him," I hissed.

Holly fell silent and Tamara twisted in her chair. "Who? Where?"

"The fae from the floodplain. He's over by the magazine rack." I pointed at the newsstand across the street. The fae, with his strange slumped stance and hawkish nose, held a copy of what looked suspiciously like *Fae Weekly*—a gossip rag—but his attention wasn't on candid pictures or exaggerated articles. His gaze locked with mine, and I swallowed hard.

"The police issued a BOLO, be on the lookout, on him, right? As a person of interest in the case? I'm calling the station." Holly pulled her phone from her clutch, but before she flipped it open, a scream rang out down the street.

For one stalled moment, the café went quiet as all conversation stopped and the patrons turned to look. My gaze tore free of the fae and I whirled around. A block up the street, cars slammed on brakes, horns blaring, and pedestrians ran inside buildings. Tamara jumped to her feet, Holly right behind her.

I glanced back to where the fae had stood, but he'd vanished. Of course, that didn't mean he was gone. *What is going on?*

A car swerved, wheels screeching as it braked, and my attention snapped back to the commotion in the street. More screams sounded as people ran, and the air tingled with dozens of charms being activated at once. Then the cause of the panic became sickeningly apparent.

A hulking form lunged onto the hood of a car, which buckled under the beast's weight. I stared, rooted to the spot. I'd never seen anything like it. I would have said the creature was a wolf, except it was the size of a grizzly bear and covered in shaggy moss green fur. *A fae beast.* It tipped its head back, its nose working the air. Then its red-tinted gaze swung toward the café. Metal bunched under its claws as it hurled itself off the car.

Oh, crap. "Let's get out of here," I said, snagging my purse.

"Two steps ahead of you," Tamara said, already breaking into a run. The air around her tingled as she activated a charm.

Between one step and the next she vanished behind the invisibility charm. I only wished I had one as well, but the best thing I had was my ability to run. So I did. Fast.

I'd just reached the door of the potion shop next to the café when the air around me chilled. Death appeared in front of me, his tight black T-shirt pulling taut over his muscles as he stepped forward into my path.

Soul collector, Grim Reaper, Angel of Death—whatever you called him, his job was to gather the souls of the dead and dying. Which meant, unless he'd picked a damn funny time for a social call, someone was about to breathe their last.

Who? I mouthed, not wanting to be seen talking to someone no one else could see. Not that anyone on the street was likely to notice amid the panic.

Death looked away, his heavy lids drooping to mask his deep hazel eyes. I turned, looking back at the street. Holly hadn't run, hadn't moved.

We were in the center of the Magic Quarter, so magic abounded. Almost everyone—witch, fae, and norm alike—was getting the hell off the street, but a handful of witches had hung back, magic snapping and crackling around them. Holly also held her ground. She stood facing the street. I could see only her profile, but her eyes were closed, her fingers twitching.

She's crafting a spell.

A web of magic catapulted across the street from one of the pedestrians. It snarled around the beast, but with a shake, the creature shrugged off the spell and kept running. It was headed straight for the café. And Holly.

I turned back to Death. "Not her," I whispered.

He didn't look at me.

No! I dashed back through the tables, tripping over toppled chairs in my haste. I reached Holly just as her eyes popped open. She lifted her hands and a ball of fire burst into existence, building between her palms. The rubies she wore on her fingers—gems where she stored raw magic—glittered in the flames, and the ball of fire burst forward.

The fireball exploded against the beast's chest, the back-lash of heat slamming into us. But the beast didn't stop. It didn't even pause. Holly's eyes went wide as she backped-aled. The cool and collected assistant DA was gone. The confident witch? Gone. All that remained was a mortal staring at her doom.

And behind her, Death, his expression grim.

Holly's legs tangled in a chair, and I grabbed her arm, trying to keep her standing, to get her moving. Too late.

The beast's red eyes locked on us, and it tipped its head back, releasing a bloodcurdling howl. It was the first sound it had made, and all other sound fell away under that howl. Then the beast was suddenly there, filling the sidewalk. Its breath, thick with the smell of rotted meat, tumbled over us. Holly could hurl fireballs, but I had no offensive magic. Hell, I could barely cast a circle. Grave magic wasn't ex-actly effective on things not already dead. But it was all I had, so I reached for it.

I dropped my mental shields so fast that pain stabbed through my head. The street washed out into shades of gray, the concrete crumbling in my sight, and the chairs rusting as the land of the dead snapped into focus. Brilliant wisps of raw magic swirled through the air. The ground throbbed with the signatures and emotions absorbed from those who'd crossed it.

And the beast disappeared.

It simply vanished. A faint shimmering outline re-mained, but nothing substantial. In the very center of the strange shape hung a clump of glowing magic.

Beside me, Holly screamed and slammed backward into the concrete. The front of her blouse ripped open, rent by unseen claws.

Glamour.

The beast was a glamour surrounding a magical construct. "Holly, it's not real!"

She screamed, thrashing under something I could barely see. Around me, the Aetheric thrummed, the swirls of raw magic scattering as someone threw a spell at the beast. The spell hit the construct and then dissolved into the space that the beast only appeared to occupy.

"It's a glamour!" I yelled as a ring of bloody bites sprouted on Holly's shoulder.

Holly's back arched, her arms thrashing at her sides. I reached for her, and the beast's head snapped up. Unreal eyes focused on me, narrowed. Then it lunged.

I jumped sideways, out of its path. Its flank slammed into my side as it turned, and I stumbled. The thing might look insubstantial, but it had some mass behind it. *Dammit.* No, it didn't.

Glamour was an illusion magic so strong that reality believed it to be true—at least for a while. If you knew something was glamour, and your will was strong enough, you could disbelieve it out of existence.

But it's hard to disbelieve in an animal actively trying to rip your throat out.

The beast's gaze locked on me, and again it howled. The sound made me flinch. The urge to hit the ground and cover my ears gripped me, but I couldn't. Holly's too-still form lay between the beast and me, far too close to its massive claws. I'd seen what those claws could do to a car. I didn't want to know what they'd do to a woman. I had to draw it farther from her.

Death stepped closer to Holly, momentarily attracting my attention as he crouched beside her. *No, she can't be . . .*

I shook my head, and the beast must have sensed my distraction. Its back legs bunched, preparing to attack. And Holly would be caught in its charge.

No! I didn't believe in the beast. In fact, I *knew* it didn't exist, and reality had bent to my will before.

I dove forward, into its attack. I plunged my hands into the misty form just as one of its huge paws landed on Holly's chest.

"What I see is true," I whispered, willing with everything in me for reality to agree. To confirm that there was no beast.

Holly screamed, and the street hung on her high-pitched note. Then the beast dissolved.

A cloud of pale mist exploded around me, and a small disk fell from where the clump of magic in the beast's center had been. It hit the sidewalk with a *ping*, a sound

quickly overwhelmed by dozens of yelling voices. Shouts
and screams that I'd zoned out when I'd been facing the
construct.

Footsteps rang out over the sidewalk, people heading
toward us from every direction. Doors banged open as
more people poured onto the street. Holly pushed herself
up from the sidewalk, her hand gripping her savaged
shoulder.

"Alex? Oh, my God. It's just gone? Alex, how did
you . . . ?" She threw her arms around me, dragging me
down. "Thank you," she whispered. Her cheek was wet
where it brushed my neck.

I stiffened under her touch, her skin hot enough that I
winced, but I didn't pull back. "It wasn't real."

Someone in faded jeans, the knees slightly worn, stepped
nearer, and Death knelt behind Holly. I stared at him over
the top of her head.

"It's going to be okay," I whispered, the words as much
to comfort her as to question Death.

He held my gaze, and then nodded, his dark hair brushing his chin with the movement. "She'll be fine," he said, but
he frowned.

He stared at the thin cloud of mist hanging in the air
around us. If the cloud had been natural water vapor, the
midday sun would have evaporated it in minutes, but this
mist hadn't dissipated. It hadn't even thinned after I'd first
disbelieved the beast.

Death reached out and twisted his hand as if he could
wrap the mist around his fist. Then he gave a small jerk. The
cloud vanished.

I gaped. The thing about soul collectors was that they
collected *souls*. But how could a glamour construct have a
soul? *Was that thing alive?*

I couldn't ask. Not here. Not with people crowded
around us. No one else could see Death.

Death brushed an escaped curl back behind my ear. "Be
careful, Alex," he said. Then he vanished as the first Good
Samaritan reached us.

"Is she all right?" a man asked and someone else yelled,
"What *was* that thing?"

An overweight witch in a hat wider than her shoulders

lowered her heft to the pavement beside me. "I'm a certified healer," she said, reaching out to take Holly's shoulders. "Let me see her."

I let her strip Holly's arms off me, and as I felt the tingle of a healing charm being invoked, I slammed my shields back in place. My vision didn't immediately revert to normal, and I squinted in the bright midday light, which I now perceived as dim and full of shadows. In the dimness, I searched out my purse. I'd dropped it—I didn't remember when. Sometime between Holly's fireball and my disbelieving the construct.

I finally spotted the red bag a couple of feet away. As I stooped to grab it, I noticed a small copper disk. *The charm from the beast.* I pulled a tissue from my purse, and, as inconspicuously as possible, plucked the disk from the sidewalk. Through the thin paper, the spells charged in the disk hummed faintly, but whatever they had been, they were defunct now. The sound of sirens rang in the distance, and I backed away, carrying the disk with me.

Tamara pushed her way through the crowd. She leaned over Holly for several minutes before straightening and glancing around. Her gaze landed on me, and she made her way over to me.

"You okay, Alex?"

I nodded, rubbing my hands over my chilled arms. "She's okay, right?"

Tamara might not have been a healer or a practicing doctor, but as a medical examiner, she knew injuries and she was definitely familiar with fatal wounds.

"She's in shock, but her injuries aren't serious. What the heck were you two doing? Why didn't you get off the street?"

I didn't answer. Both Tamara and Holly knew I was on close personal terms with a soul collector, but I wasn't about to tell Tamara that Death had been here. When I blinked at her without answering, Tamara shook her head.

"You want to tell me what happened?" she asked, sounding more like a cop than an ME—if you hang around enough cops, it rubs off.

"The beast was a glamour. I disbelieved it." Or at least, it was partially glamour. The magic in the disk felt familiar and definitely witchy, not fae. And then there was that mist that Death vanished. *What was that creature?* Had that strange fae sent it? He'd warned me that I would regret revealing the feet.

"Yeah, you disbelieved a glamour out of existence. Everyone on this street will probably relate the same thing. But how do you explain *that*?" Tamara pointed to where Holly and I had faced the beast.

Two feet above the sidewalk was a fist-sized patch of darker air. Swirling colors escaped the dark patch, reaching out of it in amorphic tendrils.

The Aetheric.

I'd merged realities.

I shot Tamara a panicked glance. I couldn't close the rift—I didn't know how. *We could cover it . . .* Maybe if we moved a table over it, no one would notice.

Yeah, like a direct hole into the Aetheric wouldn't be noticed on a street full of witches.

People were already looking up, their attention leaving Holly. Several crept forward, reaching for the escaping tendrils of raw magic, their expressions a mix of suspicion and amazement. A tangle of green energy wrapped around a male witch's extended finger, and he gasped. Then, his eyes full of wonder, he looked up, his gaze falling on me.

Crap. I couldn't explain the tear. I looked away, not even willing to try.

Tamara glanced down at the charm wrapped in tissue on my palm. "What's that?"

"It fell out of the beast when it vanished." I held it out for her inspection.

The front of the copper disk was engraved with runes. A couple of them looked familiar from a class I'd taken back in academy, but I was pretty sure they were the archaic forms. Several of the runes I'd never seen before, but despite the fact that the beast had been mostly glamour, the runes didn't look like the twisting, hard-to-focus-on fae glyphs I'd run into a month ago. Crimson wax sealed the back of the disk.

I was a sensitive, and a damn fair one. I could sense magic, could often tell the purpose and sometimes even recognize the caster. But the spells on the disk were beyond my abilities. Luckily, Tamara was an even more skilled sensitive—at least when it came to witch magic.

She studied the disk, biting her lip as she turned it over with the tissue. Leaning forward, she peered into the thick wax.

"This magic . . . There are spells twisted on top of spells," she whispered. "I can't decipher a thing in this mess, but the signature of the magic . . . it's familiar." She looked up. "Alex, whoever charmed this disk—I think they're also responsible for the spells on the feet."

Chapter 3

The panic caused by the construct's attack paled in comparison to the utter chaos that overtook the street once the officials arrived. Every law enforcement entity in the city wanted to claim jurisdiction. The FIB showed because the glamour implicated the fae, the NCPD came because it was an attack on citizens on a city street, the MCIB—Magical Crimes Investigation Bureau—arrived because of the nature of the crime, and the OMIH—Organization for Magically Inclined Humans—came because witches were involved. Even a representative from the AFHR—Ambassador of Fae and Human Relations—made an appearance.

With no one clearly in charge, I decided to side with the people who tended to bat a paycheck my way every now and then: the good old-fashioned police. I turned the charmed disk over to their anti–black magic unit. The ABMU officer dropped it into a magic-dampening evidence bag, and then, after making me repeat what happened on the street twice, turned me loose. I didn't mention Tamara's suspicions that the caster who'd charmed the disk had also been responsible for the feet in the floodplain. The ABMU had the very best forensic spellcrafters in the city; they would unravel the spells on the disk.

"Did you see where it came from?" one woman asked another as I passed beyond the police barricade.

I hoped she was talking about the magical construct and not the tear into the Aetheric. After all, a beast rampaging through a major metropolitan area was *not* an everyday occurrence. Aside from the time a bear had escaped from a Georgia zoo a couple of years back, I couldn't remember hearing of any similar situation. But the beast was gone, and the tear was still here. And it was drawing attention.

I'd merged planes of reality before, but last time—well, actually, the only other time—I had been in a private residence. A private residence that happened to belong to the governor of Nekros. He was a big mover and shaker in the Humans First Party, an anti-fae/anti-witch political group. The governor also happened to be my father, and ironically, fae, but neither of those facts was common knowledge. He must have paid a considerable amount to keep the events surrounding the Blood Moon quiet, and neither my very short arrest nor the fact that an entire suite of rooms in his home now touched multiple realties had shown up in the papers.

I didn't personally have the required money or influence to hide a patch of merged reality in the center of the Quarter. Especially not with a street full of witnesses, the media already arriving with cameras out and recording, and a whole slew of legal alphabet soup on the scene. So I did the only thing I could: I avoided questions about the tear.

Or at least I tried.

"Miss Craft, why am I not surprised to see you here?" a sharp female voice asked.

I cringed, and then tried to hide the reaction as I turned. "Agent Nori," I said to the FIB agent I'd had the displeasure of meeting the day before. "Is there something I can help you with?"

"Doubtful, but I need your statement. Tell me what happened here."

"My friends and I were finishing dessert and talking about our day. Everything seemed normal enough. Then I noticed the fae who threatened me at the swamp. He was watching me. I pointed him out just before we heard the screaming. We all looked in the direction of the sound, and that was when we saw the beast. It came from somewhere up the street." I pointed to where the cars were being cleared from the road. "I lost sight of the fae in the panic that ensued. Several witches tried to conjure against the beast. My friend Holly threw a fireball at it, and the beast charged her. When I disbelieved in the construct, it vanished."

"It takes a hell of a lot of conviction to destroy a fully autonomous glamour." She frowned at me, her dark eyes searching my face. When I didn't say anything, she continued, "So, what can you tell me about that?" She pointed at the hole in reality.

I forced a casual shrug. "Maybe something to do with the beast?" It wasn't a lie. It was a question.

Agent Nori's frown etched deeper, the movement tugging on her high cheeks. "Do you make a habit of disbelieving glamour, Miss Craft?"

I'd have liked to say no, but there was photographic proof from a month ago that showed me walking through furniture and candles at a crime scene. In my defense, I hadn't been able to see those glamoured objects, not even as hazy outlines like I'd seen with the beast. "I don't go out of my way to do it, if that's what you mean."

"And do tears into the Aetheric appear anywhere you disbelieve glamour?"

"No." At least I could answer that one definitively.

Agent Nori stared at me a long moment, as if trying to decide if I was lying. Or maybe she was trying to determine if I was *capable* of lying. Fae couldn't—though they could bend the truth until you'd swear up was down. At the floodplain, Nori had hinted that she knew I had fae blood. Now she appeared to be weighing how much sway it held over my words.

She must have reached some conclusion because after a moment she said, "The ABMU has a charmed disk in evidence. It looks like witch magic. You are aware that fae rarely use complex charms?"

I nodded. By "rarely use" she actually meant that most couldn't use witch charms. The Aetheric resisted something about the fae nature. When I used my second sight, I could see the magic bend away from their very souls.

"Knowing that," she said, "you still insist that the attack was committed by a glamour?"

I faltered. I'd disbelieved the creature, not dispelled it. That fact indicated that its form was held together by glamour. But, it was undoubtedly a magic construct. When I didn't say anything, her gaze moved past me.

"I'm sure I'll see you around, Miss Craft." She walked away, and I let out a relieved breath.

Relief felt premature as a pair of heels clicked a fast-approaching tempo on the sidewalk behind me.

"Alex Craft, a moment of your time," said a perky, and far too familiar, voice.

I didn't turn. Not immediately at least. I recognized the voice: Lusa Duncan, the star reporter of Nekros's most popular news program, *Witch Watch*. And if I knew Lusa, there was a camera pointed at me right now. Taking a deep breath, I pasted on my professional smile and prepared myself to face the press.

She pushed her mic at me as soon as I turned. "Word in the Quarter is that the police have called you in to consult on the Sionan floodplain foot murders and that the FIB is now involved. What can you tell us?"

Is that seriously what the news guys are calling the case? Not that it mattered—my answer was the same.

"No comment," I said. I gave a quick nod to her cameraman, whose name I still didn't know, though I'd seen his face often enough over the last few months that I probably should have known his name as well. Then I tried to duck around Lusa.

Not that she let me.

Lusa was a petite witch—a full head and shoulders shorter than me, even in her heels—but she was 110 percent ambition and excessively tenacious about following a story. She sidestepped, blocking my path, and shoved her mic at me again.

"What can you tell the people of Nekros about the attack in the Quarter today?"

I sighed. I didn't want to appear dodgy on the six o'clock news. "Nothing more than anyone else here could tell you. I'm not sure where the beast came from or why it was on the street. We were lucky it was only a glamour."

"Yes, lucky. Do you think this was a targeted attack?"

Possibly. It was very possible the killer was upset that I'd revealed the mound of feet in the floodplain. Tamara was also on the case. She could have been the target. But I wasn't about to speculate on the news.

Instead I said, "I think we need to wait for the NCPD's analysis."

Lusa hurried on to her next question. "What can you tell me about what appears to be Aetheric energy slipping into the street? Witnesses say the . . . tear is in about the same place as where you unraveled the glamour."

"Maybe something to do with the beast?" I gave her the same line I'd fed Nori, though Lusa seemed to swallow it as more credible than the FIB agent had. Hitching my purse strap higher on my shoulder, I stepped around Lusa. "If you'll excuse me, I need to check on my friend."

This time Lusa let me go, and I hurried toward the ambulance idling across the street. Holly sat in the back of the vehicle, two paramedics hovering over her and Tamara at her side. Holly's eyes were still a little too wide, as if the shock of the attack hadn't quite passed. A flame of freckles dusted her nose and cheeks, bright against her paler-than-normal skin. She usually hid the freckles behind a complexion charm, but the medics had taken the charm to avoid possible magical interactions with the healing spells.

"How're you feeling?" I asked as I approached.

"They say I won't even need stitches," she said, but I could tell her frail smile was held in place by will alone. "You know, I've used the expression that I felt like I'd been mauled after particularly bad days in the courtroom. I was wrong—this is worse."

"Just wait until tomorrow. You'll be stiff and sore too."

"Gee, thanks, Alex. You always give me something to look forward to." She shook her head, but her smile looked at least a little less forced.

When the paramedics finally released her, with instructions to rest and watch the bite on her shoulder for signs of infection, Holly allowed Tamara and me to help her down from the ambulance—which was a testament to how shaky she still felt.

"You're not still planning to make your trial?" Tamara asked as she grabbed Holly's purse.

Holly shook her head. "No. I'm calling it a day. I already contacted Arty about covering for me."

Of course she had. She'd probably still been bleeding when she'd had someone bring her the phone. I shook my head. If Death hadn't been there, hadn't warned me . . .

But then again, if the spell truly had been targeting me, Holly might not have been injured if I hadn't run back for her. *Had Death been here for Holly, the beast, or me?*

Holly was in no condition to drive, so we deposited her in the passenger seat of her car. I'd dropped my shields and peered across planes during the attack, and though it had been nearly an hour since I'd dispelled the construct, shadows still ate at my vision. Which left only Tamara to drive—we'd have to come back for the other cars later.

I slid into the backseat of Holly's car, but as we pulled away from the curb, I noticed Lusa standing not far away, interviewing one of the pedestrians who'd been on the street. The man pantomimed thrusting his hand out like he was shoving it through something—or, more than likely, into a beast. Then he splayed his fingers as if to demonstrate suddenness and pointed to the hole.

Oh, I didn't even want to know what kind of fallout I'd be dodging from this one.

"No comment," I said, and hit the END button on my cell phone. It immediately buzzed again. "I need an anti-reporter charm," I muttered. Yeah, and if I managed to create *that*, I'd make as much money as if I created a spell to reduce chocolate to zero calories. Of course, I was searching for a way to break glamour, and *that* charm appeared to be just as improbable.

"What do you think I should do, PC?" I asked, looking at my Chinese Crested.

The mostly hairless gray dog glanced up at his name. Then he grabbed a stuffed penguin and dropped it at my feet.

"Yeah, I don't think that's going to help, buddy."

He stared at me, his big brown eyes hopeful. When I didn't move, he nudged the penguin closer with his nose, and the crest of white hair on his head—the only hair he had aside from the puffs on his tail and feet—bobbed with the motion.

"Oh, all right." I tossed the toy across the room, and PC took off, his nails clinking on the hardwood as he scrambled for the penguin. When he reached it, he stood there, squeezing it so it squeaked. Then he took off again, prancing around the one-room apartment with the toy. What he didn't do was bring it back—we hadn't quite got that retrieve *and return* thing down. I shook my head. *Little goof.*

My phone buzzed again, and with a sigh I hit the button to turn it off completely. I wasn't likely to score a new client without my phone, but clients weren't the ones calling right now. Tossing the phone on the counter, I turned back to my computer. I'd spent the last hour searching the Web for spells and charms that could detect glamour. So far I'd run across some sketchy-sounding potions that used exotic—and probably fake—ingredients, and I'd found a couple of folklore-based glamour-piercing tricks, which, assuming they worked, would be even less feasible than my using my grave-sight whenever I left the house. After all, walking around peering through a stone with a naturally bored hole wasn't exactly inconspicuous.

But I didn't like the fact I'd run up against glamour two days in a row. I wasn't a big believer in coincidence, and with first the glamoured feet and then the construct, plus the fae from the floodplain showing up in the Quarter . . . Yeah, I'd feel better with a glamour-piercing charm.

Not that I was finding one.

I closed the search browser. I was just going to have to fashion my own charm. *Yeah, because I have such a successful history of spellcrafting.* At least none of my charms had exploded recently.

As I closed my laptop, the electronic buzz of my TV turning on hummed through the room. My spine stiffened. I'd reactivated my wards when I came home, and the door that separated my over-the-garage efficiency from the main house hadn't opened. I should have been alone.

I whirled around, groping blindly for a weapon as I turned. My fingers landed on the hard plastic of my cell phone—which wasn't much of a weapon, but it was better than nothing.

Thankfully, it was also unnecessary.

Roy Pearson, a thirtysomething former programmer—being deceased complicated the whole holding-down-a-job thing—knelt in front of my television. He was focused, his gaze locked on where he slowly depressed the channel button one click at a time. I might as well not have been in the room for all he noticed.

"Roy, you can't just materialize in my bedroom and turn on my TV!"

The ghost looked up, his concentration faltering, and his finger passed through the front of the TV's control panel. With a frown, he shoved his thick black-rimmed glasses higher on his nose and his perpetually slouched shoulders sagged more than normal. "Sorry. I wanted to see if I was on again."

I dropped the unneeded phone-turned-makeshift-weapon back onto the counter. "Shock news doesn't age well. I think your interview probably got trumped today," I said as I walked across the room to change the channel for him.

A few days ago I'd helped Roy give Lusa at *Witch Watch* an exclusive—and heavily censored—interview about his part in the Coleman case a month ago. Roy had finally been able to tell the story of how he'd died, and I'd completed my part of a bargain with Lusa that kept a damaging tape of me from being aired—win-win situation. The interview had been broadcast several times already, and one national newspaper had run an article about it, including a half-page photo capturing Roy looking spectral and spooky, me beside him, my eyes glowing pale green and my hand locked with the ghost's as I channeled energy into him so he would appear on camera. But despite all the press the interview had garnered, I had the feeling that the construct attack and the tear into the Aetheric would eclipse Roy's story.

Lusa appeared on the screen as I flipped to Channel 6. She was back in the studio, but a digitally imposed box beside her head rolled footage of the small hole in reality surrounded by crime tape. My picture popped up on the screen, and I groaned.

"What did you do this time?" Roy asked, staring at the screen.

"Hopefully nothing that will start another media circus." Once upon a time I'd actually liked *Witch Watch*—that was before I started appearing on the show semiregularly. *I'd better find out what's being said.*

I bumped the volume up and listened to Lusa's report as I sketched a plan for the spell I intended to cast.

"—are still debating jurisdiction over the tear, but the Organization for Magically Inclined Humans has officially confirmed that what we're seeing is pure Aetheric energy slipping out of the hole. Rumor has it that billionaire Maximillian Bell, founder of the controversial spellcrafting school for norms, Spells for the Rest of Us, made an offer for the property and has attempted to buy access to the tear. The possible implications and dangers of raw magic slipping into reality are actively being debated all over the nation, so for now, the tear is being contained within a circle and the area is off limits to civilians. In other news—"

I muted the TV again. All things considered, if whatever she'd said about me had been short enough that I didn't catch it before hitting the volume, it probably wasn't devastating. *At least, I hope not.*

"I'm going to cast my circle," I told Roy as I gathered a quarter-sized wooden disk and a carving knife and headed for the small circle cut into the floor in the corner of the room.

The ghost shrugged, not looking up from the cereal bowl he was attempting to shove from one side of the kitchen counter to the other. When I'd first met Roy, he hadn't been able to interact with anything on the living side of the chasm between his plane and mine. He'd received a serious power boost a month ago when I'd been overflowing with energy I couldn't control and I'd siphoned a load of it into him. Ever since, he'd become a champion poltergeist: knocking things over, pushing buttons, and even managing to hold a pen long enough to write his name in uneven, crooked letters.

"Don't break that bowl," I said, and then settled down inside my circle. If I was going to have any shot at casting a spell that would alert me to glamour, I'd need to be focused—and not on the ghost haunting my apartment.

Closing my eyes, I concentrated on the raw magic stored

in the obsidian ring I wore. I channeled it into the dormant circle, and the magical barrier sprang to life, pulsing with blue energy. Circle cast, I cleared my mind and let my consciousness sink deep inside until I reached the trancelike state I'd been taught to strive for while in academy.

I hit that place of perfect nothingness, perfect peace. Then the world exploded in a rainbow of colors.

Aetheric energy twisted around me in writhing swirls of light, but there was no land of the dead mixed in, no mortal realm. I'd reached the Aetheric plane the way a witch was meant to: my psyche, and only my psyche, projected into the magical plane. I could still feel my body sitting inside my circle, but it was a distant sensation—more a minor irritation, like a buzzing fly, than a solid connection.

In the Aetheric plane I wasn't restrained by the rules of a body. I could float. I could fly. I laughed with the freedom of it, the sound turning to bright blue notes. Magic swirled around me, and I was a part of that magic. I felt invulnerable, limitless. And that was the dangerous part.

It would be so easy to forget I needed the tether to my body. To forget that I wasn't just magic and energy like everything else in the Aetheric plane. To forget that I had a limit. So after I danced along a stream of vibrant green magic, years of training forced me to pull back and recenter myself.

I adjusted my perspective and did something that was possible only in the Aetheric plane: I moved outside myself and examined my projected self from the outside. The deep fissures where a soul-sucking spell had damaged my very being still cut through my astral body, but the wounds were clear, showing no signs of taint or dark magic. They also showed no sign of healing.

I changed my perspective again, this time focusing on the magic around me. I drew on the brilliant strands, pulling the magic into my body. I absorbed only the blue and green swirls, as those were the Aetheric strands that resonated with me. My astral body filled with the magic, shining a brilliant turquoise. I stepped out of myself once again and ensured that there were no dark points and that nothing malicious had attached to my psyche. Then, filled with magic, I free-fell back into my physical body.

When I opened my eyes, I was back in my apartment. Roy was gone, PC was stretched across my lap, and my back ached from too many hours sitting in one place. But though I registered the soreness, I was too giddy to care. Magic filled my body, rushed through my veins. I felt like I could do anything. *Anything.* But I couldn't. That was another danger of magic, and why it needed to be stored or used immediately.

I refilled my ring first, pushing as much raw magic into it as the obsidian could hold. Then I focused on refreshing my personal shields and charms. The maintenance took more than half of the magic I was holding—my capacity had never been great—but what was left was more than enough for the charm I intended to craft.

I'd found no reference to a successful charm letting the bearer see through glamour. But I could already see through glamour. I just needed to know when to look.

I grabbed my knife and the wooden disk. As I cut the first stroke of the glyph for awareness into the disk, I released a steady trickle of magic and focused on what I wanted the charm to do. Once I'd finished the first glyph, I started on the rune meaning truth.

As I carved, the charm began to buzz with magic, the spell taking hold. By the time I cut the last stroke of the final rune, warning, the charm all but vibrated with power. I released the rest of the raw magic I held, allowing it to dissipate harmlessly. Then I clipped the disk to my charm bracelet. The wood looked out of place with all the silver, but it felt like the strongest charm I'd ever personally cast.

Now I just had to hope it worked.

Chapter 4

"**A**lex," a deep voice said.

I buried my head in my pillow.

"Alex," the voice said again, more insistent this time. A finger traced the ridge of my ear, the touch light enough to tickle.

I rolled away and pried open my sleep-encrusted eyes. A confusing array of colors swirled in my vision. I squinted, trying to decipher the different layers of reality. One of the first lessons taught in academy had been how to maintain mental shields, even during sleep. But every morning for the last month I'd woken to the madness of colors and multiple planes of reality.

I concentrated on my mental shields, envisioning the vines surrounding my psyche as a solid wall with no gaps. Slowly the world resolved itself back into my bedroom, washed in morning light. I sat up. Death stood less than a foot from the side of my bed. He smiled at me, his dark hair loose around his face and his thumbs tucked in the pockets of his jeans.

"Is this a social or a business call?" I asked, brushing back a tangle of curls from where they'd fallen in front of my eyes.

"I was thinking it had been a while since I had coffee."

Social.

I collapsed back against my pillow and PC lifted his

head to grunt at me in disapproval. After voicing his general upset, the dog tucked his white-plumed tail over his nose and closed his eyes again. I seriously wished I could do the same, but Death was still standing there, watching me with a grin on his face.

"Why am I awake?"

Death shrugged. "I could watch anyone sleep."

But only I could see him. Well, that wasn't completely true. Any grave witch could see and talk to soul collectors if the witch straddled the chasm between the living and the dead, but I was the only grave witch I knew who could see collectors while not in touch with the grave. And, more important, I was the only grave witch who could physically interact with collectors. Death had been visiting me since I was a child.

Forcing myself awake, I swung my legs over the side of the bed and fought to untangle my feet from the sheets. I frowned when I realized I was still wearing yesterday's jeans and tank. *Right, I spent most of the night watching old movies with Holly.* Caleb, my landlord and third housemate, had urged me back upstairs after I'd fallen asleep on his couch. Changing had seemed overrated by the time I'd made it to my bed.

After a few fruitless kicks at the ensnaring sheets, which didn't free me, I reached down to unwind them from my legs. Death watched, his expression losing some of its playful edge.

"Nightmares again?" he asked, his voice serious.

I shrugged off the question. I'd had nightmares every night since my final confrontation with Coleman. Facing off with a madman and finally destroying him by accelerating the decomposition of his body and cannibalizing his soul? Yeah, that was nightmare inducing, but I really didn't want to think about it.

Yawning, I stretched, trying to work the kinks out of my back. The night of poor sleep—to say nothing of the nights before it—had left me sore and still exhausted, but a glance at my clock told me it was past time I should be getting up. I couldn't remember when I was supposed to meet today's client, though I was pretty sure I was scheduled to raise a shade. I'd check my calendar as soon as I got some much-needed caffeine. Snapping my jaw shut, I shuffled toward my kitchenette.

Death watched me, amusement once again lifting to his dark eyes. Unlike me with my bedraggled clothes and knotted hair, he looked good in the morning light streaming into my apartment. Okay, actually, he looked exactly the same as when I'd first seen him when I was five years old, but recently I'd come to appreciate the way his black T-shirt pulled tight over the expanse of his shoulders and his faded jeans hugged his ass. Not that I was looking, of course. I mean, he was Death.

Yeah, he was Death, and a month ago, when I lay dying under the Blood Moon, I was pretty sure he'd said he loved me. Neither one of us had mentioned it since. In fact, for the first week after that night, whenever I'd catch sight of him, he would vanish without saying anything. Then he'd started visiting again as if nothing had changed between us. Well, almost nothing.

"You want coffee?" I asked, riffling through my cabinet.

"Among other things."

And there went my pulse rate.

When I'd been in academy I'd discovered I could make the objects I interacted with tangible to Death, but the trick worked only if we both remained in contact with the object in question. As a teenager, when I'd first offered him coffee, I'd been flirting. Since I had to hold on to the mug for him to touch it, sharing a cup of coffee put us in close contact, but over the last few weeks he'd taken the flirting to a whole new level.

I focused on scooping coffee grounds into the filter. Never in my life had I measured my grounds more meticulously, though with the way my fingers trembled, I was surprised I didn't miss the coffeemaker. *Come on, Alex. Get a grip.* Death was my oldest friend. The one constant in my life.

And he'd said he loved me.

I hit the BREW button on my coffeemaker harder than needed. Then, after taking a deep breath, I turned back around.

Death stood directly behind me, much closer than I'd expected. He filled my space, his wide shoulders blocking out everything else. Once he wouldn't have been able to move so close without my noticing—his very presence would have chilled the air between us. Now our temperatures were about the same. I was pretty sure he hadn't become warmer.

"It will take a couple of minutes to brew," I said, because I had to say *something*.

"Mmm-hmm." He smiled and took a step closer.

I didn't mean to back up, but the counter was suddenly pressing against my ass, so clearly I had. Death's hands moved to my hips. I tried to draw a breath, but couldn't seem to catch it.

"That attack yesterday . . ." he whispered, crowding my space. "Who did you irritate recently?"

"Irritate? I—no one. Well, a fae in the floodplain when I revealed some dismembered feet, but—" Death slid close enough that his thighs brushed the front of mine, and I lost track of what I was saying. I mentally groped for an intelligent strain of thought. "Was that a soul you collected from that beast?"

"That's what I do." His breath tickled over my skin as he spoke.

"How did a magic construct gain a soul?" I asked, trying to focus on something other than how near his lips were to mine.

His smile stretched wider. "Magic," he said, leaning closer.

A loud knocking banged through my loft.

My head snapped up, my gaze jumping to the front door. But the knocking wasn't from someone outside. It was coming from the inner door that led down to the main portion of the house. *Saved by a housemate.*

"Come in," I called, shocked by how breathless my voice sounded.

The door opened, and Caleb bustled in. "Hey, Al, I wanted you—" He stopped. "Is this a bad time?"

"No, I, uh—" I swallowed, wondering what this must look like to Caleb. He couldn't see Death, so from his point of view, I looked like I was alone in my apartment, backed against my counter for no particular reason. I glanced at Death, and he stepped away, giving me space.

"Later," he whispered, smoothing a curl behind my ear. Then he vanished.

Later . . . I shook my head and tried to wipe away the goofy smile I felt spreading across my face.

"How is Holly?" I asked, pushing away from the counter.

PC, who'd jumped off the bed as soon as the door opened, pawed at Caleb's leg. My housemate smiled at the small dog and knelt to give the top of his head a good rub.

"Sleeping," he said as PC lathered his hand in dog kisses. "She left very early this morning and returned a little after dawn. Did she mention anything last night about having to go somewhere?"

I shook my head. She shouldn't have been leaving in the middle of the night.

I was halfway across the room when my throat tightened and a hiccup hit me like a punch in the chest. My voice broke with an undignified croak at the force of the hiccup.

"I—" Another hiccup hit me, cutting off my words.

"You okay, Al?" Caleb asked, his brows drawing together.

"Yeah, I'll"—*hiccup*—"get"—*hiccup*— "water."

I grabbed a glass, nearly dropping it as another hiccup shook me. Caleb took the glass from me, and two more hiccups, each worse than the last, hit back to back. A burning ache spread across my chest. I covered my mouth with my fingers, as if I could stop the sound and thus the pain.

Caleb held the glass—now filled halfway with tap water—out to me. When I reached for it, the charms on my bracelet clinked and twinkled.

The charm.

Caleb looked like a sandy-haired college quarterback, but he was fae, his boy-next-door facade a glamour. *And I created a charm to warn me of glamour.*

I snatched off the charm bracelet. As soon as it lost contact with my skin, the hiccups stopped and my chest stilled.

I frowned at the bracelet and the little wooden charm I'd created. *Some warning.*

I hadn't considered installing an off switch in the charm,

so it was either try to convince Caleb to drop his glamour or go without my charms until he left. With a sigh, I shoved the bracelet in my pocket. My house wards blocked grave essence, so it wasn't like I needed the extra shields the charm bracelet provided.

"Better now?" Caleb asked as I took a long sip of water. The cool liquid felt good in my aching throat and I nodded, but I didn't thank him. You didn't thank fae. Or apologize. Or in any way acknowledge a debt, for that matter. So I smiled and hoped he understood my appreciation.

"Okay, then," he said. "I'd like you to meet a friend of mine."

That was all the warning he gave before he opened the door separating my apartment from the main house. An all-too-familiar figure marched into my room, his back curved and his knees bent.

I did a double take, and PC ducked under the bed. Just the tip of his black nose showed under the bedskirt as he growled at the fae I'd first met in the floodplain. *Smart dog.*

"Caleb, what is he—"

"Alex, this is Malik, a friend of mine."

Friend? I frowned. Caleb had always had my best interests in the past, but . . . I trusted Caleb. That didn't mean I trusted his friends.

"You're not welcome here," I said, lifting my gaze to meet the large, unblinking eyes of the strange fae. He'd threatened me, and I'd seen him in the Quarter directly before the construct attack. Coincidence? I doubted it.

Malik's thin lips tugged downward and he glanced at Caleb.

"Hear him out, Al."

I shook my head. "You're wanted by the police, Malik. I suggest you leave. Now." I grabbed my phone off the counter where it was plugged in, charging. Malik was a person of interest wanted for questioning in connection with the feet found in the floodplain. John would want to know he was standing in my apartment.

I pressed the button to wake the phone, but the screen didn't light up. *Damn.* The phone was off, shut down to avoid reporters. I held the power button and headed for the main door. I jerked it open, letting the morning light stream in as I waited for the phone to power on. Either Malik would walk through that door, leaving me in peace to call the police, or I'd flee my own room. Escape plans were a plus.

"Alex," Caleb said, stepping between Malik and me. "Please, listen to what he has to say."

I gaped at Caleb. Fae don't say please, just like they don't thank you or apologize. Words had power and all of those words acknowledged a debt. Debts with fae were binding.

"Please," he said again, and I felt the imbalance hanging in the air between us. If I did as he asked, he'd be indebted to me. Not that I wanted that, but in all the years I'd lived in his house, he'd never once said please. The fact that my hearing Malik out was worth Caleb's indebting himself to me meant that whatever the other fae had to say was important.

The phone chirped in my hand, letting me know it had powered on. I glanced at it, then hesitated and reached out with my ability to sense magic. Neither fae carried any charms. Caleb was one of those very rare fae who could manipulate the Aetheric, and his skin tingled in my senses with residual magic from a ward he'd been crafting recently, but Malik didn't have a trace of residual magic on him. And he certainly didn't have a trace of the spells I'd felt in the feet or the construct. Of course, that didn't mean he wasn't involved; it just meant he wasn't carrying any charms. Still, if Caleb was willing to indebt himself . . . I lowered the phone, letting the screen fall asleep again.

"I'm listening," I said, turning to close the door. Then I stopped, my gaze stuck on the porch.

"Al?" I could hear the frown in Caleb's voice. "Alex, what is it?"

I didn't answer. I couldn't. I just stood there, shock reverberating down my spine. Outside my door, in the very center of the landing, was a dagger.

Caleb sprinted across the room. When he saw the dagger he cursed in one of the fast, fluid languages of the fae. I couldn't understand the words, but from the tone I could tell he was pissed and maybe a little freaked. Or maybe I was projecting. Caleb shoved his hand against the doorjamb to check the house wards, but I doubted he'd find anything. The dagger had been driven into the wood in the middle of the small landing. Caleb's wards didn't reach that far. I swallowed, glancing at Malik—who watched with curiosity but hadn't moved.

The reassuring weight of the phone still filled my hand. I flicked the screen lock off and opened the phone app. I got as far as dialing the nine when Caleb plucked the phone from my trembling fingers.

"Don't do anything hasty," he said, his voice low.

"Hasty? *Hasty?* You brought the fae who's been threatening me into the house and now there's a dagger driven into the middle of my porch. I think I'm already behind on calling the police. And don't tell me this isn't connected." I made a wide, sweeping gesture to include both Malik and the dagger protruding from one of the porch beams, the blade embedded deep enough that the ornate hilt touched the wood. It pinned a scrap of paper to the porch. *A note?* From where I stood, still inside the house, the yellowing parchment looked old, the edges curling and torn. The entire display looked surreal, almost innocuous, beside the saucer of milk I filled nightly for our resident gargoyle, but fear gripped my chest, made my breath harden in my lungs. Someone had come to my home, to my door, and driven the dagger into my porch. And I had a good idea who.

Caleb tucked my phone into his back pocket and turned to face Malik. "What do you know about this?"

The gangly fae cocked his head to the side, one bushy eyebrow lifting as he shuffled forward. I stumbled back, out of arm's length, and the fae hesitated. He blinked at me, as if surprised by my fear and not pleased at being the cause. We stared at each other for a moment, and when he stepped toward the door again, I held my ground.

He peered around the doorframe and after a single glance shrugged. "It's not mine."

"It has to—" I stopped. No, it didn't have to be his. He hadn't said he didn't put the dagger there, only that it didn't belong to him.

Caleb obviously came to the same conclusion. "Do you know anything about the dagger or how it ended up here?"

Malik blinked his large, dark eyes, surprise at Caleb's

clarification obvious on his face. Then the surprise hardened to anger and he straightened to his full height, his head inches from the ceiling. He tugged at the hem of his unseasonable coat, making whatever was inside clatter.

Caleb met the taller fae's gaze. "If you want her help, you're going to have to be straight with her. I told you that before we came here. Now what do you know about that dagger?"

Malik glanced at me, the conflict in his features clear, but after a moment he let out his breath and his knees bent again, his posture slumping. "I've never seen that dagger before and I have no knowledge of how it came to protrude from your porch." The clear and indisputable statement seemed to pain him, his thin lips cutting downward as he spoke.

Well, no wiggle room in that statement. But if he didn't drive the dagger into my porch, who did? I turned back to the open doorway.

PC, noticing the open door for the first time, darted out from under the bed. I intercepted him, scooping him into my arms and clutching his warm gray body tight. "Outside later," I told him, whispering the words into the soft white hair on the top of his head.

"Do you think it's a threat or a warning?" Caleb asked, pulling my phone back out of his pocket. Apparently now that Malik wasn't the main suspect he would let me call the police. "Or it could be a trap," he said, frowning.

A trap? By the same person who'd sent the construct? *Only one way to know for sure.* I took the phone from him, but I hesitated before dialing and reached with my senses. Unfortunately, the same wards that protected me from outside interference locked my own magic inside the house. To sense spells on the dagger I would have to leave the safety of the wards, which if this was a trap, didn't sound like a great plan. *Except . . .* From my spot in the doorway, I studied the intricate hilt.

"I think that's my dagger." Which didn't eliminate the possibility of a trap, especially since I'd lost the dagger a month ago when I'd exhausted the spells enchanting the blade by using it to overload a magical circle. After I'd escaped the circle, I'd lost track of the dagger and when I'd gone back to search for it, it had vanished.

I glanced at the phone in my hand. Calling the police was the smartest move, but if it was the same dagger I'd lost . . .

I've already delayed this long; what would a few more minutes cost? After all, Caleb and Malik had entered my loft from the inner door, so the dagger could have been driven into the porch anytime since I'd arrived home last night.

I lowered my mental shields, letting my psyche span the chasm between planes. The wards kept my ability to sense magic locked inside, but they did nothing to my grave-sight. Colors dulled as in my vision the wood around the dagger rotted and the note browned and curled, but the dagger remained the same. Whatever metal the fae-wrought dagger had been forged from, it had never tarnished or rusted, not even in my grave-sight, and this dagger didn't either. It shimmered with the enchantments bound in the metal, but again, my lost dagger had done the same. I glanced around the landing. The tendrils of Aetheric energy were as chaotic as ever, but I didn't see any disturbance that looked like a spell ready to descend on the unwary. I also didn't see any glamoured or spelled forms ready to spring out as soon as I stepped through the door. If this was a trap, I wasn't spotting a cage.

I snapped my shields closed and set PC down. He looked at me and then the door. Shaking my head, I nudged him and he grudgingly headed toward the bed, his nails clicking on the hardwood. Once he'd jumped onto the mattress, I headed for the door.

Caleb grabbed my arm, his fingers feverishly hot against my own lower body temperature. "I'll take a look," he said, stepping into my path. He didn't give me time to protest before he walked out onto the porch.

Nothing happened.

He squatted beside the dagger, not touching it. Caleb wasn't a sensitive, so if there were malicious spells on the dagger, he wouldn't be able to tell, not until it was too late. I, on the other hand, could sense magic. I ignored his disapproval as I joined him on the porch.

Without the shields in my bracelet or the house wards to block the grave essence, the chill of the grave swarmed around me. It clawed at my mental shields like dozens of spectral hands searching for cracks in my defenses. There was a graveyard a mile away, and there were other, smaller graves even closer than that, but I didn't want to feel them. I blocked hard, concentrating on keeping the vines encircling my psyche sealed tight. The real trick was to shield while still reaching with my ability to sense magic.

I focused on the gleaming hilt a foot from my toes. Enchantments swirled inside the metal, but they didn't feel malicious. They felt *familiar*.

Very familiar.

"It's my dagger." It seemed impossible, but somehow it was the same dagger, one of a pair. The enchanted blade could cut through almost any material. I'd thought I'd lost it forever. I reached out, tracing a single finger along the intricate design. Then I closed my hand around the hilt.

Magic purred across my palm and an eerie, alien consciousness touched the edge of my mind. But that wasn't unexpected. The enchantments forged into the fae-wrought blade gave the dagger not so much an intellect as a sense of awareness. It liked to be drawn, to be wielded, to cut through skin, through magic—and right now, it did *not* like being driven into wood.

"Al?" Caleb edged closer, the muscles in his legs bunching as if he were a moment from leaping to his feet.

I felt much the same way. I still hadn't spotted a trap, but I was ready to leave the exposed position of my porch. After a quick glance around, I tugged on the dagger. The blade slid free of the wood effortlessly, the note moving with it.

Caleb jumped to his feet and I whirled around, dagger in hand. Nothing happened. No magically constructed monsters appeared, nor did a shadowy witch or malicious fae emerge to ambush us. Not even a spell charged the air. The suburban neighborhood street was empty, nonthreatening. I scanned the dagger and note once again with my ability to sense magic. Nothing. I wasn't going to wait around for that to change. Clutching the dagger, I hurried inside, Caleb at my heels.

"What does the note say?" Caleb asked as soon as the door shut behind us.

I pulled it from the blade, trying not to damage it worse than being pinned to the porch had done. The paper was a thick vellum that rustled and cracked as I unfolded it. I recognized the neat script immediately.

"It's from Rianna." I said, frowning as I read over the carefully penned letters.

Alex,

   I need your help. Please, come to the Eternal Bloom. I'll be in the VIP section all day and through the night.

                                    Forever your friend,

                                              Rianna

   P.S. I heard about the cu sith attack. I had your dagger repaired. I only hope it can help you. Be careful, and please, come see me.

I reread the short note twice. Then I handed it to Caleb. He read it aloud. While he read, I dug through my top drawer, looking for the sheath enchanted specifically for the dagger—it wasn't exactly safe to leave a blade that could cut through anything just lying around.

Why would Rianna pin a note to my porch? It didn't make sense, though knowing she was the one who'd left the dagger actually did explain some things. Rianna, my roommate from academy, had been a captive of Faerie until recently. The last time I'd seen her I'd freed her from the slave-chains binding her and she'd saved my life. She'd been one of the few witnesses to what happened under the Blood Moon when I'd lost the blade. Also, the dagger had originally been a gift from her.

But why the threatening display? And why hadn't she just knocked on the door? *Unless she didn't deliver it.* Her note said she needed help. Was that the trap? Was someone using Rianna to draw me to the Bloom? Of course, if that was the case, why make a production of delivering the note? Why put me on my guard? The Eternal Bloom was Nekros's only fae bar, and the majority of its profits were drawn from humans gawking at the unglamoured fae who worked in the bar. But the VIP area was different—it was a pocket of Faerie.

My fingers finally landed on the sheath, its leather buzzing lightly with magic. It was still in the holster I'd used to keep the dagger in my boot through most of the Coleman case, which was probably best—it looked like I needed to wear it again. Kneeling, I rolled up my pants leg and strapped the dagger in place.

When I looked up, I found Caleb staring at me, the note still in his hand. Malik stood beside him, and I started. I'd gotten so caught up in the dagger and Rianna's note, I'd forgotten about Malik. A new wave of adrenaline flooded my system. I stood, crossing my arms over my chest.

If Malik had planned to hurt me, he'd had the opportunity while I'd been distracted—but he hadn't taken it. A good sign, I guessed. I opened my mouth to tell him I'd listen to what he had to say, but Caleb spoke before I got a chance.

"You didn't tell me you were attacked by a cu sith."

I blinked. "It wasn't like it was wearing an ID tag."

Caleb turned to his friend. "And you, you didn't tell me either. You didn't think that was worth mentioning?"

Malik's shoulders crowded his large ears as he cringed, and a tinge of color flared in his pallid cheeks. "I was holding the information as a bargaining chip."

"A bargaining chip? I told you that you'd have to be straight with her."

"Well, she hasn't so much as agreed to hear me out yet, has she?"

"Hello, I'm right here," I said, giving both men a mock wave. "Holly and I were attacked by a glamour construct built on witch magic that tried to kill us. Does the shape the glamour took really matter?"

"Yes," both men said simultaneously, and I stumbled back a step.

"Okay." I looked from one to the other. "Explain. No, actually, wait. You were on the street yesterday," I said, focusing on Malik. "I saw you. Did you have anything to do with that creature. Anything at all?"

Malik hesitated long enough that I thought he might not answer. Then he blew air out between his teeth and said, "I was following you because I wanted to talk with you. When I saw the cu sith I actually thought it was after me. Until it saw you and howled."

I wasn't convinced, and I didn't see how the beast howling at me changed anything, but I nodded for him to continue.

"Cu sith are a type of faerie dog—" he said, and I scoffed under my breath.

"That was no dog. The giant faerie cousin of a dire wolf maybe, but not a dog."

Malik cleared his throat, ignoring my commentary. "As I was saying, cu sith are a type of faerie dog that disappeared centuries before the Awakening. You said it tried to kill you, but the cu sith were never trained to kill. Inside Faerie they guarded against intruders, but when they were sent out of Faerie to hunt, their role was that of retriever. They howled only once they spotted their prey, and if their target heard the third howl before reaching safety, Faerie claimed that mortal—forever."

I shivered, remembering the beast's red eyes locking on me, its giant head tilting back, the howl that made me want to fall to my knees and cower. *Twice.* It had howled twice. I'd been afraid of its teeth, of its claws. I would never have realized I needed to be afraid of its howl.

"So it was there to steal me away to Faerie?"

Malik shrugged. "Like you said, it was a construct. But it is my belief that it intended to steal you away to somewhere."

I stared at the gangly fae, not really seeing him anymore. My knees felt weak, rubbery, and I wanted to be alone to think about this information. That didn't seem to be an option.

After the silence stretched several moments, Malik cleared his throat again. "Will you hear me out, Miss Craft?"

I nodded absently and Malik fidgeted, rubbing his fingers and shuffling his feet so that the points of his knees pressed through the threadbare material of his pants.

"As I'm sure you'll recall," he said in his hauntingly musical voice, "two days ago you trekked through my territory in the floodplain and found a pile of feet. Afterward, we had a rather unfortunate encounter."

"All of that was rather memorable."

"Yes, well . . ." He paused and glanced back at Caleb, who nodded, and Malik let his hands fall to his sides. Then he rolled his shoulders and straightened to his full height again. "My life and livelihood are in danger. I need to hire you, Miss Craft."

Chapter 5

❦❖❦

I poured coffee into three mismatched mugs and carried them to my "guests." Caleb sipped his politely, but Malik clasped his mug between both hands without seeming to be aware of it. His gaze flickered around my small apartment, never staying in one place too long. Clearly I wasn't the only uncomfortable one.

I owned only one chair, and I wasn't about to invite Malik to plop down on my bed, so after handing off the mugs, I leaned against the wall. Then I stalled, blowing on my coffee to gain an extra couple of seconds as I tried to decide how to handle the situation.

"I'm going to guess that you're not interested in having a shade raised," I said, watching Malik over the rim of my mug.

He shook his head.

Figured.

"What is it you think I can do for you, Mr. Malik?"

"Actually, it is what we can do for each other. Your actions two days ago brought Faerie's attention down on the fae in the floodplain," he said, and then paused, as if waiting for some response from me.

"I'm not going to justify helping the police in their search for a serial killer."

"I hid those feet for a reason!"

A reason? I glanced at Caleb, letting my uncertainty

bleed into my expression. The good guys didn't hide disembodied appendages.

He met my gaze, but there were no answers in his eyes. They were the same blue he usually wore while glamoured, but I'd never been more aware that the person behind that glamour was so *other*.

I swallowed a gulp of coffee without tasting it and let my hand fall casually to my pocket. I could reach my phone, but my recent upgrade to a touch screen meant there would be no dialing numbers by feel. "Are you admitting to the murder of those people?" I asked Malik, my voice just above a whisper.

"Of course not. I hid the feet, but they were already severed when I found them. And before you ask, no, I don't know how they came to be that way."

"Then why hide them in the first place?"

His fingers clenched his mug. "To avoid the very scrutiny you have brought to my home!"

At Malik's outburst, PC, who'd fallen asleep on his usual pillow, jumped to his feet with a yelp. Then he dove off the bed and ducked behind the bedskirt. *Not exactly a guard dog.* Malik set his mug on the counter and took a deep breath.

He released the breath slowly, and when he spoke again, his voice was calmer. "That scrutiny is unavoidable now. But you've also drawn attention. The best thing for both of us would be if the murderer is caught as soon as possible."

Well, I couldn't argue with that. There were seven left feet in the morgue—it would be best for everyone if the killer was found before he or she killed again. But ... "What is it you think I can do?"

Malik frowned. "You're an investigator. Investigate."

Right. Searching for a serial killer was way out of my job description. If enough of one of the bodies was recovered that a shade could be raised, I would gladly help the police question the victim, but the last time I'd gotten actively involved in a major investigation I'd nearly died. And then I'd been arrested.

I pushed myself off the wall. I'd heard enough. Malik had said he'd found—and hidden—the feet but didn't know anything more about them. Fae couldn't lie, so I had no choice but to believe him. John, and most likely the FIB, since they had taken over the case, would still want to question Malik, but I wasn't going to antagonize him by calling the police while he stood in my loft. I'd kick him out first.

"I don't think I'll be able to help you," I said, giving him a wide berth as I headed for the door.

"You're the only one in the position to help us."

I stopped, my hand hovering over the doorknob. That whole not-being-able-to-lie thing meant that when Malik said I was the only one who could help, he honestly believed that was true, and considering everything Caleb had done to make this conversation happen, I assumed he agreed. I turned back around.

"Why me, and who is included in 'us'?"

"'Us' would be the fae in the floodplain in particular, but also extending to all the independent fae in Nekros." Malik paced across my small apartment. "Yesterday *she* ordered the floodplain cleared. All fae inside were to be taken to Faerie for questioning, but the brutes she sent came with iron chains, and none of the fae they captured have returned. There's war brewing in Faerie and she's bolstering her court with our numbers."

"That is only speculation," Caleb said, but he didn't sound sure. In fact, I thought I caught an edge of fear in his voice.

"She?" I asked because they obviously both knew what woman they were talking about, but I surely didn't.

Caleb pushed away from the counter. "The Winter Queen. Nekros City is part of her territory."

"The winter court? Seriously?" I frowned at Caleb. "Nekros City hardly has a proper winter. I can count on one hand how many times it's snowed here and the snow stuck to the ground more than an hour. Hell, half the trees don't have the decency to lose their leaves. Shouldn't the winter court hold territory somewhere, I don't know, *cold*?"

Caleb shrugged. "Faerie is the ultimate contradiction. It is unchanging and yet ever in flux. Doors in Faerie are . . . inconsistent. For the past few years the door from Nekros into Faerie has opened to the winter court so Nekros City is part of the queen's territory. The door will change soon enough, and all the fae with ties to the winter court will move on, making room for the next court. Only the independent fae, those who have tied themselves to the mortal realm instead of Faerie, will remain."

That was more information than I'd ever gotten out of Caleb at one sitting before. And it was clearer than any of the lessons the one and only fae teacher the academy had hired to teach students fae history had ever been—our teacher definitely had never taught us anything about the doors to Faerie moving. I sipped my coffee, giving myself a second to absorb this information and let it infiltrate my limited understanding of Faerie. Then I put the mug aside.

"If the queen is illegally gathering the independent fae, shouldn't you go to the FIB?" After all, if the local court was kidnapping fae, someone with a lot more authority than I had needed to know.

Malik huffed under his breath. "Who do you think is doing the *questioning*?" He shook his head. "The FIB are all court-loyal—not an independent in the bunch."

"Then go to the police." I knew for sure the NCPD wasn't answering to a queen.

Malik's dark eyes widened like I'd said something unbelievable, and Caleb shook his head.

"Al, there are certain . . . restrictions to being independent," Caleb said, stepping forward. "As we don't answer to any regent, we had to take vows before leaving Faerie. Involving mortals in affairs best settled among the fae is strictly forbidden. That's why Malik came to you."

"That's why?" The blood drained from my face. If the fae couldn't involve anyone mortal . . . "You know."

Caleb nodded.

So much for my heritage being a secret. "You didn't say anything."

"Neither did you."

True.

"I only suspected in the beginning," he said. "Even with you living in my house, under my wards, I wasn't sure. Until a month ago. Now I can hardly believe I missed it. Something about you changed."

Don't I know it. Discovering I had fae blood was only the tip of my problems, but Caleb wasn't done yet.

"You are in a unique position, Al," he said, stepping closer. "We can go to you. We can talk to you. But you've taken no vows. Yet. You can work as an intermediary with the police, and they already know you, already trust you."

I swallowed and glanced over Caleb's shoulder to where Malik had stopped pacing to watch me; his large, unblinking eyes fixed on me, waiting. I didn't like the "yet" that Caleb had worked into that little statement, but I didn't doubt he was right. It wasn't like I hadn't noticed the changes in myself since the Blood Moon: the sensitivity to metals, the inability to maintain my shields, and my increased ability to sense fae magic—and that was all on top of the whole seeing multiple planes of existence. Faerie would eventually notice me.

I grabbed my mug again because I had to do something with my hands or I'd start pacing and fidgeting like Malik. I swirled the dark contents, staring at the liquid instead of at Caleb. *I could use something stronger than coffee right now.* Still, coffee was what I had. I drained the mug in two swallows, barely tasting its lukewarm contents.

Yes, eventually someone important in Faerie would notice me, but that hadn't happened yet. The fae couldn't talk to the mortal police, and the FIB, which functioned as the fae police in the mortal realm, belonged to the courts, but Malik was right that they could talk to me.

"The queen is gathering the independents because I revealed those feet?"

Malik nodded. "That was likely only an excuse, but yes. As long as a fae is suspected of the crime, she has the authority to search for the criminal."

I sank onto my bed, my mind reeling. Did I really want to get involved—or actually, *further* involved—in this case? I raised shades, got some answers, and then cashed the check. That was the kind of investigator I was. I didn't hit the street and search for suspects in murder cases.

But the independent fae couldn't turn to anyone else, and the Winter Queen had free rein to gather the independents as long as the murderer was free. On top of that, since the fae couldn't talk to the police, there might be information out there that the police desperately needed that I could access and they couldn't.

I focused on Malik again. "So, what do you know about the feet?"

"Does that mean you're taking the case?"

"I'm considering it. Do you have some fact I can take to the police that would prove without a shadow of a doubt that the floodplain fae were not involved? Or do you know where the remainder of the bodies are located?"

Malik shook his head. "There were no bodies. Just the feet. They floated down the river all at once, like a fleet of toy boats—"

Lovely image.

"—I thought I'd gathered all of them, but obviously I missed a few in the flooding. I should have made the nixies help. They are silly, frivolous little things, but they know every disturbance in the water. They could tell if a fly hit the water in their territory."

I'd taken a course on fae races during academy and I vaguely remembered reading about nixies being some sort of water nymph. "Would you be able to arrange for me to question the nixies? If they are that attuned to the water, they might be able to point me to where the feet were dumped. The police are still searching for a primary crime scene and the dump site might shed some clues."

Malik's shoulders sagged, his head dipping. "There will be no questioning them unless you want to sneak into the queen's dungeons. My poor dears. The FIB brutes went after the nixies first. Everyone knows they're harmless, but that Agent Nori chained them in iron and dragged them away."

Great.

"What about the kelpie?" Caleb asked.

Malik cocked his head to the side. "Maybe," he said, running one long finger down the length of his nose. "If those brutes haven't grabbed her as well."

I glanced from one to the other of them. "A kelpie? As in a carnivorous water horse?"

Malik nodded. "She has a . . . hungry disposition, but she claims the track of the Sionan River from north of the city down to the edge of the floodplain. She might not be as attuned to the river as my poor nixies, but if you can bargain with her, she might be able to point you toward a general area."

"That's miles of river. How do I find her?"

"She frequents the banks below the city. You know the old stone bridge?" Caleb asked, and I nodded.

The bridge, a forty-minute drive past the warehouse district south of the city, was a thing of mystery and rumor. After the Magical Awakening, when the spaces between began to unfold and the perceivable world grew, Nekros had unfolded between Georgia and Alabama. The first settlers in what would quickly grow into Nekros City noted that the stone bridge was already there, and that it was already old.

"Well," he said, "if you head out toward the bridge, the riverbanks in that area are your best bet. She's often spotted there."

Okay, questioning the kelpie would be a good starting point. Hopefully she'd know something. I could ask a few questions, poke around a bit, and hand off what I learned to John. This was legwork, the equivalent of knocking on doors. *Except I'm going to be searching the banks for a carnivorous horse.* I sighed and pushed myself off my bed.

"If I go looking for the kelpie, what kind of precautions should I take? I mean, according to folklore, kelpies drown their victims, then tear them to pieces to eat them. Is that accurate?"

"I definitely wouldn't suggest taking up equestrianism," Caleb said with a grin. "But as long as you don't climb on her back, you should be safe."

"If you have any trouble, you can use this." Malik pulled a leather harness from under his coat.

No, not a harness. A bridle. I cocked an eyebrow. My father had sent my sister and me to camp one summer and we'd learned to ride and care for horses. Cleaning hooves had convinced Casey she didn't want a pony after all, but it was the bridling and saddling that had gotten to me—the mare I picked wasn't cooperative. I imagined struggling with a fae would be incalculably worse.

Malik read the skepticism on my face and shrugged. "If you bridle a kelpie, it's obliged to grant you a request in exchange for its freedom. This particular bridle is enchanted. Toss it over her head and she'll be caught."

Well, that changed things. I held out my hand, but Malik frowned. He gripped the leather tighter.

"This is hard for me, Miss Craft. Speaking so freely and giving away treasures—it is not in my nature."

Even though he was the one who wanted to hire me? "I'll return it."

He perked up. "Twice-fold?"

Twice-fold? Like what, two enchanted bridles? "No, once-fold."

He frowned. "I could help you look for the kelpie."

"That would be fine." Appreciated even, but I couldn't say as much—I didn't want him twisting this around so he was helping me instead of vice versa.

Malik hesitated a moment more. Then, turning his head away as if he couldn't bear to look, he handed over the bridle.

I smiled. "Well, Malik, looks like you're Tongues for the Dead's newest client."

It took another hour to work out a contract for the case—and only a verbal one at that. Wording and phrasing were important with the fae. I'd known that. What I hadn't realized was how difficult it could be to agree on a contract for hire. A normal contract of service was a type of trade: I performed a service in exchange for payment for my time.

"That won't work," Malik told me. "It is my nature to get the better deal in any trade and then I'll still try to trick you out of what you've earned." He inclined his head. "It is who I am."

Well, at least he was honest.

Then there was the issue of payment. A song? The first snowflake of winter—I think that offer was meant to be ironic, all things considered. The first flower of spring?

Yeah, no. Not appropriate.

I would have lost my patience if Caleb hadn't been present to arbitrate. In the end, I agreed to gift Malik my time on the case and Caleb agreed to gift me free rent depending on how many hours I spent on the case. I had no idea what agreement Caleb and Malik reached. Caleb also made a point of adding a verbal clause stating that any assistance—including information and magical help—that Malik provided wouldn't put me in the fae's debt. Malik looked miffed by the statement, but he agreed to the terms.

Once everything was settled, I moved to the door to show them out but stopped when a shimmering form floated through the wood.

"Hey, Al, I— Whoa, who's the ugly guy?" Roy asked, shoving his iridescent glasses higher on his nose.

"Malik," I answered, and then winced when Malik turned at the sound of his name.

"Yes?"

I shook my head. Only I could see or hear Roy. I used to be so good at not talking to people no one else could see. Of course, until recently, I couldn't have heard Roy unless I'd tried. That was another thing that had changed.

"There's a ghost," I said by way of explanation. "He asked who you were."

"A real specter?" Malik looked around, his dark eyes shining with interest. "Can he frighten the living by making the lights flicker or the table rock?"

"I don't own a table."

Malik frowned and glanced around the small apartment as if he hadn't noticed that before. "True."

I turned back toward Roy. He'd been excited when he first floated through the door, before he'd gotten side-tracked by my visitors. "What's up, Roy?"

"Huh? Oh, yeah. So I was down visiting my grave, right? They delivered the headstone, and I wanted to see it again."

I nodded, waiting for him to get to the point. He'd spent twelve years watching his body walk around without him in it. Now that it was decaying in the ground like a corpse should, he visited his own grave regularly—kind of freaky in my opinion, but it was important to him, so I'd helped with the burial arrangements.

"So, yeah," he said, continuing. "I was at my grave, and this couple entered the cemetery, looking a little nervous. I didn't think anything about it, until I heard your name."

I blinked at him. Then my mouth went dry. "Crap. The Stromowskis. What time is it? I was supposed to raise their grandmother." I gave a glance at my slept-in clothes—I'd worn worse—and then I grabbed my purse. With all the excitement of Malik's case, reappearing daggers, and Faerie courts, I'd completely forgotten I had another client.

Chapter 6

It was late afternoon before I drove through the warehouse district and headed for the old stone bridge to meet Malik. Legally I couldn't drive for two hours after raising shades—the havoc that grave-sight wreaked on a grave witch's eyesight was well documented—but even after I'd waited a couple of hours for my sight to recover, the dimness under the branches overhanging the road made me nervous. Of course, taking any of the back roads out of the city made me nervous.

Like any other large city in the nation, Nekros City had its bad neighborhoods and high-crime areas. But it was outside the city, once you left the suburbs behind, that gave most human citizens pause. The fae had initiated the Magical Awakening when they had come out of the mushroom ring, as some said, seventy years ago. Their announcement altered the course of the—until that moment—technology-focused world.

And that was only the beginning.

Ancient history might have been riddled with stories of witchcraft, but in the decades—maybe even the centuries—before the Magical Awakening, magic was considered a myth. After the Awakening? Well, then, as if the magic had just been waiting for humans to be primed to channel it, the veil between the Aetheric and mortal reality thinned. Magic was accessible, and a good third of the population proved capable of reaching it, of shaping it. When space unfolded, opening new areas, both the witches seeking a place where they could practice in peace and the norms who didn't want to associate with the magically inclined moved into the new territory. The two groups didn't mix well, and several violent clashes had occurred in the years following the Magical Awakening, but witches and norms alike agreed on one thing—humans were safer in the city because strange, long-forgotten legends were waking in the wilds.

Now here I was, out in the middle of nowhere, searching for a carnivorous water horse.

I pulled my car off the road and parked under a cove of tree branches at one side of the bridge. The bridge itself was a hulking gray stone monstrosity with no obvious seams, no bolts, and no metal infrastructure—just solid stone. As I pulled up the soft top on the convertible—trees meant birds and I did *not* want to have to clean bird crap off my seats—Malik approached.

"Nice car," he said, circling the little blue convertible.

"Thanks. It's new." New used, but it was still a major step up from the hulking metal junker I'd driven until it had gotten stolen and stripped while I worked the Coleman case. Of course, since the Blood Moon, sitting inside my old car for an extended period of time probably would have made me retch. The convertible had been designed for the filthy rich or fae and had no iron in its construction. Even used, it hadn't been cheap, and I was almost surprised it didn't run on rainbows. *Actually, rainbows would probably be a pain-in-the-ass power source.* I'd used most of the money I'd made from the Coleman case on the down payment, and I still owed the bank, but business had been good and as long as that lasted, I wouldn't have trouble with the monthly payments.

Since Malik wasn't glamoured, I pulled the charm I'd made for detecting glamour from the cup holder and snapped it onto my bracelet. Better safe than sorry. I checked that the magic bridle was in easy reach in the top of my purse and then leaned across the seat to grab the plastic grocery bag on the passenger side. "I brought what you asked for. Do I want to know why we need raw hamburger meat?"

Malik's thin lips cracked into a smile full of small, yellow teeth. "We have to get the kelpie's attention, now, don't we?"

Great.

I followed him down the bank to the edge of the water. When he held out one long-fingered hand I gave him the grocery bag. He dug inside, pulling out the three pounds of raw hamburger. Tearing off the plastic, he studied the pink meat.

"Bloodier would have been better," he said, "but this will do."

He sank his fingers into the meat, and after pinching off a clump, hurled it into the rushing water. It vanished into the current, and I waited, shuffling from foot to foot on the uneven bank.

Nothing happened.

"Now what?" I asked, staring at the water.

Malik flicked his fingers, dislodging bits of pink hamburger, but he continued to watch the river. After several minutes, he shook his head. "Let's try farther upstream."

The walk couldn't be described as companionable. Malik hummed to himself, clearly not interested in casual conversation as he waltzed through the thick underbrush crowding the edge of the bank. My progress was considerably less effortless as dry twigs snapped under my steps and vines tugged at my ankles. This was the second time this week I'd tromped through the wilderness, and my boots just weren't made for it. Then there were the bugs. I seriously should have packed an insect repellent charm, or at least the spray that norms used. Not that any of this seemed to bother Malik as he led us farther upstream. In between swatting mosquitos on my bare arms and watching for raised roots waiting to trip me, I scanned the water, the banks, and the woods beyond, but nothing bigger than a squirrel moved in the wilderness.

We stopped several times, and at each stop Malik tossed more hamburger into the river. But no water horse emerged from the current.

"Do you think the court already captured the kelpie?" I asked once we'd exhausted all three pounds of meat.

Malik shrugged. "She might not be hungry."

Maybe because she snacked on some human remains? Actually, that theory didn't hold with the evidence we had. Tamara had said there were no tool marks—or any other indication of how the feet were severed from the legs—and I didn't think she'd miss something like gnaw marks on the bones.

"So how can we draw her out?" I asked as Malik handed me the grocery bag.

"We could offer her something she'd find more appetizing." Malik smiled, flashing discolored teeth. "She's not my biggest fan, but I bet she'd find you . . . sweet."

My stomach, already a little sour after tossing raw meat around, knotted tight. I backed up a step. "What are you suggesting?"

"Calm down. Kelpies are like sharks with hooves—they can smell blood in the water for miles. A few drops should be enough to get her attention."

Right, a couple of drops of blood so the kelpie could get a taste for me—because that wasn't creepy. I stared at the rushing water. The hope that the kelpie had information about the location of the crime scene was the only lead I currently had. I'd bled for worse reasons. Finally I nodded.

"So just a couple of drops in the water?"

Malik rubbed the point of his sharp chin. "Yeah, but it would be best if you could put them in at the middle of the river."

Which meant trekking back to the bridge. Well, that was where the car was anyway. If this didn't work out, I had to leave soon. We'd been walking for at least an hour, and I still needed to make it to—and out of—the Eternal Bloom before dusk. Driving after dark wasn't an option with the extent to which grave-sight had deteriorated my night vision.

The walk back was no more companionable than the first part of the hike had been, and by the time I spotted the gray stone bridge, sweat coated my skin. *Gee, I'll be pleasant-smelling company when I meet Rianna.* I wiped damp curls from my face and followed Malik to the center of the bridge. He turned to me, nodding without a word. *Guess I'm on.*

Most witches carried fingersticks for activating or personalizing charms, but the only spells I used that required blood magic were healing charms, and, well, I was typically already bleeding if I needed one, so I didn't have a fingerstick with me. I did have two daggers: the ceramic knife I used to cast circles outdoors and the enchanted dagger. I tended to drag the ceramic knife through the dirt, so it definitely wasn't sterile, but I was reluctant to give a somewhat aware dagger a taste of my blood. *But I'm willing to give a taste to a man-eating horse?* It was probably better if I didn't think about that.

I dug through my purse and pulled out the ceramic dagger. A quick examination of the blade showed a caked-on smear of mud. I scraped off as much as I could with my fingernail and then wiped the blade on the leg of my pants. That was about as clean as it was going to get, I would definitely need a disinfectant when I got home.

After pricking my finger, I sheathed the knife and dropped it back in my purse. I squeezed my finger and blood welled from the small wound. Holding my hand over the edge of the bridge, I squeezed until gravity forced a fat drop of blood to fall to the water below. Malik stepped forward after the third drop hit the water.

"That should be enough," he said, leaning over the stone railing to stare at the river's choppy surface.

I dug through my purse until I found a tissue. Pressing the tissue against my finger, I waited, watching the water rush under the bridge. Nothing changed.

After several moments, I shook my head and dropped the tissue back into my purse. "I don't think it worked."

"No, look. It did." Malik leaned farther over the edge of the bridge and pointed at a spot near the center of the river, almost directly where my blood would have hit the water.

I squinted at the dark shape. "That's a turtle."

He shook his head. "It's the kelpie. You called her. You need to identify yourself."

"Uh, hi. I'm Alex Craft," I said, feeling stupid talking to what I was pretty sure was a turtle or a fish. The shadow began to sink back under the water, and Malik's head snapped toward me. His dark eyes went wide, and his hands fluttered as if urging me to say more. "I work with Tongues for the Dead, and I'd like to ask you a few questions."

The small shadow stopped. Then it grew larger. And larger. I could have sworn the river didn't run too deep here, but the shadow grew to the size of a dog and then to the size of a cow. It headed for the bank. *Apparently not a turtle.* I shouldered my purse and ran toward the bank, Malik at my heels.

A large equine head emerged from the water. The kelpie's coat was a dank grayish brown like the dark silt and seaweed tangled in the slimy mane clinging to her long neck. She lifted one large hoof onto the bank, and then another, not so much as scrambling as she climbed from the water. Her hooves struck the ground like thunder as she trotted toward me, and I stopped short. She was massive, each hoof the size of a dinner plate, and even in my three-inch boots, I stood only as tall as her large back.

My hand twitched toward the enchanted bridle in my purse, and I forced my fingers away. I wanted to talk with her, if she was willing, not jump straight to trickery. No use making an enemy if I didn't have to. Nevertheless, it was hard to remain still as the kelpie lowered her head and drew in enough air to make the curls around my face quiver. She let the air out again, blowing her lips and revealing very sharp—and very unhorselike—teeth.

"You smell delicious, Alex Craft with Tongues for the Dead." The voice that emerged from her horse mouth was surprisingly feminine and her enunciation perfect. "Sleagh Maith with a mix of mortal? Would you like to go for a ride, little feykin?" She knelt on her front legs to give me easier access, but I backed away.

"No. That's okay."

"More's the pity." She turned her attention to Malik.

"Oh, it's you, Shellycoat." Her lips curled away from those sharp teeth. It was strange to see a snarl on a horse, but the expression was unmistakable. She huffed her breath and as the air rushed out of her the skin on her neck flared. *Gills?* "What an unpleasant surprise." She tossed her head, flinging water and muck from her mane.

I stepped back, but I couldn't avoid the spray. I wiped

the muddy water from my cheek with the back of my hand and frowned at the dark spots dotting my top, but there wasn't time to do anything about it as the kelpie turned back toward the river.

"Wait." I reached out, my hand brushing her side. Her muscles quivered under my fingers and I jerked my hand back. What I'd originally taken as fur was actually hundreds of small, sticky scales. I stepped back a bit, but didn't move far. "I need to ask you some questions."

The kelpie turned and studied me with one large, milky eye. "Part ways with Shellycoat and come to my home for supper. You may ask me any question you wish during the meal."

Was that a legitimate offer, or would I be part of dinner? Either way, she lived under the river, and I definitely couldn't breathe water. I shook my head. "I'd prefer to keep my feet on dry land."

"Then why should I answer your questions, Alex-Craft-with-Tongues-for-the-Dead-who-prefers-to-keep-her-feet-on-dry-land?"

I blinked at the title and glanced at Malik. He rolled his shoulders and stood straight so that he matched the kelpie's impressive height.

"You should answer because Ms. Craft is working to protect the independent fae in Nekros from the grasp of the Winter Queen."

Pale skin flashed beneath the kelpie's gills. "And what care I for the troubles of other independents?"

"You'll care if the queen saddles and stables you."

It was hard to read the kelpie's equine features, but I think she glared at Malik. After several silent seconds, she turned to me, her large eyes unblinking. *That's as close to permission as I'm likely to get.* I asked my question.

"A group of feet recently floated down the Sionan River and washed up in the floodplain to the south. They were tossed into the river sometime in the last four or five days. Do you remember seeing or otherwise sensing the feet floating through your territory?"

The kelpie's lips once again curled back from those sharp, predatory teeth. "The grotesque offering? The meat was putrefied by magic. It offended me."

Offering? That was an unusual way to view body parts dumped in the river, but the feet the police had found were certainly saturated with dark magic, so I guessed we were talking about the same thing. I shuddered at the idea that she'd actually tried to eat one of the feet, but if I thought about it, that wasn't really unexpected.

"Do you know where the, uh, 'grotesque offering' was tossed into the river?"

"In the place that reeks of iron, near one of the thundering gates."

Well, that's as clear as river muck. The place that "reeked of iron" was probably the city—no fae liked iron and the city had a lot of it. But what were the "thundering gates"?

I didn't get a chance to ask. A hiccup erupted in my chest, interrupting me. I pressed my fingers over my lips just as a second hiccup hit, followed by a third.

The charm. Glamour—and not from the kelpie or Malik.

I whirled around, glancing over the bank, the bridge, and the road as I turned. Nothing. My gaze shot to where the woods encroached on the river. Still nothing.

Another hiccup gripped my chest, bursting from my throat, and I cringed. *Okay, charm, I got the point.* There was glamour being used nearby, but I really wished the charm had a better way of warning me. At least I'd had the foresight to attach the charm with a quick-release clasp this time. I unhooked it from the bracelet and pried open my shields.

My grave-sight snapped into focus, painting the forest in muted shades as the landscape decayed. Several yards away, amid the forest of rotted trees, a troll moved silently through the wilted underbrush. His shoulders were wide enough that he had to turn sideways to step between two thick trees and avoid tearing the dark business suit he was wearing. His hands, each as big as my head, dragged the ground beside bare green feet sticking out under the hemmed legs of his slacks. I thought for a moment his hands were brown with moss green mounds over his knuckles, until I realized he wore gloves, the leather worn away on the top.

He moved slowly, sucking in his gut to allow more clearance between the tree trunks. But not enough clearance. Bark flaked off the trees as he brushed past. Beside me, the kelpie's ears twitched, the skin on her neck quivering as she snapped her head toward the forest. The troll's glamour might have hidden his footsteps, but we all heard the explosion of bark.

Malik wrung his hands, glancing from the forest to me. "What do you see?"

"Troll," I whispered, hoping the troll in question wouldn't hear. He'd paused when he brushed against the tree, as if waiting to see if we had noticed.

We had.

I'd met only one troll before, and it had been rather slow on the uptake. This one looked much more astute—it was probably the suit. If nothing else, the suit definitely implied that roaming the wilds wasn't part of his normal routine.

"I'm guessing trolls aren't common in this area?" I asked, but the only answer I received was a loud splash behind me.

I turned in time to see ripples and the kelpie's dark shadow fade under the surface of the water. I glanced at Malik—or at least at where Malik had been. Now there was only his retreating back.

I whirled back around, and the movement dislodged small pebbles, sending them tumbling down the bank to make *plink plink* sounds as they hit the water. The troll was running now, bounding toward me. *Crap.* My muscles tensed, preparing to send me bolting away. My car wasn't far, just on the other side of the bridge. Then the troll reached into his coat, pulling his sidearm and in the process flashing the badge at his waist.

"Freeze—FIB," he yelled as he leveled a gun large enough to be a small cannon at Malik's fleeing back.

I froze. For one endless moment, even my heart stopped. Then the next beat crashed hard, threatening to knock me forward. I lifted my hands slowly, palms open to show I carried no weapon and was preparing no spell. Not that it mattered. The troll never looked at me.

He thundered by, each stride of his tree-trunk-thick legs eating the ground in a massive gait. Still the distance between him and Malik grew.

"Malik Shellycoat, by order of the winter court I command you to stop," he yelled, his voice booming but already breathless.

Malik dove into the forest, slipping silently through the underbrush until he vanished among the trees. The troll crashed after him, trees shuddering and bark exploding like shrapnel as he shouldered through.

I remained by the bank, my hands in the air until both fae had vanished from sight. Then I lowered my arms, glancing around. I could still hear the troll's loud pursuit in the distance, and I half expected to spot the troll's partner approaching me, gun out and cuffs in hand. But there was no one.

Time to get out of here.

I grabbed my purse from where I'd dropped it when the troll appeared and snapped my shields closed. I hadn't had my grave-sight active long, and I hadn't actually reached for the grave or used my power, but darkness still swam over my vision. I dug the glasses I often needed after the ritual from my bag and blinked, giving my sight a moment to adjust. It did, and after a couple of still-rushing heart-beats, my vision cleared enough that I was confident I'd be able to drive. Then I made my way over the bridge, not exactly running, but just barely not.

The FIB was an official law enforcement entity—I probably should have waited to see if the agent's backup would arrive. There would definitely be questions about what I was doing out in the middle of nowhere with a person of interest in a homicide case. *I'm not fleeing the scene,* I told myself, but I was. And I knew it.

I'd just crossed the bridge when I noticed the shadow leaning against my car. I stopped short, squinting to make out the figure. I groaned and started walking again when I finally recognized the woman.

"Agent Nori," I said as I approached.

"Miss Craft. You have a tendency to show up where you shouldn't." She flashed some teeth. "It seems you found the fae who was harassing you."

I twisted the strap of my purse in my hands as I focused on her nose, not her eyes. "I was mistaken about his involvement."

"I see." She drew the word out so it had multiple sylla-bles. "Be that as it may, he's still wanted for questioning in an open case. If you encounter him again, give me a call."

She pressed a card into my hand. "And, Miss Craft, let me give you a little *friendly* advice. Those who don't have loyalty to a court don't have loyalty to anyone. Be careful with whom you associate."

"Right." I slid into my car and got the hell out of there, silently wishing luck to Malik as I drove away.

Chapter 7

I called Caleb on my way to the Magic Quarter to meet Rianna, but he didn't answer his cell. I didn't like the idea of walking into the Bloom alone, but Tamara was working late and I wasn't going to call Holly. That left me with only one other person.

"Thanks for meeting me here," I said as Roy popped into existence in the passenger seat of my car. A ghost for backup in Faerie probably wasn't much backup at all, but he was the best I had. If nothing else, at least he was a second pair of eyes.

"Hey, no problem. It's not like I have a lot of better prospects to haunt," he said, folding his hands behind his head. "So, what's on the agenda? A little breaking and entering? Some undercover work? Or just a little good old spying?"

I pulled into a metered spot a couple of blocks from the Bloom—that was as close a parking spot as I could find. "Actually we're going to meet with an old friend of mine." I paused, my hand still on the stick shift. There was an issue with bringing Roy along that I hadn't thought of before now. "I'm meeting Rianna."

Roy's hands fell and his face screwed up tight. "Tell me you're going to manifest me."

"Uh, no." By "manifest," Roy meant he wanted me to pump him with enough energy to make him physical in the land of the living. The first time I'd done it he'd punched Rianna. At the time that had been a good thing, as she'd still been under Coleman's control and on the opposite side, but Roy had deeper reasons to hate Rianna—she'd been involved in his death. Unwilling though she might have been, Roy was having a hard time forgiving his murderer. I guess I couldn't blame him. "Try to play nice," I said, giving him a pleading smile.

His fists balled by his side, but after a moment he gave me a sharp nod. "Fine." He stood—straight through my car, which was rather disturbing—and walked to the sidewalk.

I hurried to catch up.

He sulked as we walked to the Eternal Bloom, his shoulders slumped and his gaze down. After two attempts to start a conversation with him—which both received only noncommittal sounds in response—I didn't bother trying to converse with someone that no one else on the street could see. I would make it up to him later. Maybe I'd buy him some Legos—the little blocks were light enough for him to pick up if he concentrated. Roy floated through the main door when we reached the Bloom. I, on the other hand, had to pull it open.

"Hullo, lass. Welcome to the Eternal Bloom," the bouncer, a red-bearded man perched on the stool in the entry said, his accent thick. "Check all iron items here, and do'na forget to sign the ledger."

"No iron," I said, pulling a pen from my purse.

The entry wasn't large, just a short room with enough space for the bouncer, his stool, and the pedestal with the ledger balanced on top. I saw only one door, but I knew there was another one not accessible to the majority of the bar's clientele.

As I stepped up to the pedestal and ledger, the short man stood on his stool. Even with the stool's height, he only reached my chin, but he peered around my shoulder, watching me write my name, and most important, the date and time. I wrote as legibly as possible. I was about to step into a pocket of Faerie—I wanted to make sure I emerged on the same day I entered.

"Ah, a VIP," the bearded bouncer said once I put my pen away. He puffed on the pipe clenched between his teeth and then blew a smoke ring in the air. The sweet, tobacco-scented smoke stung my eyes and tickled my chest. I coughed, waving a hand in front of my face to clear the air. When I blinked away the moisture in my eyes, I found two doors along the back wall where there had been only one before.

The little man smiled around his pipe. "Enjoy your visit, lass."

"Right. Thank—" I stopped myself before I thanked the man. Hitching my purse higher on my shoulder, I glanced back at Roy. "Coming?"

"Yeah, right behind you," he said, but he was staring at the newly appeared door, a frown etched hard in his shimmering face.

Maybe I'll owe him more than Legos for backing me up in there.

I jerked open the door and then hesitated. Roy wasn't following.

"We won't be long," I promised.

The ghost bit his lower lip. "I can't go."

Okay, that was a little much. I knew he was mad at Rianna, I got it, but he'd said he'd back me up. He must have seen my thoughts on my face because he shook his head.

"It's not . . . *her.* It's the door. It feels wrong. Definitely not safe."

I stepped back into the entry, letting the door swing shut, and studied it. *Safe?* Well, I wouldn't describe Faerie as safe for anyone, but the fact that he said it felt wrong did concern me. The door was some sort of portal to another place—it might not be safe for Roy. *Hell, it might not be safe for me.* But that was another story.

I thought back. I'd seen a ghost, or at least a spirit, in the Bloom before. Well, actually I'd sort of *created* a ghost when I'd jerked the spirit from a dead, animated body of a slaver's pet grave witch. "I've seen ghosts in there," I told Roy, leaving off the rest of the story.

"Yeah, but did the ghost leave?" He stepped back, farther from the door. "It feels like a cemetery gate."

That wasn't good. Cemetery gates kept ghosts—and other, rarer forms of the dead—locked inside. Even newer cemeteries typically had a ghost or two, the older ones many more, though the ghosts rarely started their spirit-life in the graveyard. Like some sort of spirit roach motel, the ghosts could enter the cemetery, but they couldn't leave. While Roy might get annoying once in a while, I definitely didn't want to get him stuck in Faerie.

"Okay, stay here," I said, and realized the bouncer was studying me, his bushy red eyebrows drawn together and his pipe in his hand.

"Lass, talking to invisible faeries isn't uncommon here, but I happen to know none are present."

In other words, he thought I was crazy. I gave him a tight smile.

"Ghost," I said by way of explanation, and the little man squinted as if that would help him see the spirit among us. I ignored him, turning my attention back to Roy. "I shouldn't be long. If I'm not out in an hour or two . . ."

I trailed off. If I wasn't out soon, what was he supposed to do? He couldn't come after me, and unless he tracked down another grave witch—and last I'd heard, the closest one not in Faerie was over a hundred miles away—he couldn't communicate with the living. A ghost really was terrible backup.

I didn't finish the sentence. With a quick wave good-bye, I jerked the door open and let myself into the VIP area of the Eternal Bloom.

I signed another ledger inside the door, again printing carefully. The attendant, a sour-faced fae with long, donkeylike ears and cloven feet, nodded, taking the pen from me and shooing me farther into the Bloom when I would have dawdled in the doorway.

The Eternal Bloom hadn't changed since the last time I was here. The giant tree growing through the floorboards and blooming with an impossible arrangement of shimmering blossoms dominated the center of the room, its large limbs spreading to form a leaf-and-flower-filled canopy over the tables in the bar. I didn't stare at the tree long—it had nearly entranced me last time.

In the far corner, a new fiddler had taken the place of the one whose strings I had severed to halt the eternal dance. A small cluster of dancers spun around him, but not yet a third as many as I'd freed during my last visit. I could just barely hear the lively jig the fiddler played over the murmur in the bar, and I moved farther away so I wouldn't be drawn into the dance.

The crowd in the bar boasted a mix of the grotesque and the beautiful. While some of the patrons either still wore their glamour or were, in fact, human, many were very obviously fae, *other*. Small, large, winged, floral, too-many-limbed, too-few—they were a dizzying display rarely seen on the streets. While the fae had announced their presence and needed mortal belief, they kept their own counsel more often than not and had no interest in becoming sideshows—not that I blamed them. I let my gaze move quickly, not lingering long enough to cause offense as I searched for Rianna. I spotted her at a small round table at the very back of the room.

She stared at her drink as I approached, never glancing up. Her note had said she needed my help, but she didn't appear anxious, and certainly not fearful as she sat in the crowded bar. If anything, she looked dejected and worn down. Her narrow, slumped shoulders were thin under the drab gray gown she wore and her skin was pale, sickly. If she was in danger, I would have expected her to be watching the other patrons, to glance nervously from person to person as she scanned the room, or at least to glance at the door once in a while, looking for me, since she'd asked me to meet her here. But she didn't look up from the wooden mug in front of her, not even as my approach put me only tables away. Of course, maybe she didn't have to—she'd brought a guard dog.

The huge black dog stepped around the side of the table when I approached. The thick hair on its back stood up, and it glared at me, its black irises ringed with red as if splashed with blood. A low growl tumbled from behind rust-colored teeth.

Rianna's head snapped up at the sound, her sunken green eyes a little too wide. Then her gaze landed on me, and her thin lips spread into a weak smile. She jumped to her feet.

"Al!" She all but ran around the side of the table. Her

arms wrapped around my shoulders, the rough material of her gown scratchy against the skin left bare by my tank top. "I was afraid you wouldn't come."

She stepped back. Before I'd seen her inside Coleman's circle a month ago, I—and the rest of the world—thought she'd died four years back. It turned out she'd been kidnapped and enslaved in Faerie. When I'd destroyed Coleman, the silver chains holding her had dissolved, but she looked no better now than the last time I'd seen her. Roy called her the Shadow Girl, and she truly looked like little more than a shadow of the girl who'd been my best friend in academy. Her grayish skin lacked any rosy hint of health, her once-vibrant red hair now hung listlessly around her shoulders, and her eyes had the haunted look of someone who had seen too much pain and too much evil—which, considering she'd been enslaved to a megalomaniac, she probably had.

"Of course I came," I said as I stepped back. A pang of guilt that I hadn't come earlier, that it had taken a plea for help nailed to my porch to get me to the Bloom to see her, wiggled under my skin and whispered what a horrible friend I'd turned out to be. I ignored that voice. "It's been too long," I said, smiling. Both the smile and the statement were true—I really was glad to see her. We hadn't had any time to catch up when I'd seen her last. But even as the words left my mouth, I could feel the awkwardness between us. *What do you say to your best friend after she's been enslaved by a psychopath and presumed dead?* I fidgeted with my purse strap. "So, what's happening? You said you needed help?"

She nodded and led me to the table. The enormous dog continued growling, lower now but no less threatening. He stepped in front of Rianna, blocking her from me with his own body. Rianna cooed at him under her breath. "It's all right, Desmond. This is the old friend I told you about."

The dog stared at me, and I felt a trickle of sweat trail down my neck as he caught me in the glare of those red-ringed pupils. The growl leaking out of Desmond's throat ceased, but he kept his rust-colored canines exposed.

"New pet?" I asked as I sank into the chair across from Rianna.

Her hand moved to the massive dog's head, and he leaned against her legs, dropping his muzzle in her lap. "No, not a pet. More of a friend turned guardian. This is Desmond. He's a barghest. Desmond, this is Alex Craft."

The barghest lifted his head briefly, gave me an unimpressed glance, and then nuzzled Rianna's thigh.

Back at you, buddy. Not that I could say as much out loud. I mumbled a quick "Nice to meet you," just to be polite. I hadn't read much about barghests, but I vaguely remembered a tale suggesting that seeing one was a portent of death—*not reassuring*—but they were fae creatures, or perhaps lesser fae, so polite was the best approach. Not that Desmond seemed inclined to show me the same courtesy. *Guess we'll agree to ignore each other.*

I pulled my chair closer and leaned forward. "Your letter sounded urgent. Are you okay?"

She nodded. "I have an odd request," she said, her hand still idly stroking the dog's head. "Can I see your palms?"

I blinked at her. *My palms?* "Are you reading fortunes now?" I joked, but obediently placed my open palms on the table. Then I gasped.

Dark red liquid coated both of my hands—red liquid that looked a whole lot like blood.

I jumped to my feet. "Are you hurt?" I asked, starting around the table. The blood had to be hers. It must have transferred to my hands when I hugged her.

Desmond rounded on me, blocking my way.

"I'm fine, Alex, Desmond. Both of you, sit."

I frowned at the fae dog and then at her again. *What's going on?* When Rianna just stared at both of us, I finally returned to my side of the table and sat. We were both stubborn—spending half our lives as roommates during academy had provided plenty of opportunities for our unyielding natures to butt heads. She'd asked me to come and I wanted to hear what she had to say, so for now I sat. Desmond continued to stare over the table at me for several seconds before he sat back on his haunches and laid his head in Rianna's lap again.

"So if you aren't hurt, whose blood is this?" I asked as I lifted my purse with one finger. Thankfully the tissue I'd used earlier was still on top of the purse's contents and I didn't have to root around and risk getting the blood all over everything.

"How familiar are you with fae inheritance?"

I frowned at her. *Well, that definitely doesn't answer my question.* "Not at all. Now about the bloo—"

"I was afraid of that." She leaned forward and plucked the tissue from my hands. "That won't help."

I glared, though she was right. I'd rubbed at the blood, but it still coated my palms and fingers, as if I'd dipped my hand in paint.

"Now, about fae inheritance," she said without pause. "The fae are not truly immortal, just unaging. Death for humans is expected, anticipated, and in some ways prepared for. Death among fae is always a shock. They do not prepare for it, and as a culture have few precedents for it. Property and titles are not passed down along family lines because such things are assumed to be owned forever unless traded, gifted, or lost in duels. There are dozens of faerie princes and princesses, but none will rule a court unless they duel or kill for it."

"Okay. Why the culture lesson, and what does it have to do with this?" I lifted my hands.

She motioned me to be patient and continued. "Most duels are held under court supervision. Rules are established before the duel begins, but if it is a duel to the death, the winner takes all: property, titles, possessions, whatever the loser claimed as his own. When a fae is killed outside of a duel, it is less clear what happens to his property. But Faerie, well, sometimes Faerie has its own idea."

The sick feeling in my stomach told me I knew where this conversation was going. "Coleman?"

Rianna nodded. "You killed Coleman outside a duel, but because of the magic of that night, we were technically in Faerie. The courts tried to claim Coleman's property, but thus far, all claims have failed." She took a deep breath and looked at my hands again. "I wasn't sure, with how things played out that night, if you would be credited with his death—I mean, the Winter Queen's knight shot and killed the body Coleman inhabited. But you, well . . . you have Coleman's blood on your hands, so I think Faerie transferred his property to you."

A sour taste crawled up my throat, and I swallowed, trying to rid the taste from my suddenly dry mouth. "His blood?" I stared at the red, tacky liquid and then scrubbed my palms on the thighs of my pants, desperate to wipe them clean.

It didn't work.

"Here." Rianna dropped something in the center of the table between us.

I tore my gaze from my palms, hoping she'd had baby wipes or hand sanitizer on her. No, she'd dropped a pair of white gloves on the table.

"I'm just supposed to cover it up?"

Rianna shrugged. "Fae blood can't be washed away."

I stared at the gloves and my throat constricted. I had blood on my hands. My eyes burned, my vision clouding over as moisture gathered. I blinked it back. I was angry, and freaked, but I wasn't going to tear up. I wasn't. *I have a man's blood on my hands.* But he'd been a monster. If I hadn't stopped him, others would have died.

I took a deep breath. Then another. It took three deep breaths to ease the tightness in my chest enough that I could speak again. I picked up the gloves, sliding them on with slow, careful movements to keep from jerking them on frantically. Then I looked at Rianna.

"It's been a month. Why did the blood appear now?"

"I'd guess because this is the first time you've come to Faerie since the Blood Moon." There was no accusation in her words, but I still felt the sting and cringed anyway. One of the few things she'd had time to say to me that night was to ask me to come here, to the Bloom, to see her. I hadn't.

She wrapped her fingers around her wooden mug and stared at its contents, not meeting my eyes. "Faerie tends to take things more literally than the mortal realm does. When you're not here, you probably won't be able to see the blood."

But it would still stain my soul—not that I hadn't already felt it there.

"You talk about Faerie like it's sentient. It's a place."

The fabric of her dress rustled as she shrugged. "Faerie is . . . It just is. I wouldn't say the land is exactly a *being*, but it is certainly full of very old magic, which appears to have grown *aware*, for lack of a better word."

"And you think the land decided I should inherit Coleman's property?"

We both looked at my now covered hands. Then she pressed her lips together and nodded. "Like I said, the courts tried to claim it, but all of his former holdings moved to a type of no-man's-land, outside any of the courts' control. They are incensed, to say the least, particularly the Winter Queen, as she thought her knight had claimed it for her. You should come to Faerie and see if the holding responds to you."

Mention of the "queen's knight" again—Falin. I made it a point not to think about him, or about the fact that he'd never called or made any attempt to contact me after the Coleman case. But being back in the Bloom, remembering what had happened here—or more accurately, what had happened after we'd left the Bloom, made heat lift in my cheeks and the ache fresh again. I dropped my elbows on the table and pressed the palms of my hands against my eyes. "I think I need a drink."

"Have you tried that before?"

I looked up. "What?"

"I have heard rumors. Most are not convinced you are fae enough to hold land in Faerie, but the blood . . . If you've eaten faerie food before and left Faerie unscathed, that perhaps proves you are fae enough."

"Oh." I shook my head. Everyone knew better than to eat faerie food. One bite of food or sip of wine would addict a mortal for life—she would never be able to eat anything else, as regular food would turn to ash on her tongue. Even if someone had the willpower to leave Faerie, she would eventually starve to death. There were talks about importing regulated faerie food for those who accidentally became addicted, but making fae food available outside Faerie increased the risk that mortals would come in contact with it. Currently there were very few cases of addiction, but it was also very difficult for mortals to get into Faerie, so the chance for accidental exposure was minimal.

I was half fae. Did that give me a fifty-fifty chance of being addicted? I glanced at Rianna's mug.

Her thin fingers wound around the mug, dragging it closer to her side of the table. I didn't think she was aware of the motion. *She believes I can claim land in Faerie but is unconvinced I can eat their food?* I felt a smile crawl over my face, but I knew it wasn't a happy one. I wasn't about to take the chance of getting addicted anyway.

"Will you come to Faerie?" she asked. "See if the land responds to you? If it does, you can align to a court so the holdings move there."

"Whoa, slow down." I threw up my hands. "I don't want to claim Coleman's holdings. They can rot for all I care. And I'm certainly not going to align myself with a court."

Rianna's frown stretched across her face, and if possible, her shoulders slumped further. "Al," she said, her voice just above a whisper, "I'm *part* of Coleman's property."

Chapter 8

I blinked at my former best friend and roommate. "I thought you were freed when Coleman died." I'd seen the silver chain dissolve from her throat.

"From his compulsion, yes. But from Faerie?" She shook her head. "I'm a changeling. Four years passed for you, but I have lived in Faerie hundreds of years, danced with the fae, eaten their food and drunk their wine. I'm not mortal anymore, not truly. Like them, I'll never age, never die, but only while I'm inside Faerie."

"You can't ever leave?"

She shrugged. "I can take short trips as long as I'm careful. If I leave, the magic of Faerie will protect me except for the moments surrounding dawn and sunset. Those are the moments *between*, when the world is changing, and all but the strongest Fae magic fails. If I were caught outside of Faerie in the moments when magic fails, all the years I've seen would catch up with me and I would turn to dust." She shuddered and Desmond nudged her stomach with his muzzle. Her hand dropped to him and clutched the thick fur at his nape. "But back on topic. A changeling can't own anything or align with a court. If I had just wandered into Faerie, I could be claimed by any court, but since I belonged to Coleman, I now belong to his heir. While possession of his property is in question, I am untouchable—theoretically—but there is no one to enforce that status, and no court will help me."

"So you want me to come to Faerie and *claim* you?" The words tasted bad in my mouth. "That's crazy. You're a person. You're my friend."

She crossed her arms over her chest. "I'm a changeling. And I'm in trouble."

"I—" My protest died in my throat when Desmond's head snapped up. He lunged to his feet, his lips curling away from his rust-colored teeth as he stalked around the table.

I whirled around, my hand moving toward the dagger hidden in my boot even as I turned. *Me, paranoid? Probably.*

A woman who *looked* human, though she may have been glamoured, stopped three tables away. Her eyes widened as Desmond planted himself in her path, and her hand froze in front of her body, as if caught in a motion between reaching and blocking. Then, shocking the hell out of me, she dropped into a curtsy.

"I mean no harm, sir barghest," she said without rising.

Desmond went silent. *So the overgrown dog likes ladies who curtsy.* But even though his growling stopped, he didn't move from the woman's path.

"Is there something we can help you with?" Rianna asked, her hands disappearing in her sleeves as she spoke. When they emerged, I caught the glint of metal. A dagger, maybe? Clearly I wasn't the only paranoid one. Of course, it's not exactly paranoia when the monsters really are chasing you.

The woman straightened from her curtsy. She looked about ten years older than me, with wide, blunt features that made me suspect she was a changeling, not a fae. It wasn't that she was unattractive, just more handsome than pretty. She smiled, her wide mouth softening her face with the expression. "Actually . . ." Her focus moved to me. "I think you already have. You're Alex Craft, aren't you?"

In my experience, it was rarely good when people I didn't know recognized me. Still, it wasn't like I could deny I was me. I nodded.

"Oh, I thought you were." She pressed her palms together, her smile spreading. "I saw you on television and was sure I recognized you. You were the one who stopped the eternal dance. I know you were."

Crap. Being recognized as someone who had caused trouble in the Bloom probably wasn't a good—or safe—thing. The woman's excitement grew when I didn't dispute the claim.

She rushed forward, sidestepping Desmond. The barghest growled again, but the woman had already reached our table. She threw her arms around me, and if she'd had a weapon, I would have been dead. Instead I found myself in an emphatic embrace.

"Uh."

"Thank you," she said. The top of her head ended at my shoulders and her cheek felt blistering hot where it pressed against my bare arm. "I was caught in that dance for six hundred years. You freed me."

At her words, a balance between us shifted and whether she realized it or not, the debt she owed me became a very real obligation. I ignored the feeling. I wasn't about to start collecting favors from strangers. I patted her back awkwardly.

"Don't mention it." *Really. As in please be quiet.* I glanced over her head. Several patrons had turned our way, listening.

I extracted myself from the woman's hug gently, trying not to be rude but anxious to reclaim my personal space. She released me, but she didn't back off.

"I'm Edana. I didn't mean to interrupt your conversation." She nodded an apology to Rianna. "But I had to thank you when I recognized you. I can't believe you managed to free everyone from the dance. And you talk to the dead as well, don't you? The newscast I saw featured you with a ghost. It looked like you were holding hands, but I didn't think the living could interact with ghosts and shades. How did you pull that off?"

"I . . ." I didn't have a good answer for that, especially since most grave witches couldn't. Of course, if she'd been in that circle for six hundred years, I had no idea how much she knew about the changes since the Magical Awakening. "I have an affinity for the dead."

"But—" she started, but was interrupted as two men approached the table. Well, two male fae.

Whereas Edana appeared human, the two newcomers

were undeniably fae. The first had skin the texture of bark and wore a twisting vine of mistletoe in place of clothing. The second stood only three feet from the ground. He had eight spindly legs but a surprisingly humanoid head on the top of his insectlike thorax. Behind him, I caught sight of a curved stinger as long as my forearm on the end of a thick scorpionlike tail.

Desmond's growl rolled soft but menacing across the table. He'd planted himself between the fae and Rianna. I was apparently on my own.

"You are the one who s-stopped the endless-s dance?" the scorpion fae asked.

I gulped. The two fae weren't the only ones waiting for my answer. Conversation had all but ceased in the bar. *Why do I get a feeling not everyone is going to want a membership to my fan club?*

"There were extenuating circumstances," I muttered, dropping eye contact.

"You shouldn't interfere with situations that don't concern you," the mistletoe-clad fae said, stepping forward and making my gaze snap up to him. "Many of the dancers were imprisoned in that circle for a reason."

But not all. I knew for a fact that some were tricked into joining the festivities and some simply stumbled in by mistake. Not that I was going to say any of that. Arguing with the two fae wouldn't win me any points and I wasn't about to apologize and indebt myself to anyone if I didn't have to, so I remained silent.

My heart crashed in my chest, each beat harder than the last as the silence dragged on, but slowly the sound of murmured conversation picked up around us again. The two fae stared at me a moment longer, and then without another word they turned and walked away. The mistletoe-clad fae sat at a table with two thorn fae, and the scorpion fae joined a cluster of goblins gambling on a dice game in the back corner. *They just wanted to issue a warning?*

I sank into my chair, relief making my hands shake enough that I shoved them in my lap. Edana had slipped away at some point during the conflict, so it was once again just Rianna and me at the table. Well, and Desmond. Not that I had any delusions of privacy—there were definitely ears turned toward our corner.

"So . . ." I said, tugging on the cuff of my glove. I wished I had something in front of me—food, pen and paper, anything at all—to focus on. But I didn't. I just had Rianna sitting across from me, watching me fidget.

"You're not going to come to Faerie, are you?" She phrased it as a question, but her voice betrayed her lack of hope.

I cringed. I'd had enough of Faerie for one day. Besides, I couldn't claim ownership of Rianna. "You're my friend. I can't claim you as property. It's weird and wrong."

"So you'd rather someone else who is not my friend and who may see me only as a tool, take over?"

Okay, when she put it that way, it was the lesser of two evils, but . . . I released a deep breath, letting the air drag out of me and take with it the panic fluttering in my stomach. *But nothing.* I couldn't let someone else, someone who wouldn't have Rianna's best interests in mind, walk in and make her a slave again. The least I could do was see if Faerie recognized me as the heir to Coleman's holdings. If it did, I could try to figure out a way to free Rianna.

"What do I have to do?"

"Thank goodness." She pushed away from the table. "Now, we go deeper into Faerie."

And somehow I'd gotten talked into going to the one place that scared me the most.

Rianna led me through the club, toward the large tree growing right through the floorboards of the bar. Over our heads, a swollen moon glimmered high above the tree limbs. I frowned at it. The full moon had passed almost a week ago on the mortal plane. The full moon here was not a reassuring indication of time.

"How do we get there?" I asked, lagging slightly behind. Desmond had glued himself to Rianna's side, and there wasn't room for all three of us to walk abreast between the crowded tables.

"We'll have to pass through the winter court," Rianna

said without turning around. "Then we'll take another door to Stasis—that's the no-man's-land where the holdings are currently located."

She stopped as she reached the tree and turned back to me. Motioning me closer, she raised on her tiptoes and whispered, "I wouldn't mention where we are going. Coleman's holdings are nothing magnificent, and surely nothing to fight over, but the Winter Queen was miffed to say the least when Faerie didn't award it to her court. In her opinion, her knight is responsible for Coleman's death, even if he employed the help of a feykin. She doesn't take rejection well and she isn't the most pleasant person when displeased."

"I take it the winter court wouldn't be one to align with then?"

Rianna lifted one thin shoulder and let it drop. "I know you have . . . interests . . . in the winter court—which, by the way, I also recommend that you not mention. The queen is infamous for her jealousy. But any court you decided to join would be better than staying in Stasis, cut off from everyone."

Interests. I almost laughed. *That's one way to say I slept with the queen's pet assassin and lover.* Of course, I hadn't known he was either at the time. I shook my head. "You know that even if Faerie recognizes me as inheriting, I'm not going to automatically join a court. I don't know anything about the courts."

"I know. But at least if the holding is claimed, that will be taken care of." She gave me a weak smile. "Desmond and I can wait it out as long as we know we're not going to be tossed and traded around."

"Am I inheriting the dog as well?"

The dog in question rolled back his lips, showing fangs, and Rianna winced. "Not exactly. I'll explain later. Are you ready?"

Well, I guess this is it. I nodded and followed her as she walked around the back of the tree. I expected a trapdoor in the ground, or maybe in the tree itself—after all, folklore reported Faerie to be a subterranean land, and I'd heard Caleb say before that he was headed "under hill," but there was no door—there was just tree and the back side of the bar.

"Rianna, wha—"

"Keep walking."

I took another two steps around the tree, and the world seemed to slide around me. I wasn't moving, or at least it didn't feel like I moved in space, but the warm amber light in the bar smeared into darkness, and a cooler, bluer light filled the air.

I looked around: the bar was gone, the tree was gone, and I stood next to a giant pillar carved from shimmering glass. No, not glass. Ice.

The air had a bite to it, but it wasn't cold, and surely not frigid enough for the enormous pillar beside me, but though the ice shimmered, the intricately carved fae dancing in spirals up the pillar were sharp, the details too precise for the pillar to be melting. My eyes followed the dancing fae up the column until it disappeared into a glassy ceiling that sparkled like hundreds of small stars were caught in the frozen mass. Music emanated from somewhere, the soft, plucked notes mournful.

"This is Faerie?" I asked. *Where are the fae?* There was no one here, unless the carved ice sculptures lining the walls were alive. Which was possible.

"This is a hallway. Little more." Rianna crooked her arm through mine. "We shouldn't tarry."

She set a brisk pace, all but dragging me down the long passageway. I expected the smooth ice floor beneath us to be slick, but it was no worse than walking on marble. The only light in the passage was from the stars caught in the ice overhead, but it provided more than enough illumination, even for my bad eyes. I reached out with my ability to sense magic. The very air buzzed with enchantments and magic. It was as if I were drinking the magic of Faerie in with every deep breath. I tightened my shields before the buzz of magic overwhelmed my senses.

We'd made it only a couple of yards when three figures stepped out in front of us. At first I thought the statues really had come to life, but these were fae of flesh and blood. Not that we could see a lot of that flesh. All three wore hooded cloaks as white as freshly fallen snow, and in the gap where the cloaks fell open I could see intricate armor that looked like plated scales carved from blue-tinted ice.

Two blocked our path while a third moved to intercept us, a sword naked in his hand.

"You've entered the winter court's territory. Identify yourselves and your purpose," the guard with the sword said, coming to a stop directly in front of us. This close, I could see thin, shimmering lines of glyphs tattooed across the exposed skin of the guard's face and hands—at least I thought they were tattoos, though the ink glimmered like hundreds of ice crystals tracing the man's skin.

Welcome to Faerie.

"I'm the changeling Rianna, currently in Stasis. And this is . . ." She glanced at me, squeezing my hand once before dropping it. "My dear friend. I have permission to use this hall to travel between Stasis and the mortal realm."

The guard held out his hand, palm up. "Let's see it, then."

Rianna dug a thin chain out from under the collar of her dress and tugged it over her head. A blank pendant shaped like an ice crystal hung on the end of the chain, and she dropped it in the guard's palm.

He whispered a musical-sounding word and the pendant glowed a deep cobalt blue. With a nod, the guard handed the chain and pendant back to Rianna. "Follow me. I'll escort you to the door."

Rianna followed silently, so I did the same. Desmond brought up the rear, his nails making the softest clinking sounds on the ice. At first I tried to memorize our route, but as the guard led us down one identical hallway after another I lost track of how many lefts and rights we'd taken. *I'll definitely need a guide to get back out of this place.*

Finally the guard stopped. He gave Rianna a nod and then stepped aside, motioning us to a doorway. Except it wasn't a doorway at all. It was a large archway set into the wall.

I stared at the unbroken ice wall inside the arch. "Um."

"It's the door," Rianna said, locking my arm with hers again. "It will take us anywhere we want to go in Faerie, as long as we know where we want to go. Now you have to trust me. And don't let go."

She stepped forward, into the wall. *Oh, crap.* I squeezed my eyes closed and followed.

The world froze around me. I gasped, sucking in solid frozen air, and a sharp ache filled my lungs. Panic stung my mind, flooded my muscles, but I couldn't move. Then, as suddenly as the world had frozen, it thawed, turning as comfortable as bathwater. I released the frozen gasp I'd taken, and the pain in my chest vanished as warmth spread over my body. Again I didn't feel like I was moving, but the world slid out of focus, like a child smearing his hand through a painting that was not yet dry. Then it solidified again, and I was standing in a cavern that held a castle. Not just a big house, but an honest-to-goodness, large-stone-facade-with-turrets-and-towers castle. There was even a moat—though why anyone would build such a thing in the belly of a cave was beyond me. As I stood there staring, the drawbridge lowered and a portcullis made of twisting vines lifted to clear our path.

Rianna beamed at me. "Welcome home, Al!"

Chapter 9

※━─◦◦━◦◦━─※

"Home?" I stared at the large stone wall. At the moat of crystal clear water. At the jutting spiral towers. "This isn't a home. This is a castle!" Like a castle straight out of the Middle Ages. Or a fairy tale. *Welcome to Faerie, Alex.*

"Do you want to go inside?" Rianna all but bounced on her toes as she asked. "It opened for you. It's yours."

"And it's about time," a rough female voice said behind me.

I turned, but didn't see anything. My confusion must have shown on my face, because Rianna pointed toward the ground. I obediently looked down.

A woman who stood no higher than my knee stared up at me. She was nearly as wide as she was tall, so she looked like a waddling basketball wrapped in burlap as she gave me a quick once-over, and then, with a nod, marched past me.

"Well, get a move on," she called over her shoulder. "I'm sure there's a layer of dust on everything by this point."

I gaped at the small woman and then looked to Rianna for explanation.

"Wait, Ms. B," Rianna called after the woman. "This is Alex."

The small woman paused. "Well, of course she is." Ms. B curled her lips in what might have been a sneer or a smile—I wasn't sure which. "Now, I've work to do." She hopped onto the castle's drawbridge, the hair that exploded around her head like overgrown spider-grass trailing behind her as she walked away without a backward glance.

"Uh, Rianna . . . ?" I looked at my longtime friend.

"Ms. B is a brownie. Think of her as a housekeeper, cook, and general organizer of all things inside the castle."

"I can't afford a housekeeper!" And I certainly couldn't afford to keep a castle. I was barely able to stay on top of paying rent on an efficiency.

"Don't be silly. You don't *pay* brownies. Faerie may say you own this property, but trust me, this is Ms. B's castle. She went absolutely crazy when she couldn't get inside— tried to take the wall apart stone by stone. Not that Faerie let her. She was here before Coleman claimed the castle, and she'll still be here when the castle changes hands again." She didn't elaborate on how I might lose the castle, but hurried on. "My suggestion is to make friends with her. She never liked Coleman. On the few occasions he stayed in the castle every meal came out burned, the ceilings leaked, moths attacked every scrap of material, and sand wound up on the bedsheets. He'd leave and everything would return to gleaming order. Brownies are good at holding a grudge."

"Coleman couldn't get rid of her?"

Rianna shook her head, and the dog at her side made a huff that sounded suspiciously like a laugh. She ignored him. "You don't get rid of brownies. You could burn the place to the ground, but I've heard they will stick around to tend the ashes. Though, sometimes, if they particularly like a family or a person, they will relocate with them rather than remain attached to a domicile." She shrugged, like she used to when we'd study together at academy and she didn't think the subject was particularly interesting.

"Right." My head was spinning. *This is all a little surreal.* "Are there any other, uh, *inhabitants* I should know about?"

"Just a garden gnome. He tends the grounds, but he's shy. I rarely catch sight of him." She leaned closer. "I think he's sweet on Ms. B."

I stared at her, trying to decide if she was joking. She wasn't. *How do I get myself into these things?* I turned back toward the castle. "So are we sure Coleman's holdings are now mine? I mean, I didn't exactly claim anything—I just showed up."

"Faerie locked this place up tight as soon as Coleman bit the big one. The castle opened for you. It's yours."

Great. *A castle, really?* I turned away. "Well, then, I guess I should head back."

"You haven't even looked around yet. Aren't you curious?"

I was, but I'd just found out I owned a castle in Faerie, complete with house- and groundskeepers; I wasn't up for much more yet. "It's claimed. Everyone can get inside again." Which was what I was assuming was the real issue. Homeless in Faerie land—it sounded like a bad TV show. "You don't really need me for anything else right now, do you?"

"You'll need to choose a court," she said, quickly adding, "eventually, of course."

"What happens if I want to stay in the mortal realm and be independent?"

Rianna threw out her hands to stop my words, her head swinging back and forth and her gaze sweeping over the castle like she was afraid it might jump up and run. "Don't say that," she hissed. "Faerie might listen. Doesn't happen often, but once in a while, Faerie will try to move the independents' holdings to the mortal realm. I don't think anyone wants this castle to suddenly force itself into Nekros City."

Oh, yeah, I could see trying to explain that. And with the way reality tended to bend around me, it would be my luck that my castle would appear downtown—probably in the middle of the statehouse lawn.

"I'll look into courts," I said, though I had little intention of looking quickly. From what Caleb had said, if I wanted to remain in Nekros, I'd have to align myself with the winter court, but when that court moved on, I'd have to go as well. Not a good option. "So, you're good here?"

She nodded. "For now. Come on, I'll lead you back."

She headed toward a small arch in a cavern wall, which I assumed was what we'd stepped out of despite the fact it looked like solid stone. As before, she took my arm and we stepped through the arch. Guards once again met us in the deserted halls of the winter court, and after Rianna once again produced the pendant—did I want to know what she'd gone through to acquire that?—we found ourselves with a snow-cloaked guide leading us through a maze of icy corridors.

As we walked, I leaned closer to her. "So, what do you do here?"

"I'm guessing you don't mean 'here' as in the winter court. In Stasis, there isn't much to do, and most of the fae won't have anything to do with me. Inside the courts, there are balls—lots of them—games, arts, legal proceedings. I don't know, faerie stuff."

"And you never leave?"

She shrugged as we reached the large ice pillar I'd seen after I left the Eternal Bloom. "There is no decay in Faerie. Practically no death. That means no shades to raise, and you know what it's like if you don't raise shades on occasion."

I nodded. It hurt. A grave witch ached from the inside out if she didn't raise shades on a regular basis. And grave essence tended to slip through even carefully maintained shields, the magic reaching out and filling corpses that the witch had no intention of raising. But if there was no grave essence . . .

"I slip out every once in a while, just long enough to raise a shade." Noise and light filled the air as we stepped through the winter court and into the Eternal Bloom. "Well, I guess this is where I leave you."

I held up a hand to stall her. "Wait. Do you remember your last year at academy when we mingled our magic and raised that ancient shade? The one whose body had been found mummified in a bog and was believed to be a witch or a priestess but no one else could even sense it?"

"The one that turned out to speak absolutely no English, so even though we raised it, we couldn't get an intelligible thing from it?" She smiled—a slow, creeping smile, like the memory had reminded her how to make her lips do it. "What about it?"

"This is going to sound strange, but feet have been washing up from the Sionan. A single foot isn't enough for me to raise a shade, but if we mingled our magic . . . I thought that together we might have more luck."

The smile fell from her lips as I spoke. She was frowning by the time I finished. "I would have to leave Faerie for that."

"You said you're able to leave," I said, and her hand dropped to Desmond's coat. She did that whenever a subject she wasn't comfortable with arose. I stuck my hands in my pockets and stepped back. "Never mind. It was just a thought." Sharing magic was personal, and not always comfortable or safe, which was why I hadn't thought about it when I'd first been unable to raise the shade. But Rianna and I had successfully merged our grave magic before. I shrugged. "I'll see you around, okay?"

I turned to go, but Rianna called after me.

"That's it?"

I frowned at her. "What do you mean?"

"You could tell me to help you," she said, her gaze dropping to the floor. "Could command me."

My stomach twisted, soured. I stepped forward, lowering my voice so it didn't carry to the tables surrounding us. "Rianna, I don't care what the laws of Faerie say. You are my friend. That's it. If you aren't comfortable sharing magic or are nervous about leaving Faerie, I'm not going to force you." I smiled. "I might beg a little once in a while, but you'll remember that well enough from academy—all those times I tried to get you to help fudge the results of my spellcasting homework, or that one time I was convinced I could get the attention of that super-crushable guy in meditation if I could cast . . . I don't even remember what spell it was."

Rianna's smile was reluctant, but it slowly crept across her face. "A doppelgänger spell, so you could skip class while still being there. Didn't you end up managing to make a copy of yourself that talked backward and totally failed at wearing clothing?"

"Yeah. I never sent it to class."

She laughed, her fingers slipping from Desmond's coat and lifting to her mouth as though she could catch the sound of her own amusement. "I'd have loved to see the teacher's face if you had sent it."

"No way. She was a total prude. I'd have been kicked out of academy before anyone managed to dispel the stupid double."

She nodded, but her smile remained. The laughter had done her some good and brought color to her cheeks. "Okay," she said after a moment. "When and where do you want to attempt to raise this shade?"

"You don't have to—"

She waved away my protest. "Yes, trips out of Faerie frighten me, but trips *to* Faerie frighten you." She held up a hand, motioning for silence. "And don't even try to deny it. You glance at your boot anytime anyone around us moves, so I'm guessing that's where you stashed the dagger." She smiled. "You came to Faerie because I asked for your help. I can suck it up and leave because you asked for mine. So, when and where?"

"Just so we're clear, I'm not forcing you to do anything."

"Just a friendly favor."

I nodded. "I'll need to talk to John," I said, and then realized that since she'd been out of my life for several years, she wouldn't know John. "He's the homicide detective on the case. I'll let you know when he can set up time at the morgue. How can I contact you?"

"I'll send Desmond or Ms. B," she said. Then she reached out and hugged me. "I missed you so much, Al." She stepped back. "See you soon?"

"You know it."

We said our good-byes. Then I made my way out of the club, and no one even tried to enslave me this time.

Chapter 10

⟶⟶⟹ ⟸⟵⟵

Roy waited for me just outside the door to the VIP room. "What time is it?" I asked as I signed out on the ledger. I didn't ask what *day*, though that was what I really wanted to know.

"No worries, lass," the little bouncer said from his stool. "No more 'an five minutes have passed on this side."

I blinked at him and then glanced at Roy for confirmation. Logically I knew the bouncer wasn't lying—that he *couldn't* lie—but I'd had multiple conversations and taken a trek through part of Faerie. Hours had passed for me. It seemed impossible that only a few minutes had passed in the mortal realm.

Roy shoved his glasses higher up on his nose and shrugged. "That sounds about right."

Okay, then.

I shoved open the main door. The sun still hung in the same place as when I'd walked through the door earlier. *Five minutes.* I could use extra hours once in a while— imagine how much more I could accomplish. Of course, from what Rianna had said, if I was more mortal than fae, then time would catch up with me every sunrise and sunset. I wouldn't want to waste away years in Faerie and end up old before my birth certificate said I should be.

"Is something wrong with your hands?" Roy asked as we walked toward my car.

"What?" I glanced down and realized I was still wearing the gloves Rianna had given me. "Oh, uh . . ." Would the blood still be there? Now that I'd gone to Faerie, would I always see it on my hands? I peeled off one glove, almost afraid of what I'd find. My skin was spotless underneath. No blood. "No, nothing," I said, dropping the gloves in my purse and holding up my hands to show Roy my clean palms.

The ghost lifted both his eyebrows, but it wasn't a look of shock and disgust, just his you're-acting-odd look. I received it occasionally, and right now I didn't care. I clenched my fists and then opened them again, staring at my palms. Once I got home and didn't have to worry about driving close to dusk, I would open my senses and look at my hands with my grave-sight.

"Uh, Alex, are you listening?" Roy said, and I realized he must have said something before that.

I dropped my hands to my sides and glanced at him. "Yeah?"

"'Yeah,' we're being followed or 'yeah,' you're finally listening?"

Followed?

I turned. A dark limo crawled down the street, keeping pace with me. Or it was keeping pace, until I spotted it. Then it sped up, stopping just ahead of me. The back door opened and a man stepped out onto the sidewalk. Dark shades masked his eyes, and his hand moved into the front of his jacket—exactly where a shoulder harness would be—as he straightened and turned toward me.

"How much you want to bet the appearance of a TIDS is bad news?" Roy asked as I ground to a halt.

"TIDS?"

"Thug In Dark Suit."

"Well, I certainly wouldn't bet against it," I said, glancing back the way we'd come. There was a second TIDS, as Roy put it, behind us. *Oh, this is great.*

I ducked into the nearest doorway, but this close to the Bloom most of the shops were geared toward tourists and norms. Another street over and the shops and businesses would be like any other except with a magical twist, but here they were full of gaudy, overpriced wares and operated only on nights and weekends.

The CLOSED sign hung prominently in the glass doorway.

I jerked the door handle anyway, just in case. It shook on the hinges, but didn't open.

"I might be able to open it," Roy said, stepping through the door.

Through the glass, I saw his face scrunch in concentration as he focused on the lock. But there wasn't time, and we both knew it.

I whirled around as the first man rounded the corner of the shopfront. The second joined him a moment later. They both had severe haircuts, tailored suits, and dark wraparound sunglasses that screamed "high-class thug" or "muscle-for-hire."

"Miss Craft?" Thug One asked as he stepped forward.

"Who's asking?"

The thugs shared a glance that said they'd been working together long enough to have their nonverbals down. In the short alcove I was completely cornered and they knew it. I could go for the dagger in my boot, but I had no illusion that I'd be able to draw it before the thugs closed in on me. I glanced back at Roy. He was still working on the lock.

I shouldn't have glanced away.

One of the thugs surged forward, his hand locking around my biceps. He jerked me forward with that viselike grip. I dug my heels into the ground, trying to pull back in the opposite direction, but the thug clearly spent way more time in the gym than I did. Thug Two snatched my other arm.

"Boss wants to talk with you," he said, trying to steer me toward the limo still idling on the side of the road.

"Well, maybe I don't want to talk to him, and I certainly don't like the treatment," I told him, but I stopped struggling. It wasn't getting me anywhere and I knew only one person who would want to talk to me and had a penchant for limos. My father.

The way I saw it, I had two choices. I could scream and kick and fight, and maybe cause enough of a ruckus that someone would call the cops and they'd eventually show up, or I could cooperate and get out of this quicker and without having to file a police report. I chose the second option. For one thing, it would be dusk soon and I needed this to be over quickly enough that I could still legally operate a vehicle and drive myself home, and for another, it was long past time for Daddy Dearest and me to have a little chat about my heritage. So when one of the thugs opened the limo door, I ducked inside without a fuss. Roy followed.

The man waiting inside wasn't my father.

The stranger sat on the far side of the limo, taking up more than his fair share of the leather seat as he sprawled, knees wide apart and large meat hook–like hands balanced on his legs. He had no hair, so even behind the limo's tinted windows, his scalp shone in the sunset. His pants and jacket were flawless white—a color I would never have worn in such quantities, as I was way too accident-prone—and his dress shirt was a brilliant sapphire. Years in my father's house had taught me how much stock men of power put into their physical appearance, but he hardly needed to impress me—after all, his men had just abducted me off the street.

"Miss Craft, thank you for joining me. Would you care for a drink?" He lifted a wineglass already filled with deep red liquid.

"I think there's been some mistake," I said, trying to back out the door, but, of course, the thugs were there, blocking my way.

"No mistake. You are Alex Craft with Tongues for the Dead, yes?" He smiled, flashing teeth that had to have been paid for or heavily charmed to be that white and straight. "Please, sit down."

"Should I go for help?" Roy asked, fidgeting with the edge of his flannel shirt and pacing through the floorboard of the limo.

Go where? To whom? I gave Roy a minute shake of my head and then considered the seat my "host" had offered.

It wasn't like I had much of a choice with Thug One and Thug Two outside the door. I slid stiffly into the plush leather seat and crossed my legs. I still had the charm to detect glamour in my pocket. Getting to it might be an issue, but the man looked only mildly interested when I dipped into my pocket and slid the small disk out. I clipped it to my bracelet, but no sudden attack of hiccups hit, so what I saw was apparently what I got.

"And what would that charm be, my dear?" the man asked, his voice dispassionate but his eyes glinting with curiosity.

I ignored the question. "I don't think we've been introduced."

Again he flashed that dazzling smile. "Of course. Forgive me. I must admit, I am not accustomed to not being recognized on sight. I am Maximillian Bell the Third."

"Of Spells for the Rest of Us?" That meant not only was he human, but he was a norm. Spells for the Rest of Us existed to teach norms who had extreme determination—and loads of money—how to touch the edge of the Aetheric plane and draw magic. The slang word for such a norm was "skimmer." It was rude, but an accurate description, as they could only skim the smallest amount of raw energy. The problem with skimming was that norms weren't meant to touch the Aetheric or to channel energy—it tended to burn them up from the inside out, typically starting with their minds and driving them insane. There was legislation currently in the works to make skimming illegal, but the bills kept getting delayed. People like Maximillian Bell III were likely the cause of the delays.

I opened my senses, letting my natural sensitivity to magic loose in the confined car. Bell wore more than a dozen charms on his person, everything from a dewrinkler charm to a charm meant to engender feelings of friendliness—which was borderline gray magic. None of the charms were particularly powerful, but all were at a decent level, some stronger than I could have cast, and nothing I expected to be in the possession of a skimmer. Of course, he could buy his charms. Or he could be a witch making easy money on norms. Despite his charisma charm, nothing about this situation added up to my feeling any overt goodwill toward him.

"What can I do for you, Mr. Bell?"

"Please, call me Max. I would like to hire your services. Cigarette?" He held out a flat gold cigarette case and I shook my head. He took one of the thin cigarettes from the case and fished a matching gold lighter from an inner jacket pocket. "You don't mind if I—?"

"Actually, I do mind. There are channels to go through if

you would like to hire me. You could call my business line, use my Web site, or e-mail me." I uncrossed my arms and leaned forward. "Having your goons pluck me off the street is not an appropriate channel, nor is it appreciated. Now, it's time for me to get going. Good day."

"Please, Miss Craft, I did not mean to offend. Your line appears to be turned off, your voice mail is full, and e-mail is so *impersonal* for what I wish to discuss. I am willing to spend a tidy sum of money to retain your services."

Money is always hard to turn down, especially when working freelance. But hard to turn down doesn't mean impossible. I showed some teeth. "Good day, sir." I slid across the seat toward the door.

"You haven't even listened to my request yet," he said, and pressed a button beside him.

A click sounded as the doors locked. *Creep.* I reached for the handle anyway, hoping it would auto-unlock from the inside, but it didn't and there were no controls for the lock on my side of the limo. I turned toward Roy. I didn't want to alert Bell to Roy's presence, so I fixed Roy in my gaze and then cut my eyes toward the button near Bell's hand.

The ghost nodded and walked over to the button. I just hoped he had enough focus to push it—the TV bested him if he got even slightly distracted.

"I'm not inclined to work with anyone who holds me against my will, so you better hope the deceased has some other relation who can go through the proper channels," I said, leaning back in the seat but not moving away from the door.

"Deceased?" Bell scrunched thick, dark eyebrows, which I guessed were the same color as his hair would have been if he'd had any on his head. "I don't want to hire you to raise the dead, Miss Craft. I want you to open the Aetheric for me and a select number of my followers."

The world slowed for a moment at his words, and I felt the blood drain from my face as if all my strength slipped out of me and into the leather seat. "I think you were misinformed about what I do."

"You didn't open that hole just a dozen blocks away, right here in the Quarter?"

I wanted to say "no," but that was a bald-faced lie, and my lips wouldn't even form the word, let alone let me speak it. *Guess I'm more fae than I thought.* Scowling, I went for another tactic—misdirection. "Mr. Bell, have you ever heard of any witch, even a wyrd witch, who could do such a thing? The news implied my involvement in that tear because it made a good story. Now, I think we've taken enough of each other's time."

As the last word left my mouth, a loud click sounded. Bell jumped, his head snapping toward the lock button— which he hadn't pressed, but I was already moving. I shoved the door open and stumbled out of the limo in the same movement.

The thugs were directly outside, and they turned as I emerged. *Act casual or run like hell?* I didn't have to decide. Bell yelled, "Miss Craft!" from inside the limo, and the thugs tensed, prepared to pounce.

I ran.

The thugs started to give chase, but a resounding "Let her go" came from inside the limo. The sound of following footsteps ceased, but I didn't slow until I could touch the shiny blue paint of my car. Chest burning and my breath coming in heavy gasps, I dug through my purse, searching for my keys.

I didn't give myself time to catch my breath until I was inside my car with the doors locked. Then I closed my eyes and leaned back against the headrest as I tried to convince my heart it wasn't a world-class gymnast and my ribs that they weren't its trampoline.

"You did great," I told Roy once I could speak normally.

He beamed and sat up straighter in his seat. "I did, didn't I? He'll be trying to figure that one out for a while."

Yeah, poltergeist intervention probably isn't high on most people's list of possibilities. I cranked my car and threw her in gear, but then I had to slam on the brakes before I could pull out of the parallel parking spot. The limo pulled to a stop beside me, and a window rolled down in the back.

"I wanted to follow up, Miss Craft," Bell said from inside the limo, and I wasn't sure what kind of charm or spell he used, but his voice projected perfectly. "Do consider my offer. I'm willing to make it very lucrative for you. Now drive safely—the roads can be dangerous."

A chill crawled down my spine, as if a ghost had trailed an icy finger along my skin, but the only ghost in the car was Roy, and he was out of arm's reach. Was Bell threatening me? I glanced at him. His posture was relaxed, a smile still dangling on his wide face, but his words *felt* threatening.

He lifted his hand as he spoke to someone inside the limo, and the window rolled back up, the reflective tinting showing me as a distorted image of myself—and I didn't like how freaked out that image looked.

"Roy, do me a favor," I whispered as the limo rolled away. "Snoop on Bell. Make sure he plans to leave me alone."

Roy nodded. "Will do." He vanished, stepping further into the land of the dead, where he could travel faster.

Ghosts. Terrible backup. Excellent spies.

I called John as I drove but reached his voice mail. I didn't tell him about Bell. After all, Bell hadn't hurt me, taken me anywhere, or prevented me from leaving—eventually. His lawyers would eat me alive if I tried to press charges. When Roy returned and I found out what Bell planned, I might change my mind, but for now I left a message letting John know I might be able to raise a shade from one of the feet. I wasn't sure he could still get me into the morgue, since the FIB was now involved with the case, but I knew he'd call if he could swing the time for a ritual.

When I got home, I stopped first at the main portion of the house. I needed to update Caleb on my progress—or lack thereof—and check in on Holly. Caleb didn't act surprised that the kelpie wasn't terribly helpful, but his concern bled across his features as I told him about the FIB's arrival. Holly was antsy, ready to take on the world and none too happy about everyone babying her. I made it a short visit.

PC greeted me at the door when I reached my apartment. He bounced—I'd never realized dogs were so bouncy until PC—the movement making the patch of white hair on the top of his head flop.

"Hey, buddy," I said, picking him up before he hurt himself. He lathered a kiss on my chin and then squirmed, ready to be put back down. "All right, all right." I plopped him on his feet and he immediately charged the door, whining.

"Can I get something to eat first?"

He looked at me with shiny black eyes and whined again.

"Nature calls, I guess." Food would have to wait on tiny doggy bladders.

I grabbed PC's leash, and after hooking him up, opened the door and let him charge out in front of me. I'm pretty sure the six-pound hairless dog thought he was a sled dog—he sure pulled like one. Halfway down the stairs, we passed our resident gargoyle.

I'd never seen the gargoyle move, but it traveled around the yard. I assumed by its current position it was either headed up to the bowl of cream I kept on the porch or had just drained it and was coming down. I'd have to check on my way back inside.

"Evening, Fred," I said as I squeezed around its hulking stone wings. I didn't expect an answer.

I got one anyway.

"They come," its gravelly voice said inside my head.

I froze.

"Who comes?" I asked, ignoring PC's attempt to pull me down the last few steps. "When?"

The gargoyle remained silent. *Great.* I looked around, squinting, and trying to force my grave-sight-damaged night vision to see through shadows in the dusk-filled night. Nothing.

Gargoyles—or at least this particular gargoyle; I'd never spoken to any other—were psychic but didn't always differentiate the present from the future. Last month the gargoyle had told me it missed cream when I was away. Then I'd lost three days while passing through a door to Faerie.

"Who?" I asked one more time. *Bell's men? Fae? Hell, reporters?*

I received no answer. PC whined again, but I hesitated

another moment, listening for sounds that were out of place in the quiet neighborhood. Then I leaned down and eased the dagger out of my boot. I hadn't heard anything, but that didn't mean nothing was out there. Of course, the gargoyle's words didn't mean anything dangerous *was* out in the night. I couldn't jump at shadows because an undefined "they" were coming. Who knew how long it would be before "they" arrived?

I stuck to the path of charmed stepping-stones that led from the stairs of my loft to the front yard. They twinkled under my feet as PC zigzagged across the path, pausing at every odd piece of grass to hike his leg. As we rounded the front of the house, he stopped, one foot in the air, his ears cocked.

What do you hear? I didn't ask the question aloud. If something was out there, I didn't want to announce my presence. Clutching the dagger, I searched the growing darkness, but I couldn't see much of anything aside from the twinkle of streetlights. I'd removed the glamour-detecting charm when I visited Caleb, and I was now seriously wishing I'd remembered to clip it back onto my bracelet. Okay, so I was jumping at shadows, but it was better to be safe than sorry.

I dropped my shields. My eyes might have been bad, but I didn't need them to see on a psychic level. The yard snapped into focus in shades of gray and swirls of color. In the center of the driveway, leaning heavily against Caleb's car, was a man, his soul shimmering a brilliant silver. He stepped forward, and then he stumbled, doubling over.

I squinted, trying to pick out details under the glow of his soul. The Aetheric twisted away from him, as if an aura separated him from the magical plane—which meant he was fae. At my feet PC sniffed the air, then yipped and wagged his tail in greeting. As I made out the sharp features, the wide chest slimming down to trim hips, and the long, brilliantly white hair, I realized why.

"Falin?"

Chapter 11

Falin Andrews—the infuriating but irresistible man who had invited himself into my life, chiseled himself a place in my world, and then disappeared without a word.

Giddy excitement at his return attacked my stomach even as anger at the way he'd left burned my cheeks. Then he stumbled again, falling against Caleb's car. The side mirror snapped off with a crack and thumped against the door, swinging from a few wires. It was better off than Falin. He crashed to his knees on the pavement and neither my excitement nor my anger mattered.

I ran into the front yard, dragging PC with me by my death grip on his leash. The little dog yipped happily as he followed at my heels, but I barely heard him over the rushing in my ears.

Still on his knees, Falin swayed, his eyes half closing. One of his hands—gloved as always—gripped his side, where something dark spread along his shirt. The other hand groped outward, his fingers sliding over the side panel of Caleb's car. *He's hurt.* Bad. I was still yards from the driveway. I needed to call an ambulance, to get help. But I had a dagger in one hand and PC's leash in the other.

I dropped both.

I patted my pockets as I ran, hoping I had my phone. I didn't. *Crap.*

Falin swayed again. His hand fell from the car. *He's going to black out.*

"Falin," I yelled, trying to get his attention, to keep him focused. I was almost there. Just a short sprint left.

Falin looked up. His hair clung to one side of his face, the pale locks dark and sticky. "Your eyes are glowing," he whispered.

Then his eyes rolled back in his head.

I lunged forward, grabbing his shoulders as he collapsed. It was a messy move to start with, and his added weight overbalanced me, sending me sprawling. My ass hit the pavement as Falin's back slammed into my stomach, and the air whooshed out of me. But I caught him, his head hitting my chest instead of cracking against the pavement. Of course, judging by the blood matting his long hair, someone might have already cracked his skull.

PC ran a circle around us, dragging his leash behind him before finally stopping to lick Falin's hand. The man didn't so much as twitch.

"What happened to you?" I whispered, still trying to regain my breath. I turned Falin's head to an angle that looked more comfortable—and one that I hoped would give me a better view of his head injury, but I couldn't make out a thing under his blood-soaked blond hair. *Oh, this is bad.*

And there was more blood than just from his head wound. My grave-sight made his clothing appear worn and moth-eaten, but the remaining fabric was saturated with blood all along one side from the middle of his chest down to his pants.

"Caleb," I screamed. *Please be able to hear me.* "Caleb, help me!"

The front door opened and Caleb rushed out, Holly a few steps behind him. I tried to shift my legs from where they were pinned under Falin's body without jostling him—which I failed at miserably. His brows scrunched together, his grimace making his sharp features draw in pain, but he didn't open his eyes.

"What—?" Caleb stopped short, still several feet away.

Holly kept running. She dropped to her knees beside me. "Alex, what happened? What's wrong?"

What's wrong? Clearly the unconscious fae sprawled in our driveway. But Holly wasn't looking at him. *Was he glamoured?*

"Holly, go back inside," Caleb said, not moving.

She looked between Caleb and me, her indecision clear on her face. "What's going on?"

"Just do—" Caleb cut himself off, then lowered his voice to a more civil volume and said, "Wait inside."

I think he would have said "please" if his nature had permitted it, but it didn't. Holly's frown etched deeper and she looked at me, her eyes asking me what I wanted her to do.

I wanted help for Falin. Now. I didn't know what Caleb's issue was, but Holly couldn't see Falin if he was glamoured, so she couldn't help. Swallowing the sour taste of adrenaline, I nodded. "I'll explain later."

Holly scowled, but she pushed herself up and stomped across the front lawn. When the door slammed behind her, I looked at Caleb.

"Help him?"

He shook his head. "It would bring more trouble down on you and on my house."

"He's hurt. We have to do something."

Caleb didn't move. "Get up, Al. Let's go. I'll call someone to deal with him."

Falin didn't need "dealing with"—he needed help. And I wasn't about to leave him until he got it.

"Please, Caleb. Help him. Please."

At my words, I felt the potential for imbalance between us. He owed me a favor because I'd listened to Malik—I'd forgotten about that favor—but I'd asked him for help, and he was so against the idea that if he did help, I would be the one indebted to him. I didn't care.

"Please," I said again.

He winced. "Alex—" He shook his head and then exhaled a long breath. "For you, Al. Not for him. We should get him inside."

Caleb knelt to lift Falin off of me. Falin was easily six-five and well built, but Caleb lifted him without so much as a grunt. He hauled him into a fireman's carry and I winced.

"I think he has a stomach injury."

If Caleb heard me, he ignored me as he headed around the side of the house toward the stairs to my loft. PC pranced at his heels, dragging his leash. My legs tingled with pins and needles as I climbed to my feet, but I forced them to work anyway. After fishing my dagger out of the grass and shoving it back in its boot sheath, I jogged to catch up with Caleb.

I closed my shields when I reached the stairs. In my grave-sight the steps were rotted and pitted, and I didn't want to fall through the staircase. I hurried up the steps, my knees wobbly from the adrenaline rush as I tried to catch up with Caleb while watching Falin's disconcertingly limp head loll to the side with Caleb's swift steps. It wasn't until I reached my door that I realized, as it was my grave-sight that let me see through glamour and I'd closed my shields to the grave, I shouldn't have been able to see Falin. Of course, glamours were easier to see through when you knew they existed.

Caleb slung Falin onto my bed, careless of the other man's injuries. Then he stepped back as I made a hasty job of trying to get Falin's limbs into positions that looked comfortable—or at least natural. I peeled his shirt away from his chest, wincing in sympathetic pain as the fabric stuck to the tacky blood.

Drying blood caked Falin's torso, but dark, wet blood still glistened along a long gash that started just under his ribs and disappeared into the top of his pants. Blood oozed from the deep laceration, and my breath caught in my chest.

"We need to get him to a hospital, or a healer, or . . ." I turned to face Caleb. "Where do fae go when they're injured?"

Caleb didn't answer. He just stared at the man on my bed. Not moving.

Okay, Caleb was obviously limited help. Very limited. *So it's up to me.* "Hospital," I said. After all, the hospital in the Quarter would be up-to-date, with all the most current healing magics. I reached for my purse and my cell phone, but Caleb grabbed my wrist.

"Leave him. He'll be fine."

"Fine? *Fine?* Caleb, I'm pretty sure he's mortally wounded!"

"Yes. If he were mortal."

Oh, right. I glanced at the bed. I didn't know a lot about injuries, but this one looked bad. Definitely hospital bad. Maybe morgue bad. But I also didn't know a lot about fae healing abilities.

Was Caleb right? Could he heal from this on his own? Or was Caleb's personal dislike clouding his judgment?

I sank onto the mattress beside Falin and swiped a strand of blood-crusted hair from his face. His cheek twitched as the hair pulled away, but he gave no other response.

"You're sure?" I asked without looking up.

Caleb rested his hands on my shoulders and squeezed lightly in what was probably meant to be a reassuring gesture. The heat of his palms blistered against my skin, but only one part of my brain registered the pain as the remainder focused on the prone form in front of me.

"Let him rest," Caleb whispered. "I was making spaghetti. You should come downstairs and have some dinner."

"I can't leave him here alone. What if he wakes and doesn't know where he is?"

Caleb's grip tightened. "Exactly."

Huh?

I shrugged him off and turned to face him. He frowned at me.

"If he wakes up confused and uncertain . . ." His voice trailed off. "You shouldn't be here with him alone."

"He's injured."

"He's lethal."

I scowled at Caleb and he sighed. Then he stepped back, shaking his head at me.

"Think about it, Al. Where has he been this past month? What has he been doing? Who did this to him?"

"I don't know." I sounded miserable, and I hated it, but it was true. I didn't know why he'd up and disappeared two days after Coleman's death, or why he hadn't made any attempt to contact me since then. I didn't know what had happened that he'd ended up in this condition in my front yard, or why he'd come to me at all. I just didn't know.

"Dinner, Al. Then you can check on him."

I nodded reluctantly. There wasn't much I could do for Falin besides sit and fret, and I needed food. Pushing myself away from the mattress took more effort than I'd expected. My adrenaline had finally stopped rushing and the absence left me drained. Shuffling to my nightstand, I opened the tiny drawer and dug out the few healing charms I owned. I'd made them myself, and my spellcasting being the dismal thing it was, they weren't all that potent, but they couldn't do any harm. I'd focused the spell into small wooden disks, and I placed the three of them on Falin's chest. There was no shortage of blood to activate them, and they hummed slightly as the spell sprang to life.

Turning, I found Caleb already at the door leading down to the main portion of the house. He didn't comment on the charms, but held the door for me. PC had already trotted down the stairs, so with an unconscious and half-dead fae in my bed, I abandoned my apartment.

"Is someone planning to tell me what's going on?" Holly asked as I pushed spaghetti around my plate.

I looked up, and Caleb lifted his eyebrow but said nothing as he poured himself a second glass of wine. Guess it was up to me, but how was I supposed to explain a mortally injured man Holly hadn't even seen? Of course, there were plenty of invisibility spells on the market, and Holly knew Falin was FIB. Guessing he was fae wasn't a far leap.

"Falin's back," I said, my voice flat as if it didn't matter.

Holly dropped her fork. "Outside?"

"He was glamoured. He's hurt. Pretty badly. He's unconscious upstairs."

She looked from me to Caleb and then back. "And we're here eating spaghetti?"

I cringed. *Yeah, that's pretty much the situation.* I rolled a meatball from one side of my plate to the other.

"He's fae," Caleb said, running his finger along his wineglass. The crystal sang under his touch. "Our options were to take him to Faerie or give him time to rest and heal. The latter was more feasible."

I could feel Holly's disbelieving stare on me, and I hunched a little further over my plate. *I think it's time to change the subject.* That, or I was going to feel even worse about leaving Falin upstairs. *Maybe I should call a healer despite what Caleb said.*

I accepted the glass of wine that Caleb all but pushed under my nose, and then I looked at Holly. "So where did you go this morning?"

"Go?" She made a soft snorting sound under her breath. "I've got this crazy landlord-turned-nursemaid who's barely permitted me to get out of bed." She said it with affection, but there was definitely a strand of irritation mixed in. She looked at Caleb. "You know I'm going back to work tomorrow, right? I mean, I'm a little bruised and cut up, but I'm fine."

He smiled at her but all he said was, "If you're up to it."

I frowned as he focused on his plate again. *Hadn't he said she'd left this morning?* Maybe he'd been mistaken, but the fact that he hadn't pushed the subject made me think he'd already discussed it with her. Apparently it wasn't any of my business. Not that I could complain about anyone else keeping secrets. I had more than enough of my own.

We finished dinner in a series of awkward silences separated by short bits of conversation. Afterward, as I headed for the stairs to my loft, I found I had a tagalong. A rather large, unhappy-looking tagalong.

"You planning on babysitting me all night?" I asked Caleb as I took the stairs two at a time.

"Actually, I was planning to tell you to grab some PJs and spend the night in the main portion of the house."

Oh, he couldn't be serious. I glanced back as I pushed open the door to my loft. He looked deadly serious.

"I'll be fine." I didn't need a babysitter. He was overreacting. He had to be.

I checked on Falin. The three healing charms had puttered out already, and I tapped into the magic stored in my ring and channeled power into them, giving them a slight recharge. It wasn't much, but it was something. Then I checked the wound. It had stopped bleeding, which was good, but I couldn't have said for sure whether it actually looked any better.

When I turned, I found Caleb still shadowing me, and still looking just as determined about my not staying in my own loft.

"I want you downstairs, behind a locked door and my wards. You and PC can stay in the guest room," he said, crossing his arms over his chest. "You owe me a debt, and I'm calling it in."

He'd helped me move Falin upstairs, and while I didn't think he'd been any great help to the man other than that, I could feel the debt between us, and feel the fact that I *had* to do what he'd asked. I sighed. It wasn't like staying in the guest room was a bad option—it certainly was more appealing than the floor, which was what I'd been planning, but I would have liked to be closer at hand if Falin needed anything during the night. Now I didn't have the option.

I grabbed a pair of shorts and a sleeveless top and then headed to the bathroom to get ready for bed. When I emerged, Caleb was still waiting for me, PC dozing in his arms.

I made one more stop by the bed to tuck Falin in as much as possible with him lying on top of the unmade comforter. If you ignored all the blood, he looked almost peaceful, as if he were just sleeping. "You really think he's that dangerous?"

"Al, I don't think. I know. And he has the blood on his hands to prove it."

Chapter 12

—❖— ◈ ❖—

I woke with a jolt and slammed into the mattress a moment later as if I'd jumped in my sleep. My eyes snapped open and I blinked at the chaotic swirl of colors filling the darkness.

Something was wrong.

I snapped my shields closed and sat up, brushing aside the comforter as I moved. A comforter with a stiff, lacy trim. *My comforter doesn't have lace trim.*

But I wasn't in my room or my bed—I was in Caleb's guest room. The glowing red numbers on the clock beside the bed told me it was 3:49 a.m. *Is that it? Is it just the unfamiliar room?*

No. There was something else wrong.

I blinked, trying to figure out what felt off. The air hummed with the familiar resonance of the Glen—the neighborhoods surrounding the Magic Quarter, where most of Nekros's witches and fae lived—and the grave essence reaching from the nearest graveyard felt the same as it always did. Then I realized the issue was as much what I *wasn't* feeling as what I *was*. I felt the magic in the Glen, and not the sheltering buzz of Caleb's wards.

Why are the wards down?

I didn't know, but I was going to find out.

Sliding out of bed, I padded as silently as possible across the room, but I wasn't familiar with the layout and the moonlight streaming through the closed blinds wasn't nearly enough to illuminate anything. I stubbed my toe against a box—Caleb used the room for storage—and cursed under my breath. PC's tags clinked softly as he lifted his head, trying to decide where I was going.

"Stay," I whispered in the general direction of the bed, but I heard his paws land on the hardwood a moment later.

I reached out, feeling along the wall until my fingers traced over the light switch. Then I blinked in the sudden glow of fluorescent lighting.

I hadn't brought my boots downstairs, but I'd dropped my dagger in my purse and that was on the nightstand. I dug out the dagger and unsheathed it. I hoped I wouldn't need it, but the wards going down in the middle of the night was seriously suspicious. Besides, if I didn't take the dagger, I'd feel like that ditzy blonde in every horror movie who goes out unarmed to check on strange noises. Nothing ends well for those girls.

I crept across the room, cringing as the floorboards creaked under my bare feet. Of course, I'd turned on the light, so it wasn't like I was being super stealthy. The oblivious dog trailing me didn't help either.

Opening the door a crack, I peeked into the hall beyond. My vision being what it was, I couldn't see anything but the pillar of light escaping the guest room. I opened the door wider, and a shadow crossed the doorway.

I threw a hand over my mouth to strangle the sound that tried to escape my lips and jumped back, away from the door.

"Al, you okay?"

Caleb.

I pulled the door open wider. Like me, Caleb must have woken when the wards fell, because the light pouring from my room revealed light green skin and dark, pupil-less eyes. Caleb never walked around without his glamour intact. In one hand he held a mallet, and in the other a vial containing a spell that pricked at my senses, so it probably did something really nasty if released.

"What happened?" I asked as I joined him in the hall.

He shook his head. "Not sure yet. The wards were taken down from the inside. You want me to hazard a guess at who might have done that?" His whispered words were sharp, leaving no doubt whom he was referring to: Falin.

I couldn't think of any reason Falin would dismantle the wards. He was unconscious when last I'd seen him, and even if he did wake, it wasn't like the wards prevented him from leaving. I opened my mouth to say as much and then snapped it closed again. Now wasn't the time to argue.

"Stay here," Caleb whispered as he crept along the hall-way.

That was a good suggestion. Unfortunately, I wasn't taking it. I closed PC in the bedroom, and then, clutching the dagger tight, I followed Caleb.

Someone had turned the lights on in the front of the house, which was good for my eyes but probably not the best sign, since we'd turned them off after we'd finished the movie we'd watched before bed and I'd said good night to Caleb and Holly. Caleb motioned me to wait as he opened the door to the den. He stepped inside and then gave a sharp hiss. I followed a moment later.

What the hell? I mouthed as I gaped at the room beyond.

The front door of the house stood wide open and dozens of ravens filled the room. The inky black birds had gathered on every available surface. Four perched on the flat-panel TV, their talons scratching against the plastic. At least a dozen sat on the back of the couch, and more were on the coffee table and on the end tables.

They stared at us with beady black eyes. Every last one of them.

"Uh, Caleb?"

"I have no idea," he said, his whisper so quiet I barely heard him.

Another raven swooped through the open front door. It screeched, wings flapping as it drew near, and I jumped aside. The bird landed on the doorframe we'd passed when we entered, and I backed farther away as a second raven joined the first. Crap, we would have to walk under the birds to get to the back of the house. Two more ravens flew into the room.

"This is like that Hitchcock movie," I said, taking another slow step away from the birds. They were blocking access to the front door and the door to the hall, but there were no birds between us and the door to the garage Caleb used as a workshop or the door beside it, which led to the stairs to my loft. I backed toward those doors, trying to keep an eye on all the ravens. The birds continued to stare. "They're giving me the creeps. Aren't they big for birds?"

"That's an understatement." Caleb shifted his grip on his mallet. "I guess we call animal control? We should probably wake Holly and get a hotel room for the rest of the night."

Yeah, except how were we supposed to reach Holly? And what had attracted the birds into the house in the first place? This couldn't be normal. I reached out with my senses, looking for a spell or charm that would have attracted the birds. What I found was seriously not what I expected.

"Oh, crap."

Caleb turned halfway around, but he never looked away from the ravens. "What?"

"Those aren't birds. They're constructs."

Chapter 13

Constructs. Just like the cu sith in the Quarter.

I opened my shields, already knowing what I'd find. In my second sight, the ravens vanished, becoming instead misty shapes surrounding a nasty clump of twisting magic. I snapped my shields closed again.

"We have to get out of here," I whispered, reaching behind me for the doorknob to the stairwell. We could escape out through my room and then circle around to the back door to get Holly. My hand landed on the knob, and I twisted it quickly.

It didn't turn.

Damn it! We never locked the doors to the stairs, but Caleb had insisted since Falin was staying upstairs. I fumbled with the lock, finally having to turn my back on the birds to unlock the door. I twisted the knob again, jerking the door, but it just shuddered.

"The bolt lock too?" I asked, my voice raising with a mix of exasperation and panic.

"Alex," Caleb hissed, and as if my name were some sort of signal, the ravens screeched.

The room filled with the sound of wings beating the air, the roar almost loud enough to block out the screeching. The birds dove forward just as I threw the lock.

"Get down," Caleb yelled and shoved me back toward the wall.

The ravens swooped at us, shiny black talons flashing and sharp beaks thrusting forward menacingly. Caleb uncorked his vial with his teeth and threw it at the nearest bird. A hazy green miasma exploded around the raven. It gave a sharp croak of a cry and then dropped. Caleb kicked it aside, but two more had already taken its place.

He swung his mallet. The sound of bones snapping made me cringe, even though I knew the birds weren't real. But this bird didn't fall. Caleb's death blow smashed its rib cage and it vanished, a small copper coin hitting the carpet a moment later.

Neither one of us had time to be amazed because there were more birds, so many more birds, to take the first's place. They swooped at us, talons extended.

I lashed out with my dagger, hitting one of the ravens in the wing. It went down, but didn't vanish. Climbing to its feet, the raven spread its uninjured wing wide and rushed me, its head darting as it lunged at my leg. *Damn. You have to hit to kill.*

Another raven dove for me, its talons aimed at my eyes. I ducked, and it got a claw full of my hair instead, pulling a clump out by the roots. I yelped, but the grounded raven was still coming for me. I jabbed with my dagger again. This time the bird vanished.

"There are too many of them," I yelled over the roar of wings as I scrambled to my feet.

"You have a suggestion?" Caleb asked, never pausing as he swung his mallet, knocking birds out of the air.

I didn't.

Somewhere beside me a door opened, and I spun around. Falin staggered into the room, one arm pressed against his injured side but a large dagger clutched in his other hand.

"Get out of here," I yelled as soon as I saw him.

He didn't retreat. His icy gaze took in the situation in one quick glance, and then landed on me. He hobbled forward, his breathing hard, pained, but the dagger in his hand cut through the air effortlessly. With every twitch of his wrist a bird vanished on his blade so that small copper disks lined his path as he made his way toward me. It would have been something to watch, if I hadn't been fighting off the damn ravens myself.

My enchanted dagger buzzed merrily in my hand as I

jabbed at the birds. I could feel it making suggestions in my muscles, trying to guide my arm, and I let it, but even with the dagger's help, most of my jabs injured rather than dispelled. Frustrated, I dropped my shields. I aimed for the knot of magic in the hazy forms instead of body parts, and the birds exploded into mist around my blade.

"Where did they come from?" Falin yelled, more ravens dissolving as his dagger struck true again and again.

Caleb's mallet took out two birds with one massive swing. "Like you don't know."

"Guys," I huffed, but didn't say anything else. My chest burned, my breathing came hard, and my arm ached from continual motion, but more birds poured in through the open front door.

A figure appeared in my peripheral vision. I swung around, anticipating seeing whoever had set the constructs on us. Instead I came face-to-face with Death.

His dark eyes went wide, as if he was surprised to see me, and in my own shock, I didn't notice one of the birds diving close until it was inches from me. Death's hand shot out, his fingers jabbing into the bird. He jerked, and the bird vanished. It didn't dissolve like the ones Caleb, Falin, and I killed, but all trace that it had existed disappeared—except the disk that fell to the ground.

"You always have to interfere, don't you?" said a voice behind him, and we both turned as a soul collector—dressed for a rave, in a bright orange tube top and a pair of white PVC hip-huggers—stepped forward.

She shook her head in disapproval, making her long dreadlocks swish. Then she strolled forward, slashing through the birds with her orange talonlike nails. Another reaper, wearing all gray, followed close behind her, swinging his silver skull–topped cane through the birds.

"Welcome to the party," I muttered, aiming my own dagger at a construct that dove too close.

"Alex, down!" Falin yelled, and a large hand slammed into my back, shoving me toward the floor.

I rolled as I hit the ground, but with Caleb and Falin on one side and the collectors on the other, I didn't have anywhere to go. My roll ended with me on my back, staring straight up as three groups of ravens descended from different directions, all diving for the spot where I'd been. Not that they stood a chance against the three collectors and two fae. I covered my head as a shower of spelled disks rained over me.

Then there was silence.

I pushed myself off the floor and looked around. The front door still hung open, but no more dark shapes swooped through it. I clutched my dagger, waiting, watching, sure the reprieve would break at any moment. I think we all were. But nothing happened, and I finally released the breath I'd been holding.

Caleb immediately rounded on Falin. "What did you do?"

"They weren't after me," Falin said, wincing and leaning against the wall. Fresh red blood dripped over his gloved hand where he pressed it against his side.

"Leave him alone," I told Caleb as I stepped forward to help Falin. He needed to sit down, and I didn't care what Caleb said—he needed a healer.

A hand on my arm stopped me, and I turned, ready to lay into Caleb for being overprotective. But it wasn't Caleb; it was Death, and the look on his face killed any protest I might have raised.

"Are you hurt?" he asked, his hazel eyes scanning my face, my neck, my shoulders. He brushed aside my hair as if searching for any injury it might have hidden.

"I'm fine." And I owed him and the other collectors a debt of gratitude for that. We'd have been overwhelmed if they hadn't appeared.

My gaze moved past him and I saw the other two collectors gathering the mist hanging in the air from the vanished ravens. It dissipated slowly as they reached out again and again. *Souls. How creepy is it that we've been trudging through souls?* Not that the stuff looked like a person or a creature. Most souls I'd seen outside of a body still looked like, well, the original body.

"How does a soul turn into mist?"

"Not any way natural," Death said, running his hands down my arms.

The raver-collector glared at him. *Guess he wasn't supposed to tell me that.* It wasn't as if "not any way natural" told me much.

Death ignored her. "You're sure you're not hurt? Not one of those creatures touched you? Not even a scratch?"

I frowned, looking down at myself. "I don't think so." I hadn't exactly had time to take stock yet, but I didn't feel hurt. "Nothing serious, surely."

"Alex, who are you talking to?" Caleb asked, stepping forward at the same time Death brushed my top up so he could search my waist and back. Caleb stopped. "Anyone else seeing her clothes move on their own?"

Falin nodded. "Yeah, she's not alone," he said, and I swear he glared at the space near where Death stood, as if jealous.

Not that he had any right to be. Still, I brushed my shirt back in place and stepped away from Death's searching hands.

"I'm fine," I said again.

"Alex, those were carriers. As little as a scratch would transfer their spell."

I blanched, staring at Death. *Crap.* I was pretty sure I wasn't hurt, but the others?

I turned but didn't have time to say anything before the collector in gray stepped forward. His cane shot out, the silver skull ornament pressing into Death's chest not in a blow but more a cautionary block.

"Do you think that wise?" he asked, his eyes on Death, who glared at him in return.

Whatever passed between them made Death look away.

"We're done here," the raver said, and true to her word the soul mist was gone.

Death looked at the gray man again, who crossed his arms over his chest, his cane tapping impatiently on his thigh. Then he turned to me. His eyes swept over me again, as if he still was not confident I hadn't been hurt. He reached out, his hand cupping my face. His thumb traced over my cheekbone and for a moment I thought he was going to say something more.

He didn't.

He leaned forward and his lips brushed against mine, a ghost of a kiss that made my entire body react to the almost electric feel of his skin against mine. Then he vanished, the raver and the gray man disappearing a heartbeat later. I stared at the space where he'd been and touched my lips, still feeling the gentle warmth of his mouth. I was breathless again—but not from the fight.

Now is seriously not the time.

I let my hand drop and turned. Both Caleb and Falin

stared at me. *At least they aren't fighting with each other.* I wiped my suddenly damp palms on the front of my shorts, fumbling with my dagger awkwardly as I did so.

"I, uh . . ." I shook my head. It was Falin's ice blue stare more than Caleb's that got to me. I swallowed and tried again. "Are you hurt? I mean, more than you were when you got here? Apparently the birds were carrying a spell that would transfer with as little as a scratch." I stopped and pressed my fingers to my mouth again, but this time in alarm. "Oh, crap—Holly."

"I don't think she woke for the fight. She should be fine," Caleb said, but he was already moving toward her bedroom as he spoke.

I wasn't so much worried about tonight's fight as I was about the fact that she'd been injured by the cu sith in the Quarter. I had no doubt the raven constructs had been sent by the same person, and if they were carrying a spell, had the cu sith been as well?

I darted around Caleb as I sprinted down the hall. I reached Holly's door a moment before he did, and I threw it open.

Holly wasn't inside.

I hadn't closed my shields, so the comforter pooled at the end of Holly's bed looked both faded and rotted and whole with a vibrant geometric pattern. The sheets had obviously been slept on, and unlike me, Holly made her bed. Always. So she'd been here, but the bed stood empty now.

I whirled around. Caleb's worried, wide-eyed expression matched mine as we made a quick search of her room. The windows were closed, there was no sign of a struggle, and the outfit she'd planned to wear tomorrow was set out on her dresser. The only thing wrong with the room was the fact that Holly wasn't in it.

"Here," Falin called from the front room and both Caleb and I took off at a run.

I heard PC barking as I passed the guest room, but I didn't pause to let him out. He was safe in there.

When we reached the living room, we found Falin leaning heavily against the doorframe. He pointed at something in the front yard and we rushed past him.

A figure lay crumpled in the middle of the lawn, red hair

fanning around her head and her bare knees tucked to her chest. *Holly.*

I collapsed in the grass beside her. I didn't see any blood, any injury, but the way she was lying could have covered it. I groped for her throat.

"She has a pulse," I said as Caleb dropped to his knees beside me.

He reached for her shoulder and her eyes fluttered open. She gasped, her hands jerking toward her chest as if she were pulling a sheet over herself.

"Caleb?" She blinked, sitting up. "And Alex? Okay, guys, really, I don't need nursemaids. I'm fine. I—" She stopped and looked around for the first time. "Uh, why am I outside?"

I shared a glance with Caleb before saying, "You don't remember coming out here?"

"No." She frowned. "Should I? Was I sleepwalking?"

Good question. I hoped that was it, but the sinking feeling in my stomach was pretty sure nothing as mundane as sleepwalking could explain what had happened.

"Let's get you inside and see if we can't work this out," Caleb said, helping Holly to her feet.

She wore only an oversized T-shirt, and she smoothed it self-consciously where the hem hit high on her thighs. Caleb and I shepherded her past Falin and through the front door, and then settled her onto the couch. While Caleb fetched her a drink, I retrieved my phone.

Tamara's phone went to voice mail the first time I called. I hung up and tried again. This time she picked up on the fourth ring.

"Alex, it's four thirty in the morning. You better have a good reason for getting me out of bed."

Unfortunately, I did.

"Tam, can you get over here. I think Holly's been spelled."

Tamara lived only a few streets away—almost all the practicing witches in Nekros lived in the Glen—so her car rolled into the driveway less than fifteen minutes later. By then, Caleb had run a full diagnostic on the house wards and traced all the magical signatures. Holly had been the one who disabled the wards, and no one had entered the house and no unfamiliar magic had brushed the wards before she'd taken them down.

I'd paced around the living room until Holly complained that I was making her dizzy. Then I set about gathering the spelled disks, a task complicated by the fact that I'd released my grave-sight and deep shadows clung everywhere despite all the lights that I'd turned on in the house. Falin had disappeared by the time I got off the phone with Tamara. Holly said he'd asked for a first-aid kit and retreated to my loft. I didn't want to leave Holly and Caleb, so I hoped he'd be okay on his own. I planned to check on him soon.

Tamara's loud knock sounded just as I shoved the broom under the couch, searching for any disks that had rolled away. Holly and Caleb jumped to their feet, rushing for the door. I started to rise, but the broom hit something larger than a spelled disk. I swished the broom to the side, knocking the object out from under the couch. Then I yelped, jumping back.

Caleb and Holly whirled around at the sound, and Tamara stopped, her foot hanging in the air where she'd been stepping through the open doorway. My heart crashed hard as I stared at the raven I'd exposed. I lifted my broom like a baseball bat, but the raven only lay in a crumpled heap. It was the one Caleb had doused with the spell, and its chest lifted in slow, labored breaths, but it was otherwise still.

"Oh, eew," Holly said, and then she ran into the kitchen. She emerged a moment later with the large strainer Caleb had used for last night's spaghetti. She tossed it over the bird and then piled magazines from the coffee table on top to weigh the strainer down. "There."

"What is going on?" Tamara asked, her eyes taking in the chaos.

Caleb and I had both frozen at the sight of the raven, and even now, with the bird trapped under the strainer, I hadn't lowered the broom. I took a deep breath and pried my fingers off the wooden handle. Then I sagged into the closest chair, feeling as if my bones had melted into something not completely solid.

Caleb and I filled Tamara in on the happenings of the

night, not taking turns so much as interrupting each other. Holly joined in once we got to the end and related how we'd found her on the lawn. After we'd finished, silence filled the room.

"Have you called the police?" Tamara asked after several minutes had passed.

Caleb shook his head. "I don't know that we should get them involved."

"I think we have to," Holly said, hugging her knees to her chest. She'd added a pair of shorts to her outfit, but with the oversized shirt draping her petite frame, she looked more like a frightened child than a confident prosecutor.

Caleb often said three was the perfect number for a group—there were never ties in a decision. Since I was the final roommate, everyone turned to me. *To call the police or not?* I dodged. "What can you tell me about the spell on Holly?" And Caleb—the ravens had scored a deep gash on his forearm and raked his knuckles. If all it took was one scratch for the spell to transfer, he'd definitely caught it.

Tamara pursed her lips and motioned for Holly to sit on the couch.

Holly settled herself on the cushion farthest from the trapped raven—we were all giving the strainer a wide berth—and Tamara sat on the coffee table, directly across from Holly.

"May I?" Tamara pointed to the collar of Holly's shirt.

Holly shrugged. "I'll take it off." She turned her back to us and pulled the shirt over her head. She pressed the material over her breasts before turning back.

Yesterday the cu sith's scratch had looked like Holly had been clawed by a tiger, but today the jagged tears stretching from her collarbone to the top of her opposite breast were thinner, the skin pink and healing quickly from some of the best healing spells money could buy. The ring of teeth marks on her shoulder was a little worse, the scabs still thick and angry-looking, but by all accounts, healing in remarkable time.

I'd scanned them with my ability to sense magic already and I'd felt a tickle of magic that seemed more like a memory of a spell than anything active or malicious. Now I cracked my shields again, peering through the brilliant swirls of the Aetheric to focus on Holly's exposed wounds. When I squinted, I thought I caught a tinge of gray behind the healing skin. Maybe.

After peering at Holly's wounds, Tamara looked over at Caleb and motioned for him to show her his hand and arm. She studied his wounds for a while and then leaned back, placing her hands to the side and slightly behind her on the coffee table.

"If I hadn't been looking for it, I never would've spotted the spell," she said, shaking her head. "And it's a weird spell. I mean, it's more a trace than anything active."

Damn. That was exactly what I was getting as well. I closed my shields and blinked in the sudden darkness clouding my vision.

"Can you sense what it is or how to counter it?" Holly asked. She was an exceptional spellcaster, but she wasn't the least bit sensitive.

Tamara reached out a hand, but hesitated before touching Holly's shoulder. "This might feel a little invasive."

Holly nodded assent and Tamara pressed her palm to Holly's skin. Tamara's eyes closed, and whatever she did made Holly cringe, but she didn't pull away.

"It's like the spell is hibernating," Tamara said without opening her eyes. "It's hard to explain, but it's like the spell formed a crystallized shell. I doubt it can do anything inside all that protection, but it's barely traceable and I can't get a slip of magic beyond the cocoon it's formed."

"So it would have to be active to be dispelled," I said, following her logic, though I didn't like it one bit. "But we don't know what triggers the spell or what it does."

Tamara dropped her hand and nodded that she was finished. Holly dressed quickly.

Caleb leaned back in his chair. "Holly left yesterday morning. When she claimed she hadn't, I thought she just didn't want us to know who she went to see." He shot her an apologetic glance. "But maybe that was just a trial run for tonight."

It was possible. I drummed my fingers on the arm of the chair. "Both events happened in the middle of the night. Was the timing based on when the caster assumed Holly's absence wouldn't be noticed and when the attack would be unexpected, or does the spell's host have to be asleep?"

"Great. I'll never sleep again," Holly said, slumping.

Yeah, like that was really an option.

"I think you should go to the hospital in the Quarter," I told her. Caleb voiced his agreement and I turned to him. "You too."

"No." He pushed himself out of his chair. "Holly, yes, definitely. She should be under observation and under the care of trained physicians and healers. No offense." He glanced at Tamara. "But not me. I'm fae—the spell might not even work on me."

"Or it might." It was probably aimed at me, after all, and I was part fae. I hadn't told Tamara and Holly that little detail yet, so I kept that thought quiet. Caleb gave me a look that said he wouldn't budge, and I sighed. "So now what?"

"We need to call the police," Holly said.

I agreed. Caleb didn't. Majority vote won and Holly phoned in the call.

"You probably need to find a way to fix that," Tamara said, pointing to the far wall of the room.

I twisted to see what she meant and the blood drained from my face. In the air where we'd fought the ravens, small, pinprick-sized wisps of Aetheric energy twisted.

I'd ripped holes in reality. Again.

Chapter 14

There were seven small holes—not nearly as many as spelled disks, so apparently only the ravens I'd destroyed had caused tears. I couldn't close the rips in reality, so Caleb worked on glamouring over the holes while we waited for the police to arrive. My friends shot curious gazes my way, but none demanded an explanation. Yet.

I excused myself, gathered PC and my purse from the guest room, and then retreated to the stairs so I could dress before the cops arrived. I grabbed one of the charmed disks before I left. I had no doubt the police had their very best people working to unravel the spells on the disk, but the feet, the constructs, and the spells on my friends were linked, and once the police confiscated everything, I wouldn't get another look at the disks. I needed a lead in this case. Now more than ever. Dropping the disk in my purse, I took the steps two at a time. It wasn't until I'd reached the top and my free hand was hovering over the doorknob that I remembered my apartment wouldn't be empty.

Falin is on the other side of this door. And aside from when he'd been unconscious and when we'd fought side by side against the ravens, I hadn't seen him in a month. Now I couldn't decide if the prospect of being alone with him excited, terrified, or agitated me, but my fingers shook as I grabbed for the doorknob. *Get hold of yourself, Alex.* Taking a deep breath, I pushed the door open, not sure what I would find.

Not finding anything wasn't what I was expecting.

I looked around. The room was empty. What felt like a bag of rocks dropped in the bottom of my stomach, and I sagged against the doorframe. *He left.*

PC wiggled in my arms, and I set him down without moving a foot more into my empty apartment. PC, oblivious, pranced across the room and checked his food bowl. A couple of bites of kibble were left in the bottom and he happily—and noisily—chomped away at the early morning snack.

I stood there looking around a moment longer. Then I pushed away from the doorframe and forced my back straight.

So he left. So what? It wasn't like he hadn't done it before.

I shoved the door closed harder than needed and dropped my purse by the side of the bed—which Falin had apparently stripped before leaving. I glanced around, but I didn't spot the bedding anywhere. *Great.*

I headed for my dresser, pulling my shirt over my head as I walked. Then the bathroom door opened.

I jumped, whirling around at the sound and pulling my shirt flat against my chest in one movement. Falin stepped out of the bathroom, his ice blue gaze meeting mine.

"Alexis." My name, my real name, was a whisper around a smile as he stepped forward. Then his gaze moved down, taking in my half-dressed state. His eyebrows lifted and the smile turned rakish.

I gulped and looked away. "I, uh . . ." I'd thought he'd left, but there really wasn't a reason to say that. "The police are on their way," I finally said, and then turned my back on him so I could dig through my clothes hamper one-handed. The hamper was currently filled with clean but unfolded clothes—the dirty clothes were in the pile beside it.

I felt the heat of his body warm the air behind my bare back before his hands landed on my shoulders. His skin was pleasantly warm against mine, and I felt the urge to lean back against his body and take the comfort I'd find in his arms.

But I didn't.

He'd left without a word and appeared just as suddenly. On top of that, he was the Winter Queen's assassin—*and her lover.* Besides, I didn't do relationships. I stepped away from him.

"I have to get dressed," I said, clutching the change of clothes I'd grabbed and heading for the bathroom.

"Alex . . ." But he trailed off, not following my name with anything.

I stopped halfway to the bathroom and turned back around. "What happened to my sheets?"

He glanced at the bed. "Soaking in the tub. They had my blood on them." He gave me a weak half smile and lifted one shoulder. The movement wasn't smooth, though, and he wasn't quite fast enough to cover the wince.

He's hurt. Well, of course he was hurt. He'd shown up half dead last night and he'd reopened the wound during the fight. The idea that he could have healed all that damage in the last hour was pure faerie tale, but he did *look* healed.

His platinum blond hair hung loose and clean around his face and shoulders, and I could see no evidence of wounds on his face or scalp. His clothes were what I'd grown accustomed to when we'd worked together before— dress slacks and a crisp white oxford—but what I saw couldn't have been real because the clothes he'd worn here were torn and bloodstained, and he didn't have clothes stashed in my apartment. I almost opened my shields to see what he wore under the glamour, but what if he wasn't wearing *anything*?

And speaking of clothes, I was still only half dressed and I could hear the police sirens in the distance. *Crap.* I ducked into the bathroom and dressed quickly. When I emerged a minute or two later I found Falin sitting stiff-backed on my stripped bed.

"Don't tell them I was here," he said without standing.

I stopped. "Who? The police?"

He nodded.

"I can't lie to the police for you."

"I'm not asking you to lie. Just don't mention me."

I frowned and studied him. I didn't really know Falin.

Once I'd thought I did, at least a little, or at least I'd *felt* like I knew him. But feelings could be deceptive.

"What's going on?" I asked, leaning against the wall. I could hear the sirens in front of the house now. I needed to get downstairs, but I wanted some answers from Falin first. "What happened to you?"

Falin pushed away from the bed. He walked across the room and peered through the window before answering. "It's complicated."

"Complicated? Someone tried to kill you."

He didn't respond. *Maybe I have it wrong?* He was the Winter Queen's assassin. Maybe it wasn't that someone had tried to kill him. Maybe they were just trying to stop him from killing them.

He still didn't say anything.

"Falin, why are you here? Why now?" Had he just needed a place to hide while he was injured? Was that why he was here?

From the main portion of the house below I heard the front doorbell ring. I had to go, but . . . I looked up at him, waiting for an answer.

"I wanted to contact you," he said, stepping forward, and I wasn't sure if his words meant he had wanted to contact me during the month he was missing, or if he was here because he wanted to contact me. He reached out like he was going to place his hands on my hips.

I skittered sideways, out of his path.

"Oh, no." I crossed my arms over my chest. "You do not get to disappear for a month, say you meant to contact me, and then try to pick up right back where we were. It doesn't work that way."

His shoulders sagged as he stepped back. Then a half smile made the edge of his lips crook. "You're mad at me."

"And that's amusing because?"

The half smile spread into a lopsided grin, and he stood up straighter. "You wouldn't be mad if you didn't care. I'm on to you, Alexis."

Oh, that insufferable, arrogant—

Voices drifted up from the floor below. "I have to go," I said, turning my back on him as I pulled the door open.

I hesitated once I stepped into the stairwell and glanced

back at him. I wanted to ask if he'd be there when I returned, but I didn't. Without saying good-bye, I pulled the door closed behind me and escaped the rest of our awkward conversation to have a much easier one. It was probably a bad sign that I considered it easier to be questioned by the police.

The responding officers weren't happy that we'd waited nearly an hour to call the authorities or that we'd all dressed and started cleaning up the crime scene. Oh, well.

The anti–black magic unit took the lead in processing the scene. The room was photographed, the charmed disks were gathered and each sealed individually in a magical-dampening bag, and even the raven was caged and taken away. After we'd given the lead detective, a weary-looking witch by the name of Tepps, our statements—all of which were edited slightly to leave out Falin and the soul collectors—Tamara drove Holly to the hospital. Caleb refused to go, and nothing in the ABMU's arsenal detected dark magic on Caleb, so he couldn't be committed against his will.

"We've bagged thirty-three disks. If there was one per construct, you two were lucky to get out with just a couple of scratches," Detective Tepps said as he watched his people work.

I nodded. "Yes, sir." We were. Though there'd been six of us, not two. "Have you deciphered any of the spells on the disk from the attack in the Quarter?"

Detective Tepps looked me up and down, as if assessing why I wanted to know—and if wanting to know made me a suspect. He had a day's worth of stubble on his chin and a line around his head that made me suspect he'd worn a hat earlier in the night.

"We've made some progress," he said, but didn't offer to elaborate. One of the techs called his name and he excused himself.

I hovered on the outskirts of the investigation, hoping to pick up something useful for my own case. I didn't. This wasn't a major crime—there was no body, little damage, and nothing had been stolen. The cops tagged and bagged and then moved on. They were wrapping up when the FIB, and Agent Nori in particular, appeared on the scene.

"So, another construct attack?" she asked as she gave the bagged evidence a cursory glance.

"We have a live specimen this time," Tepps told her, and she sniffed as if that fact wasn't terribly interesting.

"Ms. Craft," she said to me as she invited herself into Caleb's house. She looked around and when her eyes landed on Caleb himself, a sharp, and not the least bit kind, smile cut across her face. *If the FIB has been gathering independents to be questioned, have I endangered Caleb?* We weren't anywhere near the floodplain, but I wasn't sure how wide a net had been cast.

"You probably need my statement," I said, stepping into Nori's personal bubble.

She glanced at me, managing to look down her nose despite my superior height. "I imagine you've already given your statement. But I have some questions. For *both* of you." She put emphasis on the last statement.

"Agent Nori," a male, and very familiar voice said behind us.

The self-satisfied smile fled from Nori's face, and she turned, her head snapping up and her shoulders back as she stood straighter. "Sir, I hadn't heard you were back in the city."

"Should I state the obvious, Agent?" Falin asked as he stepped through the door. The front door, not the inner door from my room, as if he were just now arriving on the scene. "I'll question them," he said, nodding toward Caleb and me.

"But, sir, the constructs are built on witch magic, so probably not glamour, like Ms. Craft claims. I've been working this case and—"

"And now I'm working it." Falin placed his hands on his sides. The movement caused his blazer to gape open, exposing the dark butt of his gun in his shoulder holster. Blazer, gun, and holster were more glamour—unless he had some sort of dislocation spell—but the display still oozed both authority and threat. "This case has drawn my attention, and the attention of her majesty. I want all your files on my desk by the time I reach the office."

"Yes, sir," Nori said, the muscle in her cheek bulging as she clenched her jaw. Then she stalked out of the house.

"Are you the boogeyman in the FIB?" I asked once the door shut behind Nori.

Falin flashed me a smile. "Try agent in charge."

Right, good to know. *Does that mean he's behind the snatch-and-bag in the floodplain?* No, he couldn't have been. Nori had indicated he'd been out of the city. But maybe he could help me stop it. I waited until the last of the cops had left before asking.

Falin let out a long breath and leaned against the wall, as if standing straight for so long had taxed him. "It's complicated."

This wasn't the first time I'd heard that tonight. I opened my mouth to ask for a clarification, but Caleb brushed past me.

"Don't waste your breath, Al," he said, and grabbed the mallet from where he'd dropped it earlier. "I'll be in my workshop if you need me." Then he stormed into the garage. A trickle of magic sparked through the air as he activated his circle, and he said, "Oh, and Al, be careful what you say to her majesty's bloody hands."

Chapter 15

❖❖ ❖ ❖❖

"What did he mean, 'her majesty's bloody hands'?" I asked once we were back in my apartment.

Falin didn't answer, but stepped around me as he headed for the bathroom. He'd taken the steps slow, his hand moving to his side when he thought I wasn't looking. Somewhere along the way, his blazer vanished, and by the time he reached the bathroom door, glamour no longer cloaked his ragged and bloodstained clothing.

I leaned against the wall beside the door. A door he hadn't closed. "Are you here doing your queen's bidding?"

Again he didn't answer. I pushed away from the wall and peeked around the open door. Falin stood with both hands braced on the sink's counter, his head hanging heavy below his hunched shoulders. He looked up as I slipped inside and gave me a small, tight smile that didn't match the wince around his eyes.

"Joining me in the bathroom? This is a new level of intimacy for us."

I didn't take his bait. "Let me see it."

"Mmm, and what is it you want to see?"

I frowned at him. "Stop playing around and let me see your side."

"It's fine. Don't worry about it," he said, but it clearly cost him to push away from the counter and stand up straight.

"Let me see, or I'm going to dope you with a knockout charm and drag you to a healer." It was an empty threat and he knew it, but he still moved to unbutton his shirt.

"Fine, fine." He shrugged out of the shirt, the movement stiff.

While I'd been occupied downstairs he'd done a nice job of dressing the wound. I hated to disturb the carefully taped gauze, but blood had seeped through in several places, so it needed to be changed anyway.

I shuddered once I'd exposed the wound. "Shouldn't you see a healer?"

"I've healed worse. It's dawn and the magic is weak right now. Give me twenty minutes and I'll be much better," he said, reaching for the sealed sterile gauze pads on the counter. They must have been from Holly's first-aid kit because they had official OMIH stamps on the top and I didn't own charmed bandages.

I helped him dress his side again, and as I worked I had to admit he was healing. The edges of the wound were pink, and new skin had knitted across the long laceration in several places. If he could avoid reopening the wound, he would probably heal in a matter of days. Once the gauze was taped securely in place, I stood. "How's the head?"

"Healed," he said, and smiled at my disbelieving look before tilting his head forward so I could look. "Head wounds bleed a lot, but that one wasn't deep."

I scanned the part of his scalp I could see and then laced my fingers in his hair, letting my fingers read the truth of his healed scalp even if my eyes couldn't see it. Without his glamour, Falin's hair was closer to white than blond and, like his skin, seemed to give off its own light. I ran my hands through those soft locks, following one that fell over his etched cheekbone and cascaded down his chin to his throat.

His gaze snagged mine. There might have still been pain somewhere in those blue eyes, but more than anything there was heat. He watched me look at him and his lips parted, his pupils dilating. Only then did I consider the fact that I'd just had my hands on his sculpted abs and chest while examining his wound, then in his hair, and now . . . Heat rushed to my face. While I'd been focused on his wounds everything had been so clinical, but now I was acutely aware that we were in my small bathroom, standing very close, and he was only half dressed.

He was also injured. *And taken.*

"I'll just—" I pointed over my shoulder as I backed away.

"Wait." He flashed me a smile. Dawn had come and gone, and there must have been something to what he'd said because he moved easier as he crouched and opened the cabinets under the sink. "Have you seen my toothbrush?"

I cringed. "I told you to get it out of my bathroom."

"You threw it out?"

God, I wished I had. But I hadn't. Not that I planned to tell him that. And what was with the hurt eyes? What would it matter if I *had* tossed the toothbrush?

I crossed my arms over my chest and lifted my chin, which earned the exact opposite response from what I'd expected—a lopsided grin claimed his face.

"You're mad at me again. I told you, I'm on to you, Alexis. You wouldn't be mad if you didn't care." He waggled a gloved finger at me and returned to rooting around under my sink. "So where did you hide my toothbrush?"

I stepped in front of him, blocking his access to the cabinet with my legs. "You think you've got me figured out, huh? Well, I think you missed a couple of chapters, so let me give you a quick highlight. I've got commitment and abandonment issues." It wasn't like that was a big secret— even my favorite bartender knew that. "You disappearing without a word? That doesn't help. And finding out you're the Winter Queen's lover? Yeah, no. I don't know what was happening between us a month ago. Personally, I blame it on the adrenaline from tracking Coleman. But whatever it was, it's over. Now I'm glad you are no longer dying on my front lawn, and I'm glad you were here when the ravens attacked, but I think it's time for you to go home."

He was still crouched on the floor, staring up at me, and each word out of my mouth attacked his expression like verbal shrapnel. By the time I'd finished, his face had shut down and thrown up shields of apathy. With his lips taut and grim and his gaze cold, he pushed to his feet. Then he looked around as if uncertain why he was there in the first place.

"I'll go, then," he said, stepping around me and out of the bathroom.

"Wait," I called after him, my anger dissipated. He paused at my front door, but he didn't turn to face me.

"Maybe we can meet for drinks or something if situations change," I said because as much as I hated it, seeing him again more than proved there was a spark. But I couldn't do it like this. With him injecting himself into my life without warning while I waited for him to disappear again.

He glanced back as he stepped outside. The morning sunlight streaming in through the open door caught in his hair and made it a shimmering halo around his face. "Watch yourself, Alex Craft. You are attracting the wrong kind of attention. Again. And I meant what I said to Agent Nori. You've caught the queen's interest, so be cautious."

Then the door slammed behind him, and he was gone.

I ran across the room and jerked the door open.

"What's that supposed to mean?" I called, but the landing was empty, as were the stairs. Falin wasn't like Death; he couldn't just vanish. *Glamour*—it had to be.

"I know you're still here." Or at least I was pretty sure.

No answer.

Damn. I opened my shields, just enough for my psyche to slip through. The decaying land of the dead overlaid the real world like a double exposure as Aetheric energy swirled around me, close enough to touch. I peered through it, glancing down the steps, into the yard behind. I ignored the way the wooden steps looked rotted and pitted, the grass brown and decayed. Amid all the decay what I still didn't see was Falin. *He can't have gotten far.* But there was no movement. No one.

How did he—? I turned and found him directly behind me, leaning in the corner where the porch rail and the side of the house met. After the morning I'd had, my frayed nerves didn't take well to another surprise.

I yelped, stumbling backward, and my foot smashed through what my senses perceived as a decaying board. The wood crumbled around my calf as I lost my footing, and the porch swallowed my leg up to my thigh.

Falin jumped forward, catching my arms. He lips twisted
in pain with the movement, the muscles in his jaw twitching. I slammed my shields closed, and the land of the dead
slipped away.

But the damage was already done, my leg caught all the
way to my midthigh. In fact, closing my shields might have
made things worse because the wood was once again solid
around my leg.

"Hold still," Falin said, shifting his grip under my arms.
He winced as he lifted me and I motioned him away.

"You're hurt. I can do this."

He glared at me, but I met the ice in his eyes with my
own scowl. Finally he released me, holding his hands up in
surrender and backing up a step. Of course, saying I could
do it was easier than actually freeing myself.

It took me several minutes of repositioning my arms
and my free leg before I found an angle where I could wiggle my leg out of the hole. I was breathing hard by the time
both my feet were on the top side of the porch again. Blowing a curl out of my face, I wiped my palms on the front of
my jeans and turned to face Falin. "So, was that parting
quip meant to get me chasing after you for clarification
or . . . ?"

"Just watching."

"Me? Or for someone?" I asked, but he didn't answer.
"Falin, what is going on?"

He crossed his arms over his chest. His glamour once
again cloaked his clothing and he leaned against the wall as
if he had no intention of going anywhere. I sighed. Obsti-
nacy was one of his reigning qualities.

"Well, if you are going to stick around, you might as well
come back inside." I pushed the door open, holding it wide.
He pursed his lips but didn't move.

I waited several heartbeats. Then I turned, letting the
door swing shut behind me and headed toward the bathroom. It took me only a moment to find what I was looking
for. Then gripping it hard enough that my knuckles turned
white, I headed back outside.

"Here's your damn toothbrush." I shoved it at Falin, and
he blinked, his blue eyes wide with surprise. "Now, it's
barely seven o'clock and I've already had a hell of a day.

Why don't we have some breakfast and swap notes. Maybe we can work together."

If we didn't throttle each other first.

"Alex, an oatmeal creme pie doesn't count as breakfast," Falin said, staring at the prepackaged sweet as if it had offended him.

I shrugged. "Don't knock it," I said. I perched in the one chair I owned and opened my laptop. I'd put fresh sheets on the bed and I hoped Falin would get a little more rest. He might have some super-fae healing powers, but the glimpses I'd caught of him unglamoured proved he still needed some recuperation time.

"So, did I draw the queen's attention with the tear or the castle?"

"Castle?" Falin's eyebrow lifted, and while he might have been faking ignorance, he sounded genuinely confused.

I shook my head, dismissing the question. "Okay, so I'm guessing this has something to do with the tear."

"Something? This has everything to do with the tear. What were you thinking, merging realities in the middle of a crowded street?"

"Uh, I was thinking Holly was about to get shredded," I said as I dug through my purse in search of the charmed disk. "What kind of fallout am I looking at?"

"Well, you drew the attention of at least two faerie courts. They are asking questions."

"I'm guessing their curiosity would be bad for my health?"

Falin set the untouched oatmeal creme pie aside. Then he propped my pillows against the wall and reclined against them, his hands behind his head. "If not your health, then definitely your freedom. If the courts realize what you can do, you'll likely end up sequestered in Faerie."

Sequestered? I was not a fan of that outcome. I retrieved the disk and set my purse aside.

"Fred said, 'They come.' Think that's about the courts?"

Falin opened his eyes, which had drifted closed while we spoke. "Who's Fred?"

"Oh, uh, the gargoyle?" I shrugged. "I sort of named it."

He stared at me, and then burst out laughing. "The winged one with the cat face?" At my nod he laughed harder, which made him wince and grasp his injured side. "You realize that particular gargoyle is female and holds a position among gargoyles similar to that of a high priestess or a grand oracle?"

"Oh." I guess that explained why she'd seemed so amused when I'd named her. But she'd refused to give me a name to call her, and it was hard to converse with someone who didn't have a name—even if that someone happened to be made of stone. "Anyway," I said, "just before I found you last night, she told me, 'They come.'"

"That's a fairly vague warning."

"Tell me about it."

But he didn't because his eyes had drifted closed again.

I let him rest and turned my attention to the charmed disk. The spells in it were inert now that the glamour and soul had been separated from the magic, but somewhere in the tangle of residual magic, there had to be a hint of what spell infected my friends. If I could find the spell, I'd be that much closer to finding the counterspell. And hopefully to finding the witch behind the spell as well.

I copied the runes from the disk onto a blank sheet of paper, making sure to leave each one incomplete in case it could be invoked without knowing what it was or did. I had to dig out a magnifying glass to make sure I copied them all correctly—the disk's design was intricate. And there had been over thirty of those ravens. Someone had way too much time on their hands.

Once I'd copied not only the runes but also the design they made on the disk, I flipped the disk over and broke the seal of wax. The wax covered a thin strip of paper, and I unfolded it, glancing over the heavy block-printed letters. The paper contained two words. A name. Mine.

Well, now there's no question as to whether the attacks are targeted.

I dug through the trunk at the edge of my bed until I found a small enchanted box that one of my teachers gave me when I graduated academy. Like the ABMU's magical-dampening evidence bags, the box locked magic safely away inside itself. It was one of my spellcasting instructors who'd given me the box, and I think she assumed I would eventually botch a charm so badly that it would have to be contained. I'd never used it before, but now I dumped the disk, paper, and wax inside and flipped the latch. The prickly tingle of dark magic that had been nibbling at my senses for the last hour cut off and I sighed from the sudden relief.

PC, who'd curled up beside Falin on the bed, lifted his head to see why I was making so much noise. He must have judged my activities uninteresting because after a single glance, he laid his head on Falin's calf and closed his eyes again. I shook my head and settled in front of my computer.

Out of the sixteen runes from the disk, I thought that one looked similar to the rune for health—though it would have to be an archaic form of the rune—and that another looked like something I'd seen in academy, but couldn't quite remember. The other fourteen were complete mysteries. Pulling up a search browser, I dove into the task of solving those mysteries.

Several hours later, I'd gained a serious crick in my back and learned that the rune I thought looked like health was, in fact, very similar to an archaic version of the rune, though the older version also meant life. *Is that the spell that animates the constructs?* I'd added the idea to my list of notes on the case—a very short list.

I pushed away from my laptop and stretched. I'd gone through a pot of coffee since I'd started scouring the Net, but my gritty eyes were blurring with exhaustion. I'd even switched gears at one point and searched maps for the kelpie's "thundering gate." After all, I had multiple directions from which to attack this case. Finding the killer would lead me to a counterspell for my friends and it would fulfill my obligation to Malik.

I searched the Net as well as studied several maps as I looked for the gate. The major interstates passing through Nekros had stylized gates, though they were just decoration, the recent beautification project downtown had added green space, some of which was gated, and even some "art" that looked more like gates than anything else, but none of those were near the river and thus they were not good candidates. Most of the warehouse district had chain-link fence blocking off the river, as did many of the residential areas, but I couldn't see why they'd be considered "thundering."

With my muscles cramping and my butt asleep from too many hours in a chair, I finally switched off the computer and gave the research a rest. *Time for a little legwork.* But first, lunch.

Falin woke as I ransacked my fridge.

"What else did she say?" he mumbled, still half asleep. Then his eyes popped open. He glanced at where the afternoon sun stretched across the floor and groaned. "I fell asleep? You should have woken me."

I shrugged and pulled a cardboard container of Chinese takeout from the top shelf of the fridge. *What day had I ordered it?* I didn't think it was more than a week ago.

"I got some stuff done," I said, though what I'd actually done was establish where I *wouldn't* find useful information.

Falin joined me at the fridge, his movements smoother and clearly less painful than before he'd fallen asleep. He glanced over the limited contents before plucking the carton of Chinese from my hands.

"Hey!"

He chucked the carton back on the top shelf and shut the fridge door. "I'll buy lunch," he said. Then cut off my protest with, "I need to stop by my office to grab Nori's case files. We can grab lunch afterward."

"I have a lead to follow up on as well." Okay, what I had was a plan to drive around town near the Sionan and search for a gate, but it was kind of a lead. "We should divide and conquer."

"You think I'm letting you out of my sight? Alex, you're a magnet for trouble, though, in the trouble's defense, you go out looking for it. What with tearing holes in reality in the middle of populated streets and wandering the wilds using raw meat to draw out a fae well known for tearing people to shreds and eating them, it's a wonder you're not completely entangled in trouble." He shook his head.

Like he was in any shape to help me should "trouble" come calling. Though I guess his point was to prevent the situations I occasionally—Not typically! Really!—stumbled into. Before I had a chance to respond, he continued.

"Besides," he said, "I need your car."

Chapter 16

As it turned out, Falin did let me out of his sight, and at his own insistence. He requested that I wait in the car while he ran inside his office, so I sat in my own car, in the mid-August heat, glowering. Granted, his reasoning was sound. Letting on to Nori that Falin and I were friends probably wasn't in anyone's best interest, but I couldn't help feeling that our very association was a secret he didn't want his fae acquaintances to know. Hey, girls have feelings.

When he returned he carried only a single distressingly thin folder. It was my car, so I was driving, but with the case file so close, I was tempted to hand off my keys. I didn't. I'd seen Falin drive before, and I didn't trust him behind the wheel of my car.

"So what does it say?"

"I'm still on the first page, Alex," he said, his head bent over the file as I drove.

He tore two pages from the file, folded them, and shoved them in his pocket. I twisted in my seat, never actually taking my eyes off the road, but only just barely.

"What was on those pages?"

"Court business."

Right. As in none of my business. Why was he really here? I didn't know.

He'd finished reading the file by the time we reached the

restaurant. I debated driving through to save time, but I wanted to get my hands on the file before he changed his mind and decided not to share. Folding myself into one of the uncomfortable particleboard booths that tended to populate all fast-food chains, I pored over the file, barely noticing the chicken nuggets I ate while I read.

The main thing I learned was that Nori couldn't document worth a damn, and unless she'd left out a lot—or the two pages Falin removed had contained the useful information—her investigation had gone all of nowhere. Most of the events in the files were ones where I'd been present, and my firsthand experience was much more informative than her abbreviated write-ups. If she'd heard back from the ABMU about the spells in the feet or the disk, she hadn't included that information in her report. The only exhaustive record she kept was a list of fae who'd been questioned and relocated to Faerie, and that was a big, long list.

After flipping the last page, I shoved the file away in disgust and polished off the last of my fries. "Hey, agent in charge, I think your subordinate could stand to brush up on, well, everything."

"She gets her job done," he said, which didn't quite count as disagreeing with me, but he focused on his hamburger, obviously not willing to discuss the matter further.

As we finished lunch, John's ringtone—the theme song from *Cops*—cut through the air. I dug in my purse and grabbed the phone as the song started its second repetition.

"John, did you get my message?" I asked by way of greeting.

"Good afternoon to you too, Alex," he said, his deep voice full of amusement. "I did get your message. I also heard some water-cooler gossip that you might have had some trouble this morning. Everything okay?"

I gave him the summarized version of the morning's predawn events, then asked him the question no one seemed to be able to answer. "Has the ABMU turned up any leads on the spells in the feet or the disks?"

"Definitely not on my case, but if you're correct about the caster responsible for the feet being the same as the one who sent the construct, I can probably make a case to get a copy of the results from the disks. If there are any results, that is. No guarantee, and I'm not saying I'll be able to pass it on to you, but I'll check."

"I'll owe you one," I said, and suddenly, sitting in the middle of a fast-food restaurant with John all the way across town, I felt the potential for imbalance grow between us. *Damn. It's going to take time to get used to that.*

"Yeah, well, I'm inclined to tell you to let the police handle this, but with the attacks targeting you, and with Holly caught up in the middle of it, I know you won't. Have you tried contacting Dr. Aaron Corrie?"

The name sounded familiar, but it took me a moment to remember why. "He was one of the founding members of the Organization for Magically Inclined Humans, wasn't he?" I'd had to write a paper on him in academy. As well as being one of the founders of OMIH, he was from a family that had been practicing magic generations before the Awakening and reputedly had one of the largest collections of ancient grimoires in the world.

"Yeah, but did you know he was local?" John asked. "He consults for the police on occasion, and he likes puzzles, so he might help you for a modest fee. I'll give you the address."

Now I really did owe him, though I didn't say as much—I seriously disliked the feeling of debt racking up around me. I jotted the address John gave me on a napkin and shoved it in my purse.

"So, back to the message you left me," John said. "What makes you think you'll be able to raise a shade now when you couldn't before?"

"I'll bring another grave witch. I'm not promising it will work, but between the two of us, we might be able to pull a shade out of one of the feet. Can you get us access?"

The line was silent for a long moment, and I could imagine John tugging his mustache as he considered the obstacles ahead. "Well, technically you were already hired to consult on the case, so I guess there wouldn't be much need to file additional paperwork." In other words, if I performed another ritual, the higher-ups, and presumably the FIBs, wouldn't know about it. "But I couldn't pay you for your time."

Yeah, definitely off the books. "Don't worry about that, John. The department is already paying me for my time in the floodplain. Think of this as tying up loose ends." Besides, at this point, I was being paid to investigate by Malik—at least in a roundabout way—and it would have been sleazy to bill two different clients for one ritual.

The sound of papers fluttering on the other end of the line filtered over the phone and John said, "While we haven't gotten any magical results yet, the DNA profile on the first three feet we found came in. Nothing. Not a single match. I'm still waiting on results for the second batch. I'm grasping at straws in this case." There was a muffled sound of something hitting the mic on the phone, and I knew John had rubbed his hand over his face, his knuckles scraping the mouthpiece.

"Okay," he said at last. "What could it hurt? Besides the FIB's egos if NCPD finds the killer first. Maybe your ritual will be the case-breaker. How does tomorrow evening, about six thirty, sound? Those FIB suits never stay around here that late."

I agreed to the time and wrapped up the call. Then I looked at Falin, who'd been listening avidly to my side of the conversation.

"Come on," I said, shouldering my purse. "We have to see a witch about a rune."

"This is the one?" Falin asked as he stared up at the large brick wall topped with ornate fleur-de-lis.

Fleur-de-lis fashioned out of cast iron.

I glanced at the address I'd written on the napkin and checked it against the large numbers in the brick. They matched. I nodded and shoved the napkin back in my purse.

While most witches lived in the Glen, the suburbs surrounding the Magic Quarter, Aaron Corrie lived *in* the Quarter. And not only in it, but in the very center of it. His house overlooked one side of Magic Square, the park in the middle of the Quarter. The streets this far inside the Quarter were narrow, cobbled, and reserved for pedestrian and horse-drawn carriages only, so I'd parked several blocks away and we'd walked. Now we stood on the sidewalk staring at the old house.

Okay, so in a city only about fifty years old, we didn't really have *old* houses, but in Nekros, Corrie's house was what passed as historic. Not that we could see much of it. The tall brick wall blocked most of the house from view. The only opening in the brick was a narrow walkway barely wide enough for two people to walk through side by side—I'd hate to see what Corrie would do if he ever decided to replace his furniture.

A tall cast-iron gate blocked the walkway. More fleur-de-lis had been worked into the gate's intricate design, as well as several runes. From more than a yard away, I already could feel the buzz of Corrie's wards—and the nausea from being near such a high concentration of iron.

"I don't feel very welcome," I said, staring at the gate. While cast iron had been popular pre–Magical Awakening, post– it was considered rude. And a sign of bigotry.

"I'm guessing we're going in anyway?" Falin asked.

I nodded. I needed answers and I didn't care if the person who had them happened to hate fae. Or maybe we were jumping to conclusions. Maybe he was just a fan of pre-Awakening architecture.

I scanned the wall, searching for a call box. There wasn't one, and now that I really looked, I realized the gate didn't have any electronic locking devices. *I guess we let ourselves in.* But I didn't immediately try. Instead I reached out with my senses, feeling the magic in the wards and making sure old Corrie hadn't cast anything nasty for unwelcome visitors.

His wards were powerful, but the only unexpected spell I found intensified the sting of the iron. *So much for the theory on pre-Awakening architecture.* I stepped closer to the gate and a wave of sickness washed over me. My stomach clenched, my tongue curled, and I stumbled back, farther from the gate.

"Jeez, how do you deal with that?" I whispered, wrinkling my nose.

Falin watched me, his lips tugging down at the edges. "Iron didn't used to bother you, did it?"

I shook my head.

"You'll get used to it."

"Yeah, right. If that was true it wouldn't be one of the universal deterrents for fae."

He shrugged. "Hey, I can offer you hope, right?" He gave me a smile, but there wasn't much to it. "You will grow accustomed to feeling sick, but remember that the symptoms are warning signs. Fae can die from iron poisoning, and if you're experiencing the symptoms, you might be able to as well."

"Good to know, sensei."

The quip earned me another frown, and I immediately regretted it. Like most people raised in the mortal realm, I had only dodgy knowledge of the fae at best, more than likely filled with enough gaps to hold one of Faerie's endless halls. If Falin was willing to share information without making me trade for it, I really shouldn't discourage him.

"Come on, let's do this," I said, nodding toward the gate.

The wave of sickness washed over me again, but this time I rolled with it and forced my hand to reach for the latch anyway. Falin caught my wrist before I reached the gate.

"Gloves," he said, splaying his own gloved fingers in front of me.

Right. That made sense—and explained the gloves he always wore.

Falin grabbed the latch, and as soon as his gloved fingers touched the iron, his glamour shattered, his ragged and bloodied clothing becoming visible for all to see. I noticed that this time his holster and gun didn't disappear. He must have picked them up at his office. The gun added to his bloody clothing didn't improve his appearance, and people on the street behind us stopped, staring.

I motioned him ahead of me as soon as he pushed the gate open. I followed close behind, and the moment we were inside he released the gate and let it swing shut behind us. It didn't latch, but neither of us bothered touching it again to close it properly.

I expected Falin's glamour to bounce back in place as soon as he released the gate, but it didn't. I hoped Corrie didn't peek out his window, because we certainly looked like disreputable guests at the moment.

"Give me a moment to rebuild the glamour," Falin said. He wasn't breathing hard, but the skin around his eyes was pinched and I knew that brief contact, even through the fabric of his gloves, had taxed him.

And how much worse did Corrie's spell make the effect?

"Iron does more than make fae sick, doesn't it?"

Falin nodded as his clothing returned to its immaculate glamoured state. "Iron blocks fae from the magic of Faerie."

So what would it do to changelings? We were almost to Corrie's front door, so I didn't have time to ask, but I made a mental note to avoid iron when I was with Rianna. Not that I was exactly seeking it out now.

I trotted up the front steps and ground to a halt. There was no bell at the door, but a large knocker. An iron knocker. The doorknob was iron as well.

I gave a low whistle. "Man, this guy is serious."

Falin grimaced at the sight of the knocker, but reached for it. This time I stopped him.

"Let me. I don't have a glamour that will fail," I said, and he acquiesced with a small smile that was either gratitude or amusement—I couldn't tell which.

Digging through my purse, I pulled out the gloves Rianna had given me when I visited the Bloom. I didn't put them on, as short white gloves really didn't match my emerald green halter top, but I did use one of them to grip the knocker. After banging out three loud raps, I stepped back and dropped my gloves back in my purse, waiting. I was becoming afraid I'd have to knock again when the large door creaked open.

Aaron Corrie stood in the doorway, or at least I assumed the old man was Corrie simply because I couldn't remember ever seeing anyone older and Corrie had been a young man during the Magical Awakening seventy years ago. It was obvious that he'd been tall once, but age had stolen his height and curved his back so that the top of his head with its thin wisps of silver hair reached no higher than my nose. But his green eyes were clear and bright.

"Yes? Who are you?" His voice was gravelly, as if he hadn't used it yet today.

"Hi, I'm Alex Craft, a private investigator with Tongues

for the Dead." I held out my hand. Corrie's handshake was firm but friendly, and almost unbearably painful. The heat of his skin did nothing but exacerbate the chilling ache as his ring pressed against my flesh. *Iron jewelry? Seriously?* I'd had a lot of practice recently in keeping my face impassive during handshakes, so I managed not to wince or jerk away. When he dropped my hand, he turned to Falin and I rushed on. "And this is—" I hesitated. I'd first met him as Detective Andrews, but now that I knew he wasn't, introducing him as such would be a lie. I also couldn't introduce him as Agent Andrews. Corrie was fae-phobic and "agent" was a dead giveaway for the FIB. Finally I said, "—my associate, Falin Andrews."

Falin shook Corrie's extended hand, his glamour holding against the small quantity of iron in the ring. The old man glanced at Falin's gloved hand and then gave him a slow, scrutinizing appraisal.

"May we come in?" I asked, trying to get Corrie's attention away from Falin.

"What is it you want, Miss Craft?"

As in, no, we couldn't enter. Okay. I could work with this. Somehow.

I forced a smile. "My current case involves runes I've never seen before, and I haven't been able to find them in my research." Or at least not in four hours of Internet searching. "I'm told you might be able to help me decipher them."

He twisted his thick lips and ran a wrinkled hand over the few remaining hairs on the top of his head. "Do you have a copy of these runes?"

I nodded and riffled through my purse until I found the page where I'd sketched the runes. Corrie accepted the paper, and then patted his chest until his fingers found a thick leather cord. He pulled the cord until a mass of charms emerged from under his shirt. He flicked through the charms, finally stopping when his fingers landed on a silver charm shaped like a pair of glasses. He detached the charm and flipped it upside down before reattaching it. One of the charms around him shimmered and changed.

"I'm always having to change from a nearsighted to a farsighted charm," he said as he dropped the knot of charms back under his shirt. He smiled, as if sharing some inside joke. "You'll understand one day. Now let's see what kind of runes you have here." He lifted the page and studied the runes I'd meticulously copied from the charmed disk. As his gaze moved down the page, his eyes grew wider, his bushy white eyebrows lifting. "Now this is interesting. Very interesting."

He stepped back, vanishing from the threshold. I waited, but he didn't return.

I stuck my head inside and peeked around the half-open door. "Uh, hello?"

"Try to keep up," Corrie called as he shuffled down the hall and disappeared around the corner.

"Sounds like we've been invited in after all," Falin said, pushing the door open wider.

If Corrie hadn't already disappeared deeper in the house, I'd have dawdled endlessly in the entry hall. The walls were lined with shelves and every square inch was filled with knickknacks. But this wasn't just a collection of junk—it was a collection of *magical* junk. As soon as I passed the ward on the doorway, the press of hundreds of different charms and enchantments tumbled over me, threatening to overwhelm me.

They thundered through my senses, deafening my mind to anything else. Getting out and reorienting myself would have been best, but it was too late for that, and thinking above the magical roar to command my legs to move was beyond my ability. There was nothing malicious in the room, or at least nothing obvious, and not even anything terribly powerful. I felt a train that puffed out magic smoke, a doll that made children laugh, a mirror that reflected the image the viewer desired most, a spoon that kept soup hot, and other small, frivolous charms. But there were hundreds of them. And they overloaded my senses.

I rarely shielded with more than my bracelet and my mental shield of living vines, but now I had no choice. I squeezed my eyes closed and forced my focus inward—at least as much focus as I could summon. Outside my wall of briars I visualized a second wall enclosing my psyche. This wall I saw as a bubble of unbroken mirrors, the reflective surface deflecting the feel of magic.

As the bubble solidified in my mind, the roar of magic dulled and then fell away into eerie magical silence. I always felt blind, deaf, and dumb when I shielded this hard and completely cut myself off from the ebb of the world around me, but for now, it was better than being overwhelmed.

"Alex!"

My eyes flew open at the sound of Falin shouting, and shouting extremely close to my ears.

Falin stood with his face so close to mine that our noses brushed. The warmth of his palm pressed against the back of my neck, and I realized it wasn't new warmth, but that he must have been standing there like that for some time. He must have been calling my name for a while too. When he saw my eyes open, he let out a breath of relief, and the warm air rolled over my skin. He stepped back and my gaze snapped to the gun in his hand.

"Were you planning to shoot something?" I smiled as I asked the question.

He didn't smile back. "Was it a trap?"

"What?"

"A trap? Did we walk into a trap? What happened? You went completely unresponsive."

"Oh." I shook my head. "No trap. Just a nonsensitive collector showing off his trove. Where did Corrie go?"

Falin pointed at the hall, but he didn't move, and he stared at me several more seconds before he finally holstered his gun. Then, apparently satisfied that the danger had passed, he headed for the hall. I followed, my steps slow and heavy. We found Corrie in a bedroom that had been converted into a library. He sat at a round table in the very center of the room, my page of runes directly in front of him and stacks of oversized and irregular leather-bound books piled around him.

"Where did you find these?" he asked, his nose buried in a grimoire with pages so thin and weathered that he used a tool instead of his fingers to turn them.

"Did you hear about the magically constructed beast that attacked pedestrians in the Quarter?"

Corrie looked up and squinted at me. "Oh, you're that girl. Yes, I recognize you now." He rubbed a finger against his chin, making the loose skin jiggle. "How interesting."

He pushed away from the table and scurried to one of the bookshelves. "Where are my manners?" he said as he hauled a book with a cracked leather spine off the shelf. "Take a seat. I made tea."

I'd have preferred coffee to tea, but as I saw where his finger pointed, I realized it wouldn't have mattered what he served. In the center of the table sat a black iron kettle and three deceptively delicate teacups on saucers. Iron teacups, of course. Where did he even find these things?

His book thumped on the table and Corrie grabbed the kettle. He poured the tea and passed out cups as if we were dolls gathered at a child's tea party. I gulped back the nausea clawing at my throat as he pushed a dark saucer into my hand, and I set it on the table as soon as possible. Falin held on to his cup and saucer, his gloves apparently shielding him. When Corrie turned to walk back to the other half of the table, Falin bumped my leg with his. I met his gaze and he lifted the mug and shook his head. The message was clear: *Do not drink.*

Not that I'd planned to in the first place.

"How is the tea?" Corrie asked, sipping from his iron cup with his pinkie crooked. He didn't look at me when he asked, but at Falin. And he more than just looked at him—he watched Falin, waiting.

Falin obediently lifted his cup, but he stopped before it touched his lips and blew on the steaming liquid. "Still too hot for my taste."

The old witch set his cup down, the iron making a horrid *skritching* noise as the cup ground against the saucer. "You're fae, aren't you?"

Falin stared at him for several long heartbeats, his expression unchanging. "Yes."

"Ha, I knew it!" Corrie jumped to his feet. "Get out of my house. You're not welcome here. And you." He turned to me. "Were you knowingly associating with a fae or were you tricked?"

I blinked at him. He'd asked two questions with opposite answers. I picked one. "Yes."

"Good girl. Wait . . . which is it? Did you know he was fae?"

"Yes."

Corrie's face flushed with color. "Then you're a fool and you can get out too. Both of you. Now."

Falin and I exchanged glances and then both pushed back our chairs, letting the legs scrape on the floor as we stood. The irony was that if I'd been fully human I could have lied, and probably avoided being kicked out. But I wasn't.

"What are you waiting for? Get out."

"My runes," I said, holding out my hand for the paper.

Corrie snatched it off the table, clutching the page between his wrinkled hands. He glanced between it and us and then stepped back, pulling the page closer to his chest. "This I'd like to keep."

If I'd thought he would share what he learned I'd have let him; after all, I could always recopy the runes. But he wouldn't. I knew he wouldn't. I shook my head and extended my hand farther.

Corrie took another step back. "No. I'm keeping this."

"What would you like to trade for it?" Falin asked, crossing his arms over his chest.

Corrie looked down at the page. His eyes glimmered with either greed or lust—it was hard to tell which, but whichever demon he struggled with also had to contend with his prejudice.

Prejudice won.

The old witch tossed the page toward us. "I don't trade with Faeries."

That settled that. I picked up the paper, folded it, and then left.

Chapter 17

---※·→ ◎ ←·※---

We spent the rest of the afternoon—and the remainder of my gas tank—searching for the kelpie's "thundering gate." We drove down as many riverfront roads as I could find and walked the riverside areas of two of the three parks that butted up to the Sionan. By the time we left the second park, dusk had fallen dangerously dim and I squinted at the shadows merging my blue car with the asphalt. I blinked, keys in hand. It had gotten dark fast. You couldn't tell by the weather, but winter was on its way, and the days were growing shorter. Which meant fewer hours I could be out and about.

"Want to drive?" I asked, turning toward Falin.

"You can't see?"

"Maybe I'm just being nice." I tossed my keys in his direction. I heard more than saw him catch them as I headed for the passenger door. "Just be nice to her. And obey traffic laws."

"Of course." I could almost hear the smile in his voice.

Since I couldn't see much of anything anyway, I closed my eyes, just a blink. Or so I thought. When I opened them again, Falin was parking the car. I stretched, reaching for the door handle. Then I stopped. The air didn't resonate with magic—we weren't in the Glen, which meant he'd taken me somewhere other than home.

"Where are we?"

"My apartment. We won't be here long." He slid out of the car, but leaned back in when I didn't move. "I need to pick up some supplies."

"Supplies?" I had the suspicious feeling he meant things he would need in order to move into my loft for a few days.

When I still didn't emerge, he walked around the car and opened my door. "I need an extra gun and ammo, for starters. You're being targeted and I'd prefer to be prepared."

I didn't have any response for that. His help had been indispensable this morning, but he was injured. He needed to rest, not fight magical constructs. Besides, I wasn't exactly comfortable with his jumping back into my life and playing white knight. On top of that, I wasn't sure I could trust him. Caleb seemed convinced that Falin was here on the Winter Queen's business, and I wasn't positive he wasn't. *What is his agenda?*

Falin led me into the large brick apartment complex, and we rode the elevator to the seventh floor. At his front door, he hesitated, his hands moving to his pockets but not reaching inside them. He sighed, his shoulders sagging with the soft sound. When he looked up again, he gave me a weak smile.

"Wait here a moment," he said, and walked to the door next to his. He knocked.

It took his pounding on the door several times before the music in the apartment muted and a woman in her early twenties answered. She wore her hair in a messy ponytail, brown strands escaping around her face. A long blue streak of paint decorated one cheek where it must have transferred from her paint-stained hands when she'd brushed her hair behind her ear. She scowled when she opened the door, but when her gaze landed on Falin, her features softened, her eyes widening as she smiled.

"Falin. Hey. Long time no see. I was starting to worry," she said, wiping her hands on the thighs of her overalls. "Please, come in. I'll, uh—" She glanced at her paint-covered fingers. "I'll just clean up. You want a drink or something?"

"Actually, Tess, I locked myself out of my apartment. Do you still have my spare key?"

"Oh, yeah. Of course." She opened the door wider to motion him inside, and for the first time her gaze landed on me. She froze, the door hanging half open. "Oh. You have company. Let me get you that key. I'll be right back."

She shut the door and I glanced at Falin. He stared at the molding above Tess's door, his thumbs hooked in his belt. When the door opened again, Tess handed him a small box.

From where I stood, the heavy wards draping the box were obvious, as were several nasty spells set to trigger in the event of tampering. I shook my head, and huffed under my breath. The box had been coated in a classic mass-produced pandora-trap charm.

"You got ripped off," I told Falin.

He looked up, his finger hovering over the box. His eyebrow lifted in a cocky question mark, and I held out my hand for the box.

He started to hand it to me, but hesitated before dropping it in my palm. "There are built-in penalties for getting the code wrong," he warned.

"Yeah, feels like a shock for the first incorrect code, sickness for the second, and a knockout spell after that until the box runs out of juice." I kept my hand extended and he dropped the small box in my palm.

I wrapped my senses around the box and then, with the tip of my finger, I traced the rune for loyalty into the lid. The second rune was love. The third . . . I hesitated, my finger hovering over the lid. I didn't recognize the third rune, but I traced the design I felt.

The box popped open.

Falin stared at me. I smiled at him; then I removed the key and tossed first it, and then the box, to him. "Next time shop for charms with a sensitive."

He palmed the key and stared at the box. "What's the trick?"

"Not really a trick." I shrugged. "Low-grade pandora-trap charms sit around waiting for the right answer, and if you're sensitive, they practically broadcast what that answer is. A higher-grade pandora-trap includes a blanket spell that covers that broadcast."

"Huh." He shot a disappointed glance at his spelled box

and shoved his key in his apartment door. Once he returned the key to its box, he flashed Tess a dazzling smile and handed it back to her. "You're a lifesaver, Tess."

"Yeah. I know. See you around." She shut the door and a moment later, the music in her apartment turned up again, twice as loud as when he'd first knocked.

Falin said nothing as he ushered me inside his apartment. The air inside smelled stale, like the one-room apartment hadn't been opened during the month he'd been gone. I wrinkled my nose and glanced at the layer of dust coating every surface of the otherwise immaculate room.

Falin crossed to the closet and grabbed an empty duffel bag. He dropped it beside the TV on the dresser and pulled open a drawer.

"So what was the third rune?" I asked as I looked around. "I didn't recognize it."

"Just a symbol I can remember easily." He shrugged, unbuttoning his oxford. "I know only two runes."

Love and *loyalty*. Love was no surprise. While true love spells were considered gray magic since they compromised someone else's free will, charms meant to attract love or help the bearer find love could be purchased at gas stations, to say nothing of charm stores. But loyalty—that was a rarer rune. There was probably a good story behind it, and I made a mental note to ask at some point.

"So I imagine you took a class on runes in school," Falin said as he peeled off his shirt. He winced with the movement, though his glamour covered not only the wound but the dressing as well, so his chest looked smooth and touchable. *No, not touchable. Fine. Or, er, unhurt.*

"Unhurt" was a much safer description. I tore my gaze away.

What were we talking about? Runes, that was it. Runes were a nice safe topic.

"Yeah, my academy required me to take four years of rune theory. I don't use them a lot, though, so I only remember the common ones off the top of my head. What about you? Do the fae have schools that little fae kids go to and learn about Faerie and being fae?"

"Doubtful."

"You don't know?" I asked, glancing back over my shoulder.

That was the wrong move. Falin had discarded his ruined pants and now dug through the top drawer of his dresser in nothing but his glamour—and not a glamour that included clothing. From where I stood, I had a perfect view of his broad shoulders, the line of his spine, his trim waist trailing into slim hips and a tight ass and sleek thighs. My hands clenched at my sides as the tactile memory of tracing my fingers over all that skin gripped me.

I ripped my gaze away and tucked my balled fists under my armpits before my hands did something to embarrass me. *Now would be a good time to remind yourself he's the Winter Queen's lover.* But I'd never met the Winter Queen, so she wasn't the best cold-shower solution in this situation. I needed something else to think about.

"So, do you and Tess date?" I asked, wandering around the furniture. The apartment barely looked lived in. Falin owned a large couch, a dresser with a TV on top, a computer desk with computer, a folding card table and two chairs—little else as far as furniture, and nothing that I could pretend held my interest.

"Tess? No. She stores a key for me because I wind up here without one a little too often. Occupational hazard."

I bet. "She likes you," I said, hitting the POWER button on his desktop.

His presence suddenly filled the space behind me. Then his arms slid around my waist, pulling my back against his chest.

"Jealous?" He lips brushed my neck as he asked, sending a shiver down my spine.

"Please tell me you have clothes on." I knew he didn't have a shirt—my halter top left enough of my back bare that his skin against mine was obvious.

"Mmm-hmm," he said, the sound vibrating over my skin.

His embrace was deliciously warm—not blisteringly hot, but a wonderful, content-making warm that made my body tingle with his nearness. It was also completely unacceptable. *What is wrong with you, Alex? This morning Death left your skin singing with a ghost of a kiss, and now*

you're going all melty because of Falin? I seriously needed
to get my head examined. Logic demanded that I couldn't
desire two men at once, right? But I could. Oh, it left me
confused, but it didn't drown the desire. *An assassin and a
soul collector—how screwed up is that?*

I tried to shrug away from Falin, and the movement
brought my elbow in contact with his side. He sucked in a
breath and I winced on his behalf. Half spinning as I
stepped out of his arms, I rounded on him.

"I'm sor—" I caught the apology in time. "Are you
okay? Did I reopen it?"

"It's fine." He straightened as if his posture could prove
his health.

He could say he was fine all day, but I couldn't *see* that
he was fine. Well, actually, his glamour made his smooth
chest look perfect, but obviously it wasn't.

"Drop your glamour so I can see that wound."

He grunted in response, turning away from me, and I
grabbed his arm to stall him.

"Falin?" I said his name the same way I'd normally say
"please" but with none of the debt incursion.

He turned, emotions warring for his expression. Obsti-
nate resistance flashed across his face with a quick thinning
of his lips and narrowing of his eyes and then gave way to
something softer, but by the time he stepped forward that
had faded and a smile I could only describe as sly curled his
lips.

He reached out, cupped my face with both of his large
hands, and leaned forward. "If you're that concerned, you
can kiss me and make it better."

"No."

The smile spread wider, as if that was exactly the response he'd expected. "You'll change your mind," he said,
and then turned, and with the way he said it, I half expected
him to ruffle my hair or tweak my nose as he sauntered
away.

I shook my head, not sure if I should laugh or throw
something at him.

Either way, I still wanted to get a look at that wound.

"Falin," I said again, but this time it was just his name,
meant to call his attention. As soon as he turned, I cracked

my shields. My grave-sight snapped into focus. I dropped my shields so I could see through his glamour, and as I stepped forward to study the wound, I realized that this once the decay benefited me because I could see bits of the gash through the rotted gauze—I just had to be careful not to touch it. I didn't want his dressing ending up like my poor porch. I caught sight of only small sections of the wound, which were dark against the shimmer of his soul under his skin, but I could see enough to reassure myself that I hadn't reopened the wound with my careless elbow. I also saw enough to be amazed at how much he'd healed since this morning.

Falin frowned at me when his gaze landed on my glowing eyes. "I told you I was fine," he said, turning his back on me and heading to his dresser. After pulling a shirt out of the top drawer and shrugging into it, he commenced shoving clothes into the duffel bag. "Try not to make anything in my apartment decay. I'd like to get the security deposit back when I leave."

"Right." I slammed my shields in place and my vision returned to normal—or at least to the shadowed landscape that passed as normal. I stepped closer to see exactly how much Falin was packing, and he knelt to pull a false floor out of his bottom drawer.

Another pandora-trap charm locked the safe in the bottom of the drawer. He reached out with one hand, and then paused, glancing up at me. "What, do you want to do it?"

I backed away, holding my palms up flat in front of my body. The charm on the safe had been created by the same person who cast the charm on the box, so it had the same flaws. Falin hadn't been pissed when I cracked his first pandora-trap, so I assumed that wasn't the issue now. *Note to self: He doesn't like me breaking his glamour.* Of course, if our roles were reversed and someone could willy-nilly look at anything I tried to hide, I guess I'd be peeved too.

He unlocked the safe and pulled out three guns and several magazines, as well as his FIB badge, an extra harness, and an extra pair of knives. Some of these disappeared to various concealed locations under his clothes and the rest went in his duffel bag.

I blinked at the haul. "Are you planning to go to war? Sure you don't want to pack an assault rifle as well?"

He looked up from the bag. "You have met yourself, right?" He zipped the bag closed.

"So should I get a gun too?"

"I'd fear the day." He grabbed a blazer and pulled it over his shoulder rig. "You do have a good blade," he said, nodding toward the dagger concealed in my boot.

"It was a gift."

"I never doubted as much. If you're going to carry a dagger, you need to learn to use it."

I frowned at him. "I know how to use it. I stick the pointy end in things I don't like."

That earned a cocky eyebrow lift and he picked up his duffel bag. "Ready?"

"You do know I haven't invited you to crash at my place."

"You'd rather stay here?" He gave an open-palmed wave that encompassed the small apartment.

"No, that's—" I stopped as one side of his lips twitched in a grin he couldn't hide. He was hitting my buttons on purpose. "You're insufferable, you know that?"

"And you're a danger to yourself." He grabbed my keys off the dresser where he'd tossed them when we first walked in. "Come on, let's go."

"Did you hire a maid?" Falin asked as he stopped in the doorway of my apartment.

I hadn't walked much farther than the threshold myself.

The bed, which I'd put sheets on this morning, but nothing more, was now made, with a comforter I hadn't seen since last winter tucked in and turned down. The clothes that usually lived in a pile in front of my dresser were gone, and the books I'd left precariously stacked on different surfaces in the room were now lined up neatly on my bedside table. The dishes in the sink were missing, and PC, who was bouncing at my knees, had a large pink bow in the thin crest of hair on the top of his head.

"Who was here?" I asked the dog as I scooped him up from the floor. I attacked the bow one-handed. Someone had come in my house. Had entered my space, violated the masculinity of my dog, and ... and ... *cleaned*?

I couldn't get the bow loose. Picking up on my agitation, Falin stepped forward to try to help. Of course, three adult-sized hands trying to attack one very small bit of twine securing the bow didn't actually help. PC squirmed in my arms, also not happy about the situation.

"You hold him. I'll get the bow," I said, shoving the dog at Falin.

"I take it you didn't request your house cleaned?" Falin asked, his voice a whisper near my ear as I leaned over PC.

"Of course not. I—" I stopped because I caught movement out of the corner of my eye. A mug jumped out of the dish drainer and headed across my kitchen floor. I threw open my mental shields as the mug hopped up to the counter and the cabinet opened.

As my grave-sight filled my vision, the bow under my fingers rotted, the fibers fraying and the twine holding it in place eroding to nothing. But across the room, in my little kitchenette, I caught sight of a small round figure as it jumped to the bottom shelf of the cabinet and used stubby arms to carefully set the mug next to the rest. Green quill-like hair trailed down the creature's back, over the counter, and fell almost to the floor.

"Ms. B?" I called, which made the small brownie turn. She hopped to the counter, then down to the floor.

"Just finishing here," she said as she scurried across to the other counter. She grabbed another mug out of the dish drainer and headed back for the cabinet.

I stared for a moment, feeling strangely disconnected. Then I stumbled toward the bed, which in my grave-sight sagged under the rags covering a mattress with exposed springs. "I think I need to sit down," I mumbled.

Falin caught my wrist as I reached the bed, and tugged me upright when I would have sunk onto the sagging mattress.

"Don't you think you should ..." He pointed at my eyes.

Right, I didn't want my apartment rotting away around me. I closed my shields, annoyed at the sudden darkness pressing around me. Only then did I sink down onto the bed. I pressed the heels of my hands into my eyes and said, "I'm guessing Rianna sent you?"

"That she did," Ms. B's surprisingly full voice said from the kitchen. "Came to find you and discovered cream on the doorstep but no one keeping the house."

I heard her bare feet scurrying over the hardwood floor, and then the bed shifted as she jumped up beside me. I opened my eyes to find her looking over the dingy and rotted bow that my magic had destroyed. It was large enough that she used both of her small hands to grip the frayed material, and the way her lip protruded made me feel guilty about destroying the damn thing.

"The house looks great, Ms. B," I said, because I suddenly felt like I had to say something and I couldn't apologize for the bow.

She looked up and tucked the bow in the leather belt cinching her burlap dress. She waved a hand through the air as if to dismiss my implied thank-you and then looked up at me. "The girl said you'd have a message."

I nodded, guessing that "the girl" was Rianna. "Tell her to meet me at Central Precinct tomorrow evening at six thirty."

"Consider it told." She hopped off the bed, her hair twitching as it trailed after her. When she reached the door, she jumped, turned the knob, and then saw herself out.

I stared at the door for a long moment after it closed.

"So, a brownie," Falin said, walking around the side of the bed. "You want to explain how you befriended a brownie?"

"Not really."

He looked at me, leaning back with his thumbs hooked in his pockets, and I glanced away. I flipped on the TV to have something else to focus on. Lusa's face showed up, but she clearly wasn't in the studio. *What is she up to now?* Hopefully something that would pull attention off me. I walked over and turned up the volume.

"—we're approaching the anomaly now. Ted, can you focus on that?" She pointed and the camera focus zoomed over her head.

The scene was dark. Wherever she was broadcasting didn't have many lights, and I could just make out the shadowy shapes of tree limbs. As the camera zoomed, I caught the glint of moonlight off a reflective surface. *Water?* A bad feeling crept into my stomach.

"Are you getting it?" Lusa's voice asked from somewhere offscreen, and the camera zoomed more. "Okay, folks at home, I don't know if you can see this, but it appears that we're looking at another tear into the Aetheric. The one we saw two days ago was bursting with raw power, but this one has only a couple of wisps coming through. This thing is huge."

The camera zoomed closer, and she was right, it looked like a person-sized rip in reality. *Crap.* I felt like I was moving in slow motion as I turned toward Falin. His expression darkened, his full lips pressing tight. He tore his gaze from the screen and fixed on me.

"Did you?"

I shook my head. I'd ripped open those small, dime-sized holes when we'd fought the ravens, the hole in the Quarter during the first construct attack, and, of course, the room-sized hole I'd created in my father's mansion, but unless I'd merged reality from a distance or the tears moved, I hadn't caused this one. I squinted, searching the fuzzy screen of my old TV set and trying to make out details of the tear's location.

The cameraman panned, zooming out to pull Lusa back on the screen. She rehashed information about the tear in the Quarter and about what the officials were currently debating. *Come on, Lusa, tell us where you are.*

As she spoke, someone crossed directly in front of the tear, pausing to look at the camera. Because the camera was focused on Lusa, the person's face was blurred. I was pretty sure the figure was male. His height was hard to judge, though he was taller than the tear. He wore a long dark coat, which even after the sun set, was far too warm. *A passerby? A gawker?*

"Can you tell who that man is?"

Falin tore his gaze from the TV long enough to frown at me. "What man?"

"That one." I pointed to the figure in the background, and Falin's frown turned puzzled. "You can't see him?" I asked.

He shook his head. *Okay, then.* That meant, most likely, that the man was a ghost or a soul collector. The tear in reality scared me, but the fact that it was present at the edge of the river and that there was a spectral figure near it worried me even more.

"This is Lusa Duncan with *Witch Watch* live at Lenore Street Bridge, signing off."

I was on my feet before the last words were out of Lusa's mouth. I had my purse over my shoulder and was halfway out the door before I realized Falin wasn't with me. True dark had fallen and he still had my keys, which meant I wasn't driving myself anywhere.

"You coming?"

He stared at the TV and shook his head. "I don't think you should go anywhere near that tear."

"What? Why?" I hadn't been the one to rip reality. I was sure of that. I hadn't been anywhere near the Lenore Street Bridge recently, which meant someone else had the ability to merge planes of existence. I wanted to find out who. Maybe there was someone out there who could teach me how *not* to merge reality. Also, the riverside location worried me. Call it a hunch—which was surely nothing definite—but a twisting feeling in my gut told me the tear needed to be checked out in relation to my case.

Falin shook his head again. "Alex, what you can do, when you make the land of the dead manifest in the mortal plane or bring the Aetheric here, is called planeweaving. It is a fae ability."

"You think?" The fact that the ability had gone into hyperdrive around the Blood Moon when, supposedly, my fae soul had awakened, was a good indication of the connection between the two.

Falin ignored my sarcasm. "Planeweavers are rumored to be responsible for a lot of things. The folded spaces, the fact that Faerie and the mortal realm touch only in small doorways, the fact that the fae can't reach the Aetheric . . . There are legends and myths that date back even farther than the oldest living fae's memory." *And that would be a long time.* He stepped forward. "But, Alex, planeweavers don't exist anymore."

"I think I'm going to beg to differ on that one."

One side of his mouth lifted in a lopsided smile. "Yes. Of course you exist, though it would be best if the courts don't learn what you are. What I mean is that there are no fae planeweavers in Faerie. No feykin planeweavers either."

"And outside Faerie?"

"If the courts knew about a planeweaver, they would be in Faerie whether they were mortal, kin, or fae. Which is why, if you don't want to be dragged off to Faerie, you need to keep your head down. The tear in the Quarter already has rumors circulating in the courts. You can't be seen near that one." He pointed at the TV screen and then reached out and smoothed a loose curl behind my ear. "Officially, as far as anyone in Faerie knows, the only planeweavers that exist are a pair of mortals. They serve the high king, and rumor says they are the only reason he's held the high court for over a millennium—but they are changelings, mortal captives of Faerie, which is as good as saying sterile, so there will be no more from their lines. I've heard rumors that the Shadow King has a changeling planebender, which is similar though not quite the same. Again, his planebender is a changeling, mortal, and the end of a line. There were apparently more mortal planeweavers in centuries past, but fae planeweavers have been extinct since the age of legends."

And recently the legends had been returning.

The dread I'd been feeling since Lusa's special report had aired intensified, and the clenching in my stomach moved to my lungs until it was hard to breathe. "I'm not a legend. But whoever opened that might have been." I nodded at the screen, which was replaying Lusa's footage. I'd already faced a legend forgotten in time—I didn't want to think about how much worse a legend *not* forgotten might be. "So now what?"

"I'll go check out the tear. You stay here, and stay inside. We don't know when more of those constructs could show up."

Right. I frowned at his back as he took *my* keys and walked out the door. Of course, he was probably right. I couldn't afford to add any more associations between me and the tears in reality. The only people who knew for sure that I could merge planes had been with me on the night of the Blood Moon, and that was a short list: Falin, Death, Rianna, and Roy . . . maybe Casey—I had no idea how much she remembered. My father also knew, of course, and at this point Caleb, Holly, and Tamara suspected that at least I could punch holes to the Aetheric. But everything else was speculation and rumor.

I just have to keep it that way.

I'd have to wait to check out the tear after the commotion died down. *If it dies down.* I sighed, fed and walked PC, then called Holly to check on her. They were holding her in the hospital overnight for a sleep study, but if nothing unusual happened, she was scheduled to be released in the morning. I wasn't sure if that was good or bad news. I was about to head downstairs and visit Caleb when Roy appeared in the center of my room.

"Alex, you aren't going to believe this," he said, his shimmering form all but vibrating with his excitement. "That guy you sent me to follow, Maximillian Bell? He just claimed responsibility for a tear in reality."

Chapter 18

"Wait, Roy—slow down," I said both to give myself a second to absorb his words and because the excited ghost looked like he might flit back into the deep realms of the land of the dead at any moment. "Which tear? The one at the Lenore Street Bridge?"

Roy scrunched his face around his thick-framed glasses. "I'm not sure where. A phone call came in, and then everything happened in a flurry. At first I thought I'd missed something. That his men had nabbed you despite his instructions to follow you discreetly—"

That would have been good to know before now.

"—But then Bell and a bunch of his followers—that school is a cult, by the way—piled into cars and drove down to the river."

"That has to be the same tear Lusa found." I rolled from my heels to the balls of my feet. So Bell was on the scene. *And claiming the tear?* "Roy, did you actually see Bell rip the tear into the Aetheric?"

The ghost shook his head, pushing his glasses farther up his nose when they slipped forward. "He got the call, hurried to the site, and then told the reporter and the officials that the tear was his possession and on his land, so they were trespassing."

"So Bell might not have had any idea the tear was there until Lusa ran her report." Which made a lot more sense.

After all, if he could rip a hole in reality on his own, why would he have approached me? *Unless he found someone else to do it.*

But who?

"Did you see another ghost at the scene?" I asked, remembering the figure I'd spotted in Lusa's footage, the one Falin hadn't been able to see. "Probably a man with dark hair. It looked like he was wearing some sort of trench coat?"

"You mean the reaper?" the ghost asked, and his form shimmered out of focus as he shivered. "Yeah. That's why I got the hell out of there."

A soul collector? The collectors were a secretive bunch. I'd "known" Death most of my life, but in truth, I didn't know anything about him or the other collectors—I didn't even know his name. *What was a collector doing walking around a hole into the Aetheric?*

Lusa was no longer on the screen of my TV, most likely because Bell had kicked her off his property. The studio reporter rerolled Lusa's footage of the tear, keeping his own running commentary as he pointed out parts of the tape. He paused to enlarge the shot when the cameraman had zoomed in on the tear, and a symbol scratched into the dirt caught my attention.

"Is that a rune?" I stepped closer, squinting as I all but shoved my nose against the screen trying to make out the small shapes in an already overzoomed image. The symbols sure *looked* like runes, but the magnification had degraded the image quality to the point that someone could have drawn a tic-tac-toe board in the dirt and it probably would have looked like a rune.

I leaned back as the camera panned. Then a clump of pixels at the bottom of the screen jumped out at me. "That's *definitely* a rune." It was that same damn rune I'd spent half the morning staring at because it looked familiar but I couldn't place.

"Got you," I said, jabbing my finger against the TV screen.

Roy hunkered down beside me and looked from where my finger pressed against the screen to my face. He shoved his glasses farther up his nose again. "Alex, are you talking to the TV?"

"Not at all." I jumped to my feet, unable to stay still any longer. The rune proved that the tear and the constructs were connected. Maybe they weren't from the same ritual, but they were definitely cast by the same witch or coven of witches—the chance that two unconnected witches would suddenly start casting unheard-of spells using the same rare runes was too unlikely. "This is the break we need."

"Would 'we' include me?" Roy asked, floating beside me as I paced. "Because if it does, I'm lost."

"I'm thinking out loud, but sure, 'we' can include you." I grabbed my purse and dug out the page of runes. "We've only had the end results of the witch's spells thus far. First there were the feet filled with dark magic. Then the constructs that left only a spelled disk behind. We knew the two were created by the same person or group because the magic felt the same, but we haven't been able to get anywhere with the remains of the spells. But this rune"—I pointed to the fourth rune down on the page—"was cut into the dirt around that tear. Whoever ripped that tear has to be responsible for the other two as well, but now we have a crime scene. There has to be something at that site that will lead back to the caster." And I wasn't there. I glanced at the TV but a commercial was currently playing. "Roy, can you go check out the scene? Let me know what's going on?"

"With that reaper there? No way." He fanned his hands out away from his body to accent his no. "Being a ghost might not be the best gig in the world, but I have no idea what happens *after* the reapers nab you. The devil you know and all that."

"Right, the soul collector," I said, pacing again without really hearing the rest of what Roy said. "Why is he there? Does he have a part in this? The collectors take that ... soul mist ... that appears when the constructs are disbelieved. Does he provide that?" But why would he? Why would a collector be involved at all? "He might just be passing through."

I dug my phone out of my purse. I needed to update Falin on the runes. He'd need to make sure the area was treated as a crime scene—especially if Bell had claimed ownership and had his people tromping through the place.

I woke the phone but then hesitated as I pulled up the address book. I didn't actually *have* Falin's phone number. My phone had been destroyed by the time we'd started working together on the Coleman case, and I hadn't replaced it until after Falin had disappeared. Come to think of it, I hadn't seen him use a phone since he reappeared, so I wasn't even sure he had one on him. *Damn.*

I shook my head and dropped the phone back in my purse. "I have to go to the scene."

But Falin was right—I did not want to draw Faerie's attention. If there was some other planeweaver out there ripping holes in reality, the courts could drag him or her away. I needed to stay far from the tears. And even if I wanted to go, how would I get to the scene? It was dark, so I couldn't drive. Besides, Falin had my car.

But what about the case? And Holly? And Caleb—who wouldn't be protected by anything but his wards tonight. Wards that this morning's adventure proved were easy enough for the spell to circumvent.

I chewed my lip and walked over to the TV again. They were replaying the same clip I'd already seen twice. I didn't need to see the tear's discovery again. I needed to see what was happening at the scene right now. One of Lusa's "Breaking News" bulletins would be great. Of course, I guess she'd already done that.

The anchorman rolled the film where the collector crossed in front of the tear, his features out of focus. *What was he doing there?*

"Okay, that's it. I'm going to the scene." There had to be a crowd by now. I would just try to blend in.

Picking up my phone, I hit the second number on my speed dial and then turned the speaker on while it rang. As I waited, I twisted my shoulder-length curls up on top of my head, then secured—and covered—them with a cap that read WITCHITUDE across the front. As far as disguises went, it was weak, but much more and I'd look like I was trying to hide. I'd just tucked the last of my escaped curls under the cap when a groggy-sounding female voice answered the phone.

"Alex? You woke me at four this morning. I'm trying to catch up those hours, plus I had a day full of dead bodies

with no cause of death and I . . ." Tamara said, and then her
bed squeaked as if she'd sprung to her feet. "Wait. Did
something happen? Is Holly—?"

"She was fine when I talked to her last. She's staying at
the hospital for observation tonight. But something did
happen, and I need a favor, and, uh, a ride."

"Do we know which side of the bridge the tear is located
on?" Tamara asked as we headed south toward Lenore
Street.

I shook my head. The Lenore Street Bridge wasn't a
high-traffic pass. The Sionan River separated the skyscrapers and booming metropolis of downtown Nekros City
from the Magic Quarter and the Witches Glen, but the Lenore Street Bridge was in the southern part of the city. On
the western side of the Sionan—the Quarter side—Lenore
Street was practically a country road, since the suburban
sprawl hadn't yet spread that far south. On the eastern
side—the city side—Lenore Street was a fairly minor road
in the warehouse district. It certainly wasn't a street I traveled often.

"We'll look for the crowd." And there was bound to be
one. *Witch Watch* had been replaying Lusa's footage for the
last hour, so aside from the media frenzy guaranteed to
flock to the site, gawkers had probably gathered by now.
There were always gawkers. Several law enforcement agencies would descend on the new tear as well, even if they
hadn't realized the site was a crime scene—and though I
couldn't yet prove a crime had taken place there, I had no
doubt that Tamara or I would pick up the magical signature
from the witch responsible for the recent murders. Finding
the right location wouldn't be an issue.

I was right. Empty cars dotted the side of the road as we
neared the river, and by the time the old steel bridge came
into view, the crowd gathered on the other side was easy to
spot.

"I guess I should have parked on the grass," Tamara
said, drumming her thumbs against the steering wheel as
traffic stopped, stranding us in the center of the bridge.

"I'm sure we won't be stopped long. See, we're already

moving again." Okay, it was more like crawling, but at least we were moving.

I squinted as I tried to make out anything in the shadows on the far side of the bridge. My glasses were in my purse and I dug them out. They tended to help with the blurriness that plagued my sight after a ritual, but they couldn't do much for my night blindness. Still, it couldn't hurt to try. I shoved the glasses on my face and leaned forward. Then I jumped as Roy materialized on the console between Tamara and me.

"Okay, that wasn't the spot I was aiming for," he said, glancing down at the gearstick pressed against his inner thigh. "This isn't a stick shift, is it? She's not going to change gears on me, is she?"

"Like you'd feel it if she did, but no. It's an automatic."

"Alex?" Tamara's voice sounded concerned, but I couldn't see her clearly through Roy's shimmering form. I smiled in her direction anyway. She couldn't see the ghost, so she wouldn't have trouble seeing me.

"Roy's back," I told her before focusing on the ghost again. "So, did you see anything important?" I asked. It had taken some coaxing—he was still unnerved about almost running into the soul collector near the tear earlier—but I'd talked him into doing some reconnaissance for me.

I was hoping for news about what was happening closer to the tear, but Roy was still staring at the gearshift precariously close to his crotch.

"Uh, Alex. I can definitely feel that gearshift. And the console."

"Oh, for crying out loud." I pushed the seat belt off my chest and twisted in my seat until my shoulders were catty-corner to the passenger-side door. As soon as my bare shoulder lost contact with Roy, the gearshift slid harmlessly through his shimmering leg.

Roy released a relieved breath and let his head roll back as if he'd been spared unspeakable torture. "You should warn me before you do that."

I rolled my eyes. "Hey, you're the one who materialized touching me. Not my fault."

Once upon a time, when the highlight of any week in academy was a visit from Death in which he let me experi-

ment with making objects tangible to him, I'd actually had
to focus to accomplish things like letting him interact with
a mug of coffee. Not anymore. Now if I had physical contact with something, anyone—or any being—touching me
could interact with the item as well. *Alex Craft, the nexus at
which realties converge—lucky me.*

"So, anything?" I asked Roy again.

"Huh? Oh, yeah. Bad news. Bell has private security and
barricades. He's not letting anyone but his inner circle near
the rift."

"Damn."

"What's wrong, Alex? Damn what?" Tamara asked as
the car crawled off the bridge. Traffic had improved mar-
ginally in that Tamara no longer had to sit on the brake, but
she wasn't using any gas either. I related what Roy had told
me and Tamara clicked her tongue. "I swear, if I rolled out
of bed just to stand three hundred yards from that tear, I'm
going to be pissed."

She wasn't the only one.

The taillights in front of us flashed red, and Tamara
sighed. To our right, blue lights strobed in the dark, illumi-
nating the crowd milling outside a tall chain-link gate.
News vans hugged the perimeter, shining bright spotlights
at the gate, but Roy was right: no one was being permitted
inside.

"Roy, can you go out for another look? Also can you try
to find out what Bell and his people plan to do with the
tear?"

"Nope. I've done my brave deeds for the night. That
reaper was still out there the last time I checked." He
crossed his arms over his incorporeal chest. "I'm staying
with you. Unless the reaper comes over here. Then, I guess,
I'll go hang out at my grave, or something. As far as Bell is
concerned, when I was out there a few minutes ago he and
his followers were huddling around that rift."

Great. I'd been afraid they would be. That was where I'd
seen the runes. I could only hope they weren't trampling all
over the evidence of the ritual.

Our snail's pace finally led to a gravel lot a block down
the road. We parked and headed back toward the bridge—
the walk back didn't take half the time the drive had. Roy

followed, his hands balled in the front pockets of his shimmering jeans, but his head snapped back and forth as if he thought a collector might descend on him at any moment. When we crossed Lenore he lost his nerve completely.

"I'll catch back up with you later," he said. Then he vanished without waiting for me to say good-bye.

I tugged the bill of my cap down and avoided meeting anyone's gaze as Tamara and I reached the edge of the gathered crowd. Not that anyone was looking around the crowd—everyone wanted to see the tear.

"So you have a plan to get us to the front of this crowd, not to mention behind that gate?" Tamara asked as we joined the onlookers.

I shrugged. "I met Bell once."

"Yeah? And did you get on well enough that he's likely to let us pass?" The tone she used betrayed the fact that she anticipated a no, and I didn't need to reflect on my short conversation with Bell in his limo to know she was right.

Tamara stood on her toes, her neck straining as she peered around the shoulders of the people in front of us. In my boots, I was as tall as or taller than all but the tallest men in the crowd, so I didn't have to strain to see over people like Tamara did. I strained to see, period, though the media and security lights helped.

Bell had obviously intended to invest in some sort of industrial enterprise, but judging by the vacant lot, he had never gotten around to moving forward with the project. A nine-foot chain-link fence ringed the property, but it was an old fence, rusted and dilapidated. One section of it had fallen completely, and it looked like people had been using the opening as a path for years. Two of Bell's thugs guarded the opening, stopping anyone who pressed too close, and Bell's lawyers held the front gate.

"There has never been any legislation put in place making it illegal to own an opening into the Aetheric. Unless you return with a warrant, you have no grounds for entering this property," a middle-aged man with flame red hair the same color as Holly's said to a uniformed officer as we wove our way nearer the front gate. Holly's father was a big-shot defense attorney with a high-powered client list, and while I'd never met him—Holly's relationship with her father was almost as screwed up as mine, one of the many reasons Holly and I got along so well—I had the feeling we were looking at him now.

I touched Tamara's shoulder and pointed to a clearer spot about twenty feet away. Most of the crowd had gathered around the front gate, so we might see more if we moved farther along the fence. Excusing ourselves as we stepped around people, we slipped through the crowd. I kept my head down as we passed cops and reporters, but they weren't paying us any attention. We managed to find a better spot right up against the fence, but between my ruined vision and the flashing police lights blowing any shot I had of my eyes adjusting to the darkness, I couldn't see a thing more than a yard or two into the vacant lot.

"Can you see the tear?" I asked, leaning closer to Tamara.

"Yeah, a little, and Alex, I don't like this. Those skimmers are drawing raw Aetheric energy with no filtering and minimal training. I don't even think they've drawn a protective circle." She shook her head in disbelief. "The raw magic filtering through the air is throwing off my senses, but I'm not sensing a circle at all. Lots of other spells, though."

Yeah, I was picking up on that too. Magic was everywhere. Most of the crowd wore charms, Bell's security had laid down a perimeter ward along the gate so they'd know if anyone tried to sneak in, and beyond the gate . . . I let my senses reach out, trying to sift through the magic in the air. I closed my eyes, stretching my senses, and a hand closed on my biceps. I yelped, my eyes flying open.

"What are you doing here?" a familiar and none too happy voice asked.

"Falin." *Busted.* I turned to face him. "Hey, yeah, about that . . ." I told him about spotting the rune when Channel 6 reran Lusa's footage and about the assumptions I'd made from there, as well as my thoughts on the soul collector's presence. His pissed expression didn't change through my explanation, and I ended with a shrug. "It seemed like it was worth the risk."

"It might be enough for us to get a warrant," he admitted after a moment's hesitation, and his grip on my biceps loosened. "Now you should get out of here." He wrapped an arm around my shoulders as he tried to steer me away from Tamara and the fence. "Come on. I'll take you home and call about the warrant on the way."

"No, you won't," I said, but he was already dragging me forward. I glanced over my shoulder at Tamara, who looked unsure if she should interfere or not. "I'll be right back," I told her before turning to Falin again. I was okay with him leading me to where other people couldn't hear us discuss—okay, *argue*—about why I needed to stay—after all, there were aspects of my life I wasn't sharing with my friends, let alone strangers—but I wasn't about to leave. "I came here to—"

I didn't get a chance to finish as a female voice, smooth and camera-ready, said, "Alex Craft."

Crap. I didn't bother smiling as I glanced toward the voice. "Lusa." And her cameraman, of course. *What, do I have a sign over my head attracting everyone I'd rather avoid?*

I'd no sooner had that thought than I spotted Agent Nori in the crowd. Luckily, she at least wasn't looking my way.

"So, what brings you to the river tonight, Miss Craft?" Lusa asked, pushing a mic toward me.

"I could ask you the same question."

She smiled. "A story. You?"

I glanced from the mic in my face to the blinking red light on the camera. "I imagine the same thing as everyone else." I nodded toward where I imagined the tear was located. The tear wasn't the full reason I was here, but it was *one* of the reasons.

Unfortunately, Lusa seemed to realize that. "No," she said. "There is more to it than that. You know something, and I'm betting it's newsworthy. I've got a nose for this type of thing."

I scoffed under my breath. "Lusa, I doubt your nose is real."

Her perfectly straight teeth clicked audibly, and color bloomed in her cheeks. The color faded again instantly, her camera-ready persona snapping back in place.

"Well, how about this," she said, dropping her mic to her

side. "How about I run my next story with the spin 'Alex Craft seen poking around the scene, likely checking what damage her latest tear into the Aetheric is causing'?"

At my side, Falin stiffened, his fingers digging into my shoulder hard enough to hurt, though I didn't think he was aware he'd tightened his grip. I fought wincing—which would have looked like guilt to the camera—and tried to step out of his grasp. It didn't work; he might as well have turned into a solid ice sculpture.

"You can't run that story," he said, his voice a low warning.

"Detective Andrews, the public has the right to the truth."

"Except that isn't the truth. I didn't open that tear."

"Well, the public also has the right to draw their own conclusions." She smiled, a big, hungry display of teeth.

"You can't run that story. I've already been pulled off the street once by someone who wanted me to open a hole to the Aetheric." I was appealing to her better nature, which I wasn't sure she still had under her reporter instincts, but it was Falin who responded to my words.

He stepped around me, his eyes catching, and locking, on mine. Right—I hadn't told him about my little *chat* with Bell. Not that now was the time to go into it. I focused on Lusa, who seemed much less concerned about my safety.

"Give me a better story and I'll run with it instead."

"I can't just conjure up a story."

"Well, then, I guess I already have my sound bite."

I glared at her. "You broke a major story when you discovered the tear—which I'd love to learn how you found, by the way, because *that* little tidbit wasn't in your broadcast and I can't see you heading out this evening thinking, 'I know, I'll go poke around abandoned warehouse lots and see if a story turns up.' Especially not in those heels." I nodded at her purple slingbacks. "You got your story, and because of Bell's barricade, *Witch Watch* is the only show that has footage of the rip up close. So why do you have to put a target over my head just to ride the coattails of your own success?"

"The tear will be old news soon unless I dig up something to add as a new development. My original footage is already viral and streaming from countless places on the Net. I need something fresh. Now I imagine you're here for one of the cases you're working." She lifted the hand holding her mic, not to shove the mic in my face but to point at me with one of her perfectly manicured nails. "Scratch my back and I'll scratch yours. And because you asked, I'll tell you how I found the tear—that is, as long as what you give me is good."

I glanced at Falin. He scowled at Lusa, his face hard, ungiving, and totally unreceptive to her idea. I, on the other hand, was inclined to capitulate. I'd worked with Lusa before, and I knew she kept her word. Which meant she'd help me out if I helped her, but it also meant she wasn't kidding about using me as a sound bite. But perhaps more important than that, while the woman could be extremely irritating if you were the story she'd latched on to, she was a damn fine researcher and investigative journalist.

And I happened to have a page full of runes I needed researched.

"Off the record," I said, nodding at the blinking light on the camera behind Lusa.

"Micky, take a break," Lusa said, handing her mic to her cameraman. "Come on, Craft. There are fewer people closer to the bridge."

I started to follow her, but Falin grabbed my arm, stalling me.

"You really think this is the wisest plan?" he asked, his voice a hissed whisper beside my ear.

I considered the decision again, staring at him as I tried to puzzle out which part he objected to. I hadn't learned anything from the file he took from the FIB office, so it wasn't like he could say any of the information I had on the case was privileged—everything I had I'd learned myself, mostly just by living through the events. Runes were witch magic, so though the glamour proved the constructs had some tie to the fae, the individual runes didn't, so sharing them didn't breach any rules about "issues best kept amongst the fae" as Malik had put it. No, I didn't see anything at all he could object to about my sharing the runes with Lusa.

"I'm sure." In fact, I didn't see any downside. If I gave

her the runes and she turned up nothing, then I'd lost nothing. But if she did find something . . . well, that could be very beneficial.

Falin continued to frown and Lusa sauntered back to us. She pursed her lips. She hadn't heard what we'd said, but our body language probably told her all she needed to know about our conversation.

"Detective Andrews," she said, studying him, "I heard you were jettisoned from the force for going MIA during the Coleman case."

Falin didn't answer, but pulled his jacket aside to reveal the FIB shield at his waist.

"My mistake, Agent," she said before turning back to me. "Are we still on for a little tit for tat?"

"Yeah. I'll be right there." I shot her a smile and then focused on Falin again. "It's a good idea," I told him. "Weren't you going to get a warrant?"

"I'm more concerned with getting you out of here."

And I was more concerned with my friends not spending a moment longer than necessary carrying some shadowy, crystallized spell that was just waiting to overwhelm them at an unknown moment.

"I'll keep my head down," I promised.

He huffed out a breath and rolled his eyes. "Because you're *so* good at that."

As if to accent his point, Lusa chose that moment to turn and call out, "Miss Craft."

Falin and I both cringed. Okay, so keeping my head down wasn't one of my strong suits.

"I have to go," I said, and then jogged to catch up with Lusa. Falin didn't stop me this time.

Lusa headed away from the news vans and cop cars to where the fence ended at the steel supports of the Lenore Street Bridge. The traffic on Lenore had died down. Everyone who was interested in seeing the commotion had apparently already arrived, so the bridge was still, quiet, and rather dark. Safety lights dotted the span at evenly spaced intervals, but I could have wished for a little more light, especially as Lusa trudged deeper and the bridge towered over us.

I had to say one thing for her—I'd told her I wanted this off the books, and she'd found a place where no one was likely to overhear or disturb us. And she wasn't done yet. Once we stopped, she fished a silver necklace from the top of her blouse, pulling the chain until a half dozen charms spilled over her collar. The air around us hummed as she tapped into the raw magic in her earrings and channeled it into one of her waiting charms. A spell buzzed to life around us.

"You're a sensitive, right?" she asked and I nodded. "Good, then you know that I activated a privacy bubble. No one but us can hear what we say. Now, why are you really here?"

I'd rather have heard how she found the hole in reality first, but I wasn't in a position to demand she show me hers before I showed her mine. Opening my purse, I dug out the page of runes I'd copied. Then I unfolded the paper and passed it to Lusa.

"Those are sketches of runes from a magical construct. As you can probably tell, they aren't exactly common. When I watched your broadcast, I noticed similar runes cut into the ground around the tear. My theory is that whoever sent the construct also cast the ritual that opened that tear. I'm here to prove that theory, and to find out anything I can about the witch who is responsible."

"Nice. This might actually be newsworthy."

She'd threatened and goaded me but hadn't actually thought I could provide her with a story? *Figures.*

"So do you know what the runes do?" she asked, and I shook my head.

"I did a little cursory research, but so far I haven't turned up anything definitive." I paused, letting her study the runes for a moment before I asked, "You've used Aaron Corrie as a source before, right?"

Lusa furrowed her brow, which I'd never seen her do on TV—probably because the thought lines that crawled across her forehead weren't terribly attractive. "Dr. Corrie? Yes. He wasn't able to identify the runes either?"

I made a rude sound and Lusa looked up, surprise on her face.

"He'd *like* to identify them. Unfortunately he doesn't care for the company I keep," I said, and her lips formed a perfect O, but she didn't look surprised. Since she knew the man, she surely knew his stance on the fae. I didn't ask whether she thought Corrie had disapproved of my company due to the fact that I lived in a fae's house or because I'd partnered with an FIB agent—the fae-phobic geezer had plenty of reasons not to trust me—but as long as she didn't guess *my* heritage, I didn't care. "Since *you've* worked with Corrie before . . ." I trailed off, and Lusa's glossed lips stretched in a slow smile.

"I like the way you think, Craft. I suppose you'll want to know what Dr. Corrie and I turn up on the runes?" she asked, but obviously she anticipated that I'd agree because she didn't wait for me to answer before saying, "So, we've got a tear into the Aetheric surrounded by odd runes, and a magical construct built from the same runes, that, when dispelled, opened a hole into the Aetheric."

Oh, I liked her theory—I didn't think it was right, as none of the ravens Caleb, Falin, and the collectors destroyed had torn reality, but I wasn't going to correct her. After all, if she ran with that theory for her story, the attention for the holes would shift off me.

Lusa squinted, pulling the paper closer to her face. "These are incomplete, right?"

"I left the upper left-hand corner unconnected."

"Perfect." She folded the page in half. "Can I keep this?"

I nodded. I could always draw another copy. "You were going to tell me how you found the tear."

"Yeah." She tucked away the page of runes. "Follow me," she said, and carefully picked her footing as she and her designer shoes led me closer to the bridge.

We slid around the support pillar that the fence butted up against, and then Lusa ducked under the bridge, her ankles wobbling as stones skipped down the steep incline. Somewhere in the shadows under the bridge the river rushed by with an endless murmur. She grabbed one of the diagonal support beams to steady herself and then pointed beyond the beam.

"What do you see?"

I squinted, searching for what she was pointing at, but all I saw was inky darkness. "Nothing. Grave-sight has burned out my night vision."

"Oh. I'd heard wyrd witches had trouble with their abilities burning out their senses, but I wasn't sure I believed it. Well, what you aren't seeing is a tent city established by the homeless. I was looking into possible victims for the Sionan floodplain foot murders. That many people couldn't have gone missing without anyone noticing, but there hasn't been an abnormal rise in missing-persons reports. It didn't add up."

I nodded. I knew all this from what John had told me.

She smiled and ran a hand through her brown hair, brushing it back from her face. "I went looking for people who wouldn't be missed, and one of my searches turned up the fact that a homeless man who spent the night in jail for public intoxication seven days ago found all of his buddies missing when he was released the next morning. He reported it to the cops, but transient people disappear a lot. No one looked into it. "

No one but a reporter on the trail of a story.

"When I interviewed Eddie, the homeless man, he swore everyone had to be dead. That they couldn't have just relocated because they'd left everything behind: clothes, shoes, possessions—when you don't have anything you can't afford to abandon anything. I came out here to follow up. Stumbling over the tear was a very happy accident, though if you quote me on that I'll deny saying it."

As she spoke, a car drove across the bridge and I jumped as a nearly deafening roar rumbled under the structure. The sound echoed against the supports, the bank, the columns, the water, and back again, like rolling thunder.

Thunder.

Thundering.

My head snapped up. From underneath a bridge, a bridge didn't look like a structure that joined two landmasses. It looked like a portal that the river passed through. A gate. The kelpie's "thundering gate" wasn't a gate at all. It was a bridge.

Maybe this bridge, if Lusa is onto anything with her missing-homeless angle.

I cracked my shields, slightly, ever so slightly, so just bits of my psyche crossed the planes of reality. The chill of the grave, of the dead, hung in the air, the grave essence reaching for me. Grave essence that emanated from something very close. And fresh.

I opened my shields a little wider. The shadows in my

vision rolled back to reveal the skeletal carcass of the rusted and collapsed Lenore Street Bridge. Beyond the bent and sagging support beams—which I was careful not to touch, as I did *not* want to be responsible for a bridge collapse—I could see the remains of dilapidated lean-tos and weathered tents huddled on the bank. Grave essence leaked from amid the abandoned tents. Not a lot, just the smallest string that whispered across my skin like a north-ern wind. But essence meant a body—or at least part of one. And this one was human.

"Your eyes are doing that creepy glowing thing," Lusa said, staring.

I slammed my shields shut. "Lusa, I suggest you find your cameraman. This place is about to be deemed a crime scene."

Chapter 19

❧❦❧

I hung back at the edge of the crowd as I waited for the site to be declared a crime scene. I'd told Tamara what I found before I called John. The revelation that there was a body—or really, part of one—on the scene garnered a low groan from her, but she rolled her shoulders back and went to talk to the officer in charge.

John had been at home when I called him, but by the time I finished telling him where I was, what I'd sensed, and what Lusa had uncovered, he'd already been on a second line, waking up a judge for his warrant. He, the warrant, and cadaver dogs were on their way. Now all that was left was to wait.

A scream rang through the darkness and the crowd around me went silent as dozens of heads turned toward the sound. I couldn't see the screamer, but the voice was masculine, though pained, and distant. *One of the skimmers?* I squinted even though I knew I had no chance of spotting him—after my brush with the land of the dead under the bridge, the shadows were even darker.

"What happened?" someone beside me asked.

"Not sure," another said.

"Can we get closer?" asked a third.

That question seemed to reflect the sentiment of the entire crowd. Shoulders brushed against mine and a hot hand pressed into my back as people shoved forward. The crowd surged toward the fence, carrying me along with it as everyone jockeyed for a better view.

Somewhere ahead of me the scream mutated into a full-throated howl of pain, and suddenly I could see. Not from a spontaneous reversal of years of damage, though until that moment I would have said that possibility was only slightly less likely than spontaneous combustion from magical overload. No, I could see because one of the skimmers ignited, the blaze casting the scene in grim light.

The flame engulfed the man in a single heartbeat, the raw Aetheric energy he'd gathered acting as fuel for the unnatural fire. It illuminated the group of skimmers surrounding the tear, splashing them in color as the fire spit out sparks of green, purple, and red.

I'd heard that drawing too much Aetheric energy could burn up a witch from the inside out, but the few cases of overload I knew of had resulted in madness or the inability to access the Aetheric after overexposure. I'd never heard of anyone actually combusting.

The skimmer's scream broke, his voice hoarse from his howls. He flailed, but the other skimmers never looked away from the rift. They didn't even appear to notice their burning companion.

"Let me through," a woman wearing an official OMIH tag yelled as she charged the gate. A second official flanked her. "We can help."

A contingent of Bell's guards blocked the entrance, but the redheaded lawyer threw out his arms, motioning the guards to move.

"Get that gate open. Let them through," he yelled at the guards, and then to the OMIH officials he called, "Hurry."

The two officials and the lawyer ran for the burning skimmer. Forming a semicircle around the man, they pulled the raw magic brimming under his skin, drawing it out and dispersing it harmlessly into the air. I cracked my shields.

Different planes of existence snapped into focus before my eyes, making the night around me both crystal clear despite the darkness and almost too chaotic to perceive. The skimmers glowed with mottled light. Most witches resonated with only one or two colors of Aetheric energy, but the skimmers had been drawing down every wisp of raw magic that had escaped the rift. They swelled with a noxious mix of magic, each quite possibly in danger of being the next to ignite.

The skimmer who *had* ignited dimmed as the witches drew the magic from him. The Aetheric flames died as his broken scream faded to wracking cries. But it looked like he'd be okay.

Until the soul collector appeared behind him.

"Too late," I whispered.

The witches didn't know that yet, though. They continued drawing and dissipating the magic, their faces cut with hard lines of concentration and their shoulders stiff. Then the collector I'd first seen in Lusa's footage reached forward, his hand passing through the skimmer.

The skimmer's knees locked, his face freezing in a silent scream as sound failed him. His body collapsed facefirst, the empty husk crumpling to the ground. His soul remained standing upright, caught in the collector's fist. Anytime I'd seen Death or the other collectors take a soul, they pulled it free and then flicked their wrist and the soul went wherever it was souls went. This collector didn't.

He turned, his coat flaring around him with the movement and his hand still clenching the soul. The witches rushed forward, checking on the dead man. The collector stepped around them, dragging the soul with him. A soul that was staring at his own dead body.

I'd met several ghosts over the years, witnessed Death collect a handful of souls, and was even present once when a soul resisted collection, but I'd never before witnessed the very moment when someone was forced to confront the fact that his life had ended. The shock and confusion lasted only an instant and then the skimmer's mouth fell open, his features twisting in a mix of agony and rage. He thrashed in the collector's grasp and screamed. But there were no human lungs or living vocal cords involved in this scream. It was the scream of a soul and it made me want to reel back and clutch my ears. Several of the people in the press of bodies around me flinched—they might not have been able to hear the scream with their ears, but I think everyone present felt it.

The collector ignored the soul's pitiable distress.

"Why doesn't he send him on?" I muttered the question to no one in particular.

The man in front of me must have heard because he turned, and then he startled.

"Holy Mother—" He backed up and into the person beside him. "Your eyes," he whispered. Then he pushed people aside as he retreated farther from me.

I barely noticed him, but his passage disturbed several other people, who turned. More exclamations sounded, more movement, and soon a ring of empty space opened around me. I was too intent on the events unfolding on the other side of the fence to care.

The collector had moved to the next skimmer. She held her arms above her head as if reaching for the Aetheric energy helped her draw more of the excess magic that was poisoning her body. Despite the fact that she'd exceeded her overload point, the only expression on her face was pure and unadulterated ecstasy. I don't think she even noticed when the collector thrust his hand through her sternum and jerked her soul free.

No, she isn't dying. Not yet anyway. I marched forward— my bubble of empty space had opened a path all the way to the fence—without ever looking away from the collector, who now gripped a soul in each fist. *Who is he?* I'd never seen a collector strike before the cause of death guaranteed an end to life.

A hand wrapped around my arm, jerking me back. "This is what you consider keeping your head down?" Falin asked in a voice that had turned gravelly with anger. "Do you want to be dragged off to Faerie? Because if that's your goal, I can take you there myself."

I blinked at him and then my gaze snapped back to the scene beyond the fence. "She wasn't supposed to die." Or at least it hadn't looked like she was supposed to die.

"What? What are you talking about? Jeez, Alex, your eyes are glowing like lanterns." Falin lifted his hand as if blocking a glare and green light reflected off his pale skin. Light from *my* eyes.

I didn't have time to worry about that.

"He took her and she wasn't dead yet." I pointed at the knot of skimmers, but no one except me realized the

woman was dead—apparently not even her own body noticed it was now unoccupied.

The collector—or reaper, as Roy had called him and
maybe that was a more appropriate name—looked down
at the souls he clutched. He still hadn't vanished the man,
whose screams had given way to begging. The woman's
soul just looked confused, as if she still didn't understand.
Then the reaper vanished, taking the souls with him.

The woman's body finally collapsed, hitting the ground
without her ever making a sound.

A frenzy had already stirred the crowd outside the gate,
but now it lifted to a new pitch, bordering on chaos. With
two bodies on the ground, the police didn't have to wait for
warrants. They stormed the lot, pulling the skimmers away
from the rift by force, dragging them when they wouldn't
cooperate.

The skimmers might have been blissed out of their
minds from contact with the Aetheric, but they noticed
being dragged from the source. They struggled, screaming,
fighting, and cursing. Filled with raw magic, their curses and
their very anger, took shape. As an officer attempted to re-
strain one woman, a black and red cloud of unfocused rage
lifted out of her and engulfed him. The officer jumped back,
beating at his arms and chest as if swatting dozens of sting-
ing insects. Another officer fell to his knees, grasping his
throat as a sludgelike bubble of magic encased his head.

The anti–black magic unit officers were better prepared.
Their personal wards and charms helped them shrug off
the unfocused spells, and now that the skimmers were using
magic against them, they retaliated in kind. The first skimmer went down, unconscious under a spell. Then another.
A third one got caught in a circle.

The remaining skimmers glanced at each other, and
then scattered, Bell among them. Three officers went after
the large man, and he turned. Magic pooled in his palms. A
lot of magic.

"Look out," I yelled a moment before Bell flung the raw
magic at the closest officer. Not that anyone besides Falin
heard me.

The officer might have been warded against a lot of different spells, but nothing can ward you against an assault of

raw Aetheric energy. It slammed into his chest, knocking him off his feet, and the smell of burned flesh spread over the lot. Bell ran for the river and threw himself into the current. The officers chasing him stopped at the edge of the rushing water, the beams of their flashlights skittering over the choppy surface.

"He's gone," Falin said, shaking his head.

I scanned the water, waiting for Bell to surface for air. He didn't. "Think he survived?"

"The current isn't too dangerous here."

True, and Bell had gone into the water absolutely bristling with magic. With that much raw Aetheric energy at his disposal, who knew what he was capable of? Unless the overload had completely addled his brain, which was possible. One way or another, he was gone and the skimmers' claim on the crime scene was broken.

Four people left the vacant lot in body bags, nine more in ambulances, and five in handcuffs. The rest of the skimmers escaped.

"It's a little higher," I said from where I stood outside one of the ambulances. "Like a cloud around his head and torso."

The man in question groaned as another pus-filled blister burst open in an angry welt on his forehead. The healer leaning over him lifted his hands a couple of inches and glanced at me. I nodded to let him know he was now in the center of the cloud.

"Can you sense what color strands of Aetheric were used?" he asked.

I didn't have to sense it. I hadn't closed my shields, so I could actually see the mottled miasmic cloud of magic, though that wasn't a fact I was sharing. "Red, but it's dark, so more than one color. Primarily red, though."

The healer nodded and turned toward his patient again. His fingers trembled, and he clenched his hands. His Adam's apple wobbled as he swallowed, but then he forced his fingers straight again and nodded as if he'd come to some conclusion. His eyelids drooped as his gaze focused inward, and a thin string of energy appeared between his hands.

The string grew slowly, snaking almost unobtrusively through the cloud of magic. I watched, monitoring the curse. The healer's gently glowing spell wove through the mist, building a spiderweb of green channels. The curse finally noticed and a tendril of magic shot out the side.

"The cloud is dividing. The new section is pooling over his thighs."

The healer spread his arms, making the thread of magic stretch. Muscles twitched in his face with the strain, but he kept the flow of magic even until his slowly building tapestry of magic disrupted the structure of the curse. The destructive mist shattered.

"You got it," I said as the spent Aetheric energy dissipated.

The healer's hands dropped, and he sagged where he sat. "Thank goodness," he said, even his voice raw from the effort of dispelling the ill-formed curse. "You ever think of going into curse-breaking? You're definitely sensitive enough to do the diagnostic work."

"Not really my thing," I said as I stepped back, out of the open ambulance door. The healer remained behind. I didn't blame him; he was spent. Besides, I could see Tamara helping another healer with the last officer hurt during the skimmer bust, so there were no more patients to tend.

I gave a wave to the paramedic when he jumped out to shut the ambulance doors. Then I turned away and headed back for the fence and the crime scene beyond. The police had secured the area and once again access beyond the fence was limited. Which meant I still hadn't gotten to study the ritual space I'd come to see.

"Miss Craft, I'd like to say I'm surprised to see you here," a familiar voice said, and I cringed. Agent Nori. I turned toward the voice, but when I saw her through my grave-sight, I realized I wouldn't have recognized her if she hadn't spoken first.

Nori's typical glamour resembled her fae mien only in that they shared the same basic shape. Under that glamour her skin was tinged deep blue and her features had a razor edge, her chin and nose ending in sharp points. As she strolled toward me, her wisp-thin body moved as though her hips were shaped differently from those of a human or as if walking wasn't her most comfortable way to travel. She watched me with large, multifaceted eyes, like a fly's, and I looked away before she realized I was staring.

"What can I do for you?" I asked, crossing my arms over my chest and rocking back on my heels.

"Could you stop with the glowing eyes for a moment?"

"No, actually I can't." I'd been peering across planes for at least an hour at this point, and my regular eyesight was definitely shot by now. If it had been the middle of a very bright, sunny day, and if it hadn't been going on nearly twenty-four hours since I'd last slept, I might have been willing to hope my eyesight would adjust once I closed my shields. But it was the middle of the night and I was physically exhausted even without factoring in the amount of magic I'd used. I wasn't willing to spend the rest of the night in utter darkness. Especially not here.

"Fine." But her tone didn't agree. A high-pitched keening sound cut through the air and I glanced around, startled. Nori either didn't notice the sound or it didn't concern her because she continued without pausing, "I got word that an anonymous informant clued Detective Matthews in on the presence of a body on the grounds." She nodded to where the cadaver dogs were sweeping the lot. "I'm going to assume that call came from you."

As I couldn't deny it, I decided to remain silent. A search of the abandoned tent city had turned up a single left foot, apparently still encased in a boot. The cadaver dogs were now searching the banks, but I knew they wouldn't find anything else. Not nearby at least.

When I didn't answer, the keening I'd heard a moment before sliced through the air again. *Is Nori doing that?* Or was it coming from behind her? I shuffled sideways and shot a surreptitious glance over her shoulder. A double pair of iridescent dragonfly wings almost blended in with her dark suit where they were tucked tight against her back. The wings sprouted from somewhere near Nori's shoulder blades and trailed down to her calves like a membranous cape, but I would have missed them completely if the strobing lights from the police cars and fire trucks hadn't been reflecting off the thick veins. Her wings twitched in time with the fingers she strummed against her elbow as she watched me, and as they rubbed together, they emitted the strange, high-pitched screech I'd heard earlier.

"Should I take a guess how you knew the foot was on the scene? Maybe you placed it there."

"You know how I knew," I said, and then cursed inwardly. She'd just gotten my admission to making the call. Of course, it wasn't like my ability to sense the dead was the secret I was hiding.

Nori smiled, flashing a double row of needle-thin teeth. I tried not to show a reaction, but by the way her smile spread, I knew my face had given me away.

"Here is the way I see it, Miss Craft," she said, that strange keening sound filling the air again. "There is a second rift allowing the Aetheric to bleed into the mortal realm. There is compelling proof to suggest that you were responsible for the first known tear, which means you likely caused this one as well. The proximity to a crime scene means the two are likely connected. That alone is enough evidence to have a fae summoned to Faerie while further investigations occur."

"I—"

She cut me off with a wave of her hand. "Even if the two are later proven not to be connected, the current evidence *looks* damning, so that fae should be taken back to Faerie for his or her own protection. Humans can be ruthless to those they don't understand."

I swallowed. She was threatening me. There was no denying at this point that she knew I had fae blood, and she wasn't giving me an option of *not* going to Faerie. *Will she slap cuffs on me and drag me off right here and now?* My gaze shot past her head, searching for Falin. He was near the gate, talking to two men in suits who I was pretty sure I'd seen identify themselves as working for the Ambassador of Fae and Human Relations. I met Falin's eyes, just briefly, but hopefully long enough to convey that I could seriously use an intervention. Then I focused on Nori again.

"I didn't open that tear," I said, instilling as much certainty in my voice as possible.

She frowned. She couldn't insist that I was both fae enough to be held under fae laws but human enough to lie.

Though I supposed she could still drag me to Faerie under the pretense of protecting me from humans who *perceived* me as being able to open rifts.

"Is there a problem, Agent?" Falin asked as he joined us. *And the cavalry arrives.*

"Sir." Agent Nori stood straighter, her wings flaring behind her. "I believe this . . . person . . . should be detained and transported to Faerie immediately," she said, and then repeated the scenarios and reasoning she'd given me a moment before, though this time the tone of her delivery held no threats—it was just the facts of her case.

Falin listened to her recitation and my pulse beat double time despite the exhaustion and chill as he nodded at several of her points. If she hadn't been talking about me or suggesting the gross violation of personal freedom, I'd have thought she made a compelling case, which wasn't reassuring. When she finally finished, Falin rubbed his chin for a moment, as if weighing the decision.

He won't really let her cart me off to Faerie, will he? I didn't actually know.

I glanced behind me at the cops who were processing the crime scene. I spotted several familiar faces working the site, John among them, which was a relief. The NCPD wouldn't interfere if Nori arrested me, but she couldn't just make me disappear into Faerie. I was a legal citizen and I had friends who would make sure I was granted due process. Of course, that relied on someone knowing what had happened to me. I took a step back, closer to the gate, and prepared to cause a scene if it came to that.

Thankfully, it proved not to be necessary.

After a moment of deliberation, Falin shook his head. "I think taking her to Faerie now would be premature." He turned to me. "Miss Craft, you are appearing too frequently in this investigation. If you value your time in the mortal realm, I suggest you consider your actions very, very carefully."

I nodded, trying to look properly admonished and frightened, which considering that the idea of being dragged to Faerie scared the crap out of me, wasn't hard. Besides, the pompous delivery of Falin's threat might have been for Nori's benefit, but I knew full well that he meant every word of it.

A film crawled over Nori's multifaceted eyes from the outside toward her nose and back—*a blink?*—and she said, "Sir, I'd like it on the record that I think it is in the best interest of the queen, the fae, and even Miss Craft herself if she were removed to Faerie."

"Duly noted, Agent. You're dismissed."

She stared at him, that keening sound issuing from her wings, the disharmonious notes rising in decibels until the sound grated in my head like nails down a chalkboard. Falin turned his back on her, accenting her dismissal.

"Miss Craft, since you are at the scene already, there are a few matters I'd like to discuss with you," Falin said in the same professional but antagonistic tone he'd been using since he interjected himself in the situation, but as Nori stormed off his voice dropped. "She's going to cause trouble," he muttered, shaking his head.

He ran a hand through his hair, the movement stiff, jerky, and I frowned as I studied the exhaustion written across his face. I myself felt ready to drop, and while he'd gotten a few more hours of sleep than I had, he was also healing from a nearly fatal wound.

"You okay?" I asked as I touched his arm. Why do people do that? Touch people they're concerned about? What comfort or reassurance can it really give? But I didn't even think about it; I just flowed into his space and reached out as if we had some sort of history instead of an acquaintance that would equal less than a week if all the moments we'd actually spent together were added up.

Falin looked at where I touched his arm, and a small smile crooked one edge of his lips. The expression didn't change a single line of the exhaustion in his face, but it did make him look less haggard, not quite so worn down. He covered my hand with his gloved one and squeezed my fingers gently. Then he stepped back out of reach and straightened, becoming once again the no-nonsense FIB agent in charge.

"Come on," he said, turning toward the gate. "You came out here to walk this scene. Your presence has already done all the damage it can, so let's check out this ritual and get out of here."

Chapter 20

I signed in with the uniformed officer manning the gate. I sure as hell didn't have clearance to cross the crime tape, but there were so many different agencies on the scene, I don't think the harassed man knew who was supposed to have access to where. I had an FIB escort, and that was good enough for him. Preventing the scene from being contaminated was a lost cause anyway. With the skimmers, Bell's security and lawyers, Lusa and her cameraman, the paramedics and healers, and the magical scuffle that had occurred, the week-old murder scene was a mess. I didn't envy John his job.

And speaking of . . . "Hey, John," I said as I approached my favorite, but currently very exasperated, homicide detective.

"Alex?" He cocked his head to the side, which, considering that he was the lead detective and I'd just walked into a crime scene, was a better response than I'd expected. Then his gaze landed on Falin and his posture stiffened. "Detective Andrews, this is a crime scene."

"Agent, actually," Falin said, flashing his FIB badge.

I could almost see wheels turning behind John's eyes as he looked at the badge and refit Falin into a new box in his mind, reevaluating the events of a month ago and the Coleman case with the new knowledge that Falin was FIB. Finally he nodded.

"Alex, I don't particularly need you here, so unless . . . ?" John tilted his head, the implied question going to Falin.

"I'd like her to walk the scene."

"Fine." John jerked his head in a curt nod. I don't think he meant to project it, but when he focused on me I caught the disappointment in his gaze. Then he turned back to the CSI and ABMU officers he'd been talking to before we'd approached.

The dismissal stung almost as much as the look I'd seen in his eyes, and I stood there stunned for a moment. I mean, I'd been the one who called him with the tip about the body, and we were both out here in the middle of the night searching for clues about who'd caused this nightmare. Of course, he was a cop, so looking for murderers was his job, not mine, and the FIB and the police didn't have the most solid working relationship. My showing up on the scene with Falin probably made it look like I was throwing my support to the enemy. With that in mind, I tried not to take it personally, but as I walked away my footsteps felt heavier than they had before, the exhaustion pressing on me worse.

I would have liked to head straight for the rift, but as far as anyone knew, my specialty was only the dead. I had appearances to maintain, so Falin led me to the bridge and the dilapidated tent city first. The booted left foot had been found amid a pile of shoes inside a fire barrel. No one had told me how many shoes had been collected as evidence, but I'd heard two techs mention that all the empty shoes had been rights. The one left in the bunch contained a foot. *So what is happening to the right feet?* Or the rest of the bodies, for that matter.

I stretched my senses as we walked. Many of the tents and lean-tos sported charms and one or two were even warded, which surprised me, though I guess it shouldn't have. I didn't spend a lot of time considering Nekros's homeless, but it could happen to anyone—norm, witch, or fae alike. I took a moment to examine each of the charms my senses brushed against, but most were charms to prevent leaking or to discourage spiders. None felt malicious or carried the magical signature from the feet or constructs.

"Let's move on," I said once we'd walked the entire encampment.

As we headed back up the bank, I tripped on an empty bottle half buried in the loose stones and only Falin catching my elbow and steadying me kept me on my feet. I glared at the offending bottle, but the real problem was my own exhaustion. I wasn't sure when I'd started trembling, but I'd been doing it for a while and I couldn't stop. I'd been straddling the chasm between the living and the dead—as well as a couple of other realities—for too long. *I'm going to pay for this later.*

But for now I needed to hold on to my grave-sight a little longer. At least until I could get a good look at whatever ritual had happened around the rift. It might have been better if I'd walked the whole scene and not drawn attention to my interest in the rift, but if I was going to see that hole, I needed to do it now-ish. I said as much to Falin. His lips thinned to a grim line, but he nodded and led me on a more direct path.

"I think we have enough cadaver dogs on the scene already," a snide voice said as I drew near the rift.

The skin along my neck prickled. Jenson. *Haven't I dealt with enough for one night?* Unlike Nori or even Lusa, Detective Jenson wasn't someone I could hope I'd never see again once the case was over. He was John's partner, and I didn't know if he blamed me for John's getting shot and that was what was with the attitude for the last few weeks, but it would be better for everyone involved if we could at least be civil toward each other. So I forced a smile I didn't feel as I turned toward his voice. And then I froze in my tracks.

Jenson stood a couple of yards away, his thumbs in his waistband, his right hand suspiciously close to his gun. But that wasn't what stopped me; what gave me pause was his face. His jaw was wider than normal, and it jutted forward in an underbite that provided room for the two tusks protruding from where his lower cuspids should have been. The tusks curled over his upper lip, the skin around them dark and calloused from years of contact.

"What are you staring at, Craft?" he asked, glaring at me.

I shook my head, blinking. His image didn't change. The rest of his face was normal and exactly the same as always.

It was just his jaw and mouth that were different. His soul glimmered a normal bright yellow, which I'd come to associate with humans.

"Troll blood?" It was a testament to how tired I was that I asked the question out loud. I tried to bite the words back as soon as they escaped my mouth, but of course, by then it was too late.

Jenson's expression darkened as the color built in his face. "Oh, so you can figure that out, can you?" He stalked forward. "Look at you. Homicide's darling is a fucking faerie in hiding. Who would have guessed?"

As Jenson crowded my space, Falin moved to block his path, but I touched his arm, stopping him. This was something Jenson and I had to work out for ourselves. In the years I'd been working with the cops, I'd learned that for some of them, there were only two ways for me to earn any respect: be helpful in putting the bad guys away and be able to hold my own. Jenson had always been one of the former—or so I thought—but if he was swinging toward the latter, Falin running interference for me would only make things worse.

So I stood up straighter, exaggerating the inch or two of height I had on Jenson and tried to minimize my trembling. Jenson had decided to get in my face, and though I wasn't about to get in a catfight at a crime scene, I would meet his challenge.

"That's a rather ironic insult, all things considered," I said, my voice low since it didn't have to carry far at this distance. I let my gaze flicker to one tusk so he knew exactly what I was talking about.

The blotchy color filling his cheeks flushed a deeper crimson. "You think that's funny?"

Funny? "I'm not following. Do you have a problem with me?" My newfound heritage? My job? My abilities? What exactly was he lashing out at? Yeah, I'd figured out he was feykin, but it wasn't like I was going to out him.

"Yeah, I have a problem with you."

I stared at him, waiting. "Okay. What's the problem?"

Jenson sneered, his upper lip rolling back from his tusks. Then he brushed past me, knocking me with his shoulder hard enough to send me stumbling. I kept my feet under me, but only just barely. *What the hell was that about?*

I glanced at Falin, who looked just as perplexed as he watched Jenson's retreating back. Jenson's issues with my, or maybe his, heritage—or whatever his issue was—wasn't a problem I needed to waste energy on tonight. Time was slipping away from me, the night speedily rushing toward morning. I closed my eyes for a moment, no more than a second, and the world felt like it swayed around me. *Damn.* I needed to wrap this up, get home, and get some sleep before I collapsed where I stood—which was starting to feel like a real possibility.

I turned my attention to the tear in reality.

I wasn't sure what the area looked like if viewed just on the mortal plane, but with my psyche crossing several planes of existence, the scene was a mess. Residual magic hung in the air and pooled on the ground in murky patches. The smell of burned grass stung my nose, and the evidence of a struggle showed both in the way the Aetheric moved around patches of magic it didn't like and on the ground. Numbered plastic markers littered the area, alerting the techs to evidence that needed to be processed. Most marked footprints, but here and there I saw a rune drawn in the dirt. Or at least what was left of a rune. Footprints obscured most, and the one that had drawn my attention on TV had a long tunnel of dirt bisecting it where it looked like someone's heel had been dragged across the ground.

Damn.

I walked closer, trying to find some pattern in what remained of the runes. I felt the residue of the circle as I reached the outer edge, and I stopped before crossing it, letting my senses stretch. Unlike the charms I'd felt in the tent city, the circle definitely held the signature of the witch behind the murders and I shivered at the touch despite the fact that a magical circle was completely neutral magic.

"This is where the witch cast the circle."

"I guessed that much," Falin said, and when I glanced at him in surprise, he pointed toward the ground. "That's where the dead grass starts."

I blinked and looked around. *All* the grass was withered and gray in my grave-sight, so I never would have known that if he hadn't told me. *What kind of ritual kills all the grass in the area?*

I had no idea, but there was only one thing left to do.

I crossed the edge of the circle.

Crossing someone else's circle, even one long ago dispelled, into someone's ritual space is always a little uncomfortable for a sensitive. The area is almost guaranteed to be saturated with that witch's magic, and even the trace of beneficial and friendly magic can be overwhelming. Not that I was expecting friendly spells on the other side of this barrier.

What I expected even less was to find no magic at all, but that was exactly what I found.

I blinked. Over the last few hours I'd grown so accustomed to seeing the world through hazy swirls of Aetheric that their sudden absence was jarring. I glanced behind me. Outside the edge of the circle the Aetheric still hung over the world, but inside the circle there were only a few thin wisps, like what the skimmers had been drawing from the tear. I'd heard of magical dead spots before, but that wasn't what I was looking at, and I knew it. This was more like depletion. *But what kind of spell uses* that *much energy?*

Something major, that was for sure, and whatever it was, I definitely didn't like it.

I squinted. I wasn't used to my grave-sight opening multiple planes of existence to me, but I knew there were more planes than I had names for. I occasionally caught glimpses of different planes that didn't "fit" with the land of the dead or the Aetheric, though those two were my only constants. Now I *tried* to look for another plane, one that might give me a hint of what had happened in this circle.

Colors splashed across the world. They weren't the vivid, swirling colors of the Aetheric, but colors that seemed to emanate from inside objects and space. I'd seen this plane before, and from what I'd gathered, it absorbed the emotional resonance of the people who brushed against it. Around the rift I could make out the bright, blissed-out spots where the skimmers had stood, but those were just splashes of color, already fading. Under them, in the very center of the tear, was the most brilliant light I'd ever seen. It was no color, or all colors—I couldn't be sure. It created a silhouette of light instead of shadow. I stared at it, realizing this was the profile of the witch we were looking for, but

I could glean no details from the shape except that the witch had stood in that very spot and felt hope . . . joy.

Hope and joy? What had happened in this circle? Had I been wrong about who cast it?

I turned, walking farther from the tear, and then I stumbled because as soon as I left the glow of the witch's hope, the air turned thick with a deep stain of pulsing red.

The color bled up from the ground and throbbed against my skin. *Fear. Pain. Desperation.* I crashed to my knees. I could almost see the shadows of rage closing in around me, as they twisted and writhed in the circle. The very air hummed with anger, prickling my flesh and burning my lungs. I couldn't breathe. Couldn't move.

I slammed my shields closed, blocking out the dead, the color, the rage, the pain. Darkness fell over me, and I welcomed the sudden lack of sight as I sucked down gulps of the night air.

"Alex, what happened?"

Falin.

He was beside me, his hands on my arms as he tried to help me stand. I let him.

"They died here," I whispered. "So much pain. So many people." And the witch had stood in the center of all that misery and had felt hope.

I didn't tell the police what I'd seen. The anti–black magic unit had both an auramancer and a wyrd clairvoyant who could tap into the reality I'd touched if the cops really wanted to know what the victims had felt, though I wouldn't have wished what I'd just felt on anyone. When I saw John tomorrow—or really, later today, as it was long past midnight now—I would tell him that I'd sensed only one witch in that circle. That was something he needed to know. The rest? I didn't see how it would help.

I fell asleep on the ride home and woke to Falin lifting me from the car.

"M-mm. Put me down; you're hurt," I mumbled, the words coming out slightly garbled in my half-awake state.

"I'm not *that* hurt."

Right.

But he did put me down, and I stumbled up my stairs on my own. I let him use my keys to unlock the door, as I'd have just fumbled the job in my trembling, half-blind condition. I'd spent way too much time peering into other planes of existence. What I really wanted now was a hot shower and a good night's sleep, though not necessarily in that order.

PC danced around us, his little gray body burning my legs where he brushed against my pants. Crap, I hadn't even raised a shade and I was chilled to my core. I glanced longingly at my bed, but I'd made a promise to myself to stop sleeping with Falin—in any sense of the word—until I figured out how I really felt about him. And I'd made that decision before he'd gone and disappeared on me. Now? Yeah, I was sticking to my resolve.

"So," I said, turning toward Falin.

"So?" He slid his jacket off and hung it on the back of my solitary chair. His holster followed.

"Do you want the bed or the floor?" The good-host thing to do would be to offer him the bed, but he'd invited himself, so I'd let him be gallant and take the floor.

"You're kidding, right?"

"No," I said, and I meant it, but even to my own ears, the single-syllable word sounded feeble. Maybe that was because I was staring at the smooth skin being revealed as Falin unbuttoned his oxford.

"Really?" He pulled the shirt free of his pants so he could get to the last button, but he didn't take the shirt off. It gapped as he stepped forward, exposing small glimpses of pale skin and hard abs.

He lifted a hand, brushing a strand of hair back from my face. He'd stripped off his gloves at some point, so his fingers were bare and warm against my cheek.

"I—" I started, but he leaned down. His lips brushed mine, the kiss tentative, a question with just a touch of breath and heat.

Whatever I'd planned to say vanished.

I lifted on my toes, inviting more, and he didn't disappoint. His lips closed over mine, firm and soft all at once as he deepened the kiss. One of his hands slid into my hair, the other around my waist as he pulled me closer, surrounding me with his heat, his scent, his touch.

Someone cleared their throat behind me. "Please tell me I get a veto in this."

I jumped, breaking contact with Falin in midkiss.

Death leaned against the counter, his thumbs hooked in his pockets and his dark hair spilling into his face. I couldn't do anything more than stand there staring at him as my heart thundered in my chest, though I couldn't have said if I was more breathless from the kiss or from the fact that it was Death who had caught me at it.

"I'm not interrupting, am I?" he asked. Death may have looked casual and sounded bored, but his eyes were fixed on Falin with dark intensity.

Yes. Very much. Not that I shouldn't have been thankful—I *had* made a promise to myself, after all—but I couldn't quite summon up that particular emotion as Falin's hands slid over my shoulders.

"Alexis," he whispered, his lips pressing against my hair, his breath tracing my ear.

A shiver that had nothing to do with the chill filling me and everything to do with the sensations his touch woke in my body rang through me. Aside from the awkward, teasing dance that Death and I had been stumbling through recently, I hadn't been touched, *really touched*—in a month. The feel of his skin on mine sent a thrill through me as if it had been a lot longer than that. But I couldn't do this. Especially not with Death watching every change in my features from beneath his heavily hooded eyes.

I shrugged away from Falin's hands. "I'll just take the floor," I said, no longer caring who got stuck with the floor so long as his hands, and lips, and eyes stopped lighting a fire in my skin. I turned to Death. "What are you doing here?"

He lifted his shoulders in a slight shrug. "At the moment? Chaperoning."

Right. *Of course.* I groaned silently and realized I could almost hear the ringing absence of movement as Falin went still behind me.

"Who's here?" he asked.

As answer, I reached out my hand toward Death. I wasn't sure he'd accept it. Roy enjoyed becoming visible, but Mr. Super Secretive Soul Collector? Him I wasn't sure about. Hell, for all I knew, he might vanish just because I'd let on that he was present. But if he was going to stand around making commentary, I wasn't going to be the only victim listening.

Death looked at my outstretched hand for a moment, and then smiled, flashing a row of perfect teeth before placing his palm against mine. I dropped my shields and Falin let out a curse.

"What's he doing here?" he asked, the question directed at me and not the collector, though I knew he damn well was now visible. Falin crossed muscular arms over his chest and glared from Death to me.

I frowned at him. *The point of dropping my shields was so they didn't talk* through *me in the first place.*

Death lifted my hand to his lips, drawing me several steps forward in the process, but he didn't so much kiss my knuckles as smile into my skin. His eyes watched me as he did this; then, as if we were dancing, he spun me so my back was to him. Dropping my hand, he wrapped one arm around my shoulders. He was tall enough that he could prop his chin on the top of my head.

"I heard Alex was having a slumber party and decided to crash," Death said, and though I couldn't see it, I could hear the smirk in his voice.

I'm tall—I have been ever since I turned twelve and in a single year shot up from a respectable twelve-year-old height of four-eleven to a gangly height of five-ten. I'd slumped for the rest of the year, until I'd left the academy for summer break and my father had threatened to make me spend my entire vacation in a social polishing camp if I didn't stand up straight. I'd soon stopped caring that I towered over my female peers and learned to enjoy the fact that I could look most guys in the eye. It was some time after that when I decided kickass boots that added an extra three inches to my height were the only way to go. All that said, I wasn't used to feeling short. But with Falin towering in front of me looking like some sort of pissed-off Greek god carved out of marble, and Death pulling me back against his wide chest, I felt downright petite.

I also felt like I was suddenly caught in a situation that was about to spiral wildly out of control.

"You shouldn't be wasting energy. We need to get your body temperature back up, not invite in the chill." Falin stepped forward and, apparently deciding the best thing to do was ignore Death completely, rubbed his hands over my arms—which was more annoying than helpful.

Death's arm wrapped tighter around my shoulders. "I have body heat."

"Stop it, both of you." I shrugged away from Falin's hands, which earned me a frown from the fae, until I ducked out from under Death's arm. Then I garnered frowns from both men.

But I couldn't escape Death's touch. He and I had to be in contact for him to be visible unless I wanted to start channeling major amounts of energy, which I didn't, maybe even couldn't at this point. So I stood there for an awkward moment, my hand clasped in his, but my arm outstretched to add space between our bodies. *How do I get myself into these things?* Well, there was always one safe topic: business.

"There was a collector at the crime scene earlier. Or at least I think he was a collector. But he collected the souls before death." Well, with the female skimmer he did, though I could have sworn the male was going to make it before the collector showed and snagged the man's soul. "Can you guys do that? Get impatient and collect a soul early?"

I'd been focusing on studying the layer of dirt coating my boots from my recent misadventures in the great outdoors, but as the silence stretched I looked up and found Death staring at me. Not the dark but intense I'm-imagining-you-with-a-lot-less-clothing stare he'd been prone to giving me lately but a you've-stumbled-into-something-over-your-head stare.

"What did he look like?" he asked.

"Male. Average height. Late twenties to early thirties. Dark hair. Long dark trench coat. What are you thinking?"

Death frowned, his gaze moving past me.

"Could he be involved?" Falin had snapped into cop mode while I wasn't paying attention. "He was at a murder scene that had a rift into the Aetheric. Could a . . . collector"—the way he said the word made it clear it wasn't a title he was accustomed to using—"have ripped through to the Aetheric?"

Death shook his head, but I wasn't sure if he was disagreeing or simply dismissing his own thoughts. Then his eyes focused on me again. "You're trembling."

"I'm fine." I should have saved my breath.

"She needs sleep," Falin said, his gaze going icy again.

"With you, I suppose?" Death asked.

Falin crossed his arms. "It's an option."

"I'm fine," I repeated. Not that either of them noticed—they were too busy attempting to stare holes into each other. *Perfect. Just what I need.* I was cold to the core, magically drained, and far beyond the point of exhaustion.

"You know what, guys, maybe you're right. Have fun with the pissing contest. I'm going to bed." I dropped Death's hand, closed my shields, and marched over to collapse fully dressed on my bed. I was asleep almost as soon as my head hit the pillow.

Chapter 21

I woke trapped under a warm arm. A quick status check showed I was still in my own bed and fully dressed, though my boots had vanished at some point in the night. I was sure the warm body curled around me belonged to Falin only because Death was staring at me from where he leaned against the wall across from my bed.

"Did you stay all night?" I kept my voice low, trying not to wake the man behind me.

Death lifted one shoulder in a shrug. "Wasn't much night left. More morning and early afternoon."

"You know, that is kind of creepy stalker–esque."

"I'm not the one who crawled into bed with you after you were asleep."

Point. The men in my life were . . . complicated. *And so much for my resolve.* I craned my neck to glance back at Falin. His face was relaxed, peaceful with sleep. Good. *Now to get out of this bed without waking him.*

Easier said than done.

I tried to slide out from under his arm, but the more I wriggled, the more his muscles flexed, tightening around me. He dragged me back against his chest without waking, like it was a reflex.

Crap.

I grabbed his wrist, hauling his arm off me. Then he did

wake. The bed shifted as he moved, and he lifted his wrist from my hands, wrapping his arm around me once again.

His breath tickled along my jaw as he placed a kiss on the sensitive skin under my ear. "Good morning," he whispered, his voice still rough with sleep.

My mouth went dry, my body waking to answer his in ways I really wished it wouldn't—especially with Death still standing three feet away, watching me.

"I, uh—I have to pee." I broke free of Falin's arm and rolled to the edge of the bed.

As I crossed the foot of the bed, Falin flopped over onto his back. Staring at the ceiling, he bunched both his hands in his hair. "How many hours should I wait to start breakfast?"

"What? I—" Okay, so I *had* hid out in the bathroom the last time I woke with Falin in my bed, but this was different. "I'll be right back."

Death trailed me. I ignored him until I reached the bathroom—I had no intention of making him visible and encouraging a repeat of last night's posturing. Once I closed the door, I rounded on him.

"Out. This is alone time."

"You're cute when you're flustered."

I frowned at him. "I'm being serious."

"Then you should seriously make *him* leave." He jerked his chin toward the inner wall and the one-room apartment beyond.

"He's not here in the bathroom."

Death gave me a look that said I knew what he meant, and I sighed.

"He's helping me, okay?"

Death just continued to frown, and I turned my back on him. His reflection in the mirror watched as I tried to drag a brush through the snarls that my curls had turned into after they'd been slept on, and before that, hours of being tossed around in the wind while crossing over from the land of the dead.

"How do omelets sound for breakfast?" Falin's voice called from somewhere in the kitchen, and Death's reflection shook its head.

He muttered the word "omelets" under his breath and then focused on me again. "He has his own agenda."

I shrugged and turned on the water. "Most people do." I shoved the brush under the faucet, and then dragged the wet bristles through my hair to calm the frizz.

"Alex." He stepped closer, his hands molding around my hips. "What do you really know about him?"

I twisted in his grasp, not to get away but to face him. The position was close, intimate. If I had lifted onto my toes, I could have kissed him. As it was, I was close enough to see the kaleidoscope of colors hidden in his dark hazel eyes.

"What do I know about you?" I asked, and the skin around his eyes tightened in a small flinch, as if my question could wound. I lowered my gaze.

When I was a teenager, I'd had a major crush on Death. Yeah, imagine that, a teenager with a crush on Death—it took emo to a whole new level. He'd visited me less often then, stopping by apparently at random for reasons unknown. I think, back then, my company was an amusement or maybe an interesting novelty—a mortal who could see him, interact with him. For me, he was that dreamy, dark and mysterious older guy. I guess he was still all of those things, but I'd thought I'd outgrown that teenage crush. Clearly it had just grown up with me.

I took a deep breath, relishing the thrill of his hands on me, of his touch. Of the fact that we *could* touch. A month ago it would have been uncomfortable, him too cold and me too hot. But now things had changed.

Looking up again, I studied his face, recognizing every line of his jaw, the curve of his eyebrows. In some ways, he was my closest friend. In others he was a complete stranger. But even with our relationship in this strange, awkward, morphing mess of, well, whatever it was, I still felt like I could talk to him. Could tell him anything, everything, even if he couldn't do the same. After all, no one kept secrets like Death.

"You've always told me not to push," I said, moving my arms to his, my hands at his elbows, my forearms on top of his. We were too close for me not to touch him without making things more awkward. "Not to push for answers you can't give me, for secrets you can't reveal. Well, now it's my turn. Don't push me for commitments I can't make."

He closed his eyes and then leaned forward, propping his chin on the top of my head. The movement brought me in contact with his chest, and I leaned into him as well, feeling the softness of his T-shirt against my cheek—a T-shirt that I was pretty sure didn't exist, at least not in the terms with which I was familiar. I felt the sigh that escaped him as he wrapped his arms around me.

"Okay." His fingers trailed over the sliver of skin exposed between my halter top and my hip-huggers. "Okay, I'll stop pushing. But I expect you to tell *him* the same thing."

"Trust me, I intend to." Now, if Falin would listen? That would be a miracle.

As if he could hear my thoughts, Death laughed, one hard bark of air. "He's stubborn. You know he continued to talk *at* me—at empty air, for all he knew—for an hour after you fell asleep."

I hid my smile against Death's shoulder. "Yeah, he's stubborn."

"You could kick him out."

I groaned and pushed away from Death. "I told you, he's helping me with my investigation." I hadn't intended to rub Death's nose in the fact that he *wasn't* the one helping me, but it was there, in his eyes. He looked away, as if he knew I could see it.

"What marks the end of life?" Death asked, hooking his thumbs in his pockets.

"What?" *Where did that question come from?* Death didn't answer, or repeat himself; he just looked at me, his eyes intense, as if the words he *wasn't* saying were trying to burn through his gaze.

"Philosophically, scientifically, or . . . ?" I let the question trail off and lifted my hands, palms up, as I shrugged.

Still he didn't answer.

"Okay." I frowned and leaned back against the sink's counter. "Science would say life ends after the last breath leaves the body and the heart ceases to beat, or perhaps when brain activity stops. But . . ."

Death inclined his head, as if encouraging me to continue. He was a collector and I talked to the dead, so a scientific explanation probably wasn't what he was looking for. I'd seen bodies continue to have scientific signs of life for up to a minute or two after their souls had been collected, but I knew from experience that if I raised the shade of one of them, his memory would last only until the soul left the body. I'd also seen, though thankfully not often, bodies that had lost all signs of life but retained souls—their shades remembered being dead. "Mortal life ends when the soul leaves the body."

Death smiled, but it wasn't exactly a happy smile. "So what is the fuel of life, and where else have you seen it?" he asked. Then he vanished.

I stared at the space where he'd been. *Souls*. Souls as fuel. And I knew exactly where I'd seen souls recently—the constructs.

When I left the bathroom, I found Falin poking around my fridge, wearing only a pair of jeans.

"You need to go shopping," he said without looking up.

"Typically."

I grabbed PC's bag of kibble and flicked the coffeemaker on as I passed it. The coffee had only just begun brewing by the time the small dog was chomping away at his meal. I pulled a mug out of the cabinet, then jerked the pot out of the coffeemaker and held my mug directly under the steaming liquid. When I looked up I found Falin grinning at me.

"Impatient?"

"In a hurry."

"You always need that stuff to wake you?"

No, having two of the best-looking guys I knew in my bedroom had pretty much taken care of getting my pulse moving. Not that I was going to tell either of them that. I shoved the pot back under the stream of coffee and cupped my half-full mug in my hands.

"You never answered me about the omelets," he said, still grinning at me over the door of the fridge.

"What's with you and cooking?"

He shrugged. "I live alone and I don't like eating junk."

Well, at least he didn't say he serves the Winter Queen breakfast in bed every morning. I also lived alone—when Falin wasn't randomly inviting himself into my house—but I'd never gotten into the cooking thing. Of course, eating junk tended to be cheaper, and that was a factor too. The only reason I had eggs in the house was because I'd had a craving for brownies last weekend and the supermarket didn't sell just two eggs.

"So yes or no on breakfast?"

I glanced at the afternoon light streaming into the room. *Not exactly breakfast time anymore.* But I wasn't going to pass up real food.

"Breakfast," I agreed.

I walked PC and showered while Falin cooked. Then, after our afternoon breakfast, I paid a visit downstairs. Caleb was unhappy that Falin was still in the house, but he told me Holly had been released from the hospital—and then promptly reported to work. He swore he hadn't felt any effects of the spell, but I still sensed the crystal-armored dormant spell where the ravens had scratched him. By the time Falin got out of the shower I'd brewed a second pot of coffee and was pacing around my apartment as I mulled over the case.

"I know that look," he said as he towel-dried his hair. "You feel like you've got a dozen pieces of the puzzle but not only do they not seem to fit together, they don't even seem to reflect parts of the same picture."

"Yeah, that sums it up." I set my mug down on the counter. My mind kept circling back to what Death had said, or really, what he'd not said. I was sure he meant the constructs when he mentioned where else I'd seen souls, but he'd made me go through all that bit about the end of life first. Or, put another way, the cause of death. I grabbed my purse off the counter. "I'm going to head to the morgue a little early. I want to test a theory."

Falin returned the towel to the bathroom. "Okay, I'll be ready in five."

I stopped halfway to the door. "I don't think you should go with me." After all, John hadn't had the greatest reaction to my showing up with Falin at the crime scene.

"What if the constructs attack again?"

"If they get inside Central Precinct, past the wards, the guards, all the cops, and down to the morgue, I'm pretty sure I'm screwed. Even if you were there, I think it's a safe bet we'd all die."

Falin dropped me off at Central Precinct. I wasn't thrilled about his driving around in my car, but he hadn't replaced his after it was totaled a month ago, and he needed wheels to work the case. Besides, I wouldn't be able to drive after I raised the shade—if Rianna and I managed to do it—so it made sense for him to take the car.

After I passed through security and signed in with the attendant in her fishbowl office, I clipped on my visitor badge and headed down to the morgue in the subterranean levels of Central Precinct. Halogen bulbs lit the unadorned corridors, making the underground halls bright, if not cheery. I hadn't asked which medical examiners were working this afternoon. Considering that Tamara had been at the crime scene most of the night, I assumed it wouldn't be her, so I was surprised when I ran into her outside the coroner's office.

"I was already on the schedule," she said, covering a yawn with the back of her hand. "So what's happening? It best not be another emergency because I get off at seven and I swear if I don't make it home to my bed and sleep through the entire night there will be hell to pay."

"No emergency this time. Remember when we were at lunch the other day and you mentioned that you had several bodies in the freezer that you couldn't find a cause of death for? Did you ever find one?"

She blew air through her teeth and pushed open the door to the autopsy room with all its stainless-steel gurneys and scary-looking medical equipment. "No, and now I have more of them. Why? You think you know?"

I had a theory.

"This is them," Tamara said, rolling a second gurney to the center of the morgue.

I nodded. Tamara and I had discussed it and she'd picked

the two most inexplicable deaths for me to question. She hadn't given me any specifics about the victims, but even fully shielded I could feel that the bodies belonged to a male and a female. Young, too—my age or a little younger. I couldn't tell more than that through my shields, but the grave essence in them clawed at the edge of my mind.

"I'm at my wits' end," she said, watching as I dragged the tube of waxy chalk I used to draw indoor circles on the linoleum morgue floor. "In the last two weeks, I've had over a dozen suspicious deaths of undetermined cause cross my table. These two came in together. They're young, in good health, with no signs of foul play or disease. And yet they're dead." She shook her head, as if the movement could clear away the mystery. "I feel like the universe suddenly changed the rules and no one told me."

I knew exactly how she felt.

Standing, I recapped my chalk and walked to the center of the circle I'd drawn. Then I turned to her. "Ready?"

At her nod, I tapped into the magic stored in my ring. I spindled out the smallest amount of energy and funneled it into my circle, which shot up around me, glowing slightly blue to my senses.

With the barrier separating me from the outside world, I unclasped my charm bracelet and dropped my mental shields. A frigid wind whipped around me, through me, and my grave-sight blazed into existence, making the world wither and decay. The grave essence in the corpses on the gurneys reached for me, raking at my body and mind with icy claws. I opened myself and let the chill in, let it fill me. Part of me railed against the invasion of the grave. My warmth boiled in my veins, trying to remind me I was a creature of life, of—at least limited—heat. I pushed that living heat out of me, sending it into the two corpses. Only then did the chill of the grave settle comfortably under my skin, as if I'd reached some sort of balance, a kind of equilibrium with the grave and the land of the dead.

I took a deep breath, and as I exhaled, I reached out with my magic. Using the part of my psyche that touched the dead, I guided the magic into the corpse of the girl, sending it deep into the shell that had once been a person. Her soul was long gone, everything that had once made her someone lost, but a shade, a collection of her memories stored in every cell of her body, had remained. She was recently deceased, and the shade was strong, emerging easily when I pulled with power.

A vaporish form sat up through the sheet that topped the body. She might have been nineteen when she died, her pixielike features round as if she hadn't yet lost all her baby fat. There was no shock in her face, no sorrow. Any trace of personality or sentience had left with her soul; now all that remained was a recording of who she'd once been.

"What's your name?" I asked, and the shade turned her head toward me.

"Jennifer McCormic."

"And how did you die, Jennifer?"

The shade cocked its head to the side. "I don't know. I stopped living."

That's what I thought.

"What was the last thing you remember?"

"I met my boyfriend, Andrew. We were going to go for lunch. We were walking across campus and . . ." She fell silent.

"And what?" Tamara asked, stepping up to the very edge of my circle.

"And she died," I said because I knew the shade wouldn't. Once her soul was gone, her body had hit the stop button on the record of Jennifer's life. That was it. The end.

"Did anyone approach you before you died?" I asked the shade.

She shook her head and I chewed at my bottom lip. Sometimes people caught a glimpse of their collector before they died, but not always, and Jennifer clearly hadn't. Since she hadn't seen the collector, it was possible that something else caused her death and she hadn't been reaped, but the unsettled feeling in my stomach had me leaning toward cause of death being soul snatching.

"Rest now," I said, pushing the shade back into Jennifer's body. Then I turned to her boyfriend, Andrew.

"We were walking and Jennifer got this funny look on her face and collapsed," Andrew said without a trace of emotion in his voice, though watching his girlfriend die in front of him had probably made his last moments some of the worst in his life. Of course, it didn't sound like that moment had lasted long. "I turned, trying to catch her, and I saw this man. He stuck his hand in my chest."

Bingo.

"The man you saw directly before you died, what did he look like?"

"Older than me, but not too old. He could have been a grad student or a postdoc. He had dark hair and he wore a long, dark coat."

A trickle of icy sweat ran down my spine. That description sounded *exactly* like the collector I'd seen near the rift.

"How many of these unexplained deaths did you say you had?" I asked Tamara after I returned Andrew to his body.

Her cheeks caved inward as she chewed the inside of her mouth, and she glanced toward the cold room and the bodies stored inside. "More than a dozen. Maybe fourteen? But those are only the deaths deemed to be under suspicious circumstances."

Which meant that if the reaper had hit a hospital or anywhere else that deaths would be written off as due to natural causes or at least expected, it was probable there were a lot more victims than we knew about. But we were fairly certain of fourteen victims, plus the two skimmers I saw him take. *Sixteen souls.* I wasn't sure what process turned a soul into fuel for a spell, but the ravens had each dissipated into only small amounts of soul mist, so I guessed that the soul fueling them had been broken up somehow. *So what, maybe three or four souls among the thirty-two birds?* Adding in the soul for the cu sith attack, that accounted for no more than five of the victims. There were a lot of unaccounted-for souls out there.

And the potential for a lot of constructs.

Chapter 22

John arrived at the morgue at six thirty on the dot wearing the same clothes I'd seen last night, now wrinklier, and with bags large enough to house a pixie under his eyes.

"Jeez, John, did you get any sleep?" I asked, as Tamara pushed Jennifer's body back into the morgue's cold storage room.

He pressed his palm against one eye and dragged it down his face. "Recently?"

The air around John buzzed slightly with magic, which was weird because John was a null—no magical affinity at all. He could walk through a magical barrier without even noticing it existed. He had nothing against magic—obviously; he was, after all, my first contact with the police—but he never used charms. I let my senses stretch, tasting the magic.

"A stay-awake charm? John, those things are dangerous."

"Yeah, well, it was this or an IV of caffeine. The charm was easier." He focused on me for the first time. "You okay?"

I shrugged, a movement that turned into a tremble. Raising a pair of shades probably wasn't the best way to prepare for a difficult ritual, but I now knew the reaper was stealing souls. I wasn't sure what to do about that fact—I mean, what does a mortal do about a rogue reaper?—and I couldn't yet prove he was supplying the souls for the con-

structs, but I was starting to put things together. Hopefully
we would learn even more when we raised a shade from
the foot.

"Rianna should be here soon," I said, glancing toward
the large steel doors. At least I hoped Rianna was on her
way. I'd never sent messages via brownie before.

John rubbed a hand over the ever-expanding bald spot
on his head. "So, what is the story with you working for the
FIB?"

Crap. I'd seriously been hoping he wouldn't ask. *A little
overoptimistic there, Alex.* "It's complicated."

"Yeah?" His mustache twitched, a quick swish of displeasure, but I was saved from having to answer any more
questions by the morgue door opening.

Rianna stood in the doorway, looking unsure until her
deep-sunk eyes landed on me. Then a feeble smile broke on
her face and she scuttled across the room, her wooden-
soled shoes clunking on the linoleum floor.

"I'm glad you made it," I said, since I couldn't thank her
for coming. Then I accepted her hug as she tossed her arms
around my neck.

She pulled back quickly. "You're cold."

"It happens." I introduced her to John and Tamara, who
both gave me questioning glances when I used Rianna's
name. It took me a second to realize why. They were both
good enough friends to know that my roommate in academy was another grave witch, named Rianna McBride—
they also knew she'd disappeared a handful of years ago. I
hadn't told anyone I'd found her, and I certainly wasn't
going to get into her being a captive of Faerie. "So which
foot do you want us to try to raise a shade from?" I asked,
trying to keep the focus on the business at hand.

"How about the one from last night? It's a good puzzle."
John glanced at Tamara, who nodded and walked back to
the cold room.

She returned pushing a gurney covered with a white
sheet. A sheet with only the smallest lump in the center.

"That's it?" Rianna asked.

"I know it's not much to work with, but we'll try."

She nodded, but her lips turned down in a grimace. I
didn't blame her. Even together, if we managed to raise the

shade from such a small specimen, it would be a miracle. With Rianna terrified of leaving Faerie for extended periods of time, my asking her to venture out for a nearly impossible task probably didn't rate high in her book. Still, the two of us had raised some seriously impressive shades in the past. We *might* be able to raise this one.

"So, you know where the foot was found," Tamara said as she rolled the cart to the center of my already drawn, but inactive, circle. "Like the other feet, it was severed by unknown means just above the ankle bone. And like all the others we've found, it's a left foot."

Why only left feet? Why no other body parts?

"We won't know gender until DNA results come back," she said, "but from an initial examination the foot appears to have belonged to a—"

"Male," Rianna and I said in unison. There might not have been much of a body, but there was enough to sense gender.

John shook his head. "Okay, geniuses, you'll get your chance to show off in a minute." When we'd first met, John hadn't believed I could always tell the gender of a corpse. Always. He'd rolled gurney after gurney out for me to identify. "Here's what I bet you don't know," he said. "The boot the foot was found in was laced and double-knotted. Not like it was being pinched shut but like there was a leg in it when it was laced. And here's the real mystery. The foot was severed almost four inches below the top of the boot, but there's not a drop of blood inside the boot and there's no more damage to the boot than what would be expected of an old, worn-out shoe."

"So the foot was shoved inside after being severed?" And drained of blood. But why? "Or are you thinking the person throwing feet in the river missed it because it was hidden inside the boot?"

"Yeah, that's one of several theories floating around— none of which is leading us anywhere." John rubbed at his bald spot again.

"Any luck untangling the spells on it?" I asked, glancing at Tamara.

She shook her head. "I was hoping that since this one

hadn't spent any time in the water maybe I'd glean something. But it's just like the other feet we've found."

If we were lucky, we'd be able to ask the shade. I turned to Rianna. "You ready to try this?"

She nodded and held out her hands, palms up. "Are you leading or am I?"

Rianna was the better witch when it came to spellcasting, but I'd always had a stronger connection to the grave. "I'll lead."

I placed my palms flat against Rianna's and then looked at John. "We're going to start now," I told him, and he reached over and flipped a switch on the video recorder. I turned my focus inward.

It took only a small string of magic to reactivate my circle, and it sprang up around us, buzzing softly. Once it was in place, I nodded at Rianna.

"My magic to your will," she whispered, and though the words themselves held little meaning, she laced them with magic, giving them shape and purpose.

"I will guide it," I said, tapping into the energy stored in my ring and giving power to my own words.

The spell activated like a key sliding home in a lock, and where Rianna and my palms touched, her magic poured up to the surface, slipping into my flesh, my blood. Sharing someone else's magic is a strange, personal, and innately wrong feeling. Like drawing a breath directly out of someone else's lungs. Being the one giving up magic feels even worse.

Rianna didn't complain, though the skin around her eyes pinched in a wince. *Time to get on with it.* I dropped my shields.

Only the smallest tendril of grave essence reached for me from the foot. I drew it into me, accepting the chill into my body as I released what little heat I had left into the amputated part. Wind tore through the circle, whipping curls that escaped my ponytail into my face and making Rianna's lank red hair fan out around her. A patina of gray crawled over the room as the linoleum under us wore away, revealing crumbling concrete underneath. The sheet on the gurney turned dingy and frayed, the worn holes exposing rusted metal. The Aetheric bloomed into twisting colors around us, strands of magic glowing in a low ebb and flow, like a giant magical pulse.

"Is this what it's always like for you?" Rianna asked, her green eyes glowing brightly as she looked around us.

"The land of the dead? Yeah, recently." I wasn't going to mention anything about the Aetheric, especially not while being recorded. I hadn't realized that she would share my ability to see across the planes when we shared our magic.

I reached out with magic before she could ask any more questions. My ability to raise shades had nothing to do with the amount of Aetheric energy I could channel and everything to do with the wyrd ability that both Rianna and I had been born with. I reached out with that portion of me that touched the dead, and Rianna's magic answered, reaching with mine. As I poured the two magics into the foot, they flowed together, twisting, twining, not like they were one single note of music, but like two harmonious notes vibrating together, building toward a crescendo.

I reached deep with the magic, searching for a shade. In theory, every cell in the body stored the life's memory—the trick was having enough magic or the body having enough copies of those memories to give form to the shade. A new body with lots of cells took only a little power to raise. An old body reduced to dust and bones needed a lot of magic to fill in the gaps between the memories. With just a foot? We needed to pump enough magic into the shade to fill out the missing body. Difficult. Impossible alone. But together? Maybe. Just maybe.

Our magic filled the foot and flowed beyond it. I felt the shade forming before I even opened my eyes.

It worked.

Or not.

I stared, horrified, not at the shade of a man but at the single, ghastly glimmer of a foot. Just a foot.

The foot-shade hopped across the gurney, and though we'd poured enough energy in it to raise ten shades, the stump at its ankle led to nothing.

"What the hell?" John stepped *through* my circle, making both Rianna and me shudder—I *had* talked to him about crossing active circles. He leaned closer to the foot, watching its strange dance. "Where's the rest of it?"

Good question. One I had no answer for. I glanced at Rianna. Her eyes were wide, the whites glimmering as she watched the ill-formed shade bounce across the gurney.

"Does that mean it was severed prior to death?" Tamara asked. She at least respected the edge of my circle. Of course, as deeply entrenched in magic as she was, she'd have had to shatter the circle to cross.

"No," I said, and Rianna shook her head. "I've raised shades that have been dismembered. This isn't the result. Remember that case three years ago when the parts were found in three different trash bags?" And the bag with the head and right arm had been found almost a week after the rest. The vic had died of exsanguination as his limbs were sawed off one at a time. It still made me sick to think about that case, but even though I hadn't had the full body to raise a shade from, and several of the limbs had been severed prior to death, the shade had still remembered that it once *had* a full body—the parts had just appeared dismembered. This shade . . . it was like the foot was all the man had ever been.

"Okay, so then what is this?" John pointed to the flailing foot.

"I don't know." Unhelpful. That's what it was. How could a foot forget it had been part of a body? "It's like the rest of the body just ceased to be."

John grunted. "You sound like the tracker I consulted. Good reputation, best tracking spells in the country. But he tried to track the rest of the body on each of the feet, and each spell failed. He said he'd never seen anything like it and it was like there was no rest of a body out there to find. How is that possible?"

I had no idea. The shade jumped off the gurney and hopped across the floor. It bounced against the edge of the circle, sending a tremor through the barrier. I shook my head. "Why is it stuck in perpetual motion?" I asked aloud, though I knew no one could answer. *Would the other dismembered feet do the same?*

I thought back to the circle at the vacant lot and the rage- and pain-filled shadows I had almost been able to see around me. They'd been writhing and circling. Was this shade still stuck in whatever had happened inside that circle? I watched the foot hop about. There seemed to be a pattern to its movement, but with only the one foot I couldn't guess what it was.

"We should put it back," Rianna said, her voice wavering. Chill bumps had broken out down her arms, though I wasn't sure if they were from fear or cold, and she looked exhausted, overused. Not that I wasn't.

I nodded and began drawing the magic back, preparing to lay the shade to rest. Then the morgue door banged open. I jumped at the sound and a familiar silver-souled fae stormed into the room.

"Alex," Falin said, coming to a stop inches from my circle, "we have to go. Now."

Chapter 23

John rounded on the FIB agent. "We're conducting an investigation here," he said, the shiny bald spot on the top of his head flushing to red.

"And it's over. Alex, let's go." Falin rapped on the edge of the barrier as if he were knocking at a door.

Sparks of light flashed through the circle around his knuckles, and my knees locked as spikes of magical backlash tore through me. *Reminds me of the first time we met.* Unfortunately, I wasn't the only one affected.

Rianna swayed, her eyes rolling back to show too much white. I grabbed her wrists before her hands fell away from mine. We were still sharing magic. If we broke contact at this point, the results could be disastrous. Possibly deadly.

"Unless you want to drag me out of here unconscious, get the hell away from my circle," I said, glaring at Falin as I tried to keep Rianna standing.

Falin glanced at his fist, as if only now considering the result of his action. Then he dropped his hand and stepped back a foot. The urgency in his face didn't change, though, and I didn't ignore it. Something must have happened. Regardless, certain magics couldn't be rushed, and I was in the middle of one.

I drew back the power that gave the ghastly foot form, and it vanished, the sound of its clomping dance fading. Rianna let out a breath, swaying as she did so, and I squeezed her fingers. I hastily pulled my heat from the corpse, the bit of living warmth accenting just how cold I'd grown while immersed in the grave. I shivered, but I wasn't done yet. I still had to break the ritual with Rianna.

"What's mine is mine and what's yours is yours." As the power-laced words left my mouth, Rianna's magic washed out of me.

She dropped my hands and sagged into herself, then sank to her knees. Her already pale skin blanched to the gray of a corpse, and she gasped, as if she couldn't quite catch her breath. She was the better witch, hands down. I'd seen her cast spells I could never dream of attempting. Hell, she'd healed me from being half dead after my fight with Coleman. But the gap between our grave abilities? It had clearly widened in the years we'd been apart.

"You okay?" I asked. I was exhausted, but I was still standing, and I'd raised way more shades today than I should have—I would probably pay for that one soon. And hard. I was already trembling, and I hadn't released my hold on the grave yet, which was never a good sign.

Rianna hugged her knees to her chest, and I watched her blink furiously. Finally she looked up, her eyes unfocused.

"Al, I can't see." Her voice was thin, frightened.

Crap.

I knelt beside her and put an arm around her shoulders. She'd just shared my magic and looked through several planes of realities for the first time. And now she was paying the price.

"It'll come back. Give it time."

A tear leaked from the corner of her blind eye. *Okay, I'm officially the worst friend ever.*

"Alex. We have to go," Falin said again.

Damn. I couldn't abandon Rianna blind and in the middle of the mortal realm. It would be dusk in a few hours, and if her magical backlashes were anything like mine tended to be, it would be a while before her sight recovered.

"We'll have to take Rianna . . . home," I said to Falin as I climbed to my feet, pulling Rianna up with me.

"We don't have time."

I frowned and Rianna's nails dug into my bare arm as if she was afraid I'd walk away and leave her. I patted her hand, partially to reassure her and partially in hopes that she'd let go before she drew blood.

"I can take her," Tamara said. "I was supposed to clock out eight minutes ago."

I gave her a feeble smile. "That's okay. It's on our way." Okay, so I didn't actually know where Falin was dragging me out of here to go, but Rianna had to make it into the VIP section of the Bloom and then beyond to Faerie and finally to Stasis. It wasn't exactly a mortal-friendly trip.

"Fine," was all Falin said, but I could hear the irritation as well as the unspoken *"Just hurry up."*

I turned to John. "I have to go. I—"

He cut me off. "Yeah. I see that. I'll wrap things up here." But he didn't sound happy about the situation and I had the feeling I'd be getting a lot fewer calls for cases in the future.

Oh, good, now Rianna's blind, Tamara thinks I'm brushing her off, and John is upset with me. I was doing absolutely splendid things to my friendships today.

Falin crossed his arms and drummed his fingers on his elbow, and I released my connection to the grave. The icy wind that had been ripping through me died as the vines surrounding my psyche closed and darkness fell over my eyes like a heavy blindfold.

Well, not like that was unexpected. Or something I wasn't getting used to navigating through.

I dispelled my circle and then knelt, fumbling for my purse. Someone pressed the leather strap into my hand.

"You can't see, can you?" Falin asked, his voice low and close by.

Rianna, who still gripped my arm, was probably the only person close enough to hear. Her fingers tightened. "Al?"

I shrugged. "The blind leading the blind, and all that."

I couldn't see Falin's expression, but I swear the sound he made was some sort of growl. His warm fingers lifted Rianna's clammy ones from where they gripped my arm, and his arm slid around my waist.

"Come on. We have to go." He set a quick pace, nearly dragging me as I stumbled along beside him.

"Wait. Rianna—?"

"I'm with you," she said, her voice broken by her gasps but sounding like it came from the other side of Falin.

I knew we'd reached the morgue doors only when I heard him press the panel for the automatic doors—a feature that no one typically used. I twisted back around, almost grateful I couldn't see John or Tamara's expressions as Rianna and I were hustled out.

"Bye!" I yelled and received halfhearted replies. Then we were out of the morgue, our shuffling steps squeaking and echoing in the long hallway.

"What's going on?" I asked once I felt us turn the first corner.

Falin was quiet for so long that I thought he might not answer. Then he said, "The Winter Queen sent down an order. The FIB is coming to drag you to Faerie."

"Stay inside. Don't even answer the door," Falin said as he ushered me into his apartment.

Rianna was still downstairs in the car. Falin didn't want to risk taking me all the way to the Magic Quarter, and his apartment wasn't far from Central Precinct and the morgue. The hope was that no one would think to look for me at another FIB agent's home. He would drop Rianna off at the Bloom, and then—well, I hoped he had a plan because I didn't.

"I'll be back in half an hour," he said, but then hesitated.

"Go. I'm fine." Okay, so I couldn't see and I was being sought by the FIB, but other than that . . . *All right, maybe* fine *is a gross exaggeration.* "Go," I said again.

"Alexis." My name, just my name. His heat filled the air around me, like he'd moved closer or leaned in toward me.

My lips parted as his breath tumbled against my skin, but the touch was just air. He'd said orders had reached the FIB that the queen wanted me taken to Faerie. So why was he helping me escape? I reached toward him, or toward the heat that filled the space between us, and that heat withdrew.

"Stay inside," he said again. The door clicked shut.

I stood in the spot where he'd left me, listening to the

sounds of his neighbors drifting through the walls. *Damn, this is really happening.* I was on the run from Faerie.

I felt the need to *do* something, to prepare or retaliate. But there was nothing I could do but wait.

Well, I can at least tell my housemates what's going on. Not that I'd tell them not to worry about me because I was definitely worried about me, but maybe they'd have some suggestions of how to get out of this. Caleb, at least, might have some idea.

I dug through my purse, searching by feel for the cool plastic case of my phone. Finally I found it. There would be no dialing blind, but my eyes had been an issue often enough that I'd purchased the phone knowing this could happen. I traced my fingers along the edge until I found one of the few non–touch screen buttons on the phone.

"Call Caleb," I said, speaking as clearly as I could for the voice-recognition software. A moment later the phone beeped as it dialed.

The phone rang seven times, and just as I was sure it would switch to voice mail, Caleb's voice answered on the other end.

"Thank goodness. The FIB are after me. They plan to drag me to Faerie and—"

"No, I'm sorry, Holly isn't here right now," Caleb said, cutting me off.

What? Oh, no. "Are they there? At the house?"

"Yeah. She said something about a headache and went to lie down, but she must have felt better because she left shortly after. I haven't seen her since."

My heart, already hammering in my chest, dropped. "Caleb, is Holly missing?"

"Yeah, a letter? I found it. Her bed, sure."

A letter? It must have been important or he wouldn't have mentioned it.

I stopped talking, my throat too tight to pass words, but my part of the conversation wasn't important anyway. Caleb paused for a moment, as if listening to someone on my end of the line; then he said, "I don't know if I'll be here when she gets back, but if I see her, I'll tell her."

Didn't know if he'd be there? Oh, fuck, they were going to haul Caleb to Faerie. Agent Nori had threatened that acquaintances with independent fae were dangerous, but I'd thought she meant dangerous to *me*, not to my friends.

"What should I do?" I whispered the question around the lump clogging my throat.

Caleb was silent for a long moment before saying, "Good luck." Then he disconnected.

Chapter 24

❖━━━❖ ❖━━━❖

I paced around Falin's apartment, my shins occasionally scraping this odd bit or my hands hitting that one. It was a good thing he didn't have much furniture.

I still clutched my phone, but I had no one left to call. Holly wasn't answering, Caleb was on his way to Faerie, and Tamara's phone was off, presumably because she was sleeping.

"What do I do now?" I asked the darkness hanging over my eyes.

As if in answer, a loud metallic groan cried out behind me. I turned slowly, trying to identify the sound, but the only thing I could compare it to was the scream of an over-taxed support beam. *Maybe the building is settling?* I wasn't sure I wanted to be on the seventh floor if the building was making noises like that. Another creak sounded, this time followed by a loud *pop*.

What are the chances this isn't bad?

I tore down my shields, blinking at the explosion of color and light as I saw the world through my psyche. I glanced around, orienting myself as best I could in the suddenly crumbling landscape. I was in front of the large sliding glass door that led out onto a balcony—a balcony currently groaning under the weight of two massive paws that led up to muscular legs as thick around as my torso and covered in tan fur. But though the fur suggested mammal, when the front legs landed, they were hairless and ended in talons, like a bird. Huge feathered wings beat the air, blocking the sun. Folding the sixteen-plus wingspan against its back, the beast hopped off the rail and ducked its massive eagle-shaped head under the base of the upstairs balcony.

Gryphon.

Or at least it looked like a gryphon. It was a magical construct, definitely. Its outline shifted slightly, its form slightly unreal, but where the other constructs had been misty outlines—this one looked more . . . congealed. *I guess I found the missing souls.*

Now I wished they would leave again.

The gryphon smashed one massive paw through the door. The glass shattered in an explosion of sound and shards of glittering shrapnel. I ducked, clutching my arms over my head, but the deadly part wasn't the flying glass. It was the damn gryphon.

It screeched as it tore at the metal support bar. *That's not going to hold it back for long.* I glanced at the front door. I could run. Having to tear through the building would slow it down, but I was guessing it had another tracking charm tied to me. If I ran, it would find me, and who knew how many people would get hurt in the process? Plus, the damn thing could fly—if I left the building I'd make myself an easier target. At least inside the building it wouldn't be able to swoop down on me.

But I can't just stand here.

I pulled my dagger. It buzzed in my senses, excited about the prospect of being used. I frowned and glanced from it to the gryphon. I had a five-inch enchanted blade and it had talons as long as my forearm and reach to go with them. *But it's not real.*

But it wasn't completely *unreal* either.

I stumbled back as one giant taloned foot swiped at me. The creature shoved its arm all the way to the shoulder through the busted doorway, and in the part of my vision peering into the land of the dead, the mass of shimmering souls twisted. A face floated to the surface, a face caught in a never-ending scream, and one I recognized. The skimmer from the rift.

I didn't have time to stare. The gryphon stuck its head through the space where the sliding glass door had been, wriggling to get that taloned foot closer to me. *Tell me it's stuck.*

I've never been that lucky.

It wriggled more, making enough room for its other foot. *Damn.* I looked down at the dagger in my hand again. *That thing will tear me to pieces before I get anywhere near close enough to do damage.* The dagger didn't agree. I could feel that it thought we'd be fine. I wasn't as confident, and I was the one with the rendable skin. The dagger wasn't a good option. What else did I have?

The skimmer's face was still screaming silently as it stared out of the gryphon's shoulder. Being able to see souls had always creeped me out. They were shimmery, full of light, and looked so tempting to touch. Typically a bad idea, but maybe ...

I reached into the creature with the part of me that touched the dead. There was more than just the skimmer in that congealed soul mist, but he was the one I could see, could focus on. Centering my magic on the little bit of the skimmer I could see, I pulled with my power.

Souls don't like the touch of the grave. It's unnatural for them. They are what make a person alive, and the grave is for the dead. But these souls were already outside their bodies and more ghost than not. I pulled, pouring power into the effort. The unearthly wind of the land of the dead whipped around me, mail blew off the table and whirled around the room, the cushions on the couch rumpled, billowing in the onslaught, and the gryphon's feathers quivered around its head. Still I pulled, and like warm saltwater taffy being tugged on, the soul peeled away from the rest of the soul mist.

As the soul separated from the mass, the gryphon shrank, as if the construct couldn't support its massive size with its diminished energy source. The gryphon shrinking was definitely good—except that it was now small enough to fit through the door.

It hurtled forward, its talons grasping for me. I dove sideways, the air rushing out of me as I hit the ground. *And people on TV make it look so easy.* The skimmer soul I'd freed hovered in the air, looking confused as he blinked at me. Then his eyes landed on the gryphon and he screamed.

"Don't just scream. Help me. Distract it!"

Shades have to obey me. Ghosts don't and he didn't.

The gryphon was still large enough that it had trouble turning in the tight space in the small apartment, which bought me a couple of seconds. I used them. Thrusting with my power, I grabbed another soul in the mist. I wasn't being picky. I just grabbed and heaved. I poured power into the mist, and another soul, this one an older woman I was pretty sure I'd seen at the morgue, jettisoned free.

The gryphon shrank again. We were now the same height. Of course, it still had two long-taloned front legs and a razor-sharp beak, so it wasn't exactly an even fight, but it was at least closer.

It lunged at me, that sharp beak open as it screeched in rage. I dropped, intending to roll out of its way. Unfortunately, my coordination wasn't quite up to the task. I ended up under the gryphon as its talons pierced the couch. The sharp claws on its back feet were dangerously close to my face, but the position did give me an unobstructed view of its belly.

The dagger in my hand buzzed, urging me to move, and I thrust the enchanted blade into the soft skin under the gryphon's rib cage. A shock ran up my arm as I encountered muscles harder to pierce than I'd expected, but the dagger sank to the hilt. "You don't exist," I told it, twisting the dagger to drive the blade deeper.

The gryphon exploded into a cloud of shimmery soul mist. A copper disk the size of a dinner plate dropped onto my chest, knocking what little air I had left from my lungs. Coughing, I let my arm drop, barely managing to hold on to the dagger as my hand hit the carpet. *Too close. Way too close.*

I rolled to my knees. My whole body felt like jelly as the spike of adrenaline drained from my muscles. It took me two tries to climb to my feet. I closed my shields.

Nothing changed.

I blinked. I'd expected to go blind again, but the Aetheric still swirled around me, the land of the dead showing me the world as ruins. But I wasn't touching those worlds. The wind from the land of the dead had stopped cutting across my skin and whipping my hair into a frenzy and I couldn't feel the Aetheric energy I saw swirling through the air.

Okay, so I push my magic and I go blind and I push it more and I end up seeing but not touching other planes. I think I prefer it this way. Though as I looked around I realized I wasn't seeing the mortal realm at all. I was only seeing how it reflected in other planes of existence. *That could get confusing.*

I brushed my hands against my rotted pants—I seriously hoped they weren't that way in reality—and resheathed my dagger. When I looked up, the cloud of souls around me had thinned. The raver-collector moved silently across the room, gathering souls and sending them on their way.

"I could have seriously used your help earlier." Like ten minutes earlier. Before the gryphon had almost taken me apart.

She shrugged and tossed her bright orange dreadlocks over her shoulder as she snatched the soul of the woman I'd pulled free of the gryphon. "Didn't know they were here earlier." She grabbed the skimmer. With a flick of her hand, he vanished. He'd been the last lingering soul.

"Wait!"

She glanced at me, lifting one arched eyebrow.

"Can you tell Death I need to talk to him?"

"Death?" She gave me a genuinely confused look.

I cringed. Of course she wouldn't know my nickname for Death. *Damn him not telling me anything, not even his name.* "You know, smoking-hot collector. Dreamy eyes. Easy smile. Favors faded jeans and tight black shirts."

"And you call him Death?" She snorted a laugh, and the dreads snaking over her shoulders quivered as she shook her head. "Girl, you really are *special.*"

"Will you tell him I need to see him or not?"

She cocked a hip forward, placing her hand on it. "I'm not a messenger." Her fingernails made soft thudding sounds as she drummed them against the bright orange PVC material. "And I'd rather he stay away. There are reasons for our laws."

Laws? "Fine, then I'll talk to you." I pushed myself upright. At my full height I was taller than she was, even with her wearing platform boots, but she didn't look impressed. I hoped I was about to change that. "You have a rogue reaper on your hands. He's jerking souls out of people who aren't dying, and those same souls are showing up powering magical constructs. I want to know how to stop him."

The haughty expression dropped off her face. Then, without a word, she vanished.

Well, that could have gone better. I looked around at the destruction that was Falin's apartment. The couch was shredded, the TV was overturned and smashed, the iron supports in the walls were visible behind busted drywall, and glass shards littered the carpet. Oh, yeah, and then there was the fist-sized hole into the Aetheric. *So much for Falin's security deposit.*

Sirens sounded in the distance, drawing nearer. *Damn.* I couldn't stay here. Once the cops got to the scene, the FIB wouldn't be far behind. There was no way a giant gryphon flying around downtown Nekros had gone unnoticed, but I needed to.

Chapter 25

I managed to hail a cab as soon as I reached street level, which I took as a good sign that I was supposed to get the hell away from the scene. I wished I could have left a message for Falin, to let him know I was all right, but I had no idea who else might find it first. He would know by the disk and the hole into the Aetheric—which I was leaving around like calling cards these days—that a construct had attacked and that I'd dispelled it. Hopefully I'd be able to let him know I was okay once I got, well, wherever I was going.

Unfortunately, you can't just tell a cabbie to drive you somewhere safe. An actual address is a must.

I gave him an address for two streets away from my house and then spent the entire drive fretting over that decision. The FIB had been at the house earlier, so what was the chance they weren't watching it and waiting for me to return home? Of course, only an idiot would go home, and if I worked on the assumption that they assumed I *wasn't* an idiot and thus wouldn't go home, it would actually be one of the safest places possible.

Yeah, okay, it was crappy logic, but the letter Caleb had mentioned was there. I knew the fae had taken Caleb, but I had no idea what had happened to Holly. Caleb's cryptic message made it sound like the letter would give me a clue.

It took the rest of the money in my purse to pay the cabdriver, and that was with so little of a tip that he almost ran over my toes as he drove away. Night had fallen while I'd been in the car, and I was actually thankful that my vision was on the fritz—light didn't matter so much when you weren't looking at the world through physical eyes.

I walked through backyards, stepping around forgotten toys and over sprinklers. As I neared Caleb's yard, I tried to stay out of view of the street. I didn't know where hidden watchers might be lying in wait, but whenever I'd had to stake out a place—not often, but for one case involving a falsified will and some misappropriated items—I'd stayed in my car, watching for movement in the house.

"Hey, Alex," a male voice said, and I was so tense I actually dropped flat to the ground before I realized the voice belong to Roy. "Man, I've been looking all over for you."

I pushed myself out of the dirt. "That's good, because your timing is perfect."

"Oh, you have no idea. I saw Bell run off last night, so I went after him. Man, that glowy stuff messed with his head."

I guessed that by "glowy stuff" Roy meant raw Aetheric energy. I nodded. "Okay, but, Roy—"

He didn't even pause, but paced as he spoke faster, his hands doing half the talking with him. "Well, he and a few of his followers got away, and they were, like, high on magic. Casting all kinds of random shit. Until they crashed. Now they want more. Bell sent his men to find you. Said he was going to make you open a path for him."

Great. "He'll have to get in line."

I waited to see if Roy would continue, but he'd apparently exhausted the story.

"So, uh, why are you hanging out here in the dark?" he asked as if he'd only just noticed the location.

"Because the FIB are after me. I need you to do me a favor. Can you see if anyone is in the house?"

"No. I just came from there. It's empty."

Perfect.

I stayed low as I crossed the backyard. Once I reached the back porch, the *wrongness* in the house hit me and I stopped. The wards had been busted open from the outside, and they had clearly put up a good fight before they went. I let my senses stretch beyond the now defunct wards, searching for any traps or alarm spells. There weren't any. At least, not any of witch creation, and that was as good as I could ensure. I eased the back door open and slipped into the kitchen.

When I looked around, my sight showed everything in ruins, but the ruins were all where their unruined counterparts usually sat. Cracked plates were in the dish drainer, pots and pans with rusted-out bottoms hung above a stove that should have been condemned, and even the broken chairs were tucked neatly under the bowed table—all of which I took to mean that in reality, the house looked exactly like it always did. I think I'd expected the place to be trashed, left with obvious signs of a struggle from Caleb's capture. But if the wards hadn't been cracked open, I would never have been able to tell that anything at all was amiss in the house.

I didn't turn on lights as I passed from room to room— the darkness made no difference in my vision at the moment, so turning on the lights would only alert anyone watching the house to my presence. As I didn't know where the letter was, I didn't know how long it would take me to find it, so it would be best to keep evidence of my search as quiet as possible.

Caleb had mentioned Holly's bed when we'd been on the phone, and I wasn't sure if that was where he found the letter or where he put it, but it was as good a place as any to start looking. I crept to her room, pushing the rotted door open soundlessly. A large, weathered envelope sat in the center of a tattered comforter. I snatched it and dropped it in my purse. I needed to read it, but here definitely wasn't the best place, as I had no idea when the FIB would be back.

"Now to figure out where to go next," I mumbled, more to myself than Roy. I turned, and a low scream crashed through the room. I ducked, my eyes flying wide. Then I realized the sound wasn't a scream; it was singing—and coming from my purse. *Phone.* I hadn't even thought about turning the damn thing off before sneaking about. I sent the call to voice mail. The phone went silent and then, before I could even turn the ringer off, began singing again. *Who?*

I could just make out LUSA on the cracked screen. The last time I'd seen her I'd given her a diagram of the runes used in the construct disks. It was possible she'd learned something, which might help me find Holly. Or she could have heard there was a warrant out for my arrest.

I didn't have time to be indecisive; I had to make the thing stop ringing. I slid my finger across the display to answer.

"What is it?"

"Alex Craft? Why are you whispering?" Lusa's amiable voice asked on the other side of the line.

"That's complicated. Did you contact Corrie? Were you able to learn anything about the runes?"

"You better believe I did. I took the runes to *Dr.* Corrie, like you suggested. We had to search back, way back, in his old tomes to find mentions of these runes and we still haven't identified most. Even his library gets a little spotty once you go back a few centuries, but it looks like none of these were in use as late as four centuries ago, and if you're looking for when they would have been common, you have to search back at least six centuries. Though remember, that wasn't exactly an age of sharing for witches, so the variation among practitioners and covens was pretty vast."

So either someone had dug up a *really* old grimoire or we were dealing with a witch who had been around a *long* time. I thought about the glamour-coated constructs. I knew a place where a witch could live long enough for magic to revolutionize around her more than once. *Faerie.*

I asked about what spells the runes might have been used for, but Lusa and Corrie were still in the identification stage of research, so I wrapped up the call in several hurried whispers. Lusa wasn't happy, but I couldn't afford to keep playing twenty questions with a reporter when it might get me caught crouching in the dining room by the FIB.

Now to get out of here. As I turned toward the door, a dog started barking upstairs. *PC.*

I stopped, stuck in indecision. I was on the run. I didn't know where I was going. I didn't know if I'd even be okay in the end. But Caleb was in Faerie by now, and Holly was missing, so there was no one here to take care of PC if I didn't make it back soon.

I couldn't leave my dog. I took the stairs as quietly as possible. When I reached the top, I cracked the inner door and PC barreled out.

"Hey, buddy," I said, dropping my purse on the top step so I could pick him up. "I'm going to put you in my purse, and then we are going to be really, really quiet and sneak out of here, okay?"

He yipped, just happy to see me, and I sighed. It was times like this when I wished someone had invented a charm that made dogs understand English. *Well, here goes nothing.*

I slipped the dog inside my purse. He was a small dog, but it wasn't *that* big of a purse, and his front legs and head popped out the top. I placed the strap of the purse across my chest, and PC didn't squirm, so he seemed to feel secure. Still, I kept a tight arm on the purse as I crept down the steps and out the back door.

"Two steps sideways to one step forward. When the world decays, you must do what is against your nature to do or the knights will fall."

I startled at the voice in my head, and whirled around. "Fred?"

The large stone gargoyle crouched down on the side of the porch, its wings curled tight around its body. If I hadn't been able to see the slight blue tint of the soul, I would have thought the gargoyle nothing more than a small stone boulder.

"What does that mean?" I whispered, but the gargoyle didn't answer. I waited several moments, but I couldn't stand there waiting for an explanation of the cryptic ... *premonition? Riddle?* I had to get away from the house and out of sight.

It wasn't until I reached the street where the cabbie had dropped me off that I really considered where I was going. Or really, realized that I had nowhere to go. If I called a friend, I might put him in danger either from the constructs hunting me or the fae trying to drag me to Faerie. Not to mention the fact that the FIB probably had fabricated some sort of warrant for my arrest by now, and most of my friends were in some branch of law enforcement.

Where could a girl with a newfound tendency to merge

realities, a ghost, and a small dog go to hide? Well, there was one option, though I hated considering it. There was one place no one in his right mind would ever look for me. I pulled out my phone and called my father.

I huddled under the sheltering wings of the granite angel that had stood overlooking a cemetery three blocks from Caleb's house for the last forty years. The statue protected me from the casual onlooker, but I could peek out to see the gate and a bit of the road beyond. It seemed to take a lifetime before I heard gravel crunch under tires and saw a black Porsche with mirrored windows roll to a stop outside the small cemetery gate.

I wished I could have sent Roy to check out the driver and make sure it wasn't the FIB or one of the skimmers, but he hadn't been able to enter the cemetery. The gates of a cemetery were meant to keep the dead inside, which also effectively kept ghosts trapped if they entered. He'd headed out to check on Bell's activities—and maybe actually get an address this time—so I was on my own. *Well, let's hope for the best.*

I hopped down from my perch, my legs protesting after being curled against my body so long. I ignored the pins and needles as I turned and collected my purse—and the dog currently sleeping in it. Then I made my way around the grave markers toward the car.

The Porsche's doors clicked, unlocking as I approached. I still couldn't see who was inside, which made my hair stand on end and my scalp feel a little too tight. If it was in fact my ride, I'd be happy about the heavy tinting, but if it wasn't . . .

The passenger door popped open. "Get in the car, Alexis," a crisp voice said.

I blinked in surprise, recognizing the voice. I hadn't thought my father would come *himself*.

My father and I didn't exactly get along. I'd like to say it was nothing personal, but that would have been a lie. It was very, very personal.

I'd spent most of my life believing he hated me because I'd been born a wyrd witch, and wyrd witches, especially wyrd children, can't hide what they are. I didn't fit his image of the perfect norm family he'd built. Then a month ago I'd learned he was one of the Sleagh Maith, the nobles of Faerie, and it made me reevaluate everything I knew about him. The end result? I'd decided he was playing at something bigger and further stretching than I even wanted to know, and I wasn't interested in being a pawn in his game. Continuing with the status quo of ignoring each other's existence had seemed like a good plan. *Until the fae forced me to go home crying "daddy."*

"I thought you'd just send someone," I said as I slid into the plush leather seat and pulled the door closed behind me.

"Not for this."

What's that supposed to mean?

"How are you, Alexis?" he asked as he pulled the car away from the curb.

I didn't answer, but just sat studying his profile. My psyche was apparently now touching both a plane that accepted glamour and one that didn't because I could see both the glamour that made him look like the clean-cut, just past fifty, respectable politician who walked around Nekros as governor and a leader in the Humans First Party and the face he hid under that glamour that appeared only a few years older than me and featured the striking bone structure of the ruling class of fae.

But from which court?

There weren't many Sleagh Maiths in the mortal realm. They were the royal blood of Faerie. Oh, they'd been front and center when the fae came out during the Magical Awakening, as they were humanlike and beautiful—at least by human standards—but of the openly fae, aside from some figureheads and some movie stars, it was rare to see Sleagh Maith. Unglamoured, at least. I guess there was no telling how many were in hiding. But now that I thought about it, I didn't know any independent Sleagh Maith— except, hopefully, my father.

Okay, way to think myself nervous. "You are independent, aren't you?"

My father looked over at me. "No."

Crap. Why hadn't I thought of asking him that *before* I

asked for his help? I hadn't been paying attention to where we were headed, but now that I glanced outside, I realized we weren't going toward the mansion he called a house.

"Let me out of this car."

"Sit down, Alexis, before you dump that poor dog on the floorboard," he said, and I noticed that the purse, with dog, in my lap was teetering. A lot. "I am not winter court, nor do I care what that impetuous and selfish queenling has to say."

"Oh?" *Tell me how you really feel, Dad.* But he couldn't lie, and there hadn't been much wiggle room in that statement. I sank lower in my seat and clutched PC to my chest. "What court are you, then? And if you aren't winter court but you are aligned, how are you here? I thought court fae had to move with their courts."

"Typically," he said, but didn't expound on the answer.

I frowned at his profile. I admittedly didn't know enough about fae, but it really irritated me that people kept breaking the rules I had heard. I noticed he also didn't tell me which court he belonged to—which theoretically, I also belonged to. *Except Faerie acknowledges me as unaligned.* I knew the fae inside Faerie were born into courts. They could change, but initially they belonged to the same court as their parents. So did Faerie not realize I was his daughter? *Is he that deep in hiding?*

"Does your court know where you are?"

"Alexis, I do believe that is the most intelligent question you've asked all night."

"I'll take that as a 'no.'"

I was surprised when that statement earned a smile, and not the one he gave to voters, but a grin that made his hidden fae face look mischievous. "Very good, Alexis."

Deep hiding it is. "So how do I hide what I am?"

"Right now? You don't. Your fae mien is undergoing a kind of metamorphosis."

Great. I guess I should be happy I hadn't woken as a cockroach.

"Tell me, Alexis, did you inherit in Faerie?"

The question switched gears so fast it caught me off guard. "Should I have?"

"It is a simple enough question. You destroyed the body thief. Did you inherit his holdings?"

I stared straight ahead, not making a sound. After a couple of moments, my father chuckled under his breath.

"You have finally learned the value of silence." He sounded strangely pleased by that fact. "Now I must decide if I know you well enough to decipher your silence. Perhaps you are silent because you are so uncomfortable with your fae nature that you do not wish to admit it. Or perhaps you didn't inherit and you still possess the desire to earn paternal approval so you do not wish to tell me. Or perhaps you simply do not trust me."

That almost got a reaction from me. Almost. I did *not* seek George Caine's approval. But I managed to keep my face completely clear as I stared out the window at the world flying past. We were in a part of the city I didn't venture to often. You can't have a truly *old* portion of town with a city that has existed for only fifty or so years, but we were now in what was left of the original norm homes built after the space unfolded.

"What are we doing here?"

"I am here to drop you off. You are here to get some rest."

He turned onto a street filled with narrow, one-story houses built so close together you could reach out your window and touch your neighbor's flower box. The whole neighborhood was in need of a refresh-and-repair charm—or at least some paint. My grave-sight didn't even make the houses look that much worse than reality. We turned into the driveway of a dingy gray house, and my father cut the engine.

A Porsche is really going to stand out in this neighborhood. I could imagine the neighbors looking out windows, but when I climbed out of the car, I found myself staring at a double image. A Porsche was underneath, but a boxy monstrosity with two different colors of dull paint was what the rest of the world was seeing. *Glamour. When did he do that?*

I looked up and found myself staring at a stranger. I was no longer with the governor of Nekros, but an older man in his mid-seventies with a bent back and a limp as he walked. Of course, under that image was the fae. My mouth went dry. How did I know this fae even really was my father?

Actually, I did know he was. He acted just like him. But still, it was creepy to see him turn into someone different.

"Don't dawdle," he said, limping his way up the drive to the front door.

I wonder if he changed what I look like, too?

I expected him to drop the glamour once the door closed behind us, but he remained an old man. "Here is a key in case you decide to leave—though I don't suggest that course of action. The wards on the house will prevent tracking spells from locating you as long as you are inside. I'll stop by in the next few days to check on you. In the meantime, I have a brownie who tends the house. He'll provide you with anything you need." He stopped and turned his head toward the back of the house. It was built shotgun style, the front door leading to the kitchen, then a combo den/living room, then a hall with a couple of doors along the walls and a back door at the end exactly parallel to the front door. "You heard that, Osier—whatever she needs."

No response came from the old house, but that didn't seem to surprise or upset him. He turned back to me, and I looked around the kitchen. All the appliances looked like they'd been new in the same decade as the now decrepit house.

"Have you owned this house all these years?" I knew from the face he hid that my father had once gone by the name Greggory Delane, and had been the governor of Nekros back when it was first named a state. He'd been openly fae then, one of Nekros's few fae governors. Fifty years later he was part of the Humans First Party—the thorn in the side of witches and fae everywhere. *Go figure.*

My father shrugged. "On paper? No. I'll check in on you."

The ancient hinges of the front door squealed as he let himself out. I caught the door before it could close.

"Can you get a message to Falin Andrews for me?"

His face darkened. "No. Have a good night, Alexis."

Chapter 26

"Well, PC, looks like this is our temporary home base."
I set my purse on the floor, letting PC hop out onto
the worn shag carpet that I was guessing had once been red.

"Oh, no," a voice yelled from somewhere to my right. One
of the cabinet doors under the sink opened and out stormed a
little man. He wore a green suit, a pair of green suede shoes,
and a small green hat. White hair escaped from under the hat
on all sides. "He says take care of the girl, so I'll take care of
the girl. Wipe her snotty nose if I have to. But I will not have
that"—he pointed a large wooden spoon at PC—"in my
house. Won't have it. Won't have it!" The brownie swung the
wooden spoon like a lacrosse stick, and I scooped PC off the
floor before the little man managed to hurt my dog.

"You must be Osier."

"Must be? Might be."

I frowned at the small creature. "Okay, then who are
you?"

He crossed short arms over his chest, the spoon tucked
under one armpit. "I am much put out."

Right. "Can he stay one night?"

"Hmph."

"Just one night. We'll leave in the morning." I was being
run out of a house by a man who didn't even reach my
knees. How sad was that?

The wooden spoon lowered, and I got a begrudging nod

from the small fae. "One night only," he said. Then he turned and marched across the kitchen, climbed back under the sink, and slammed the cabinet door shut.

"Well, it's good to be welcomed," I said, setting PC back on the floor.

"Heard that," Osier's voice cried, but thankfully he didn't venture back out from under the sink.

I took a few moments to explore the house—and it took only a few. The rooms off the hall proved to be a master bedroom just big enough for a full-sized bed, a dresser, and a couple of lamps, and on the other side of the hall, a second, smaller bedroom that was used as storage and a dated bathroom. PC and I headed to the master bedroom, and I dropped my purse on the bed. Sleep sounded awfully tempting; after all, I had used a whole lot of magic in the last twelve or so hours. But there was still too much to do.

Digging through my purse, I pulled out the letter I'd picked up at Caleb's house. It was a little the worse for wear after having been in the purse with PC. I flipped it over. At one point it had been sealed with crimson wax, but Caleb must have broken that when he read the letter. A small clump of crimson remained, and I frowned at the buzz of a spell locked in the dark wax. Reaching with my senses, I immediately recognized the magical signature—no surprise that it was the same as the constructs. The spell itself was a simple alarm spell meant to alert the caster when the seal was broken. *So they know it's been read.* But not by me yet. I hoped it wasn't too time sensitive.

I pulled the letter out of the envelope and unfolded the parchment. *Crap.* I still wasn't actually seeing with my eyes, and what my psyche saw was badly weathered. I squinted, struggling to read the neat but small letters. A lot of staring, looking away, and moving closer to and farther from the paper was involved before I finally pieced together the message. Not that it was long.

Alex Craft,

> *Your friend, while useful, does not have your abilities. If you would like her returned safely to her home, come to the old bridge. Two a.m. Tonight.*

There was no signature, but what did I expect, the bad guy to leave a forwarding address? I paced around the small room, PC following at my heels. "The old bridge" had to refer to the stone bridge below town. *And how exactly am I supposed to get there?*

My head was pounding. Probably from the mix of exhaustion, expending too much magic too many days in a row, and the frequent rushes of adrenaline that had been flooding my system. I dipped my head, burying my face in my hands as I rubbed my eyes and temples.

If I went to the bridge, I'd be walking into a trap. *But what happens to Holly if I don't?* I needed some sort of backup. An edge. But what did I have? A dagger and a six-pound dog. Maybe a ghost if he popped around.

I wished I knew how to contact Falin. Not that he was likely to agree to my going to that bridge. Digging my phone out of my purse, I called Information, but, of course, Falin had no listed number. I briefly considered trying to call the local FIB branch. If anyone knew how to reach him, it would be the FIB. But, one, they probably wouldn't give me a number even if they had one, and two, with my luck they'd figure out who was asking and trace the call. Wards that protected me from being tracked did little good if I let technology pinpoint my location.

I continued to pace. If I went to that bridge alone, there was no guarantee that whoever had Holly would release her. I had to go to the police. I called John.

He answered on the second ring. "Alex? Girl, where are you? Actually, don't answer that. I don't want to know. Did you know the FIB has a warrant out for your arrest?"

"Yeah. It's . . . complicated."

"You keep using that word. What the hell is going on? You're working for the FIB. Then Andrews shows up, causes a scene, drags you out of the station, and an hour later I find out a warrant's been issued."

I cringed. John was my friend, but he was a cop first, and I knew I wasn't instilling a lot of confidence. I could almost hear him thinking that he was going to have to report the fact that I'd contacted him. I took a deep breath. "I wasn't ever working for the FIB, but I think I'm sort of, accidentally, involved with Falin. I had no authority to be on your crime scene."

The line was silent a moment longer. Then a low chuckle rumbled over the phone. "Accidentally involved? Only you, Al," he said, apparently forgiving me for the trespassing without a word. "You have broken more of my boys' hearts after a one-night stand than I can even guess, and then you end up 'accidentally' dating the biggest asshole to ever walk through this place. You're right. That's complicated."

By "boys" he meant cops. I had a bit of a reputation at the station, so I let John have the laugh at my expense. I knew the next thing he would say would be on a more somber note.

"So tell me what you did to piss off the FIB. It has to be more than trespassing on the crime scene. The warrant is sealed. All anyone around here knows is that you are to be detained and turned over to the FIB."

"It's bullshit. The reason they're after me is tied in with the fact that I can see through glamour." Which was true—it was just that the reason I could see through glamour was because I could peer across realities. I wasn't going to share that detail with anyone, though, not even John. Folklore was full of stories about mortals being struck blind because they could see through glamour, so my ability to See was reason enough for John to believe the FIB would take an interest. "And, John, their timing sucks."

I told him an abbreviated version of Holly's kidnapping, the most recent construct attack, and the meeting at the bridge tonight. I left out the bits about independent fae getting spirited away to Faerie, the constructs being fueled by souls, and my theories involving the reaper.

"Damn," John whispered when I finished. He and Holly weren't terribly close friends, but as an assistant district attorney and a homicide detective, they had worked more than a few cases together.

"So what do I do?"

"You need to file a missing-person report. As there's a ransom note, it's clearly an abduction." He paused. "Actually, let me take care of that. You can't walk into a station while the FIB is looking for you." His chair squeaked again and I could tell he was pacing. Well, so was I. After a moment he said, "The detectives in charge of missing-persons inquiries will cast a tracking spell, though I have to warn you that most kidnappers are smart enough to hide victims behind wards, so there probably won't be a quick solution. The detectives in charge will also likely try to make contact with the kidnapper. That will probably be hard since you're in hiding, but they will try to buy time and get the kidnapper's demands."

"We already know what they want."

"Alex, you can't go to that bridge. This isn't a money drop that can be done quietly and hope for the best. Whoever this is wants you for her, and it's not like you've had any confirmation she's even still alive."

My throat tightened. "She's been gone less than a day."

"I know," he said, and his voice had that raw sound people get when they don't have the right words. "This is not my type of investigation. If I get handed this case, something has gone very, very wrong."

Considering that John worked homicide, I couldn't agree more.

We were both silent for a moment, the only sound the static buzzing as the house wards interfered with my cell signal.

"You're going to go, aren't you?" he finally asked.

"Yeah."

His heavy sigh carried through the phone. "I'll make some calls, see if I can get you some backup on that bridge at the very least. But, Al, if this goes down, I can almost guarantee the cavalry that swoops in to the rescue will also arrest you."

I sank down onto the bed. "Yeah. I know."

There was really nothing left to say after that. He disconnected with a promise to get back to me and a warning to be careful. I checked the time. Nine thirty. I had four hours before I needed to leave to reach the bridge at two. *Well, I can always get some sleep.* Rest could only help. I set my phone alarm for midnight. Then I collapsed on the bed, settling in for what I was afraid might be the last bit of rest I managed to snatch for a while.

By the time I woke, my eyes had recovered and my psychic vision had faded until the other planes were visible only as ignorable washes of color. At twelve thirty I called for a taxi. I didn't have any more cash, but I had my bank card. It would leave an electronic trail I didn't want, but it wasn't like the cops didn't know where I was headed. John had sent two text messages while I slept. The first said missing persons had no hits with the tracking spell and the second said we were set for two.

I'd already taken a shower—and I'd been shocked to find my clothes clean and folded and my boots buffed when I got out—but I still wasn't fully awake, so I headed for the kitchen while I waited for the car to arrive. I was on the hunt for coffee when a cabinet door smashed open behind me.

"Outta there. Outta there," Osier yelled, charging out from under the sink. He swatted my calf with his spoon hard enough to sting through the thick leather of my boots. "My kitchen."

I jumped back. "I was looking for coffee."

"Little girls shouldn't drink coffee. It'll stunt your growth."

I wasn't sure which I should object to more: that he thought I was a girl or that he thought I'd be growing any taller. "Point me in the right direction and I'll be out of your kitchen in a minute."

"Sit," he said, using the spoon to gesture toward the white table by the window. "Suppose you want grilled cheese. Always did like grilled cheese best."

What I wanted was coffee, but now that he mentioned it, real food would be good too. "What do you mean, always?" I asked as he shooed me to the table.

"Boy would say hamburgers or spaghetti. But, no, you'd cry grilled cheese, grilled cheese. Cried more than the baby. Always had to leave to get more cheese."

I gaped at the little man. I did have an older brother and a younger sister. "Have I met you before, Osier?"

"Helped raise you, didn't I?" He waved his spoon, and a tub of butter and a chunk of cheese floated out of the fridge, a pan jumped down from a cabinet over the stove, and the bread took itself out of the bread box.

Osier marched along the counter like a general overseeing his troops as he directed the grilled cheese sandwich to assemble itself. A moment before, I would have been mystified and intrigued by the magic required for a sandwich to cook itself, but now, with his words still ringing in the air, it was his statement that left me speechless.

I had absolutely no memory of the brownie. Hell, I would have sworn I'd never seen a brownie before I met Ms. B less than a week ago. If Osier had "helped raise" me, as he put it, I must have been young. Really young. I'd spent most of my time at academy after I turned eight, and my brother, Brad, had disappeared a year after that.

The sandwich, lightly browned on the outside with a runnel of cheese escaping between the thick pieces of bread, floated out of the pan and hovered as it crossed the room. A plate followed, a tall glass of milk right behind it.

"So you knew my family when I was a kid?" I asked.

Osier jumped onto the table and sat cross-legged in front of me as first the plate, then the sandwich, and finally the glass settled between us. "Still know the family, don't I? Though I've never seen much of the baby and I've been told the boy is gone. Sad, that. He was a good boy. Liked more than just grilled cheese." As he spoke, he looked from the mentioned meal to me, his gaze asking why I wasn't eating.

"It's not faerie food, is it?" I thought it was a perfectly legitimate question; after all, it *had* just prepared itself.

Osier jumped to his feet and slammed the butt of his spoon against the tabletop. "Ungrateful. Selfish. Spoiled—"

"Look, look, I'm eating," I said, and true to my word, I picked up the sandwich and took a bite. "It's good." And it was. I mean, it was grilled cheese, so it didn't exactly take refined tastes to enjoy it, but it was crispy on the outside and gooey in the center, which pretty much classified it as perfect.

As I ate, a car stopped out front and honked its horn. I crammed the rest of the sandwich in my mouth and jumped to my feet. "That's my taxi."

"Taxi? It's the middle of the night. Girl should be sleeping."

I didn't disagree, but unfortunately, going back to bed wasn't an option. I whistled for PC, and Osier bristled as the small dog pranced into the room.

"Outta my kitchen," he yelled, charging forward with the spoon.

I scooped up PC before the brownie could reach him. "He'll be out in a second," I said, and then looked around for my purse. I'd left it in the bedroom. The taxi horn honked a second time as I dropped PC on the bed before opening my purse and encouraging him to crawl inside. I didn't like the idea of taking PC with me to meet the kidnapper and make the exchange—even if I would have police backup—but leaving him alone with Osier wasn't an option.

The brownie was muttering about good girls, curfews, and bedtimes when I walked out the door. I left him to it, and I actually hoped to see the grumpy little guy again—more so because if I didn't see him again, it would probably mean I was in jail. *And headed for Faerie.*

Or dead.

The cabdriver wasn't happy when I told him where we were going, but at least he didn't grumble too loudly as I slid into the backseat. I was headed to the bridge almost an hour early, but I was hoping for time to prepare before Holly's kidnapper arrived. I hadn't decided if I would wait inside a magic circle or if I'd just have one ready, but I definitely wanted to have enough time to draw one.

We'd just reached the south side of the city where the tall skyscrapers vanished in favor of sprawling and dimly lit warehouses when Roy popped into the car.

"Uh, Alex, bad news," he said.

I had time to turn, my mouth falling open in preparation for a question. Then a car pulled out of a side street directly ahead of us, the glare of its headlights flooding the interior of the cab. The new car skidded to a halt in the middle of the intersection, and the cabbie stood on the brakes.

If the brakes had been powered by cursing, the cab would have frozen in space. As it was, they squealed loudly, and the car skidded to one side. I grabbed PC as the momentum threw us forward. My forehead bounced off the seat in front of me and the seat belt cut tight, bruising my hips and chest. But the cab stopped.

What the hell? I jerked my head up, squinting into the headlights that still washed us in a blinding glare. "Bell?" I asked, twisting to look at Roy.

He nodded as two more cars jetted to a stop behind the cab.

Crap. I had to get out of here. The warehouse district wasn't big on traffic at one in the morning, so no chance the cars belonged to tourists.

"When I said warn me, I meant before they were to the point of setting up roadblocks," I hissed, struggling with the seat belt. The cabbie must have still had his foot on the brake, because the belt was locked around me with not an inch of give.

"Bell's been in hiding. I didn't know until his men emerged," Roy said, his gaze riveted on the back window. The light filling the cab dimmed for a moment, as if something—or someone—had passed in front of the headlights. "Alex, you need to get out of here."

No shit. The seat belt finally gave way and I tugged the strap of my purse over my shoulder as I slid across the seat.

"Your company has my card information," I yelled to the cabdriver, who'd thrown the cab into park and was climbing out of the driver's seat. I didn't try to stop him but wrenched my own door open.

Too late. Skimmers were already descending on the cab. *Now what?*

"Find Falin," I whispered to Roy as I jumped out.

"But he can't—" the ghost began.

Yeah, Falin couldn't see Roy. I knew that. Still, someone had to know the skimmers had come for me, and my phone was in my purse, under the dog, so I didn't exactly have time to call 911.

"Just find him. Tell him what happened." *Somehow*.

I hit the pavement running and darted around the closest skimmer. I dashed for the sprawling warehouse across the street—not that I had a plan for once I reached it. The purse in my arms shook as PC trembled, but I didn't have time to comfort him.

Behind me, the cabbie cursed, yelling at the car blocking the road. I didn't see the spell that sent him to the pavement, but I sensed it: a medicinal-grade sleeping charm. I also sensed a couple of tracking charms—probably the best that money could buy. *No wonder they found me so fast.*

I had one foot of the sidewalk when a guy who spent way too much time in the gym grabbed my arm. He jerked me back, shoving me toward the rear bumper of the cab.

"Hey!"

"Boss wants to see you," he said. Then he pushed my pelvis against the side panel of the cab and wrenched my arm behind my back. No sleep charm for me. He snapped a handcuff around my wrist, locking it tight with a click. The cold metal instantly heated against my skin and began to itch and a wave of nausea rolled through me. Crap. High iron content. *Asshole.*

"I think there's been some mistake," I said, struggling in his grasp as I tried to twist free. My efforts might as well have been those of a child. Without missing a beat, he grabbed my other arm and jerked it behind me.

"Watch the dog!"

His hands actually hesitated, and I think he realized for the first time that PC was there. The dog's presence seemed to stump him. *What, he's never seen a dog in a purse before?* That or he thought PC was some sort of hairless rat—that happened. Either way, I used his distraction to my advantage and slammed the heel of my boot into his foot.

"Bitch." He grabbed my hair and shoved my face against the car. Pain exploded across my cheek, my vision blaring red for a moment. By the time I could feel anything other than the sting, my hands were both cuffed. The goon hauled me back, dragging me away from the taxi.

Goon Two—I'd wondered where he was—opened the door to an ancient square monstrosity of a car as I was shoved toward it. The other skimmers just stood and watched, or ran to their own cars as I was forcibly abducted. PC ducked low in my purse.

I was a foot from the car when the raver chick popped into the space in front of me, blocking the door.

"Okay, we've reached a consensus," she said, hands on her hips and nails boring into the plastic of her pants.

"But for the record, I'm still opposed." The gray man popped into the space beside me.

I looked from one collector to the other, and the goon gave me a shove. "I said to get in the car."

Okay, so he might not have been able to see the collectors, but they were very real, and very physical, to me, and right now the raver was blocking my path. As if she'd just realized that, the collector glanced back at my abductor and then ducked into the car. I followed because the goon gave me no choice. I expected the gray man to follow, but the body that slid across the seat after me was much more familiar.

Death.

"What's going on?" I whispered as I scooted over to give him and the gray man more room.

Death didn't answer, but reached out and touched the cheek the goon had slammed into the taxi. Muscles clenched along his jaw as he gritted his teeth. His gaze went dark and shot to where the two goons were climbing into the front seats. The gray man pressed the length of his cane against Death's chest, not holding him back exactly, but more like giving him a reminder.

The backseat really wasn't meant for four people, especially when two of them were well-built guys. The old beater lurched into motion and I ended up squished, my hips wedged between the raver and Death, my hands still cuffed behind my back and a dog in my lap. The raver was crammed against the far door, and the gray man ended up twisted, with one hip more on the door than the seat.

As my bare shoulder pressed against the raver's, she jumped, her eyes flaring wide. "What the—"

"It's Alex," Death said, wrapping an arm around my shoulders, which gave everyone a smidgen more room. "She's touching you and the car."

The raver's eyes were still a little too wide, like she wasn't sure if she was impressed or pissed. She trailed her fingers over the molding on the door, and I wondered, not for the first time, what the collectors actually saw and felt in this plane. She had, after all, climbed *into* the car, but clearly it hadn't been entirely real to her until now. *Just as long as I don't accidentally pull them far enough across for them to become visible.* Or maybe I should. It would give the goons a good scare if three extra people appeared in their backseat.

"Freaky," she said, dropping her hand.

"So, uh, hi, guys. You might have noticed, I'm handcuffed in the back of a car and am being taken against my will. So is this a social visit, or are you planning to help?"

Goon Two twisted in his seat and looked back at me. "Did you say something?"

I dropped my gaze, focusing on PC. He was trembling in the purse, clearly aware that something was very wrong but not sure what to do about it.

"What do you expect us to do? Rip out their souls?" the raver asked, and I frowned. "Even that one"—she pointed at Death— "isn't that foolish—yet."

"And we intend to keep it that way," the gray man muttered from the other end of the seat.

Why do I get the feeling I've landed in the middle of a long-running argument? "So why are we all crammed in this backseat together?"

"Like I said, we reached a consensus." The raver twisted so she could look at me better. "You already know too much—"

"Though he swears he didn't tell you." The gray man tapped the skull-topped cane on Death's knee.

"—So we've decided to employ your help," the raver said, though she didn't look happy about it. "You can go places we can't."

The gray man cupped his hands over the skull. "Namely, Faerie."

I frowned at the collectors. "You can't go to Faerie?"

The raver shrugged and her dreadlocks brushed my shoulder. They were stiffer than they looked. "Our planes don't touch. There is no *death* in Faerie." She smiled like she'd made a joke.

I didn't laugh. "If you want me to go anywhere, I have to get out of this car first."

"We can't interfere with such mortal matters." The gray man focused on Death, not me, as he spoke.

Right. So much for this being a rescue. "So what's in Faerie?"

The raver glanced at the two male collectors. Then she said, "You are aware we have a . . . situation."

I nodded. *The rogue reaper.* "But if you can't go to Faerie, he can't either, right?"

"No. But he has a mortal accomplice."

"Who is the one who cast the constructs," I said. I'd already reached that conclusion. While the constructs might have been fueled by stolen souls, they were controlled by witch magic. Those copper disks existed in the mortal plane—a collector wouldn't have been able to touch them.

The raver nodded. "Our magic debased to vulgarity and tarnished with mortal conjurings," she said, her mouth twisting like talking about it carried a bad taste.

Nice to know her apparent dislike of me is nothing personal—she dislikes mortals in general. I rolled my shoulders, trying to ease the pain in my arms and back. Not exactly easy in this situation. Or really, more like not possible. The itching around my wrists had turned to a dull burning and my fingers were slowly falling asleep.

I glanced at Death. He'd been awfully quiet throughout this conversation. "So you want me to find the accomplice in Faerie?"

"No, I don't," he said, and the gray man rapped him on the knee again with his cane.

"But we do *need* you to find the accomplice," the gray man said, shooting Death a glare.

The constructs were souls wrapped in glamour and controlled by charms etched with runes that hadn't been used in half a millennium. That did *seem* to point to Faerie, but . . .

"The accomplice isn't in Faerie. Holly was kidnapped and a note was left demanding that I go to the old bridge at two tonight. The magic in the seal is similar to that in the constructs. The accomplice you're looking for will be there." Which was all the more reason for me to get free of this car.

Death's arm tightened around my shoulder, but it was the gray man who said, "Then we will be at that bridge, but this rendezvous has the markings of a trap. The accomplice might not appear."

Like I don't know that. I slouched lower in the seat. Of course, at this rate, there was a good chance *I* wouldn't show either.

"What makes you sure the accomplice is in Faerie?" I asked. After all, it was possible that a fae living in the mortal realm was working with a witch who found an old grimoire, maybe a book passed down through a family. Then an even better question hit me. "And how are they com-

municating with the reaper?" The only mortals who could
see collectors at any time other than the moment of their
death were grave witches. There might have been some va-
rieties of fae with the ability, but I wasn't sure of that.

All three collectors went still.

They glanced at one another, not saying a thing. The car
hit a bump, jostling me. They still hadn't spoken by the time
I resituated myself. From my lifelong acquaintance with
Death, I knew that a collector couldn't be pressured into
speaking, so I glanced out the window, trying to figure out
where Bell's goons were taking me. We appeared to still be
headed south, out of the city. The gray man shook his head,
one quick twist of his neck, but the raver shrugged. Finally
Death turned to me.

"We . . . lost one of our own. He was hunting for the accomplice and was on Faerie's doorstep when it happened."

Lost? *What could hurt, let alone destroy, a soul collector?*
I chewed at my bottom lip. "How is that possible? You guys
aren't physical." Well, to most people, me not included.

And maybe to the two planeweavers belonging to the
high court. Or possibly an awoken legend. I thought about
the tear and the fact that all the grass inside the circle had
been withered, as if brushed by the land of the dead. Counting the facts that the magic used originated in three realms:
mortal, faerie, and spirit; and that a collector had been
physical enough to be killed, it all added up to someone
touching multiple planes.

In a voice quiet enough that I hoped the goons in the
front seat wouldn't hear, I laid out those thoughts to the
collectors. They looked surprised by my conclusion, as if
they hadn't considered it.

"I cannot discount that possibility, but there is another
explanation that is more likely," Death said after I finished.
"There is a relic. It was either lost or hidden in Faerie centuries ago, but the last time it surfaced, it allowed mortals
and our kind to meet in—" He paused. "A fold in realities.
Sort of a *between* space where both touch."

"So you think this accomplice found the relic?"

I must have asked the question louder than I meant to
because the goon in the passenger seat turned around

again. "Who *are* you talking to?" he asked. "And why are you sitting like that?"

Yeah, it had to be pretty strange to look squished when nothing appeared to be around you. Not much I could do about it, though. I shrugged. "I'm uncomfortable. Could you take the cuffs off?"

He snorted and shook his head. "We'll be there soon." Then, thankfully, he turned back toward the front.

Death readjusted so he could bend his arm behind my head. He rubbed his thumb in small circles along my spine, massaging the sore muscles. I nearly moaned.

"Yes, we believe the relic has resurfaced," the gray man said as if the goon's interruption hadn't occurred. "It transcends several realities, but it causes ripples, small disturbances."

"What does the relic look like?"

The collectors exchanged another long glance. *Oh, come on, they want me to go looking for someone who found a relic, but they won't even tell me what it is?*

The raver finally shrugged. "It has changed through time, depending on who used it and for what reasons."

"And now someone is using it to kill?" Would that make it a weapon of some sort?

"The situation is more dire than a dozen untimely deaths," Death said. "From the evidence we've seen from the accomplice's ritual sites—"

Sites, plural. Which meant there were more than the police knew about.

"—we believe they are attempting to use the relic as a focus to open permanent paths between our planes. You have looked across the planes. I'm sure you understand the possible implication of the space between realities becoming too thin."

I swallowed, or tried to, but my mouth had suddenly gone dry. If the Aetheric was always in reality and anyone could grab magic, burn themselves out like the skimmers . . . I shivered. *And the land of the dead?* The world as we knew it would be changed forever.

"That's why they want me?" I whispered.

Death nodded. "With your ability to merge planes and

the relic as a focus . . . But, Alex, they may want you, but they don't *need* you. The last ritual was close. The next may succeed."

Which would destroy the world. I thought back to what Fred had said about the world decaying. *Let that be a warning and not an unchangeable outcome.* "We'd better hope the accomplice shows at the bridge."

And speaking of a bridge, the car crossed the river and then turned onto an old gravel road. I frowned. The only thing in this direction was a cemetery.

"We will be at the bridge," the gray man said. "But in case the accomplice does not show . . ."

"Trust me, I'm already looking for the bastard. Knowing they are attempting to royally screw up reality definitely doesn't give me *less* reason to search." But first I had to get away from the skimmers.

The gray man nodded as if pleased with my answer. The crunch of tires over gravel fell away and the car slowed to a stop. *Why the hell are they taking me to a cemetery?*

"If you manage to find the accomplice, call us," the raver said.

"Call—?"

"With this." Death leaned forward, his lips brushing mine, but there was more than just smooth lips to the kiss. Power rolled into me, cold, foreign magic, and I felt the spell sink into my very flesh. It tingled, burning like ice against my skin. Then Death's warm lips soothed away the sting.

"Was that really necessary?" the raver asked Death as he broke the kiss. "You could have passed her the spell through any contact."

Death smiled, his eyes glittering in the light from the streetlamps. "Yes, it was necessary," he whispered, answering her but staring at me.

I looked away, ignoring the twisty, fluttery feeling filling my stomach. "So how does this work?"

"You can feel the spell, yes?" the gray man asked, and at my nod he said, "Good. When you find the accomplice, and they are outside of Faerie, use the spell. We will feel it. We will all feel it."

As in all the soul collectors? I imagined every soul collector in the world appearing around me and then I shivered,

making a mental note not to poke at the spell. I nodded as
the goons jerked the back car door open. *Time's up.*

"Be safe. We hope to see you at the bridge," the gray
man said before vanishing.

The raver swiped her hand through the air, orange nails
flashing like claws. "What he said." Then she also disappeared.

I glanced at Death, expecting him to vanish as well, but
he didn't. As the goon dragged me out of the backseat,
Death followed. He locked one hand on my arm and used
the other to steady my purse against me so PC didn't tum-
ble unceremoniously to the ground. The goons pulled me
away from the car, Death right beside me. Then the raver
appeared next to him.

"What is the holdup?" She cocked a hip as she stared at
him. "It's not like you can enter." She nodded at the cemetery gate. "Come on."

He didn't fight her when she wrapped her hand around
his arm, but he didn't look away from me either. "I'll be at
the bridge," he said.

Then he vanished and I was left with the goons as half a
dozen skimmers poured out of vehicles. All of us headed
for a graveyard.

Chapter 27

❖⸺⚬ ⚬⸺❖

The goons hauled me around tombstones and monuments, heedless of my dragging steps. I really could have used a moment to focus on my shields, but they didn't give me one. The media had a tendency to portray grave witches as creepy goths hanging out in cemeteries. While it was true that I tended to do most of my work in cemeteries, I certainly didn't enjoy hanging out in them. There were too many bodies, too much grave essence clawing at my shields and searching for weak spots. It was always a relief to leave a graveyard.

The moon provided the only light, so I was once again relying on my psychic vision and not my eyes. I'd been happy when I woke to find it had mostly faded, but now as I stared out at the darkness, I wished it had lasted a little longer. My psyche was touching the other planes, but only slightly, so the scene around me was like a watercolor of crumbling monuments that had been left in the rain, so the image faded and blurred until it could barely be seen. I could have cracked my shields and straddled the planes properly, but without a circle and with so many bodies surrounding me, the tidal wave of grave essence would be dangerous.

"You guys picked a cheery spot, didn't you?" I said, rambling because I tended to do that when I got nervous.

Neither goon answered, but a rotund skimmer with rings

on all of his pudgy fingers frowned as he kept pace with us. "It's temporary." He hugged his arms over his chest as if guarding against a chill. Even at one in the morning, the temperature had to be in the high eighties and there wasn't a breeze. I guessed he wasn't cold. The man looked around, a little too much of the white of his eyes showing. "You don't think ghosts really exist, do you?"

He's asking a grave witch that? Not only did ghosts exist, but this graveyard boasted several, and currently they were doing what most ghosts stuck for eternity in a graveyard tend to do—they were following the strangers. Us.

There were no truly old bodies in Nekros, but this was one of the oldest and largest graveyards in the city. Or really, below the city. We couldn't have been more than a dozen miles from the old bridge. *Not like they're going to take me there.*

The goons stopped in front of a large mausoleum. The engraving over the arched doorway read BELL.

No surprise there.

They pushed me into the cool, stagnant air inside the mausoleum. The pudgy skimmer pulled out a cell phone and used the LCD screen as a flashlight. Goon One had a Zippo. *Way to come prepared.* Still, what they could see with their makeshift lights was probably more reliable than the washed-out ruins I saw, so I let the goons guide me. That way I wouldn't slam PC into anything that didn't exist in my vision.

They stopped in front of a sarcophagus and Goon One fumbled with something under the carved rim. The *click* was loud in the dark stillness, and the skimmer with the phone jumped. Then the large stone lid swung aside to reveal a staircase.

Okay, this is a little too spy movie for me. Tell me Bell doesn't have a secret hideout under his family mausoleum.

But he did.

I descended the stairs into a well-lit room. A generator roared somewhere out of sight, and a hiss whispered around the room as fresh air was pumped into the underground space. Judging by the number of cots pushed against the far wall, Bell wasn't the only person staying here. No wonder Roy hadn't been able to warn me until Bell made his move—they'd been hiding in a cemetery this whole time.

"Welcome," Bell said, not rising from a large wooden chair that had been placed in the center of the room like it was a throne. *Would that make him the king of sewer rats?*

He smiled at me, and his dark eyes glinted, but not with mirth. No, with madness.

Magic clung in clumps around him. They weren't spells exactly, but high concentrations of magic forced with no skill into crude charms—like square pegs pounded into round holes. With a jackhammer.

"Forgive the unorthodox manner of your employment," he said, but he slurred the words. I didn't think alcohol had anything to do with his condition. "You see, we ran out of magic. You will be well compensated."

Bullshit. He was a fugitive, and from the hungry look of the gathered skimmers, the lot of them were addicted from their brush with the Aetheric. They wanted a fix. Even if I did open a rift for them—which wasn't an option—most would burn like a moth in a flame.

"Like I told you before, you can't hire me to open a hole into the Aetheric." I'd have liked to say I *couldn't* do it, but that would have been a lie, and the words stuck in my throat.

Bell blinked at me. Then he nodded at the goons behind me. The rasp and clack of a gun cocking filled the room. A cold shiver shot down my spine and I froze, rooted to the concrete under my feet. The hard muzzle of the gun pressed into the flesh under my ear. My heart crashed in my chest, knocking the air out of my lungs, but I didn't dare breathe too hard.

I could die right here, in this hole in the ground, and no one would ever know. The skimmers were crazy enough to do it. No one even looked surprised as they watched the goon press the gun hard enough against my skin to make my pulse burst like explosions in my ear. *And I'll be just another cemetery haunt.* Death wouldn't be able to reach me, and I'd be stuck until I was forgotten and faded away.

I glanced at the ghosts who had followed us into the mausoleum. They flitted about, chattering to themselves. One woman, so indistinct that she was barely a shadow, smiled at me. I don't know if she realized I could see her, or if she just thought I'd join her soon.

Not tonight I won't.

Okay, points for bravado, but even if I could open the rift in reality—which I wasn't sure I could do on command—there were no guarantees that Bell would release me. And who knew how much damage the skimmers could do in their blissed-out madness if they had unlimited access to the Aetheric? It just wasn't an option. I had to find some way out of this that didn't endanger an unknown number of people while the skimmers fed their addiction.

"You're awfully silent, Miss Craft," Bell said, and the gun barrel ground harder into my skin.

I swallowed, tasting acidic fear. My dagger hummed in my boot, but even if my hands hadn't been bound, the only thing I would be able to accomplish by drawing it would be to get myself shot. Of course, I did have one other thing. I had the whole damn graveyard. The idiots had dragged me off to a grave witch's seat of power. Not that grave magic was the least bit effective against the living, but what I really needed was a big enough distraction for me to get the hell out of here.

My gaze shot to the ghosts still flitting about the room. *They might just provide me with one.* But first I had to persuade Bell to remove my cuffs.

"Okay, Bell, you made your point. I'll perform a ritual." I didn't specify which ritual, but I doubted he'd notice.

"Splendid! And I told you to call me Max. Now, how long will the ritual take to prepare?"

"Not long." Or at least I hoped not. "But if I'm going to do this, I'll need your men to uncuff me"— *and get the damn gun away from my head*—"so I can draw a circle."

"My people can draw the circle for you."

No. That wouldn't work. I needed the cuffs off. Getting out of here would be a hell of a lot easier if I could use my hands. "I need to draw it. My magic is . . . peculiar." Okay, that was almost a lie. My magic was peculiar, that was true, and I did need to draw the circle to have an excuse to be freed, but the two statements had no connection. It was amazing what vagueness and implication let me get around. I'd remember that the next time I dealt with fae.

Bell frowned, but after a moment he nodded and the goons unlocked the handcuffs. The release from the irritating constraints was a shock, which made being free more painful than being bound. I pulled my arms to the front of my body and rubbed my aching wrists, which were red and puffy. PC licked my hands, offering his own comfort.

"Do you need something to draw the circle with?" Bell asked, and before I could respond, a young woman with hair she clearly hadn't brushed since she woke stepped forward and handed me a stick of chalk.

It wasn't the nearly invisible wax chalk I usually used for indoor rituals but a fist-thick stick of neon pink sidewalk chalk. *Right.* I accepted it, frowning as the powder coated my fingers, and then I looked around. The ghosts in the room were losing interest in the skimmers and floating off. That wasn't good. I needed the ghosts to be interested. Very interested.

The ghost who'd smiled at me earlier hovered near the stairwell. I started to make my way toward her, but one of the goons grabbed my arm before I made it two steps.

"Where are you going, Miss Craft? You wouldn't think about double-crossing me, would you?" Bell asked and nodded to Goon Two, who leveled his gun. "Betraying me could be very bad for your health."

"Just trying to decide the best place for my circle."

"How about right here in the center of the room?"

Because there are no ghosts in the center of the room? But in truth, as I had no plan to invoke the circle, it didn't matter where I drew it. I moved to where Bell had indicated and began dragging the neon pink chalk across the concrete floor. It would have been easier if my purse and PC hadn't been dangling around my torso, but I wasn't sure how the next few minutes would play out and I wanted PC with me, just in case I didn't have time for anything but running.

"Pssst, hey," I whispered, trying to get the closest ghost's attention as I drew the most meticulous—and fluorescent—circle of my life.

The ghost didn't look at me, but one of the skimmers did. "Are you talking to me?"

"No." I flashed him some teeth and then drew the last foot of my circle.

Once I straightened, I handed the chalk back to the woman who'd given it to me. My entire palm was coated in bright pink powder. With a grimace, I wiped my hand on my thigh and then moved to the center of the circle.

"I'm going to start now," I told Bell, but I didn't activate the circle.

I glanced around. There were only three ghosts left in the room. *Damn.* Not that there was anything I could do about it. *Well, here goes.* Resituating PC, I clutched the purse and dog to my chest and closed my eyes. Then I took off my charm bracelet, shoved it in my pocket, and threw my shields open wide.

Grave essence crashed into me. I'd never worked in a graveyard outside of an active circle before, and any other time, I would have said it was a suicidally stupid idea. Now it was a matter of necessity. Taking on the essence of dozens of graves was like diving headfirst into an iceberg, but I didn't stop or even try to slow the flow. I let the essence pour into me, fill me, and mingle with my magic. Wind ripped around me, tearing at the underground room. More than one of the skimmers made strangled, startled sounds.

And I've only just begun.

I opened my eyes. *Now* the ghosts were staring at me, more flowing into the room as my body filled with the grave. Roy had once told me that normally I looked like any other mortal, maybe just a little clearer than most, but once I started channeling the grave I lit up, glowing like a beacon. That was another reason I raised shades only inside a circle—not everything in the land of the dead was friendly.

I could feel the dead all around, the bodies calling to me and promising release from the war raging in my body as my life, my heat, railed against the grave essence seeping into every cell of my being. So many bodies, so very many bodies, and many so much older than the graveyard was reputed to be, far older than Nekros. My power brushed against something ancient, powerful, and *aware*, and I recoiled, drawing back before it noticed me. *I have enough.*

Now to get down to business.

The ghosts hovered around me, their faded and shimmering clothes and hair whipping violently in wind blowing across the land of the dead and through me like a violent storm, but though the ghosts were curious, they kept their distance. My gaze skittered over the female ghost who'd smiled at me, and I reached out toward her, palm up, arm extended. She stared at me, and then ever so slowly, floated forward to take my hand. As soon she touched me, I pushed the grave essence mingled with my magic and life into her. I'd manifested Roy several times over the last month. Usually I siphoned only enough power into him to make him visible, occasionally tangible, but this ghost I poured magic into, like I had that night under the Blood Moon.

"What is that? Is that a tear?" one of the skimmers asked.

"It looks different," another said.

"It looks human shaped," said a third.

The swarm of ghosts realized what I was doing before the skimmers did. As the woman's form filled out, her dress blooming to a deep burgundy and her hair darkening, the other ghosts swarmed forward.

"Help me," I pleaded to her as I released her hand.

I'd filled her with my own life force as well as my magic, but I couldn't compel ghosts. They didn't have to obey me. I couldn't make them.

But this time I got lucky.

As the other ghosts closed in around me, I saw the woman rush toward the goons. Screams filled the room, but I couldn't see beyond the press of shimmering bodies surrounding me. The ghosts reached for me, their translucent fingers clawing at me as they all tried to touch my skin, my power. And I gave it to them.

My magic poured out of me, into the greedy, spectral hands, and each ghost that touched me became more solid, more real. None manifested as forcefully as the first woman, but they crossed over enough to be well and true poltergeists.

Chaos erupted as the now visible ghosts took full advantage of their mostly corporeal state. They rushed at the skimmers, and screams shook the underground space. The pudgy skimmer I'd spoken to before I reached the mausoleum turned sheet white and hit the ground in a faint. Two other skimmers scrambled over him as they fled toward the stairs.

The ghosts howled and laughed and screamed as they soared around the room, knocking beds askew, tossing things against the walls, and shoving skimmers. Some were actually trying to help me, but most did it just because they could. That was just fine with me. It worked. The skimmers were scattering, the ghosts giving chase.

A gunshot sounded, deafening in the tight underground space, and I hit the floor, crouching over PC, who gave a terrified yip. A second, then a third, and a fourth shot banged through the room, and as I hadn't been hit yet, I chanced a look up.

Both goons had pulled guns and were emptying their clips into the ghosts. But you can't kill what's already dead. The ricochet off the concrete walls could do some damage to the living, though. *Time to get out of here.*

Bell was the only one watching as I dashed for the stairwell, but his bellowing yells were lost in the chaos. I was still straddling the land of the dead, which made the stairs treacherous. Several of the steps crumbled under my feet as I ran, and I knew I was doing real damage, but I didn't care. I burst out of the mausoleum.

Up in the graveyard proper, ghosts were chasing the skimmers who'd fled. If the skimmers had run for the gates, the ghosts wouldn't have been able to follow, but either they didn't know that or they were too frightened to realize which direction was out. Instead they dashed around tombstones, tripping over grave markers, while the half-manifested specters followed close behind.

PC was like a furnace against my chest as I ran. I was cold. Really cold, and the chill still sank into my skin from all sides. But I didn't dare release my touch on the grave yet.

I made a dash for the gates, but stopped just short of rushing through them. If I crossed those gates, I might not be able to reclaim my heat. I couldn't afford to leave a chunk of my life force behind.

Turning, I reached for my power. The mausoleum was on the opposite side of the cemetery, ghosts still underneath and others spread across the large graveyard. I'd

never tried to use my power to reach across a distance anywhere near that far. Not that I had a lot of choice. I found
my heat, my power, and I pulled. It followed the well-worn
path through my psyche back into my body, which did little
but make me feel even colder. I slammed my shields shut,
blocking the essence still clawing at me. Then I turned and
ran on shaky legs out of the graveyard.

Chapter 28

I ground to a halt in the parking lot. A couple of the cars that had arrived with us were now missing, so I knew that some of the skimmers had managed to escape, but plenty of cars remained. *Now would be a good time to know how to hot-wire a vehicle.* I could even see. Sort of. In an I-just-channeled-a-massive-amount-of-power-and-my-psyche-took-over-for-my-eyes kind of way. Driving wouldn't be *safe*, but I could probably keep the car from hitting a tree. Unfortunately hot-wiring cars wasn't part of my repertoire.

Well, I can't just stand here. Now that I'd reclaimed my heat from the ghosts, they would be a lot less corporeal, which meant the skimmers would be after me any minute. If the goons hadn't accidentally shot them all.

I dashed across the gravel lot, the rocks shifting under my feet and doing nothing for my already precarious balance. I had the option of sticking to the road or tromping through the woods. I'd make it farther, faster following the road, but the skimmers would also have an easier time catching up with me once they reached their cars. Not that I didn't think they'd find me in the woods—they still had those damn tracking spells, no doubt—but the odds were at least slightly more in my favor.

My lungs burned like ice in my chest, and the muscles in my thighs itched with exertion. I stopped, sagging against a tree as I gulped down air. I was shaking so hard PC would suffer whiplash soon, but I had to keep running. I squeezed my eyes closed. *Once I catch my breath.*

If I survived this, I was going to have to take up running.

Digging my phone out from under PC, I glanced at the time. *Nearly two.* Somehow I had to make it to the bridge *and* elude the skimmers, who I could hear crashing through the woods in the distance behind me. I could call John, but I wasn't familiar with the area. Where would I tell him to meet me? Hell, right now all I knew about my location was that I was somewhere west of the cemetery and I could hear the river.

I shoved the phone back into my purse and my fingers brushed the enchanted bridle Malik had lent me before we went looking for the kelpie. I stopped. I could hear the river, so I wasn't far, and a horse could cover ground a whole lot faster than I could.

"It's a crazy idea," I told PC between wheezing breaths.

He looked up at me with his big brown very freaked-out eyes. The sound of the skimmers crashing through the underbrush was getting closer. I had to get moving again.

I headed toward the sound of running water. Tricking a carnivorous horse who liked to drown and eat people who climbed on her back *was* a crazy idea. But I didn't have any better ones.

Once I reached the riverbank, I pulled my dagger and pressed the point into the flesh of my finger. The last cut hadn't even healed yet, and here I was bleeding into the river again. I only hoped her curiosity would get the better of her and she would answer.

I stood on the bank, shivering and waiting with the bridle clutched behind my back for what felt like a long time. Every sound from the wood made me turn, expecting to see the skimmers rushing toward me. Then the water swirled as a large dark head emerged.

"You do taste tempting," she said, her large nostrils flaring as she inhaled my scent. "Have you changed your mind? Care for a ride?"

"Actually, yes."

The horse blinked at me. I hadn't spent a lot of time around horses, only one summer when my father sent Casey and me to camp, so I wasn't familiar with all of their expressions. I hadn't realized that a horse could project pleased surprise, maybe even anticipation. She swam for the bank and then climbed up onto the damp sand. I'd forgotten quite how big she was until I found myself staring at an eye-level flank.

She leaned forward, stretching her front legs and lowering herself. "Climb on."

Okay, this is it. I stepped forward, reaching for her thick neck. Then I tossed the bridle over her head. Malik had said as long as I tossed it, it would catch her.

It worked.

The kelpie screamed, a loud, equine yell of fury. "Release me this instant."

"A favor, and I will let you go."

Her dark eye rolled in the socket, focusing on me, and she whipped her large head around like a dog shaking out his coat. Water and seaweed flung off her, hitting me, but I didn't release the reins.

After a moment, she huffed and turned her head toward me. "Name your request."

Now the tricky part. I had to get the wording right or she'd find a loophole, which she would probably exploit as on opportunity to eat me.

Goon One, or maybe Goon Two—hard to say which, stepped out of the forest beside me. *Damn, out of time.*

"I request a ride for myself and my dog, above the water. You will carry us to the old bridge as fast as you can and allow us to dismount unharmed." I hoped I hadn't missed anything.

"Fine."

The kelpie lowered her front legs again and I scrambled onto her back as the goon ran toward us. I had time to see him lift a gun. Aim it at me. Then the kelpie went from standing to an unnatural gallop and the world flashed by me.

I clung to the reins with one hand, my purse and PC with the other, and kept my knees pressed hard against the kelpie's sides. I'd never ridden bareback, and I expected to fight to keep my seat, but the kelpie's scales were sticky, holding me in place. *Well, how else would she keep her riders locked on her back while she drowned them?*

The trees blurred as she galloped past, and then the giant arch of the bridge loomed ahead of us. She slowed to a canter and then stopped at the base of the bridge. I slid down to my feet, my legs trembling with more than just exhaustion.

The kelpie shook her head and the bridle slid free. She looked at me, and huffed a breath smelling of rotted fish in my face. Then she turned, stepping into the river.

"You have not made a friend this day, feykin," she said as she sank under the water.

"I know." But I didn't apologize.

She stopped with just her dark eyes and pointed ears above the water. "Perhaps your pursuers will desire a ride." Then she vanished.

Maybe I'd grown jaded, but I couldn't force myself to care if she ate the goons.

The collectors were waiting for me in the center of the bridge. I didn't see the cops as I made my way along the bank, but I imagined that wherever they were they could see me. *Wonder what they thought of that entrance?*

I put PC and my purse under the bridge, tucked away out of sight behind a support pillar.

"Stay," I said, pointing at him. He whined, but lay down, the bag shifting with his movement.

If I had to get out of here quickly, it was going to be hard to reach him, but he'd been through a lot tonight. If things went badly, I wanted him out of harm's way.

Death smiled as I climbed the bank, relief making his hazel eyes brighter. I didn't bother fighting the answering smile that his summoned in me, but joined him and the other two collectors. The center of the bridge seemed as good a place as any to draw my circle. A circle that I actually planned to use this time.

"Looks like you made it just in time," the gray man said, and pointed with the skull that topped his cane.

The water on the far side of the bridge bubbled and whirled as a large shadow expanded under the surface of the river. A giant green head emerged. It looked like the head of an alligator with a long, leathery snout stopping in a flat forehead and thick eye ridges—but the head alone was the size of an alligator.

Sea serpent?

Then another head emerged. And another. I stumbled back against the railing of the bridge as two more heads on long, scaled necks emerged. *How many of these things are there?*

Seven. Heads, at least. Then the first huge taloned foot grabbed the side of the bridge as the creature hauled itself up, and I realized that all the heads were attached to one beast. *Hydra.*

And another construct. *How many souls are fueling that thing?* The mist under its glamoured form was solid, completely obscuring the charmed disk in the jumble of souls.

The police, whom I hadn't seen, shouted into radios, calling for backup. I glanced at the edge of the bridge, wondering if I even had a chance of making it to the bank—this thing's reach was massive. Then my senses picked up on familiar magic that was *not* part of the construct.

I let my eyes follow my senses. There, around the center head's neck was a large collar, and dangling from the collar was a ruby saturated with Holly's magic. I'd never seen her without the charm.

The police surged forward, opening fire on the hydra. Their bullets were too small in caliber to do much against the hydra's thick hide, but the collectors were a lot more effective as they lunged at heads and jerked souls free.

"Wait! It's wearing one of Holly's charms. Maybe it's supposed to take me somewhere," I yelled, staring at the head with the jewel strapped to its neck. I met its red eyes, looking for a sign of intelligence, of intent.

It blinked large, reptilian eyes at me. Then lunged.

Huge fangs hurtled toward me, but Death reached me first. He tackled me to the ground, his hand behind my head keeping my skull from cracking against the stone. The hydra's head sliced through the air above him, taking out a section of the bridge railing where I'd been standing. Death twisted, watching the head withdraw. Then he turned back toward me.

"Love, the only way that thing is supposed to take you somewhere is if it passes off the spell in its fangs. Don't try to reason with it," he said, his face close enough that his breath drifted over my lips as he spoke. His face wasn't the only thing close. The entire front of his body pressed against mine. He seemed to realize that fact at the same time I did because a grin spread over his face. "I really wish there wasn't a hydra here," he said, his voice pitched low. Then he rolled off me and helped me to my feet.

Damn hydra.

Death stepped away, his focus on the hydra again. Oh, I wanted to destroy that construct. Bad.

I glanced at my dagger. If my reach had been a handicap with the gryphon, it was astronomically worse with the hydra. The dagger was just too small. *Only one other option.*

I dropped my shields.

I could feel graves in the darkness. The essence from small dead animals, some not so small, and some that were most definitely not animals, reached for me. Fresh graves. Old graves. And some graves that felt ancient as the essence clawed at me, trying to sink under my skin.

I didn't have enough time to do more than try to block out the encroaching essence as one of the hydra's heads snapped toward me. I dove to the side, reaching with power. As the head recoiled for another strike, I pulled with magic. A soul popped free. The head shrank. *One soul down.*

Someone released a sharp scream and I whirled around. Beside me, the raver pressed a hand over her arm—an arm soaked in blood. *The hydra can hurt them?* My racing heart stumbled in my chest, missing several beats as my gaze snapped to where Death dodged the lunging heads, his hands darting out whenever one got too close. The head always drew back smaller, down one more soul. Then two heads rushed him at once.

No!

I thrust my power into the head lunging for his back, and jerked at the souls inside. One. Two. Three souls popped free. Then I was falling forward, the bridge rushing up to slam into my knees. The gray man stood above me, jabbing his cane into the nostril of a head filling the space where I'd been.

"Watch your own back, girl. He'll watch his," he said as he pulled his cane free. "We could use more room to maneuver. The beast is targeting you. Lead it to the bank. We'll cover you."

Right. I pushed to my feet, then immediately dove to the side as another head lunged forward. I made it only a few feet with each sprint, but true to his word, the gray man covered my dash off the bridge. Two men in uniform met me on the bank.

"Bullets won't pierce its skin," I said, turning back to reach with my power again. The hand I lifted shook too hard to hold straight.

"It's fae, right?" one of the men asked as he snapped a clip into his gun. A gun I wasn't familiar with but bigger than the Glocks that most of the homicide detectives carried. It was also spelled. He pulled the trigger and one of the heads exploded.

I blinked at him, wide-eyed, as he squeezed off three more shots. Another head scattered into mist. We'd already destroyed two, and while he lined up another shot, the collectors finished off the last three heads. Then all that was left was a lumbering body. The collectors tore into it as the gunman squeezed the trigger twice more.

He smiled as the beast vanished and a disk the size of a tabletop hit the ground. "Spelled iron," he said, clearly thinking his bullets had done the trick. I *so* wanted to disillusion him, but I didn't. He turned to me and held out his hand. "Name's Tucker."

"Alex Craft."

Tucker's vest had ABMU stitched on the front. *anti–black magic unit?* When John arranged backup, he didn't skimp. Or maybe I was earning a reputation for trouble.

I left Tucker showing his gun to several of the uniformed officers and used my ability to sense magic to track where Holly's ruby amulet had fallen. I found it in the grass near the foot of the bridge. Then, clutching the amulet in my fist, I made my way to the three collectors, who were huddled over the charmed disk.

"You okay?" I asked, nodding at the raver.

She shrugged the shoulder of her uninjured arm. "I'll heal, but this has gone too far. We've got to find that accomplice."

"I don't think they're going to show here," the gray man said, spinning his cane like a baton, his colorless eyebrows drawn tight. "I told you this sounded like a trap. And judging by the escalation of the aberrations, I believe you have gone from potential tool to potential threat. That one was out for your life, the compulsion spell included just for good measure."

I didn't disagree.

I clutched Holly's amulet tight as my trembling fingers threatened to fumble it to the ground. "So, what now?"

Death moved closer to me, wrapping his arm around my waist, which earned him a frown from his companions. Not that he seemed to care. "Now we try to figure out where the accomplice will go next. We have to find him, or her, before the ritual is attempted again. And hopefully before any more of these"—he hiked his thumb at the copper disk—"are created."

I agreed. There must have been thirty souls in that construct. Where was the reaper collecting the souls? He had to be reaping in more than just Nekros—we'd had a lot of unexplained deaths, but not *that* many.

I frowned at the disk. "Are you thinking the accomplice is a witch who can work glamour or a fae who can craft spells?"

They looked at each other and shook their heads. Yeah, okay, the accomplice was a big mystery. I'd never heard of a human who could use glamour. Of course, even those fae who could use Aetheric energy—like Caleb—couldn't create a jumble of spells like those contained in the disk. So a really, really rare *something*, who had found a relic that allowed interaction across planes. I gnawed at my lower lip. Occam's razor said the simplest solution was typically right. *So maybe we're not looking for one accomplice who can use multiple types of magic, but two accomplices.*

I fidgeted with the amulet in my hand. There was more than just Holly's magic woven into it. Tamara's was also present. As a gift last year, Tamara had charmed all of Holly's favorite pieces of jewelry with a spell that would all but prevent her from losing them. She could not only track the amulet, but the charm made the amulet actively try to return to Holly by urging whoever found it in Holly's direction. I could feel the charm, and it was active, but it wasn't urging me anywhere. That meant Holly was either dead—*unacceptable*—warded, or otherwise out of the spell's range.

Possibly somewhere like Faerie. The glamour, the archaic runes, the location of the lost collector—*everything keeps pointing back to Faerie.*

"If we assume the accomplice is a witch, and judging by the runes she's using, a very old one, we are most likely looking for a changeling." I glanced at the sky. We were far enough from the city that the light didn't reach here, so for as far as I could see, everything was inky darkness speckled with hundreds of pricks of light. I had no idea how much time had passed, but it felt late, or early, depending on your perspective. "Rianna told me that the magic of Faerie protects changelings except during sunrise and sunset. If changelings are caught out of Faerie during those times, all their years catch up to them. We can't be more than a few hours from dawn. The changeling is probably heading back so he or she isn't caught by dawn."

Which meant I was going to Faerie.

Decision made, I collected PC and waited for the FIB to arrive. The gray man and the raver left, but Death waited with me. I sat on the bridge, leaning against his shoulder.

"Wake up, Alex," he said, shaking me gently.

I pried my eyes open. Agent Nori, her suit as crisp as if she'd just finished starching it, strolled across the bridge. I pushed to my feet, resituating PC in my purse as I stood.

"Miss Craft," she said, hitting all the consonants hard. "As I'm sure you've heard, I have a warrant for your arrest."

"But you aren't really arresting me, are you? Because I haven't done anything."

She frowned, her eyes cutting to the side as if judging who was in hearing range. "No. I'm not. You're being taken to Faerie for your own protection."

"Great. Then let's go."

The look she gave me was torn between suspicion that I was pulling a trick and the possibility that I was an idiot. I seriously hoped I wasn't the latter.

The accomplice was acting in Nekros, and the only door to Faerie led to the winter court. Rianna had demonstrated that it was possible to not belong to a court and still use its door, but I was hoping I'd find the accomplice in the winter court. I was also hoping that going willingly would earn me some favor. Yeah, lots of hoping and not a lot of facts, but I had to work with what I had. I wished Falin were here. He knew Faerie, and he would know the best way to search for the accomplice—and Holly—once I got there.

"What's with the dog?" Nori asked as she opened the back door of her sedan.

"Long story." I slid across the seat, Death following me.

I fell asleep on the drive and felt no better for the rest when Death woke me. The steps of the Eternal Bloom loomed outside the passenger-side window. I swallowed the dread crawling up my throat and clutched PC a little tighter.

"Please check— Oh, hello, Agent Nori," the Bloom's bouncer, who appeared to be either a faun or a satyr, given the hooves evident under his loose pants, said as we entered. He stepped aside, leaving the path to the VIP section of the bar clear.

Agent Nori removed her gun and handed it to the bouncer, who, in return, gave her a claim stub. Then she headed for the inner door.

"Shouldn't we sign the ledger?" I asked as Nori marched me past it. They were always so insistent about that damn ledger. I glanced at the bouncer, hoping he'd back me up, but his attention was devoted to cleaning his fingernails with the tips of the horns sprouting from his head.

"Time isn't an issue for you, Miss Craft," Nori said, motioning me forward.

I stared at the door. *This is it.*

Death followed me all the way to the threshold, and that was apparently as far as he could go. Still he held on to my arm, his fingers sliding down to my wrist, my hand, until he clutched just the tips of my fingers. Then we were too far away to touch.

"Come back to me," he whispered as the door closed.

Oh, I intended to. But now I had to visit Faerie.

Chapter 29

There were fewer fae in the bar than in my previous visits. Those who were present glanced up as we entered, and then immediately looked back down, apparently intent on their beers. A hush rolled over the bar.

They're afraid of Nori? Or more likely, the authority she represented.

I clutched PC tight, hugging him to my chest. As I did, I caught a glimpse of my hands. Once again blood stained the undersides of my fingers and coated my palms. *Damn.* I'd forgotten about that. I stopped to dig my gloves out from under PC and Nori turned. The thin membrane slid across her eyes as she blinked and her wings released a sharp keening sound, but she said nothing as I pulled the gloves on. She, I noticed, didn't have blood on her hands.

No one tried to stop us as she escorted me to the old hardwood growing out of the center of the room. Then we were in the frozen halls of the winter court, stars caught in ice over our heads and silent ice guardians lining the sprawling cavern. I faltered, coming to a complete stop a step past the pillar.

"The ice is neither cold nor slick," Nori said, misinterpreting my hesitancy. Of course, she had no way of knowing I'd passed this way before. She made a sweeping motion with her hand. "It's just a hallway. A passage that joins places."

I nodded, falling in step behind her again. When Rianna had brought me here, I'd seen Faerie only with my eyes. This time my psyche reached across the planes, but as soon as I'd stepped around the pillar, the wisps of Aetheric energy and the rot of the land of the dead had vanished. Both had been thin inside the Eternal Bloom, but they'd been visible. Now they were gone. *Did my shields suddenly snap back in place?* I stared around as I walked. The ice-encrusted walls glowed with some force I'd never seen before, and shimmering glyphs of power floated on the surface of the carved guardians. *Well, I definitely didn't notice that last time.* Clearly I was still seeing multiple planes. But . . .

"Nothing decays here, does it?"

Agent Nori turned toward me. "There are ancient battlefields from the early ages. The fallen still stare at the sky, the red blood soaking the ground."

A "no" would have been sufficient.

I continued to look around in amazement. I knew I wasn't seeing primarily with my eyes—or possibly not with my eyes at all. I was seeing Faerie as it was, just pure Faerie with its strange magics and interesting concept of reality. And it was beautiful.

Agent Nori paused. "A moment," she said, and then seemed to shake herself. The double image around her shimmered, the human face vanishing so that only the sharp, blue-tinted fae mien remained. A sigh escaped her as she stretched, and her iridescent dragonfly wings caught the light from the frozen stars as she fanned them behind her.

"Does it hurt?" I asked, earning me another look, which on her now-foreign features was either bemusement or confusion. I couldn't tell which. "Being wrapped in the glamour," I said to clarify.

"It is . . . confining."

"Then why do it?" I didn't really expect her to answer. I was talking because I was nervous, and silence made the strange icy hallway more ominous. "Fae depend on mortal belief, and yet most fae hide behind glamours. Wouldn't it be more beneficial to be seen? If the glamour is also uncomfortable . . . ?"

"I'm not like you, born in a world of iron. Nor have I spent enough time in the mortal realm to build the tolerance that many of the independents boast. I must wear my glamour. It helps insulate me from the poison. But here ..." Her wings blurred as she lifted off the ground. Now that we were in Faerie, Nori acted more relaxed, friendlier. *Apparently that stick up her ass was glamour.* Not that I wasn't thankful for the change.

For a moment, I thought she might flitter away. Then she glanced back at me and tugged her suit straight, as if the movement helped her regain her serious role, but she didn't land. Flight was clearly more natural for her.

"Hurry up," she said, and I got the distinct feeling that she barked the order only because she felt the need to re-establish her authority.

I didn't resist, but matched the pace she set. After all, she didn't know it, but she was taking me exactly where I needed to go. As I walked, I fumbled Holly's amulet out of my purse. Relief washed through me as the charm woke. She was alive. And she was here in Faerie. I frowned. *Some-where.* The charm urged me in several different directions at once. Either it was malfunctioning or the landscape of Faerie confused the magic. The latter wouldn't surprise me, not with the way doors worked. *The layout of Faerie could have been designed by Escher.*

The guards—or at least, similar guards—I'd seen on my first trip to Faerie nodded to Nori as we passed, clearly recognizing her right to be in the halls, and she led me on a twisting route through the icy caverns. She finally came to a stop in front of a doorway. I peeked around her to look inside. It was a small, empty room. I frowned. *And where does it really lead?*

"This is it," she said. "In you go."

Right. Well, only one way to find out where I was going. I walked across the threshold and stepped not into a small room but into a cavernous ballroom filled with people.

The room was massive, the ceiling lost in shadows far above my head. Thousands of snowflakes fell lazily, sparkling in light coming from no discernible source. The only time I'd left Nekros for an extended period was when I was in academy, and that had been even farther south. I could count on my fingers how many times I'd seen snow, so I couldn't help smiling as it drifted around me. I held out my hand, but the snowflakes vanished as soon as they touched my skin, not even leaving a drop of moisture behind.

I looked around. Music filled the great ballroom, the singer a deep baritone whose voice seemed to bypass the ears so his melody was heard by the very soul. I wanted to close my eyes, to just enjoy the sound of his voice, but I couldn't rip my eyes away from the dancers. Fae of every shape, every size, every color, and every nature swirled across the floor. None wore glamour, and I'd never seen so many fae in one place before. I couldn't even name all the kinds I saw. I'd expected the court to be filled with Sleagh Maith, and their strikingly beautiful faces were evident in the crowd, but most of the dancers had horns, or wings, or tails, or tusks. They danced in large circles, wearing fashions that might have come right out of King Louis XIV's court in France during the golden days of the arts.

I stood just inside the doorway—which on this side appeared to be a large gothic arch—and gaped. *It's like I stepped into a dream.* Except dreams always felt slightly fuzzy and unreal. This ball whirled around me in full color, deep sounds, and, I realized, a mix of intoxicating scents, like walking by a bakery next to a kitchen cooking any food you could ever desire. My mouth watered, and I turned to see banquet tables lining the walls, each piled with meats, breads, and sweets. *Do not eat Faerie food,* I reminded myself, though my stomach was pretty sure the risk was worth taking.

"Welcome to the winter court," Nori said, floating around me. She snatched two frosted champagne flutes off a tray carried by a fae with floor-length vines of mistletoe growing out of the top of her head. Nori handed me one glass and then motioned me forward.

I accepted the glass, but I didn't drink the glistening blue liquid inside. The amulet in my palm had finally made up its mind. It wanted me to head back out the door. Which made sense—there was only one door to this ballroom and Holly wasn't present. Of course, that didn't mean the accomplice wasn't. I attached the amulet to my charm bracelet. The large ruby felt heavy around my wrist, but I wanted access to it without having to dig under my dog every time I wanted to check the charm.

As Nori led me into the throng of dancers, I stretched

my senses, scanning the crowd for magic. I searched for any signature of magic, even the smallest charm, that felt like the spells in the copper disks that animated the constructs. Nothing. Not a single charm or spell. The dancers stepped aside as I passed, some casting curious glances at me, others smiling, flashing all manner of tooth, tusk, and fang. A Sleagh Maith with hair so pale it was almost transparent lifted his glass in a silent toast as I walked past. I smiled but didn't return the gesture. I didn't know the rules here. Best to err on the side of caution. I kept scanning as I walked, my free hand idly rubbing the top of PC's head. Then I saw a familiar face.

Caleb, glamour free so the skin left visible above his elaborate coat and cravat was pale green, smiled at me. It was a big, boisterous smile displaying lots of his flat, dark green teeth—and it was completely at odds with the dire warning in his eyes. But he made no move to speak to me as he turned back to his partner, a fae who looked like she'd been carved from living ice. As he stepped forward I noticed the cord of ice binding him to the dance floor.

I did a double take. The chain was thin, hardly substantial, and it vanished into the icy floor, stretching to accommodate his dancing steps before vanishing again, but I had no doubt it constrained him.

I scanned the crowd again and noticed that several of the fae were tethered with cords that dripped down their ankles and disappeared into the floor. *Prisoners?* Not all of them. Not even most of them. But enough to be more than a small number, and all were the wilder type of fae who tended toward declaring themselves independent of a court.

I frowned at the extravagant ball around me. *Extravagant farce might be more like it.* The magic snow falling around me lost its charm, the beautiful and horrendous dancers their appeal. I was gritting my teeth by the time we broke free of the crowd of dancers to approach a dais of carved ice.

The singer I'd been hearing stood at the base of the dais, his pointy elbows sticking out at awkward angles as fingers with their too many joints plucked notes from a large harp. His oversized nose bobbed, his voice lifting in melodies that would pack any concert hall. As I approached, he fixed dark, reproachful eyes on me. *Malik.* An icy cord bound him in place, but he never missed a note.

Above him, in the center of the dais, a woman sat on a large, glimmering throne of ice. Her soul shimmered a brilliant silver under her already pale skin, making her radiant as she gazed down at me with a stare that threatened frostbite if met too long. Her features were sharp enough to wound, but her red lips were plump, offering a touch of soft femininity to her face. Icicles dripped like diamonds from her long gown and a glimmering layer of frost encased the perfect dark curls falling around her face.

Even if she hadn't been on the throne, I doubted she could have been mistaken for anything but a queen. She was breathtaking, and I stared. I couldn't help it. She was the kind of beautiful you wanted to be near, hoping it would rub off. I wanted to make her smile just to see the expression soften her face. To make her laugh to know if her voice would be musical. I stumbled forward, barely aware of my own feet. From the bag still slung across my chest, PC let out a loud, happy-sounding yip.

I blinked, snapped out of my daze by the sound. Oh, I still felt the need to make the Winter Queen smile, felt it with every nerve in my being, but the need was no longer all-encompassing. *Enchantment?* I didn't know, but I would be more careful from now on. I looked away and realized for the first time that she wasn't alone on the dais. Beside her, standing with one hand on her shoulder, was Falin.

Chapter 30

"Welcome to my court, planeweaver," the queen said, leaning forward.

I barely noticed. I was still reeling from the sight of Falin. Of him standing beside her. Of him touching her. My mouth went dry, and even Malik's soulful voice faded to a buzz in my ears. Something in my chest had frozen. Maybe it was my lungs, because I couldn't seem to breathe.

He's with her. And of course he was. *Look* at her. She was . . . And look at me in my tank and hip-huggers with a giant pink chalk handprint on one thigh, my hair in a snarl of tangles after being whipped around by the wind tearing out of the land of the dead. I clenched my fists at my sides. I'd known Falin was the queen's lover. I'd *known.*

Falin wasn't looking at me, but staring straight ahead, over the dancers. Heat burned in my cheeks. Embarrassment, maybe. Anger, definitely. At him. At me.

I tore my gaze away. I had work to do: a reaper's accomplice to unearth and a friend to rescue. Well, actually, more than one friend—I wasn't leaving Caleb a slave in the winter court.

When I turned I found the queen's sharp gaze on me, watching, assessing.

"You're staring at my knight," she said, reaching up to stroke his hand where it rested on her shoulder. "Are you wondering about the chain? He has been ... unpredictable, of late. Let it not worry your mind."

I blinked, and only then did I realize that a finger-thick chain, the links formed of glimmering ice, bound Falin to his queen. *What the hell is going on?*

He didn't act like a prisoner, but then again, he also didn't act like he wanted to be there. Aside from the hand touching her shoulder, he didn't acknowledge her any more than he acknowledged me. Of course, the chain binding him was thin, and it was only ice. If he wanted to break it, I was sure he could. *Stop thinking about it, Alex.*

"I have thrown this ball in your honor," the queen said, drawing my attention back to her. "Do you like it?"

I opened my mouth and then snapped it closed again. *Play this smart, Alex.* It didn't matter if I wanted to pull out all of the queen's perfect hair right this minute. I was talking to a regent in a place where I didn't know the rules. I had to be very, *very* careful. But I also couldn't lie. *That complicates things.*

I looked around. "It's enchanting."

"It is, isn't it?" She smiled. "While I firmly believe one never needs a reason for a ball, I also think one should celebrate a newly awakened Sleagh Maith joining a court."

Uh, except I hadn't. From what Rianna and my father had said, I was pretty sure that choosing a court was, well, *a choice.* I pasted on a smile and rubbed PC's ears. "Congratulations. And who aligned with the winter court today?"

She frowned. "My dear, you awakened in my territory. Of course you will join my court."

But she said "will join," which meant my assumption was correct: the choice came down to me. "I intend to see a bit more of Faerie before I commit to anything," I said, and then added, "I've heard the high court has golden halls."

"Make merry with us, planeweaver," she said, and I wasn't sure if she was ignoring my statement or just continuing with her apparent plan of awing me with the grandeur of her court. "Let me find you a partner."

She pointed and a man who appeared to be around my own age stepped forward. Judging by the bright yellow of his soul, I guessed he was a human changeling.

"Jarrid is a splendid dancer," she said as he approached the dais.

I smiled at him, but said, "I am not interested in a dance." After all, from my experience, dances in Faerie were dangerous things. Okay, so the ball had none of the frantic, addictive energy of the Endless Dance, but still, better safe than sorry.

The queen frowned and dismissed Jarrid with a flick of her hand. Then she pointed into the crowd again. "This is Alrick, one of the last remaining of his kin."

The fae she motioned forward was shaped like a man, but instead of skin, fine scales that glittered like cut sapphires covered him. When he reached the dais, he bowed to me, holding out a hand tipped in golden nails.

"I'm not dressed to dance."

It was an excuse, and a flimsy one, which the queen dismissed with the wave of her hand. Or at least, I thought she was dismissing the excuse. Then a draft ran across my shoulders.

I looked down. My tank top and hip-huggers had vanished, replaced by a pale off-the-shoulder gown shot through with silver embroidery and accented with delicate ice flowers. My red purse was also gone, PC now hanging in an icicle-studded silver sling. I could see through glamour, so I saw reality waver, both my street clothes and the gown solid. Then reality settled on the gown, and my own clothes simply ceased to exist. *Oh, that is so not fair.* And for the queen's glamour to not only fool reality, but actually *change* it, meant she was extremely powerful.

Her glamour had also vanished the gloves Rianna had given me, and a hushed gasp traveled through the ballroom as my bloody palms were exposed for all to see. The queen's thin eyebrows lifted, just a notch, and she waved her hand again. Pale gloves of the softest material I'd ever touched appeared on my hands. They matched the dress, with threads of silver woven through them all the way to where they ended at the middle of my biceps. Holly's ruby amulet dangling from my silver charm bracelet stood out like a wound against all that snowy fabric.

"It is a beautiful"—*unwanted*—"dress. But I must pass on the dance."

The queen pursed her lips. Then she scanned the crowd, as if uncertain. Finally she pointed at the Sleagh Maith who had toasted me when I first arrived. "This is Ryese, the son of my beloved sister."

I looked at the crystal-haired fae. The queen had now offered me three partners, each of higher rank than the last. There was often significance in actions made three times, and I had the feeling that if I declined again, I would not only be dismissing the offers of her court but insulting her bloodline. *What do I do?*

I glanced around the assembled fae, my gaze stumbling over more than a dozen with the icy cords binding them. "A magnificent partner, but I must pass."

Ryese looked stunned, but the queen just looked irritated. "Is there no one in my court who interests you?"

"There is."

"You are the guest of honor. You must join one dance before the night is through. So pick your partner, planeweaver. My court is yours to choose from."

I didn't look at Falin. It took every ounce of self-control in my body, but I didn't even glance at him. He was *chained* to the queen—I doubted she'd give him to me, even if I asked. *Which I won't.* But the way the queen said "must" made me believe I actually did have to join the dance. I turned, searching the crowd of fae.

"Him." I pointed at Caleb.

"An unusual choice." She waved him forward. "Do unburden yourself first."

I looked down at PC. I didn't want to get separated from him—he was an awfully small dog—but the look the queen gave me said this wasn't a negotiable point. I unslung the bag and set it on the edge of the dais.

"Stay," I whispered.

He whined, and then immediately jumped out of the bag and pranced across the dais. He stopped in front of Falin and pawed the man's leg. Falin didn't move, but the edge of his mouth on the side facing away from the queen twitched upward, just a hair, and I swear I saw his gaze flicker toward me.

"Bad dog," I mumbled, and then Caleb was leading me to the dance floor.

I don't dance. It's sort of a personal rule. I've never been good enough at it to reach the point at which dancing became fun. And this wasn't mere dancing. This dance had *choreographed steps*.

The dance started with a bow, and I didn't realize I was supposed to be curtsying, not bowing, until the woman beside me cleared her throat. Then the women made a line and danced in a small circle. I was pretty sure there was some move I was supposed to be doing with my feet, but my feet weren't visible under the gown anyway, so I just tried to keep pace. Then the men danced because, of course, this couldn't be a dance where the men and women did the same thing at the same time. I was gritting my teeth again by the time the lines of men and women joined.

"Are you okay?" I asked as Caleb and I circled each other, our right palms pressed together.

"I'm not in the dungeon anymore, so that's a plus." He flashed me a bright smile, which was completely fake. "Good behavior wins rewards, if not trust." Then he turned and held up his left hand. The couples around us switched directions, but it took me an awkward moment to figure that out and by the time I spun around the dance had moved on to the next step.

I remained perpetually one step off throughout the dance. I didn't care. I was watching Caleb and the cord binding him. He appeared to be able to move anywhere he wanted to in the ballroom, but I had the feeling he couldn't leave. Which meant it had to go. It was definitely magic, but I had no idea how it worked. I'd only just started being able to feel fae magic. *But I do have my dagger.* The dagger was enchanted to cut through anything, and from its pressure against my leg in its sheath, I could almost feel it agreeing that it could get the job done. *First I have to get to it.*

The queen hadn't changed my shoes, probably because the gown dragged the ground, so it wasn't like anyone was going to see my feet. The problem? Getting to a boot holster underneath a ball gown was a real bitch. I waited until the end of the song, when I was once again curtsying, and even then, drawing the dagger was anything but smooth. It was more of a hike-the-skirt-and-dig-through-layers-of-material-until-I-found-my-leg kind of move. I had no doubt that I'd been noticed. But with what I was about to do, I couldn't avoid being noticed. Dropping from the curtsy into a kneel beside Caleb, I slid the blade through the half-real cord. It dissolved.

"Al, what did you do?" Caleb hissed, his gaze darting around the room as if to see who noticed. Most of the fae had moved into the next dance already, but the queen pushed herself to her feet. I could feel her staring at us. I wasn't the only one, Caleb clearly sensed her gaze as well. "We have to get out of here." He wrapped an arm around my waist and dragged me forward.

"No. Caleb, I—" I had a job to do. And PC was here. And—

Caleb didn't give me the option to protest. His arm around me tightened and he lifted me off the ground, running with me in tow as he dodged dancers.

"Stop them! Bring them to me," the queen's voice yelled just before Caleb dove through the doorway.

The music went silent, the sound of dancers disappeared, and the smell of food vanished as the stillness of the hallway settled around us. Caleb set me on my feet, glancing first to the right and then to the left. Both directions looked exactly the same, and he cursed as he grabbed my arm and dragged me down the corridor to the right.

I tried to pull away, bracing with my feet. "Caleb. Let go. I have to stay."

He just tugged harder. "No. We have to get out of here, Al, before—"

He never got to the next word. I expected the guards I'd seen earlier to catch us, but it was the ominous statues along the wall that lumbered into action, and I had a good idea what he'd been worried about.

The guardians each carried a huge, three-foot-long sword. Who the hell carried a sword? Of course they were more "whats" than "whos," and there were a lot of them. Caleb skidded to a stop as three guardians barred the passage in front of us. We both twisted around, but there were more guardians behind us, and more were stepping forward from the walls, their swords lifted. *Surrounded.*

"How do we fight them?" I whispered, and Caleb shook his head.

Great. I could see the glyphs on the guardians, but I didn't know anything about the fae glyph magic, and I certainly didn't know how to dispel the enchantment. My ability to peer over the planes wasn't showing anything useful either. They weren't like the constructs I could disbelieve out of existence, but ice given purpose. Even the dagger in my hand, which was always eager for a little action, felt unsure.

The guardians pressed closer, until Caleb and I were forced back to back just to keep from being skewered.

"Stand down," a familiar voice yelled. Falin rounded the corner at a dead run.

"No," Caleb whispered.

I spared a moment to glance at Caleb before focusing on Falin. The chain was gone, and he was alone. Or at least he was far ahead of anyone else pursuing us.

He reached a row of guardians and, grabbing two by the shoulder, jerked them back to open a path with no pointy ice swords between him and us. The guardians turned, and then as one, stepped back. They didn't lower their swords, but at least I had room to breathe.

"We're not going back," Caleb said. He grabbed my dagger, wrenching it from my hand.

I yelped, my wrist smarting. "Hey!"

Caleb lifted the dagger, pointing it at Falin.

I grabbed his arm. "Caleb, stop."

Falin stepped closer. "I don't wish to hurt you."

Which didn't mean he *wouldn't*. I'd seen Falin kill before. That had been the bad guys, but I guess "bad" was a matter of perspective.

Caleb lifted the dagger higher.

Falin glanced at the ice guardians. Two advanced, faster than I would have thought possible for automatons, and grabbed Caleb's arms, dragging him down.

"What do you think you're—" I didn't finish because suddenly I was wrapped in warm, strong arms.

Falin pulled me tight against his chest, holding me close. "I was so worried," he whispered, his breath dancing through my hair.

He was *worried*. So he told me here. In a hallway. Away from *her*. "Don't. Touch. Me."

Falin jerked back, as if my words scalded him. "Alexis . . ."

"No. Don't." I crossed my arms over my chest and stared at him. A nerve twitched under my eye. "Just don't, okay? Now tell them to let go of Caleb."

Falin's shoulder sagged. "I can't."

"What do you mean you can't?"

"My queen commanded I bring you to her."

Well, that proved it, didn't it? If I'd needed any further proof of where I stood, he'd just provided it. That conclusion must have shown on my face because Falin stepped forward again. He lifted his hands as if he was going to touch me, but then he dropped his arms by his sides.

"Try to understand. I *must* obey her commands. I have no choice."

He couldn't lie, I knew he couldn't, and yet the hurt part of me couldn't believe him. I glanced at Caleb, who'd finally stopped struggling with the guardians. He wore a sour look, but he gave one curt nod, confirming Falin's words.

He has to obey? I shook my head. The rules seemed to keep changing, and I barely understood the game. But the stakes were high. Deadly.

Falin stepped forward until the hem of my dress brushed his legs. "Alexis, I would reorder all of Faerie for you if it were in my power."

The *"but it isn't"* went unsaid everywhere but his eyes, where I could almost see the words echoing. He reached out, his warm hands sliding over my bare shoulders. I didn't pull away, but I didn't move toward him either. He leaned forward, closing the distance between us. Still I held my ground, and his lips grazed mine, the touch light enough to be a kiss from the wind.

"Forgive me," he whispered. He meant the words, meant them so much that the imbalance that swung between us made us both flinch. Then his hands slid from my shoulders to my wrists. His fingers locked around me like manacles.

What?

"Oh, now isn't this touching?" a crisp female voice said, and I jumped.

Falin released my arms and whirled around, dropping to his knees in the same movement. "My queen."

The Winter Queen stood in the middle of the hall, her hands balled into fists at her waist. PC, who had apparently followed her, rushed past the ice guardians. I scooped him up and clutched him tight as the queen strolled forward, holding the skirt of her long dress. She stopped directly in front of Falin's kneeling form.

"Did you really think you could keep secrets within my own halls, knight?"

Falin didn't answer, and she slid her hand into his hair. The movement started as the caress of a lover and ended with her fist clenched in the hair at the back of his skull. She jerked upward, and he rose with the motion. She was petite, so she had to release him before he reached his full height. She stepped around him, dragging him by the front of his shirt until he faced me.

"I had wondered," she said, running her hand down his chest. Not a muscle in his body twitched. "I called my knight home, and he came, as he should have, even though he knew I was angry that he'd failed to kill the body thief in a timely manner. And then, when he knew I would have forgiven him soon, he went and broke out of my prison, at great personal expense to himself." She jabbed her fingers into the side where he'd been sliced open when I'd found him. The edges of his eyes betrayed his wince, but he gave her no other reaction. "We had just heard rumor of a planeweaver. I thought that perhaps he'd gone to retrieve the planeweaver himself. Perhaps to present her to me as a gift to regain my good graces. But that did not happen. Now I can guess why." She rounded on me.

Falin was injured escaping the winter court? To get to me. I didn't know what to say, so I met the queen's eyes, saying nothing.

She hissed under her breath. Then she turned to Falin. "Take yourself to Rath." She glanced at me over her shoulder. "That would be the court torture chamber. Since you have no interest in my banquets, perhaps a visit there would interest you more."

"My queen—" Falin started, and she dug her fingers into his side again.

"If you beg for yourself, knight, I will forgive you. But if you beg for her, you will not like the results."

He glanced at me, and then he squeezed his eyes shut and remained silent.

The queen turned toward the guardians holding Caleb. "Take him to the dungeons with the rest of the resistant independents. You"—she pointed to two more guardians— "take her to a chamber where she can await the return of my patience." She turned to me, the frost in her glare deadly, hateful. "You should hope it returns quickly. A planeweaver who will not join my court is of limited worth."

Chapter 31

I struggled to keep a safe grip on PC and not trip and fall over the damn gown as the ice guardians dragged me away from the queen, Falin, and Caleb.

"Slow down," I yelled, stumbling. PC squirmed.

They didn't slow. They didn't even pause to let me get my feet under me. I twisted, glancing back at the queen. She watched, looking regal, delicate, and utterly smug.

"Are you holding a Sleagh Maith not of your court against her will?" a deep masculine voice asked in the corridor ahead of me. A corridor that had been empty a moment before.

I turned around.

In the center of the hallway stood an unfamiliar fae—another noble Sleagh Maith, from the look of his almost-too-handsome-to-look-at features. He had black hair pulled back tightly behind his head, so I couldn't see how long it actually was, and a dark beard that formed a sharp point at his chin and probably saved his jaw from looking too delicate for a man. Behind him, the hall vanished into a large room shrouded in deep shadows. But the shadows were only in a diamond-shaped area around the fae; the ice cavern was visible everywhere else, as if a doorway had been torn open in the center of the hall.

"You." I couldn't see the queen, but her voice held all the warmth of a glacier. "You have no business here."

"I beg to differ." He made a motion with his hand and a scream crashed through the chilled cavern.

Two inky black forms surged forward. Wraithlike, in tattered robes with their hair streaming in tangles behind them, the newcomers swung swords that trailed darkness in their wake, as if they leaked shadows. Of course, the wraiths appeared to be little more than animated shadows themselves. The ice guardians released me as they reached for their swords.

The cavern shook with the impact of the guardians and shadows. I clutched PC, stumbling back a step. The clang of swords rang in the air, and I ducked as an ice blade was deflected straight toward me. *Not good.*

"Alexis, this way," the man in the rift yelled.

"No!" The queen's voice cracked through the hall. "After them, all of you. Detain her."

I whirled around. The queen's ice guardians surged forward in force. Even the two that were holding Caleb released him to grab their swords and join the fray. Caleb looked at me, looked at the man in the rift, and then turned and fled in the opposite direction. I didn't blame him.

More shadow wraiths flew out of the rift to hold off the fresh assault of ice guardians, but the ice guardians weren't the only ones coming. Falin darted forward, parrying blows from the wraiths.

"Alexis, hurry," the stranger said, holding out a hand. He was definitely no white knight here to save me, not with all his oiled black armor that nearly blended in with the shadows around him, but he was definitely rescue of some sort.

A sword passed through the air inches from my chest— and PC. The white crest of hair on the top of his head fluttered and he trembled. *I have to get out of here.* I glanced at the fae still extending his hand toward me. Well, the winter court was a bust for the accomplice and Holly anyway. Maybe I'd have better luck elsewhere. *And maybe I can manage not to piss off the ruling regent.*

Tucking PC under one arm, I gathered the skirt of my gown with the other hand, hiking it up to my knees, and then I ran for the rip. The man reached for me. I dropped my skirt and grabbed his hand just as someone grabbed my arm. The stranger hauled me forward, up and through the tear. The ice cavern vanished; the hand on my arm didn't.

I stumbled into an enormous anteroom filled with giant gothic arches and spiraling columns. And Falin followed. The fae who'd pulled me through turned, leveling a sword that reflected no light, as if it were crafted of pure shadows. He swung at Falin, who jumped backward. Falin lifted two daggers long enough to be short swords.

I stepped between them, my back to Falin. His hands immediately closed on my arms, the flat of his blades pressing against my bare skin.

"Don't hurt him."

The stranger cocked his head. Then he turned toward the rift. "Now, boy," he yelled, and a robed figure I hadn't noticed standing to one edge of the tear stepped forward.

The figure was the size of a child, but that didn't mean anything, as fae ranged in size from very, very small to enormous. He thrust his hands into the space on either end of the tear and seemed to grab the hole at the very edges. I stared, amazed, as he tugged the rip, closing it. *The shadow court's planebender?* The tear was less than a foot wide when an ice guardian reached it. The guardian dove for the opening, his sword leading, pointed directly at the planebender.

"Down!" my rescuer yelled, charging forward.

The planebender hit the ground as a dark sword swung over his head, parrying the guardian's blow. The stranger grabbed the ice wrist and shoved, trying to force the arm back through the opening while avoiding the frozen blade.

The planebender rose to a crouch and grabbed the edges of the tear again. I could feel the magic—not Aetheric energy but a magic that felt both foreign and extremely familiar. He tugged, forcing the tear around the guardian's arm.

"Knight," the queen's voice said, cutting into the room through the still partially open rift. Falin cringed behind me. *Crap.* "Knight, capture the planeweaver and—"

A loud crack snapped through the air, followed by the sound of ice shattering. The queen's voice broke off in mid-sentence, and the guardian's arm, still clutching the sword, fell to the ground. It melted immediately, leaving only a large puddle behind the planebender, and the tear in Faerie knitted itself back together, closing without so much as a seam.

My jaw dropped. I could feel it hanging open in amazement, but I couldn't seem to convince it to close. The planebender stood, dusting his hands on his trousers, and the stranger nodded at him.

"Well done," he said affectionately and reached inside the hood as if tousling the wearer's hair. There was no decay in Faerie, so I couldn't glimpse anything under the shadowy cloak, not even a glimmer of his soul. The dark fae then touched the figure's shoulder, and as if he'd been dismissed, the figure scurried away into the shadows. Then the fae turned back toward me. "Now what do we do with him?" He nodded over my shoulder at Falin.

Falin's fingers tensed around my arms. He leaned forward until his lips were level with my ear. "My queen commanded I capture you and . . . I guess the 'and' is left to my discretion." He made the last bit sound suggestive enough that heat rushed to my cheeks—and some lower places—despite my best intentions.

Damn. I'm supposed to be mad at him. I *was* mad at him.

The dark-haired fae glanced at Falin's hands on my arms and then lifted his sword. "Release her. She is a guest of my court and under my protection. If the Winter Queen or her bloodied hands wish to have her against her will, you will have to go through me."

Falin's grip on my arms tightened and he dragged me back a step, but this time there was nothing suggestive to it. He cursed, his voice a low growl, and I could almost hear how hard his teeth gritted. Then he leaned in and whispered, "Alex, she commanded me to capture you. I can't release you until you are either incapacitated or submit to being my prisoner."

"Do no such thing, Alexis," the dark armored fae said, jumping forward, his sword swinging. "I wear my own blood, boy. You'll not find me an easy opponent."

Falin lifted one of his large daggers to block the shadow sword and in the same movement swung me behind him. "I've no quarrel with you, Shadow King."

King?

The other fae kept coming, his sword trailing darkness in its wake. "You threaten my own kin, so you most definitely have quarrel with me, boy."

Kin?

"Stop. Both of you. Stop!" I didn't step between them this time because their swords were just blurs as they moved and they seemed damn determined to kill each other and I wasn't about to get in the middle of it. They didn't stop at my words, so I said, "Falin, I submit. You captured me and I'm a prisoner or whatever."

"Alexis, no," the stranger said, his sword wavering for a single moment.

Falin took the moment to jump back, disengaging. He didn't drop his blades, but he lifted his hands and turned his daggers sideways so that the edges and point were not aimed at the other fae. It wasn't a surrender, simply a motion to cease the fight amicably. "Does this mean you forgive me?" Falin called back over his shoulder.

Did I forgive him? Probably not. I almost said as much, but then I realized what he was doing. If I forgave him, that enormous debt between us was mine to call him on.

The Shadow King glanced between us, his sword finally lowering as if he had just figured out what we were playing at. Falin nodded to him and lowered his weapons as well. He walked over, his blue eyes locked on me, cautious but expectant.

I felt the debt between us. It was still only potential. I couldn't forgive him in words alone—I actually had to mean it. But could I forgive him? I considered what I'd seen in the halls of the winter court. He did as his queen commanded. He obeyed and came to her call, but he had no choice. Caleb had agreed that Falin had to obey. I could forgive him what he had no choice in. I nodded to him and felt the debt between us solidify.

"You owe me a favor," I said, choosing my words slowly. "I'm your captive, but release me and your debt will be cleared."

He winced and bowed his head. "I cannot grant you a favor that contradicts a direct order from my queen."

Well, crap. Maybe I'd been wrong. Maybe he really only wanted to know I forgave him and it had nothing to do with the debt. He looked up at me again, and there were questions in the cool blue depths of his eyes, almost a plea. *No, he wants me to ask him for something.*

But what?

What would help me but not contradict the queen? He couldn't release me, but she hadn't given him the rest of her command, so what was he supposed to do with me next? Probably drag me back to the winter court. *That would be bad.*

"Fine," I said. "I'm your captive, but I request that you not return me to the winter court."

"Done." He gave a sharp nod, relief smoothing the dip that had gathered above his nose. He looked up at the other fae. "Is that sufficient for you, Shadow King?"

"Quite." The king sheathed his sword. "Now, my most darling Alexis, we have so much to discuss," he said, walking toward me with his arms open as if he meant to hug me.

The Shadow King might have just rescued me from the winter court, but the old saying about frying pans and fire was how my life tended to go, so I wasn't about to drop my guard. Or be hugged by a strange fae. I took a step toward Falin and the king stopped, frowning. The look he shot Falin was more than just unfriendly.

"I don't welcome the Winter Queen's bloodied hands into my court. You should go, boy," he said.

I shrugged. "Point us to the exit."

The king faltered, his handsome features showing true shock for a moment before he recovered. "But you've only just returned home, my dearest niece."

Chapter 32

———◦◦———

*H*ome? And perhaps an even bigger question—"Niece?"
The Shadow King smiled, and while there seemed
to be genuine affection in the expression, there was no
softness. His handsomeness had a deadly edge to it so that
even when he was relaxed, there was an alertness to his
movements, the possibility of violence. "Actually, my
great-grandniece, but such distinctions are tiresome. Kin
is kin."

I blinked at him and let PC slide to the ground. *An
uncle?* The world seemed a little more out of focus than the
moment before, even more unreal. *I have an uncle?* Well, a
great-granduncle. I'd never known any of my extended
family. My mother had died when I was young and my father refused to discuss the subject. Now I had an uncle. *And
he's the king of a Faerie court.*

"My father . . . ?"

The king shook his head and took both of my hands in
his. "He is, at times, a dear friend of mine, but not kin and
not of my court. No, it was your lovely mother, a darling of
a feykin, who was of my blood."

My knees went weak, and suddenly the king's hands
weren't grasping my hands but supporting me as I sagged
toward the ground. If the world had blurred at the idea that
the king was my uncle, the revelation that my mother was
feykin turned it upside down completely. I shook my head,

the idea battling with everything I knew and understood to be true.

"Maybe we should take a walk and get some air," the king said.

"That might be good," I mumbled, and even to me my words sounded far away, as if I were hearing them from the other side of a long tunnel.

The king helped me to my feet. He wrapped one arm around my waist to help steady me and held my hand in his so that my arm stretched across the front of his dark chest armor in a pose like some sort of shock-induced promenade. As he steered me toward the door I noted how much softer the armor was than it looked, and that it had been heated by his body. It was that almost blistering heat as well as Falin's voice calling my name that snapped me out of my stupor.

I yanked my hand back from the king's and spun out of his arm, nearly tripping on my full skirt. As I moved, I caught sight of the hands that had held me and I stopped, as if stuck between one step and the next. Like mine, his palms were coated in blood, but the blood on the Shadow King's hands looked thicker, darker, and fresher than the blood on mine. I shot a glance at my glamour-created gloves. They were spotless, despite his having touched them.

He must have seen me staring, because he glanced at his hands and shrugged. "The blood of my enemies and the enemies of my court. Unlike some, I don't hide it away." He shot a meaningful glance at Falin.

Okay then . . .

I grabbed the front of my enormous skirt and lifted it high enough that I could move freely. Then I bustled back to where Falin stood. He'd picked up PC at some point—for which I was extremely grateful; I didn't want to know what lurked in the thick shadows hugging every corner of the room. And with all the flying buttresses and recessed arches there were lots of corners. Whispers, thousands of them, seemed to crawl from the shadows, though I saw nothing in them. *I'd rather avoid them.*

I smiled my thanks to Falin for helping bring me back to my senses and then turned toward the king. "Sir—"

"You may call me uncle."

Uh, no. I couldn't. "Do you have another name?"

"The King of Shadows. The King of Secrets. The king of all things hidden in the dark."

Yeah, all of those titles fit the king, and his court. Well, actually, of his court I'd seen only the planebender so far, but secrets, shadows, and things hidden in the dark were apt descriptions of this room. Not really the name I was looking for, though.

"Do you have a shorter name?"

He laughed, and then gave me a small bow from the waist. "King Nandin, at your service." He smiled as he straightened, and it was a good, friendly smile that morphed an almost too handsome face into something softer. "I was saddened when your parents decided to leave Faerie, and more so to learn how cruelly the mortal world treated my poor grandniece. Disease, what a waste." He shook his head.

Even nineteen years later, mention of my mother's death sent a cold chill through my veins. The pang of loss never really fades, but eventually you just forget to feel it unless something happens to remind you. Tonight it washed through me with a sharper edge than it had in years. *Would you have told me what you were, what I am, if you'd lived?* I had no idea, and no way to ask. Her shade couldn't be raised.

"But look at you, my dear," Nandin continued, unaware of my dark thoughts. He circled me as if I were some unusual doll on display. In the dress the Winter Queen had made, I did *feel* like a doll, but I still didn't like the scrutiny, though I had to admit that at least some part of me was pleased that this long-lost uncle looked at me with approval. His warm smile was kind as he took my hand again. "I'd have never imagined that my grandniece's daughter would have blooded true. And a planeweaver at that. I am truly thrilled you have returned to my court."

I froze. *Is that what all this is about?* I looked into those kind eyes, which were so dark that the pupil was lost inside the black iris. They reflected nothing back at me. *This isn't about family. This is about adding a planeweaver to his court.* I looked away.

"I haven't—" I began, but Nandin cut me off.

"My dearest, you look ready to fall where you stand. Here I am, talking your ear off when what you really need is some sleep. We can continue this conversation in the morning. I had a guest suite prepared for you." He clapped his hands and two women stepped out of the shadows at our side.

Well, not exactly women.

The two fae were definitely female—their bare breasts attested to that—but their noses and top lips merged and extended into hooked and deadly sharp beaks. Neither woman had arms, but large wings where their arms should have been, with scythelike claws at the middle joint. They also had large talons sprouting from their toes—of which they had three per foot—as well as their heels, which at second glance might have actually been a fourth toe. Each fae had a motley covering of feathers, one a black so deep it reminded me of the raven constructs and the other a spotted brown that reminded me of a hawk.

Harpies. They had to be. I'd never actually seen a harpy before, but even if that wasn't the name the fae used for them among themselves, it had to be one of the names humans had given them at some point in history. I considered myself fairly open-minded, but there was something about the conglomeration of human and bird features in the harpies that made them hard to look at.

"Follow us," the hawk-feathered harpy said in a harsh, squawking voice.

I wanted to fall back a step and not follow them, but that was just fear, and I refused to be controlled by prejudice. In Faerie appearances meant even less than in the human world. The beautiful could be the most cruel and deadly, while the hideous monster might be the one most likely to help and bless you. I glanced at Falin.

Tight lines of worry creased the edges of his eyes and dipped at the corners of his mouth. He leaned closer to whisper, "It would be rude to dismiss the king's hospitality."

And then I might have enemies in two Faerie rulers.

I frowned and touched Holly's amulet. As it had in the halls of the winter court, the amulet told me that Holly was in multiple directions at once. *The spell really doesn't like doors in Faerie.* Of course, the doors in Faerie seemed terribly inconsistent, so it probably wasn't the charm's fault.

I sighed. Nandin wasn't wrong: with the amount of magic I used in my little trick with the skimmers and the fight with the hydra, not to mention the adrenaline-filled escape from the winter court, and then the shock of learning I had family in Faerie—*and that it was more than just my father who wasn't what he appeared*—I was ready to collapse. I hadn't actually expected that I'd waltz into Faerie, find Holly and the accomplice, and saunter back out all in one night. *Though a girl can wish, right?* I wasn't up to having to fight my way out of the shadow court if I refused and Nandin took it badly.

"Okay, we'll follow you," I finally said because there was no way in hell I was going to thank him for the room and open a debt between us.

The two harpies cocked their heads in a movement that was more birdlike than human. Then they glanced at Nandin as if seeking some answer to a question I hadn't heard anyone ask. *What did I say?*

The king ran his pointed beard through his thumb and index finger. "I suppose a room can be arranged for the Winter Queen's bloodied hands as well."

Falin stepped forward as if about to say something, and I grabbed his arm.

"He can stay with me." Because I'd feel a hell of a lot safer if he was with me, even if he might betray me to his queen at a word.

The king blinked in surprise and then his mouth twisted with distaste. "Your father surely does not approve of him."

Like I gave a rat's ass what my father thought. I didn't share that particular opinion with the king, though, as I doubted it would help my case. When I just stood there without saying a word—*the one skill I can credit my father with teaching me*—Nandin turned away.

"Fine. We will talk again at a late breakfast. Gilda and Naveen will provide you with anything you might need this night." He turned, his cloak fluttering behind him as he swept away. He paused just before he reached one of the arches. "Sweetest dreams, my dearest niece," he said, al-

most as if it was an afterthought. There was no affection in
the words this time. Then he stepped through the arch and
was gone.

That left us with the harpies, and I shuffled my feet, for
some reason even more uncomfortable with their presence
than I was before. They watched me with eyes that were a
little too round, but they said nothing as they led Falin and
me through countless dark corridors. Our footsteps echoed
in the seemingly endless space, contrasting with the whispers trickling out of the shadows.

We saw no other living soul until the harpies stopped in
front of a large wooden door. Then a short cloaked figure
stepped out of the shadows. It looked like the planebender
who'd opened the door through Faerie for me. I wasn't
positive, but he was the right height. I'd have liked to question him and ask him how he'd closed the tear like he had,
but the raven-feathered harpy turned on him.

"His majesty said you're not to talk to her. Not tonight,"
she said.

The figure stood very still for a moment; then the front
of the cloak split open and a hand emerged. It was a small
hand, somewhere between the size of a child's hand and a
teenager's, and the soul beneath shimmered with just a hint
of yellow. *Human.* He reached out as if he would touch me,
and the harpies swooped between us, their wings spread as
they squawked.

I stumbled back, away from the flutter of massive wings,
and Falin was just as suddenly in front of me, passing PC to
me as he drew his blades. And then, as fast as the squabble
had started, it was over. The harpies folded their wings,
stepping back, and the cloaked figure was gone, presumably back whence he had come.

Why doesn't Nandin want his people talking to me? Or
perhaps it was the planebender in particular.

I didn't have a chance to ask. Not that the harpies were
likely to tell me even if I did. The hawk-feathered harpy
used the claw at the joint of her wing to pull a circular handle, and the wooden door swung open.

The suite they showed me into included three rooms,
two of which were each as large as my entire apartment
and more opulent than my father's mansion. The hawk-

feathered harpy walked Falin and me through the whole suite while the raven-feathered one waited at the door. Once we'd seen the entire suite she turned back to me.

"Do you need anything?" she asked and then eyed my completely inappropriate ball gown. "Clothing? Food?"

"I'm good," I said, and then glanced at Falin. He shook his head, which was fine with me. I'd rather not accept any gifts from the fae, and my goal was not to eat while in Faerie—which meant I hoped I found Holly and the accomplice soon.

The harpies nodded and then left without a word. It wasn't until the door shut and I heard it latch that I realized there was no doorknob on the inside. Falin and I were locked in the suite, the rooms our cage. While it might have been the nicest prison I'd ever seen, a gilded cage is still a cage.

Chapter 33

⟶═◦ ◦═⟵

PC had thoroughly investigated the suite to his own sat-
isfaction and curled up in the very center of a bed that
looked big enough to sleep ten, but I was still pacing. I'd
told Falin the basics of what I'd learned since he left me at
his apartment. I didn't tell him everything—the shadows
in the room whispered, and I was afraid they listened
too—but I told him about Holly and the gist of what the
accomplice was attempting. Then it was my turn to demand some answers. "So why are you here? In Faerie, I
mean. I was more than a little shocked to see you at the
winter court."

"If you stop pacing, I'll tell you." He patted a spot on the
bed beside where he sat on the edge.

I didn't join him. If I crawled onto that bed I'd end up
asleep. Hell, I wasn't sure I wouldn't fall fast asleep still
standing, but I wanted to talk before I surrendered to sleep.
I did stop pacing, though, forcing myself to be still.

"I might have shocked you, but you scared the hell out
of me." He stood and walked across the room to join me,
since I wouldn't go to him. "I returned to my apartment
and, well, I imagine you know exactly what I found."

The aftermath of the gryphon attack.

"The police and the FIB were already there. At first I
thought they'd already grabbed you and shuttled you away
to Faerie. When I learned they hadn't, I went out searching

for you. I spent most of the night searching any spot I could think of that you might go. Where were you, by the way?"

"You wouldn't believe me if I told you," I replied, which was probably true, but again, with the shadows whispering in the corners, I didn't want to reveal too many secrets, even if these secrets belonged to my father.

"Well, sometime after midnight I returned to your apartment and these wooden blocks flung themselves at me. Then a pen lifted itself and started scratching out letters."

"Roy." He'd actually managed to find Falin and get a message to him. Of course, it sounded like it was the wrong message. "So if Roy told you I'd been nabbed by the skimmers, how did you end up in Faerie?"

"It took him thirty minutes to write '*Alex kidnap,*' and once he got that far, I just assumed . . . Incorrectly, apparently." Falin looked away.

"It worked out," I said, and shrugged, but the movement went off course somehow and ended up a slight sway.

"Come on, let's get some sleep," Falin said, his arms moving to mine to steady me. "You can't save the world if you fall over from exhaustion."

I let him lead me toward the bed, but as we walked I muttered, "I'm not trying to save the world. I'm just helping my friends and—" I cut off as we passed a large ebony desk. In the center of the desk sat a five-inch dagger with an ornate hilt. A dagger that looked suspiciously like *my* dagger, which I'd last seen when Caleb had dropped it in the hallway of the winter court. I shrugged off Falin's hands and moved to the desk, the sight of the dagger pushing back my exhaustion, at least a little. "How did this get here?"

The dagger buzzed lightly as I picked it up. It was definitely my dagger.

"Any number of ways," Falin said, looking at the blade from over my shoulder. "It's enchanted. This is Faerie and things move unexpectedly. The dagger likes you. Maybe a combination of all that. Maybe something else entirely."

Right. I fought the layers of skirt in the gown and shoved the dagger back in its holster. However it got to me, at least I was armed again. *Like that will do me a lot of good if I need to draw it fast.* What I wouldn't give to have my hip-huggers back, even with the pink chalk print. I resumed my pacing, using the energy that the short adrenaline burst had given me. Falin sighed as I passed him.

"If I could figure out how to open a rift like the plane-bender's door, I could search all of Faerie for Holly," I said, fidgeting with the amulet attached to my bracelet. I'd seen the boy close the rift. *Could I open a door as easily?* The accomplice could be preparing to attempt the next ritual while we were stuck as *guests* of the shadow court.

I stopped, rocking back on my heels. I could *try* to open a rift. I could think of several worst-case scenarios, but none quite as bad as the land of the dead merging with mortal reality, and preventing that was one of the items on my to-do list—once I got out of this room. I lowered my shields. I hadn't been able to completely drop my shields outside a circle or heavy wards for years without grave essence reaching for me. Hell, even inside a circle, the world always decayed around me and chilled wind tore at my skin. But there was no land of the dead in Faerie. I dropped my shields, and it was as if I'd shrugged off a weight I'd been carrying so long I didn't even notice it until it was suddenly lifted.

No wonder Rianna prefers staying in Faerie. I could get dangerously used to this freedom. There wasn't even Aetheric energy to entangle my psyche or for me to accidentally pull into reality. Of course, that also meant I had no magic except the energy stored in my ring, and I couldn't draw on the grave. The feeling of freedom washed away in a sense of powerlessness, though there was still magic in the air, just not a magic I was used to. But I could feel it, which meant I could touch it.

That didn't mean I *should*. I thought back to the skimmers standing around the rift by the river, drawing down energy they never should have been able to touch until one skimmer actually *ignited*.

I would leave the foreign energy alone.

Taking a deep breath, I concentrated on the space directly in front of my face. There was no Aetheric, no land of the dead, but there were multiple realities. I could feel them. *Okay, here goes.* Lifting my hands, I focused my will on parting the air in front of me as I forced my hands farther apart.

Reality moved but it didn't open.

I frowned at the air in front of my nose. I hadn't managed to open a rift, let alone a door. *And I've been opening rifts by accident all week.* It was just my luck that *trying* to do something I'd been doing by accident would lead to utter failure.

Well, not *utter* failure. The space in front of me was empty, as in, no other realities existed inside it. I'd actually cleared a space so nothing but Faerie remained. I reached out with my power and shoved. Reality moved again, bunching around the edges of empty space like a sheet shoved away from the edge of a bed. I waved my hand through the space, using no power.

Nothing happened.

I pushed with power, and reality shifted. *Which is weird, but not helpful.* Moving layers of reality didn't help us get out of this room. I reached out again, and then swayed as my knees buckled.

Falin caught my shoulders. "Okay, now I'm insisting that you go to sleep."

"I'm fine."

"You're trembling and you can barely stand."

Okay, he had me there. I leaned back against his chest, my eyes heavy. "You just want to get me in bed."

He chuckled, the sound vibrating through me where we touched. "I won't deny that, but I don't think you'll be much fun until you get some sleep."

True.

He leaned down and scooped me off the floor. I lifted a heavy arm around his shoulders and leaned into him.

"Do you love her?" I whispered the question so softly I wasn't even sure it made a sound, but Falin went stiff around me, every one of his muscles locking as he froze.

"What?"

If he'd heard me, he knew who I was talking about, so I didn't ask again. As the silence stretched, my chest tightened as if the dread I felt had become a hand pressing down on my lungs, slowing my heart.

Finally Falin said, "Once, I think that I thought I did."

"Do you still?"

"She's cold, calculating, and cruel, except for when she wants to be kind," he said, which I noticed wasn't exactly a "no," but he did start walking again.

"Why do they hate you? The other fae, that is?" Caleb, my father, and Nandin all disliked him, and I hadn't seen much evidence that the members of his own court liked him any better. "And why do they call you the queen's bloodied hands?"

"Your second question answers your first, at least in part," he said as he set me down on the edge of the bed. Then he took a step back, and conflict showed clearly in the hard angles of his face. He stared at me for a moment before he reached some conclusion, though it didn't seem that he liked what he'd decided. He closed his eyes and peeled off his glove. He opened his eyes again as he opened his hand, palm out so it faced me, but he kept his gaze down, not looking at me.

Thick, dark blood coated, or more accurately, *saturated*, Falin's palm. That didn't completely surprise me. I'd seen Falin kill before. Hell, he'd killed, or at least mortally injured, a gremlin to rescue me before we were even friends. The depth of the blood did shock me, at least a little. I could almost see it pooling on his skin, as if it would drip at any moment. *How many had to die at his hands for there to be so much blood?*

He looked at me, just a quick cut of a glance, and whatever he saw in my face made his shoulders tighten so fast his hand jerked back an inch. I don't know what I'd shown him, or if he'd only seen in my expression what he expected, but as he started to pull on his glove I jumped to my feet. I reached out for him, for his bloody hand. Yeah, the blood freaked me out, the fact he'd killed that many people scared the hell out of me, but I trusted that they needed killing. And besides, I wasn't exactly in a position to judge anyone for the blood on their hands.

When I reached for his hand, he jerked away from me. "Don't."

"I know it doesn't spread or wipe off." I told him.

He took a step farther back, still out of my reach, and studied my face as he pulled on his glove. "That's right, you touched the Shadow King." He shook his head. "I would never touch you with these hands, Alex. Not here."

I stared at him. Then I rolled down the top of one of the long opera gloves the queen had created for me and pulled it off my fingers. I held up my own bloody hand.

Falin's eyes flew wide. "No," he whispered, shaking his head. Then he grabbed my hand in both of his gloved ones. "No, Alex. Who—" He stopped. "Coleman."

I nodded. "I'm not exactly lily white either."

He gently pushed my fingers until they curled over my palm, then closed my entire fist in his hands. "You shouldn't be stained by this. Let me take it from you."

"What do you mean?"

"Let me take the stain from you." He led me back to the bed as he spoke, which was good, as I was starting to get that electrical vertigo that happens every time you blink when you're really, really tired. I covered a yawn with the back of my still-gloved hand as I sank down onto the bed, and he said, "I don't know if I can take it from someone outside my court, but let me try."

I blinked at him, my exhaustion making the conversation harder to follow. Then a very important fact from what he said hit me. "Wait—so the blood on your hands, it's not all from people you killed. You took the stain from other people?"

"I have killed enough, Alex, believe me. But no, only a drop of it is blood that I personally spilled. I carry all the victims of the winter court. The taint from every duel, every monarch who killed to rise to or ensure power, and every soldier who killed in every war since the very first winter came to the world."

My stomach gave a little somersault. "How old are you?"

"Not so old as you're thinking right now," he said, and he smiled for the first time since this conversation began. "I was born after the Magical Awakening, and I took on the role of the queen's bloodied hands only a few decades ago. There have been many more before me who killed at the queen's bidding and carried the court's taint."

"So, circling back to my original question, they hate you because you have the worst job ever?"

He smiled again, but this time it was not a happy one. "Some hate. Some fear. Some are simply repulsed. I carry a lot of death on my hands. Nearly immortal beings do not like to be reminded of their mortality. The blood also gives me some benefits that make the other fae distrustful. Any weapon that I wield is deadly, even if it might not normally be so to fae. Wounds that I inflict are more likely to be fatal, while I can survive wounds that would normally kill—"

Yeah, I've seen that one firsthand.

"—The blood also passed to me knowledge and skills from the warriors who came before me, so despite the fact that I am little more than a child according to many of the fae, I can battle the ancients and possibly win. That scares the fae, and makes me rather unwelcome."

I could see why. I crawled farther up on the bed and Falin followed.

"Let me take this taint from you. It would make no difference to me, but all the difference to you."

"No." I pulled my hand from him and fought the opera glove back over my fingers. While I wanted the blood gone, it wouldn't be right to give it away. I'd been the one who killed Coleman. Hell, I'd more than killed him, I'd cannibalized his soul, which had to be worse. While Falin might be able to take away the blood that Faerie forced to manifest on my hands, he couldn't remove the fact that I'd taken a life. I'd made a decision, and even if it haunted my nightmares, I still thought it was the right decision.

Once I'd pulled on the glove, I collapsed in the middle of the bed beside PC. The pillows were down and soft, the sheets under me silk and smooth. My eyes closed.

"Alex, you want to lose the dress, or at least the boots?"

I didn't bother opening my eyes. "Not really." I was going to sleep—probably whether I liked it or not. Besides, I didn't know what kind of wake-up call the king planned for the morning. I didn't want to be caught half dressed or barefoot.

The bed didn't even shift as Falin joined me. I was lying on top of the turned-down covers, so he didn't try to crawl under them. He slid his arm under my neck, and I scooted closer to him, resting my head on his shoulder. PC stood, circled twice, and then apparently decided he wanted human comfort more than a pillow. He climbed over me and tried to wedge himself between our hips, though six pounds of muscle didn't give him a lot of moving power. He ended up stretched out across both of us.

"I really messed up with the queen, didn't I?" I asked, close enough to sleep that I was thinking out loud.

Falin's arm tightened around me. "You did okay in the beginning. The dancers were a test. The first was an insult. If you'd accepted the changeling it would have acknowledged that you were not fae enough to be treated with the respect a Sleagh Maith deserves. The second was closer to your status, and was to appeal to your uniqueness. Offering the third accepted you as royal, and had you danced with Ryese, she'd have been planning your wedding ceremony by the end of the night. I think you threw her when you refused all three and then chose your independent green man." His thumb drew small circles where it touched my arm. "It was my actions that likely bought you an enemy."

"So why serve her?"

"I have no choice. I am bound to her, to her will and her word. When I became her bloodied hands, I became hers completely and truly. A monarch's bloodied hands can be her deadliest subject, so the bond is the curse's fail-safe. It makes me both a weapon against my queen's enemies and ensures that I pose no threat to her." He pulled me closer to him. "I won't be bound forever. The curse will pass to the next bloodied hands when my service to her is complete."

I thought about this as sleep pressed hard against me, but I wasn't quite ready for it to come yet. "Why did you become her bloodied hands? Why would anyone?" Power, maybe, though it came with the loss of choice and will, so it didn't seem worth it. *Love?* I cringed, fearing that would be what he told me.

His gloved hand moved up to my face, and he brushed back my curls. "I was born to be what I am." When I stretched to look up at him, he went on. "I was switched as an infant, and I grew up believing I was human. When I was sixteen I was brought to the court for the first time, to learn what I was, what I was meant to be. The queen's assassin. Her knight. Her bloodied hands. Sleagh Maith, while one of the most human-looking fae, have the lowest tolerance for iron and technology. With the changes in the world since the Awakening, she wanted her knight to be able to function as her great champion in both Faerie and the mortal world. That's why she had me switched." He paused. "I see the fae woman who birthed me once in a while. She let the baby she switched for me grow until he is about four. He's a handsome boy. I wonder who he would have been, if it hadn't been for me."

I wrapped my arm tighter around him and hugged him because I didn't know what to say. Though his delivery of the information was casual, there was a rawness to it that spoke of old pain. I recognized it. I'd heard it in my own voice before. So I held him, and he held me back, neither of us saying anything. I was drifting when he finally broke the silence.

"Alexis?"

"Mmm?"

He was quiet for so long that I thought he might have fallen asleep. I cracked my eyes open and found him looking at me. Then, as if he'd changed his mind about what he wanted to say, he pressed a kiss against the top of my head. "Go to sleep."

I did.

Chapter 34

❦❦❦

I was having the nightmare again. The Blood Moon hung red and swollen over my head. Coleman stood by my sister's bed, a dagger in his decomposing hand. He looked at me, half his face sloughing off as he leered. He lifted the blade.

I screamed and tried to run but tripped over the hem of my gown. A gown trimmed with delicate ice roses. I'd never worn a gown in the dream before.

"Alex! Alex, wake up."

Falin was suddenly in the dream, standing beside me. He shook my shoulders. "Wake up."

I blinked at him. The Blood Moon vanished. So did the bed and Coleman. But I was still standing in the exact same spot, Falin holding my shoulders. PC pawed the air in front of me.

I looked around. We were surrounded by shadows with no discernible source. And nothing else. I took a step forward and loose sand shifted under my feet. *Where in Faerie is a desert of sand and shadows?* I frowned. And why could I tell there were shadows in the darkness? I didn't know, but I did know that the shadows were somehow separate from the darkness.

"Where are we?"

Before Falin could answer, a scream shattered the darkness. My head shot up as a man in striped pajamas hurtled through the air, headed straight for us. His arms flailed around him, but that did little to slow his free fall. I ducked, which wasn't the most rational decision, but how often did people fall toward me? Not exactly a situation I prepared for. When the man was still a dozen or more yards over our heads, he vanished as suddenly as he had appeared.

I straightened, gasping for breath I didn't remember losing. "What was that about?"

"I don't know," Falin said, staring at the sky, "but he's done that a couple of times. He never hits the ground."

Right. I grabbed PC, cuddling him in my arms. The trembling dog didn't object to the attention. "Where are we?" I asked again.

"If I had to guess? The realm of nightmares."

Oh, now that sounded like a fun place. "How did we get here?"

Falin shook his head. "When I woke to your screaming, we were already here."

Perfect. Had someone brought us here? But who? The Shadow King? And, more important, why?

"How do we get out?" I asked, searching the darkness and shadows for a door, or even a wall.

The darkness looked exactly the same on every side.

"I think we're picking a direction at random," Falin said, and then pointed left. It looked as good—or, really, as creepy—a direction as any.

The powder-fine sand shifted under our feet as we walked. We had to stop at one point as a troupe of clowns with bright hair and fake noses chased a woman across our path, leaving behind the sound of squeaking shoes in their wake. Then we passed a man in a dentist's chair which appeared to spring right out of the sand. A teenage girl stood butt naked in front of her locker as groups of teenagers stood around her, laughing. A small boy huddled under his blanket, clutching a stuffed tortoise as something with gleaming claws and slimy scales crawled out from under his bed.

"They aren't really here, are they?" I asked as I watched walls attached to nothing close in on a cowering man. Both he and the walls vanished as the walls fell over him.

"Yes and no. They are real human psyches dreaming. But physically? No," Falin said, keeping a hand at the small of my back. I wasn't sure if the contact was for my benefit or his. *What would his nightmare be?* I probably didn't want to know.

"No chance we're just dreaming at this point, huh?" I asked as an airplane dove toward the sand, disappearing on impact.

"The same dream? You, me, *and* the dog?"

Okay, he had a point.

The shadows around us had been pressing closer. I thought it was probably my imagination—after all, I still wasn't convinced there even *were* shadows—but between one step and the next, the shadows surged forward. A solid wall of darkness sprang up around us on all sides. There is an old saying about an abyss and the abyss staring back. This darkness stared back.

I swallowed, clutching PC tighter. Falin unsheathed his daggers. The blades gleamed, as if reflecting light I couldn't find. I fought my enormous skirt, trying to reach my own dagger, but with PC clutched in one arm, reaching the top of my boot was no easy matter. My heart hadn't exactly been at a calm and steady pace before, but now it crashed so loudly I could hear nothing else. I wished I wasn't able to see either.

There were shapes in the darkness. The mind tends to try to shield itself from what it can't handle, so it accepted only pieces. Dozens of claws here, three-inch-long fangs there, some patches of molted fur, a large pus-filled abscess, scales. The nightmares pressed closer. *This is where I pinch myself and wake up, right?* Except I couldn't seem to make my body move. My mouth hung open, but I'd long since run out of air from screaming.

The darkness loomed closer. Then the nightmares poured over me. I lost sight of Falin as dozens of rough hands grabbed at my skin and tangled in my hair, my gown. I huddled around PC. He whined, a loud, high-pitched cry of panic.

I lost the ground to darkness. Lost any sense of up or down. There was just darkness and *creatures.* I felt like I was flying, or sliding, or maybe the nightmare realm moved around me. I didn't know. All I knew was that the nightmares had found me. And the nightmares were taking me.

Chapter 35

A growl, low and rumbling, cut through the skittering and gibbering of the nightmares. I'd long since given up on reaching my dagger, or fighting the dozens of hands grabbing me, and now I simply clung to PC, trying to keep him from being ripped from my grasp. As the threatening growl sounded again, PC gave another whine of pure terror. His heartbeat fluttered against my palm, his trembling threatening to shake him apart. I wished I could comfort him, but I felt exactly the same way.

The growl sounded a third time, and then I heard a loud, meaty *thunk*.

The nightmares' chittering rose in pitch before falling completely silent. Then, as quickly as the nightmares had descended, they recoiled, releasing me and drawing back. Sand crunched under my boots again, and I collapsed to my knees.

My breath escaped me in fast, shallow huffs—too fast. I was close to hyperventilating. I forced myself to take a deeper breath and hold it as I glanced around. I was alone in the darkness. All alone. No shadows. No nightmares. And no Falin.

I swallowed and took another deep breath. PC's front paws were locked around my arm, his claws digging into my biceps. I already had several bright pink scratches from them, but as far as I could tell from my quick assessment, that was the only injury I'd sustained in the ordeal, despite the nightmares' horrific appearances. My dress wasn't even torn.

The darkness surged again. I tried to jump to my feet, but my legs buckled and I landed on my ass in the sand. But the darkness didn't touch me. It churned several yards away from me and then drew back like a curtain, revealing Falin.

I climbed to my feet, forcing my shaking legs to cross the uneven sand. I stumbled more than once, and he met me halfway.

"Are you okay?" he asked, grabbing me by the elbow and helping me keep my balance.

"I should be asking you that." Whereas the nightmares had left me uninjured, he was covered in deep scratches, his fancy suit ruined and stained.

He looked me over, and then nodded. "I'll be fine."

He dropped my arm as he glanced around. Apparently satisfied that we weren't in immediate danger, he ripped a section of more or less clean material from his ruined shirt and meticulously wiped the blood from first one and then the other dagger.

I watched for only a moment, then turned to stare out at the oppressive darkness. "Why do you think they pulled back?" I asked, searching for shadows with no source.

Falin shook his head, and the low, rumbling growl I'd heard earlier filled the darkness in front of me. I froze. Falin's head shot up, the daggers gripped in his hands and ready to kill.

A hulking shadow separated itself from the darkness, its gait slow and cautious. At first all I could make out was its bright, red-rimmed pupils, but then I recognized the dog-like form and realized I'd seen a similar creature before. It was a barghest, like the one I'd seen in the Bloom with Rianna. In fact, it might have even been the *same* barghest.

"Desmond?" I asked, my voice sounding every bit as frightened and unsure as I felt. *So much for putting on a tough act.*

The barghest inclined its head, which might have been acknowledgment or might just have meant it was preparing to attack. Its eyes flickered toward Falin, focusing on the still-exposed daggers, before moving back to me. Then the doglike fae reared back onto its hind legs. He balanced like that, straightening, and as he straightened, he changed, so by the time he stood completely erect he was a man, not a beast.

"You should not be in the nightmare realm, old friend of my Shadow Girl," he said, striding forward.

Falin stepped in front of me, blocking the barghest's path, and the beast-turned-man stopped. It regarded us with eyes that hadn't changed in the least, still dark with pupils ringed in red. His hair had the inky blackness of his beast form's coat, and it blended with the dark cloak he wore like living shadows pulled around his body.

I placed a hand on Falin's arm. He would be able to feel the tremble in my fingers, but I didn't want him to attack the barghest unless he truly posed a threat. Shadow Girl was a name the fae had given Rianna, and I hadn't missed the possessive he'd used when he referred to her. Besides, I'd heard him growl before the nightmares had retreated. He may well have been the reason they'd fled. Whether that meant he was helping us or not was yet to be determined. First I wanted to confirm that he was who I thought. "You're Desmond, aren't you?"

He nodded. "That is one name I've used. Now we must leave this place. The denizens of Faerie are forbidden in this realm."

Why would they want to come here in the first place? I didn't ask that question. Instead I asked, "Do you know the way out?"

Again Desmond nodded. I glanced at Falin. His eyes were narrowed, his expression wary, but he shrugged. What choice did we have? It wasn't like we were doing so well at finding a way out on our own. Falin sheathed one dagger, but he kept the second one in his hand, though he pointed it at the ground, not at Desmond.

"Which way?" I asked, turning my attention back to Desmond.

"Oh, this is good," a new voice said, making me jump. "The Winter Queen's bloodied hands, a barghest, and a planeweaver all walk into a nightmare. What will the punch line be?"

I whirled around. There had been nothing but sand behind me before, but now, not three feet away, stood a large black chair covered in intricate carvings that reminded me a little too much of the nightmares. And in the chair was a fae, his feet kicked over one ornate arm, and his back leaning against the other, his hands behind his head. He wore a grin that looked comfortable on his face, a very Cheshire cat–like expression, as if he had a secret that amused him at our expense. Dark hair fell around his high cheekbones in the kind of chaotic rumple that had to be intentional. I realized as I looked at that goth-emo hair that he was the first Sleagh Maith I'd seen with hair shorter than shoulder length.

PC growled, and I rubbed his head absently, trying to shush him as I stared at the newcomer. He hadn't been there a moment before, but I could see through glamour, and both he and the chair were real. Judging by the throne-like seat, I guessed we must have found the local royalty. But hadn't Desmond said this place was forbidden to the fae?

"Are you the king of the nightmare realm?" I asked.

"There is no king of the nightmare realm," both Falin and Desmond said, nearly simultaneously.

The new fae's smile widened. "Ah, but if there were one, I would be he. Kyran, at your service." He didn't rise but from his reclined position made small loops with his wrist like someone putting on airs while bowing.

"He's an outcast," Desmond said, his voice all but a growl. "A scavenger scraping up the refuse the courts have discarded."

"I like to think of myself as an opportunist," the self-proclaimed king said, swinging his feet off the arm of the chair so he could stand. "Why should this magnificent place go to waste simply because the high king fears mortals?"

"What's going on? What are they talking about?" I whispered to Falin. He'd armed himself again, but for now he only watched the other two fae.

Falin glanced at me, and for a moment I thought he wouldn't answer. Then he said, "From what I've heard, when the high king and the court royalty decided the fae would announce their existence to mortals, it was also decreed that courts would no longer be allowed to build power using mortal fear. It was determined that if mortals knew fear was as powerful a magic source as belief, they'd turn against us. The Shadow King was forced to sever the nightmare realm from his court, changing it from one of the most powerful courts before the Awakening to the least powerful after the Awakening. I don't know who he is"—Falin nodded at the cocky fae—"but he's clearly trying to establish a court in the nightmare realm."

"Trying?" Kyran said. "*Trying?* This court will build itself. Faerie may have severed its connection to this realm, but mortals have always feared the dark. They have always imagined monsters in dark shadows, and here those monsters take life from that fear."

"But they are trapped here," Desmond said. "Only the sleeping enter this place, and when they wake, the nightmares are left behind."

"For now." Kyran grinned again, a grin that said he knew something that no one else did. "For now I am merely a king of dreams, but one day?" He lifted his hands in an exaggerated shrug.

"Why did you bring us here?" I asked, holding PC tight.

"Me bring you here? My dear, you're the planeweaver. You dreamed yourself and your friends right into your own nightmare. You should shield better." He slung his feet around so he sat fully facing us in the chair and leaned forward. "I must say, that was an original entrance. I give you nine points for style, but only three for the nightmare itself. I mean, really, what was that? You must have a better imagination than just rehashing that same dream night after night."

I looked away. The only person I'd told my nightmare to was Death, and that was because he'd been there and I needed to talk to someone. I didn't like it that this random wannabe king had been watching my nightly terror.

"We should go," I said, glancing at Desmond.

The barghest nodded, the red in his eyes flashing despite the lack of real light.

"Going so soon?" the nightmare kingling asked. "But we still have time." He reached around the back of the throne and retrieved a slender pole with a large hourglass suspended in a ring at the top. Currently all of the sand was in the bottom of the hourglass. The kingling jumped to his feet, studying the glass. "Wait for it," he said, holding up a single finger. "And . . . now." He flipped the glass over and the fine white sand inside began trailing down from one hemisphere of the hourglass to the other.

"See, plenty of time," Kyran said, and then glanced at the glass again. The sand wasn't pouring out of the top globe, but it wasn't crawling either. "Well, maybe not *plenty*."

"Time until what?" Falin asked, his own gaze fixed on the hourglass.

Kyran only smiled that Cheshire cat grin again.

I leaned in closer to Falin. "Are we sure this guy is supposed to be king and not court jester?"

"I heard that! And here I was going to help you." He left the pole with the hourglass stationed in the sand and then tossed himself onto his throne again.

"Help us with what?" Falin's voice sounded more than just suspicious.

"Why, with finding the door she's looking for." Kyran pointed at me.

Door? Was I looking for a particular door? Actually, maybe I was. I placed a hand over Holly's amulet, feeling for the charm. Unlike almost every other time I'd tested the charm in Faerie, this time it gave me a strong pull in only one direction. My heart fluttered. *Found her.* Or at least found the right direction.

"This way," I yelled, starting off at a run.

"Oh, this should be good," Kyran's voice said as I dashed in the direction Holly's amulet had pointed.

I didn't bother glancing back. At least, not until Falin's hand closed around my arm. Then I looked back. I was still running full tilt, or at least my legs told me I was, but he was standing still and I wasn't pulling ahead of him. *What the hell?*

"Nightmare realm, remember?" Kyran said from his throne, which was still right behind me. "Nightmares don't exist in real space and yet they exist everywhere. It makes for a very interesting landscape, don't you think?"

No, I didn't. Right now it made for an irritating landscape, especially when I'd thought I had my first lead since reaching Faerie.

"May I?" Kyran asked, holding out his palm. When I just glanced at him, he jerked his chin toward the ruby amulet clipped to my charm bracelet.

"Why?"

"Didn't I tell you I was going to help you find your door? Now, you're wasting time. Look at how much sand you've already lost."

We all glanced at the slowly filling bottom globe of the hourglass.

"What time is it counting down to?" I asked.

As when Falin had asked, Kyran only smiled. Then he threw his arms high over his head and stretched. "Ask me again. Maybe I'll tell you next time."

Right. I turned to Desmond. "You said you could get us out of here?"

He nodded.

"Wait!" Kyran leapt off his throne. "The barghest can lead you out of this realm, but he cannot lead you to what you seek. Let me find your door, and it will be the one you want."

"And why would you do that?" Falin asked, sizing up the nightmare kingling. Now that he was actually standing up straight and not slouching or leaning over the hourglass, he proved to be as tall as Falin, but thin, as if someone had stretched him to that height.

Kyran smiled. "So suspicious, but then, look at whom you serve. You've reason to be." He walked around Falin in large, exaggerated steps without bending his knees. "Perhaps my goal is to be remembered kindly by Faerie's youngest plane-weaver. Would that explanation have enough political maneuvering to ring true for you?"

It wouldn't surprise me, though he hadn't actually said that was his purpose.

"If you find me my door, I will owe you nothing? I'm not asking for your help," I told him, and he gave me a small bow.

"Of course not. You will take on no debt to me."

I stared at him, looking for the loopholes in his statement, but if he would really help us just to earn my goodwill, I didn't see a downside to that.

"How does it work?" I asked, still cautious as I searched for the catch.

"Simple. The nightmare realm touches every dark shadow where anyone has ever feared what might be hiding in the depths or believed was cast by a monster—which means as long as your room has a shadow, I can find the door."

"And we'll come to no harm by going through the door?"

"My vow on it," he said, holding up his hand in an oath.

I glanced at Falin. He still looked skeptical, but he shrugged. It was my decision.

Finally I nodded. "Okay."

"Splendid," Kyran said at the same time Desmond stepped closer to me.

"If you follow his path I will not follow," the barghest said.

I studied him. I didn't know his motives for helping me either, but I was interested in his opinions. "Is his path dangerous?"

"Not more than any other," he said, and then took a step back. "Be safe, old friend of my Shadow Girl. She needs you." He fell forward and by the time his hands hit the sand they weren't hands but paws and he was the same over-sized black dog I'd first met. Then he turned and was gone.

"I'll still need the charm," Kyran said, holding out his hand again.

The amulet was the only link I had to Holly, and my only chance of finding her and the accomplice. If something happened to it . . . I chewed at my bottom lip.

"You'll return it?"

"I think you're even more skeptical than he is. You're too young for that," he said, but when I still didn't hand it over he glanced at the sand in the hourglass and then said, "Yes, damn it, I'll return it. In the same condition and a timely manner even. Happy?"

Taking a deep breath, I unclasped Holly's amulet and handed it over. As Kyran's hand closed around the ruby, the shadows around us shifted, racing past. I expected the nightmares to return and grab us, but eventually the shadows settled again. Directly in front of me stood a vaguely rectangular shadow, as if it were being cast by an unseen dresser.

"This would be the one, I believe," he said, handing me back the amulet.

I wrapped my fingers around it. He was right. The amulet pointed toward the rectangular shadow.

"Now what?" Falin asked, and I noticed his daggers had appeared again. He must have also thought the nightmares were returning.

"Now we step through." Kyran held out his hands to us.

We were going to walk through a shadow? Well, why not? Since arriving in Faerie I'd walked through walls, doorways that didn't show the correct room beyond their thresholds, and a hole in reality. Why not walk through a shadow?

I clasped the amulet back onto my bracelet before accepting the kingling's hand. "I suggest a deep breath," he said. "This will be cold." Then he stepped forward and the shadow overtook us.

Disorientation hit hard as between one step and the next my boots left sand and landed on crimson-colored carpet. My stomach flipped, like the moment at the top of a roller coaster when you're hanging upside down but gravity hasn't caught on yet so you hang suspended before crashing into the shoulder harness. If I'd looked around and discovered I was standing on the ceiling, waiting for reality to realize it and drop me, I wouldn't have been surprised. But I wasn't on the ceiling. I was in a plain, sparsely decorated room. The shadow we'd stepped through was cast by a large wardrobe that dominated most of one wall; a small bed huddled against another wall; and in the far corner of the room was Holly.

I let PC slide to the floor as I crossed the room in three steps. Her eyes were open, and she sat perfectly straight, her hands resting on her knees. She wore a pair of pink silk pajama bottoms and a white camisole that she must have changed into before lying down and the curse overtaking her. She didn't move as I approached.

"Holly?" Not so much as a twitch. I waved my hand in front of her face. "Hey."

Falin joined me. He gently moved her face toward us, but she didn't even blink. "She's entranced."

"But a pretty doll," Kyran said.

I startled, spinning around to face the nightmare king-

ling. I hadn't realized he was still in the room. I'd expected
him to return to his realm after he'd delivered us to Faerie,
but as he settled against the wall, he looked like he planned
to hang around.

I frowned at him. "She's not a doll."

"All changelings are dolls. Some are just more autonomous than others."

Dread slid under my skin. She wasn't a changeling. Was
she? How much time in Faerie could pass during a day in
the mortal realm?

"Damn, Holly, snap out of it." I shook her shoulders. She
slumped forward, and the dread sank deeper into my skin.
I had found her. I'd traipsed through three courts, but *I'd
found her.* And I still couldn't rescue her.

"It won't help," a squeaky, high-pitched voice said, and I
jumped.

A wooden birdcage hung in the corner of the room, but
the creature inside wasn't a bird. It was a small fae. He was
no taller than five inches and covered with fur, but his face
was more human than animal and he wore clothes like a
man.

I stood and walked over to the cage. "What won't help?"

"Calling, shaking, or any means you use to gain her attention," the little creature said, stepping closer to the edge
of the cage, but not approaching the bars. "The mistress
wasn't sure if she'd need her, so the fire witch waits. Nothing will wake her but the mistress."

I shook my head. "That's unacceptable." We'd carry her
out of here if we had to. Well, I'd probably ask Falin to do
it, but we'd get her out of Faerie.

I stepped closer to the cage and then faltered. Something was wrong in that corner of the room; I could feel it
with every atom of my being. "Iron," I hissed as I recognized the slight tingle. "There's iron encased in the cage
bars." Which meant this fae was not a pet but a prisoner. I
reached for the door, but Falin grabbed my wrist, pulling
me back.

"You don't know what he is, why he's in there, or what
he'll do if released," Falin said.

I frowned and studied the little creature. It had small
pink ears that looked like soft mouse ears where they stuck

up around its brown hat, and big round eyes atop a human nose and mouth. It didn't look particularly dangerous—but looks could be deceiving.

"Who are you?" I asked the small creature.

"Tiddlywinx, best glamour spinner in the oak ring," he said, doffing his pointed hat and giving me a deep bow.

"Is the oak ring a place?" I asked Falin under my breath.

"Probably just a ring of oaks, and this little guy is as likely to be the only one who lives there as he is to be the best glamour spinner," he said.

I mouthed, *Oh,* and Tiddlywinx balled his small fists on his hips as he glared at Falin. "You ruin a good title, Sleagh Maith."

A glamour spinner, huh?

"I think I met a hydra you made," I told the small man.

He shot up at that, his hands clasped in front of him. "My hydra? You saw it? Was it the best hydra you'd ever seen?"

"It was the only hydra I've ever seen." Well, now we knew where the glamour on the constructs originated. The question was whether Tiddlywinx was a willing participant, as his excitement suggested, or coerced, as the cage made it appear.

Falin must have had the same thought because he asked, "Why did you cast those glamours?"

"Because if I refused she brought in more iron." He shuddered. I imagined a fae as small as he was couldn't handle very much iron.

"And what will you do if released?" I asked him, because as long as he wasn't a creature of ultimate darkness, I was letting him out of that cage.

"I will owe you a massive debt, Sleagh Maith."

My brows creased as I glanced at Falin. "He means you," he whispered.

"Oh, I'm not—" Actually, I had no idea what I was or wasn't at this point. I dropped the sentence halfway through and changed direction. "And after that where will you go?"

"Back to my oak ring. I have to see if the squirrels stole all the stores I've been gathering for winter."

Good enough for me. But I still had one more question.

"Your mistress—who is she and where did she go?"

The little man shook his head. "A witch of power. She was trapped until recently and now that she's free, she still can't be with her lordly love. I think it addled her brain. As to where she went, I know not."

Well, at least it was more than we knew before. I released the latch on the cage and opened the door. Falin didn't try to stop me this time, but stepped aside as the little man jumped free.

"Oh, so much better," Tiddlywinx said, scampering in a small circle around the carpet. PC, who'd been lying with his head on his paws, jumped up to give chase. When Tiddlywinx saw PC, he gave a loud squeak, which did nothing to convince the dog the little fae wasn't a toy.

"No! Bad dog!" I yelled, but PC was already into the game, which I became part of once I started trying to grab him.

Tiddlywinx turned suddenly, and he wasn't a cute mouselike fae anymore, but a giant wolverine. PC yelped, stopping so fast that his back legs skidded out under him. The wolverine charged.

"No! Don't you hurt my dog."

The beast stopped and abruptly transformed back into Tiddlywinx as Falin scooped up my now terrified dog.

"I meant no harm," the little fae said. "I'm indebted to you, dear lady. What do you wish of me?"

"Can you break the curse on Holly, or at least tell me how?"

"That is magic far outside my power."

Okay, that sucked. I glanced at Falin, and his lips thinned a moment before he said, "Could you provide us transport to a bar called the Eternal Bloom?" When I gave him a questioning look, he said only, "We can't pass through the winter court."

Right. The queen was probably out for my blood, and Falin—well, if he returned, he'd be hers again.

Tiddlywinx slumped, his lip protruding. "I could spin a glamour of the most beautiful horses you've ever seen, but I cannot create a door they could carry you through."

And that would be a long-winded "no." I sighed. *How the hell are we going to get back to Nekros if the only door*

that opens to the city is attached to the winter court? I
guessed we could take the next-closest door and rent a car
to drive back. It would suck, but it would work.

"I might be able to assist you," Kyran said, pushing off
the wall, "but if you plan to help your friend, you'd best
hurry." He reached into the shadow and pulled the hourglass on its pole into the room. I didn't bother asking him
about it this time.

But he was right. I needed to figure out what to do about
Holly. I turned toward her, and Tiddlywinx scampered
around me. He vaulted onto the leg of Holly's pants and
scurried up to her knee.

"Good lady, I still owe you a favor," he said, balancing
on the top of Holly's thigh.

She didn't flinch. Her focus didn't even move, and she
was rather squeamish about anything that the word "ro-
dent" could be applied to. I had the feeling that Tiddlywinx
would count as one of those in her opinion. *This is not a
good sign.*

"We'll work out the details later," I told him.

"But—"

"You heard her," Kyran said.

I turned around and frowned at him. I noticed Falin did
the same. *What's the deal with this guy?* He reminded me of
that kid at school who really wants to be friends with you,
but you just don't like him. Not that I'd really known Kyran
long enough not to like him; I just didn't trust him.

Tiddlywinx waited a minute more. Then he said, "Fine"
and vanished.

I rocked back onto my heels and studied Holly. *There
has to be something I can do.* Reaching with my senses, I
scanned the curse on her. It was active now, draped over
her like a net made of spider silk. I didn't have the magic
needed to be a curse-breaker, but maybe now that this one
was out of its shell, I'd be able to do something with it.
Maybe. Just maybe.

"Alex?" Falin stared at me, his eyes sweeping over my face.
"What is it? You have that look like you have an idea and you
know it's a bad one but you're going to try it anyway."

I did have an idea. And he was right. "I can see magic," I
said, moving to stand directly in front of Holly. "I mean,

ever since I began seeing the Aetheric, I started to be able to see the shape of magic and the color of spells."

Anyone could see magic while inside the Aetheric, and most witches checked their spells when they were there to make sure that no darkness or corruption had contaminated the spell or their bodies while they were spellcasting. Inside the Aetheric magic could be touched and pulled apart, separating light from dark. If a witch was cursed, and she could get to the Aetheric, she could pull the curse off her psyche, bypassing the need for counterspells. Of course, she had to do it herself. Healers had been working for years on a way to pull patients to the Aetheric with them, but so far no one had found a way to make two psyches end up in the same place.

But I didn't need to travel to the Aetheric to see magic—or to touch it. The Aetheric plane was thin to nonexistent here, but magic still functioned. *Which means this might work.*

I opened my shields. Holly's soul, which I'd already been seeing as pale yellow, became clearer, almost outshining her features. But not all of it was glowing. The bite marks from the construct had healed and vanished from her skin, thanks to healing spells, but they scarred her soul with a snaking cobweb of magic. The spell was a deep gray with veins of red. Not the most malicious spell I'd ever seen, but clearly effective enough.

Well, here goes. I reached out both with my hand and with my psyche. Part of me wanted to squeeze my eyes shut because I was terrified that I would accidentally grab her soul instead of the spell, but if I closed my eyes, that chance increased. *Just be careful.*

The spell felt slimy to my senses. In contrast, her soul underneath was a thing of heat and life. It was easy to tell the two apart, but not quite as easy to separate them. I needed something for the spell to latch on to, or maybe something to disrupt it. Drawing on the power stored in my ring, I sent a focused tendril of pure magic into the spell. In theory, the spell would either latch on to the new source of power and try to jump to me—though hopefully I'd be faster and have time to cut off the stream while the spell was between hosts—or the magic would give the spell a bit of a jolt. Or it would do nothing, but that was a bad option so I didn't think too hard about it.

The outline of the spell turned fuzzy as my magic hit it. The edges curled like the legs of a dying spider, and I seized my opportunity. I snatched the spell in the very center and tugged. It pulled free, wiggling in my grasp for a moment. Then, without the physical connection to Holly to sustain it, the spell dissolved.

Holly blinked. "Alex? Oh, my God, Alex!" She threw her arms around my neck. "Is it really gone?" The heat of her skin burned against my bare shoulders and she jerked back. "God, Al, you're cold. Are those icicles on your dress?"

"It's a long story." I stood, pulling her up with me. "Holly, do you know what happened to you? Who did this?"

"I remember." She wrapped her arms across her chest as her green eyes took on a distant, haunted look. "Al, she's crazy. She left not long ago, saying she had one more spell to cast. She said this ritual would set her free." Holly shook her head and then suddenly went completely still. Her hand flew to her mouth, her fingers pressed against her lips. "I didn't," she whispered.

"Didn't what?" Oh, crap, what sick thing had the accomplice made Holly do while she was under the spell?

Tears slid down Holly's cheeks. "I ate it. I ate Faerie food."

Chapter 36

❖

Faerie food. It was addictive to mortals. Always. Even a single bite.

I gave my friend a hug, because she needed it. "We'll figure something out," I promised. We could get it shipped out or something. We'd find a way. It didn't have to be the end of the world. But if we didn't find and stop the accomplice before she managed to merge realities, the world as we knew it would change. "I know this is going to sound cold, but we're going to have to deal with the food later. Right now I need you to tell me about the witch. She's performing the ritual tonight? Did she say where it would take place?"

Holly's eyes squeezed shut, blocking more tears as she shook her head. I turned to Falin.

"We have to get to the mortal realm, now."

"Alex, I'm not even sure what court we're in." He stalked across the small room, glancing at the contents as if the sparse furnishings would give him a clue. I didn't know enough about the courts to make a guess, but nothing about the room made me think of a season.

Could we be in Stasis?

I froze. Stasis. A powerful witch who was a changeling. A changeling who'd recently been freed but was still not truly free.

A sick feeling crawled down my skin. I knew someone who fit all those qualities.

Rianna.

"Holly, what did the witch look like?" I asked, and my voice came out low, distant.

"I—" She shook her head. "I don't know. She wore a cloak."

Damn. When I'd first seen Rianna under the Blood Moon, when she'd still been Coleman's bound and subservient Shadow Girl, she'd worn a gray cloak. No. I couldn't suspect my childhood friend of being a heartless murderer.

Or could I?

I'd felt the killer's hope, her joy in that circle by the river. Tiddlywinx had said the witch wanted to be with her love. If the ritual was opening a way to be with true love, that might cause a lot of hope and joy. Love can cause great and terrible things.

I sank down on my heels, falling away from Holly as I clutched my own knees.

The pieces fit. The timing fit. Rianna knew what I could do. She'd asked me for help around the same time this started. She'd also returned my dagger, which was now following me around and had a tendency to tear holes in reality when used. It fit.

"Alex, what is it?" Falin asked, staring down at me.

I looked around. This room might be in my own castle. It couldn't be Rianna. But it all fit.

No, not all. What about Desmond? I suspected that he loved her, and there was nothing keeping them apart. And if Rianna was the accomplice and already hunting me when I came to Faerie, why didn't she trap me then?

So it doesn't all fit. I breathed out a sigh as that little bit of hope created enough room in my chest for me to breathe. But not much. The sick, dread-laced feeling still gripped me hard.

I stood and turned toward Kyran. "You said you can get us to Nekros without passing through the winter court?"

He flashed me a grin. "My dear, I can most likely find the shadow of the witch you seek, but I believe we must hurry. Time is running out." He peered into his hourglass again.

I stared at the rushing sand and again asked, "What happens when it runs out?"

"A moment in time, nothing more. But one I do not wish to miss."

Right. "Let's go." We had a shadow to find and a ritual to stop.

"This would be the one," the nightmare kingling said as the shadows in the nightmare realm separated to show the one, or really, the shadows, that he meant.

The shadows danced, leaping and twisting against the pale sand. Not just one or two shadows either, but more than a dozen, all in constant motion. I stared at it. *This can't be right.* There was too much movement. Too many people. It looked more like a party.

"Perhaps a little farther from the action." Kyran lifted his arms and the shadows slid across the sand. The shapes that replaced them were large and too formless for me to decipher what had cast them, but at least they were still. "This, I think, shall do nicely," he said.

I nodded. As long as we ended up safely in the city we had a better chance of finding the accomplice—*not Rianna, please not Rianna*—than if we were stuck in Faerie. I waited, but Kyran made no move to lead us through the shadow.

"I have a confession," he said, turning toward me. "This is the door you need, but I can't open it."

What did he mean he couldn't open it? Falin's hand on my waist twitched.

I swallowed around the lump suddenly lodged in my throat, but tried to keep my voice level as I asked, "Do we need another shadow?"

Kyran shook his head. "My power does not let me open doors into the mortal realm. But yours will."

Damn. And this would be the catch. "What happens if I open a door?"

"You can freely walk from the nightmare realm to the mortal realm until dawn moves the shadows and the realms no longer touch."

No wiggle room in that statement, so it had to be true. *What does he stand to gain?* It hit me suddenly. "If we can walk through, the nightmares can, too."

"Very good," he said with a smile, genuinely pleased.

"Alex, what is he talking about?" Holly whispered, stepping closer to me. I hadn't told her anything about the whole feykin planeweaver thing. Looked like I'd have some explaining to do—if we survived this. But not now.

I shook my head. "Later, Holl." I focused on Kyran again. He stood with his hands in his pockets, all his weight on one leg, the other knee slack, as if whatever decision I came to made no difference to him. "What will the nightmares do in the mortal realm?"

He shrugged. "The same thing they do here. Cause terror. Fear nourishes them." He glanced at the hourglass. Only a thin line of sand remained in the top globe. "You are running out of time."

I looked at the hourglass. "What happens when the sand runs out?"

He smirked. "Ah, finally, you've asked three times," he said, and I remembered too late that three was often significant. A weight stretched between us. It wasn't quite the same feeling as when a debt opened, but it was the same sort of magic. "The hourglass counts the moments until all doors open when the planes merge—or the moment in which that is prevented. Hard to say which, but one way or the other, it will happen soon."

Damn. He really had been screwing with me this whole time. I glanced at the hourglass. At the rate the sand was falling, it had maybe twenty minutes until the top globe ran out of sand. *And then the world as we know it will change. Or someone will stop the ritual.*

I swallowed the bitter taste in my throat and stared at the shadows surrounding me. *A few hours of nightmares, or a world where all known and unknown realities converge.* Or maybe I was overestimating my evolvement. Maybe the collectors would stop this all on their own. Or the cops. Or some random good citizen who just happened to stumble by. *But can I take that gamble?*

I looked at Falin. "What do I do?"

He shook his head. "I would say the lesser harm for the greater good, but I cannot make this choice for you."

"I'm voting for stopping the bad guys," Holly said. She

was a DA—her life was all about putting the bad guys away. She wiped her palms on her silk PJ bottoms. *Nervous sweat?* "I guess this will be a little more hands-on than my normal approach," she said, flashing me a weak smile. "But someone deserves a hefty serving of revenge."

Nightmares it is. Except one problem. "I don't know how to open a door." I'd tried before; it hadn't worked.

"Yes, I did see your attempt in the shadow court," the kingling said as he circled the hourglass.

"You *saw*?" That meant he'd been watching me long before I'd fallen through that nightmare. For all I knew, he'd sent my bad dreams.

He clasped his hands behind his head so his elbows framed his face. "The planebender bent Faerie—hence the name. He took two places that normally don't touch and shoved them until they collided and a door could be opened between them. Very messy and very forceful. Your power is not. It is not your nature to shove realities around. Your power is to weave planes together."

"And why do you know so much about planeweavers?"

Kyran only smiled. "This shadow exists both here and in the mortal realm. They sit directly on top of each other. All you need to do is tie them together so you can walk between them."

Oh, yeah, real easy.

But I had to try.

I handed PC to Holly. I didn't want to be holding him while I tried to manipulate unfamiliar magic. If something went horribly wrong, I didn't want him caught in the side effects.

Then I lowered my shields and focused on the shadow closest to me. I mentally reached for it, touching it with my power and trying to concentrate on the fact that it not only existed here but also was being cast by something in the mortal realm. At first all I saw was a shadow over sand. Then the shadow deepened, darkened, and I could tell it was being cast by a tree. Actually, more than one tree. I could see them. *It worked?*

A chattering sounded in the dark around me. Then the darkness surged forward. Somewhere behind me Holly screamed, but the nightmares weren't after us. They were aiming for the door and there was no stopping them. The nightmares poured through the door I'd opened—dozens, hundreds. Maybe thousands.

I swallowed, watching the monsters I'd released escape into the unsuspecting mortal realm. *Let this have been the right choice.* Then the nightmares were gone, the darkness strangely empty without them.

"What were *those*?" Holly asked, still breathless from screaming.

No one answered. Falin scowled at the opening, and I wondered if he still thought the reaper and accomplice's threat was more dangerous than what I'd released. But it was done now.

Kyran lifted the hourglass, using the pole it stood on as a walking stick. He damn near skipped as he headed for the door. "Coming?" he asked, glancing first at me and then at the hourglass. Only a sliver of sand remained. "Looks like the end, one way or the other, will be soon."

Chapter 37

❧═══◦ ◦═══❧

I stepped through the shadow into total darkness.

Oh, the nightmare realm had been dark and full of shadows that were more physical than any shadow had a right to be, but during my hours in Faerie I'd become accustomed to seeing the world illuminated with no obvious source of light. When I stepped through the doorway I'd created, reality crashed down on me with a darkness that crawled across my vision and left me blind. The weight of the grave, which I'd been blessedly free from for several hours, also returned to bash its chilled fists against my shields.

"Fuck," I whispered, my head swinging back and forth as I tried to make out something, anything.

A hand closed over my mouth as an arm snaked around my waist and I froze, a scream brewing in my chest. But the arm dragging me backward was a familiar warm without being hot.

Falin.

I let him move me as I continued to blink, trying to focus. Cloth brushed against bark as he pressed us both into the cover of a tree, but still I couldn't see. I blinked at the impenetrable darkness filling my vision. It didn't help. I was blind. I probably had been since the fight with the hydra. Faerie just liked my eyes better.

Damn. I cracked my shields, trembling as the first traces

of grave essence dug deeper into my psyche, but as I released my shields, the shadows parted.

"Cut the light show," Falin hissed, his voice a harsh whisper.

"I need to see." Because I definitely wasn't hot on the idea of walking around blind, especially if Kyran was correct and this was near the accomplice's ritual. I looked around, trying to get my bearings.

When I'd first realized the shadows were cast by trees, I'd thought we were in a forest, but now I saw we were in a small wooded patch in one of Nekros's parks. In the distance I could hear the rush of the river, and a few feet in front of the tree Falin had pressed me behind was a large, emerald green wall.

A wall that was breathing.

"Is that a dragon?" Holly asked from where she knelt behind an unkempt bush huddled against my tree. Her fingers trembled as she clutched the amulet that she once again wore around her neck with one hand and PC with the other. Or maybe it was PC trembling. He was remarkably quiet, so he obviously realized something was wrong.

"A construct," I said.

"Yeah, and there are two more," Falin whispered as he eased his daggers out of their sheaths.

His blade glimmered in the moonlight drifting through the tree limbs as he pointed. On the other side of the clearing a blue dragon stretched wings that must have been twenty yards across, which caused a silver dragon to pause as it paced the outskirts of the clearing. No, the dragons weren't pacing. More like patrolling.

The three constructs were guarding a circle that had been erected in the center of the clearing. The barrier buzzed a faint red in my senses, preventing me from feeling the magic inside the circle, but I could *see* the energy and it swirled in a chaotic storm. The shadows we'd seen in the nightmare realm truly were dancers. They spun and leapt through the air as the magic whipped around them like they were cogs in a giant magical conductor. And in the very center of the circle stood a hooded figure playing a pair of panpipes that looked a little too real in my second sight. *The relic the collectors are searching for.*

"Come on, be here," Holly whispered as she patted her pockets. A smile broke across her face and she pulled out her cell phone. She cued the phone to display our GPS location—the riverwalk park not far from the Magic Quarter—and then dialed 911.

"Tell them to bring the really big guns," I muttered, staring across the clearing. The accomplice stood inside the circle, but where was the reaper?

He wasn't in the clearing, or in what I could see of the trees beyond. I peeked farther around the tree and Falin dragged me back.

"You'll give away our position. Look at me," he said, and then reached up and placed his palms over my eyes. When he pulled back an extra weight pressed against my face. I lifted my fingers, but he grabbed my hand, stopping me. "They're just sunglasses to dampen the glow of your eyes, but don't touch. Your magic tends to screw with glamour."

Good point. I dropped my hand as I peeked out from our hiding spot again. Still no reaper, but we did have the accomplice. *Death said to summon him once I located the accomplice.* I activated the spell he'd pressed into my skin and a blaze of unfamiliar magic surged through me, building, until it burst from my skin.

I rubbed my gloved hands over my arms to chase off the tingle the spell had left behind. *Well, now I know how a flare gun feels.* I looked around, expecting Death to just miraculously appear. He didn't.

Okay, then. I glanced back at the ritual. Magic continued to build in the circle as the dancers twisted and jumped. I shivered, remembering the pain I'd felt in the last ritual site.

"We've got to disrupt that spell." The amount of energy in the circle had grown thick enough to stain the air like multicolored fog. I blinked. *That can't be.* Clutching PC, I peeked out from our cover. Falin grabbed my shoulder as if he was afraid I'd rush into the clearing, and I pressed myself against the tree. "Is it just me, or are the tops of their heads vanishing?"

Everyone peeked out to see. Holly threw a hand over her mouth and made a small strangled noise, but she didn't scream. Falin only nodded, his face grim.

Goose bumps prickled over my skin, my dread reaching the saturation point and trying to pour out of my skin. Death had said souls were the fuel of life, and I'd thought he was hinting only at the souls powering the constructs. But this ritual . . . I stared at the slowly dissolving bodies. This ritual was being fueled by the dancers—by their movement and by their very essence, body and soul. *Those feet . . .* All those feet. All lefts, and none with tool marks. *And when I raised the shade, the foot had forgotten it had a body, and it had danced.* It was the dance. They would dance until there wasn't enough left of them to complete the next dance step. Until they were only a single foot. *We have to stop this.*

I turned to Falin. "I suppose suggesting that you shoot the piper would be too easy a solution to actually work?"

"We were in Faerie," he said with a grimace. *Which means no gun.* "The only weapons I have on me are the daggers, but they're enchanted and would never make it through the circle."

Damn.

"So we have to break that circle." *But how?*

"I have an idea." Holly said. "Can I borrow a knife?"

I nodded and squatted as I struggled with the skirt of my gown. Curses burned my tongue as I wrestled with the material blocking my boots, but I bit them back. Once I drew the dagger, I passed it to Holly and she handed me PC. The small dog's ears quivered, but he looked up at me with eyes that trusted I'd get him home safe. I wished I had the same confidence.

Holly used the dagger to scrape a sheet of bark from the tree and I felt her tap into her stored magic as she used the blade to carve small runes into the bark. Her magic surged, settling into the makeshift charm, and she let out a breath that sounded like she'd been holding it a long time. Jabbing the blade of the dagger into the dirt by her feet, she lifted the bark, examining the carvings. Then she passed it to me. "Disruption charm."

I accepted the charm, feeling it tingle over my fingers. Damn, she was good. I couldn't have crafted this charm on a good day, and she'd done it without a ritual or a circle and with only the magic she had stored on her person.

With a disruption charm, all we would have to do was touch it to the circle and the charm should bring the entire barrier down. But first we'd have to get the charm past the dragons guarding the ritual.

"Think you could hit that circle from here?" I asked, passing the charm to Falin.

Falin balanced the bark-turned-charm in his hand, bouncing it to check the weight. Then he shook his head. "It's too light. I'd never be able to throw it that far."

Which meant that one of us had to carry it to the circle. *But how do we get past the dragons?* I chewed at my bottom lip. One dragon we might be able to take. It would be a hell of a challenge, but probably not impossible. But three? I shook my head. We needed help.

Where are those collectors? I poked at the spell again, just to make sure I'd really activated it the first time. No rush of magic this time, so I trusted that the first wave I'd felt worked.

"I have another idea," Holly said, but her eyes didn't meet mine when I turned. "We can cause a disturbance, draw the dragons away, and someone small, someone who wouldn't be noticed, can affix the disruption charm to the side of the circle."

"Someone small?" That definitely knocked Falin out of the running, and I was far from short. Holly was petite, but I didn't think she meant herself. Her eyes darted to where PC sat in my lap. "No. No, no, definitely not. Holly, he's a dog."

"He's tiny, and the dragons are huge. They probably won't even be able to see him."

She had a point, but . . . I clutched PC closer. Still shaking my head.

"It's not a bad plan," Falin said. "Though I suggest we plan to become dragon bait only if they notice PC. Holly and I can take positions on either side of the clearing and you can send him at the circle from the center. If one of the dragons notices him, the person closest will attack. I'm sure the beasts are charmed to protect the circle from human-shaped threats, not from tiny dogs."

His argument didn't make my head stop shaking. If anything, it made me dislike the plan more. If someone did have to distract a dragon, that someone would be alone. I didn't like it. Not at all.

I glanced at the circle. The dancers had dissolved to the point that most no longer had eyes, so their faces went up to the center of their noses and then stopped. They were dead. All of them. Oh, they kept dancing, but there was no saving them now. Of course, there was more than just the lives in that circle at stake. I shuddered, staring at the energy coalescing behind the piper. *How much does she need to smash all the planes into reality?*

"Alex?"

Death. I spun in my crouch, expecting dozens of collectors, but found only Death, the gray man, and the raver.

"I was expecting more."

"More?" Holly asked, unable to see the collectors.

"We were the closest," the gray man said, crouching to stay out of view. Right, Holly and Falin might not be able to see the collectors, but the constructs could.

The raver shook her head as she sank into a crouch. "Damn, those things are huge."

Falin had clearly figured out that the collectors had arrived because his narrowed gaze was fixed on the space I was talking to. "Three of them?" he asked.

He was good. I nodded.

Death scoped the clearing, his jaw set hard as he knelt again. "We have to find a way inside that circle."

And we were back to the circle.

Falin explained the plan currently on the table despite my running protest. He might not have been able to see or hear the collectors, but he knew they could hear him. And, unfortunately, they liked the plan. I was outvoted five to two—because I figured if PC understood what was going on, he'd vote against the idea.

But they were right. If one of us tried to run to the clearing and place the charm, the dragons would be on us in seconds. Using PC, we might avoid detection by the dragons until after the barrier was down. *Maybe*. I hated the plan, but they were right.

Falin affixed the charmed bark to PC's collar with a bit of ribbon made from glamour. In theory, since PC was a null, he would soar through the barrier as though it didn't exist, but the glamour and the charm would stick and the disruption spell would activate. Or at least that was the plan.

"Ready?" Falin asked.

Holly nodded, her freckles standing out hard on her pale face. I let out a deep breath that tasted of sour fear, but I nodded. Then the gray man went with Holly and the raver went with Falin. Death stayed with me.

I knelt in the underbrush, rubbing PC's head, Death by my side.

"We're going to watch out for him," he said, and I nodded again. I noticed he didn't say that PC would be okay. The same quality that made PC useful for this job would make him hard to keep tabs on once things turned nasty. "They are in position by now."

I know. I crab-walked forward, carrying PC until we were almost in the clearing. If the dragons focused on my hiding spot I was screwed, but PC needed a straight line of sight for the circle.

I placed the small dog in the grass in front of me. He turned, immediately trying to climb back in my lap. *Smart dog.* I set him down again and shook my hand like I had a toy. He looked at my hand, his ears pricking with curiosity. I made a soft squeaking noise with my mouth, and PC's tail lifted, wagging. It took a moment of shaking and squeaking, but I riled him up enough about the imaginary toy that he wouldn't take his eyes off my hand. Then, in the ultimate act of deception, I reared my arm back and pretended to hurl the toy at the circle.

PC dashed after the imaginary toy. The small dog was a tiny streak of gray and white crossing the grass. As planned, he charged the edge of the circle. Cleared it. The disruption spell stayed behind. Streaks of red lightning shot through the barrier around the spell, the sparks spreading like a fast-creeping frost.

Come on, PC, come back. He stopped just inside the circle, his tail tucked as the dancers pounded past him, but he was still searching for the toy, his little head swinging back and forth.

I hadn't exactly forgotten about the dragons, obviously, but I was so focused on my dog that I didn't notice the ap-

proaching green dragon until a huge muzzle filled the space
in front of me. The muzzle stopped, one giant nostril ridged
with shiny green scales inches from my face. I froze, not
moving, not breathing, not even blinking.

The dragon's nostril flared, and the force of its inhaled
breath dragged air across my face, making my hair and
gown flutter. The dragon lifted its head and the giant muzzle disappeared. The muscles in my legs went soft with the
sudden sense of relief falling through me. Relief felt too
soon.

The head reappeared, the dragon peering into my hiding spot with an enormous red eye. The slitted pupil con-
tracted, focusing. *Damn.*

I threw my shields open farther. Each construct I'd
fought had been more solid, more real, than the last, and
the dragon was the most real yet. But I knew it was a spell
fueled by souls and wrapped in a glamour. I *knew* it. I just
had to convince reality.

In my second sight, the eye was a swirling mass of nearly
solid mist, the color and shape superimposed over top.
Clenching my fist, I thrust my hand into the construct's eye.
My skin encountered a moist resistance, and I rejected the
sensation. It didn't exist.

The eye vanished. The dragon didn't.

The dragon roared in rage as its eye disappeared, only
an empty socket of white mist remaining. It jerked back,
swiping me with the edge of its head. My breath exploded
out of my lungs as I flew backward, but there was no time
to recover before the enraged beast charged. One massive
paw uprooted a tree as it reached for me and missed. Death
grabbed me under the arms, hauling me to my feet, but
then we both had to dive out of the way as the dragon
lunged.

We scurried behind a tree, but we needed to either keep
moving or turn and fight because the tree wasn't going to
stop the construct. And worse, its bellows of rage had the
other two dragons running toward us. *Fuck! Now what?*

I peeked around the tree in time to see a silver blur dive
in front of the dragon. Falin's soul blazed brightly in my
vision as he dodged the dragon's swipe and then grabbed
the talon on the back of the dragon's foot and used it to

vault onto the beast's leg. He grabbed the wing where it connected to the body, and hauled himself higher, scrambling for the creature's long neck. The rampaging beast didn't even seem to notice Falin until the fae wedged his daggers between the dragon's thick scales, digging for its spinal column.

Then the dragon thrashed.

It craned its neck and beat at Falin with its wings, but Falin clung to the daggers, wedging them deeper. Unable to reach the source causing it pain, the dragon rolled, its claws swiping out as it hit the ground. Falin dropped, diving into his own roll to avoid the beast's lethal talons. The daggers didn't follow, but the dragon didn't die. It straightened, climbing to its feet and shaking dirt and uprooted grass from its scales.

"We have to help," I yelled, picking up the skirt of my gown and rushing forward.

I reached with my power and grabbed at the souls inside the beast, ripping them free. I'd forcibly ejected three souls by the time I reached the edge of the clearing, and Falin had scrambled back up the dragon's back. Death and the raver joined the fight, jerking souls free with every move. Previous constructs had shrunk with each soul freed, but either the spell had been improved or this thing had a lot of extra souls fueling it, because it didn't change.

I fell back, avoiding a large claw, and jerked another soul free as Falin ripped his daggers out of the dragon's neck. He thrust the blades between another pair of scales, and the dragon froze. Its jaw dropped, as if shocked; then its form exploded into a cloud of fog. A copper disk the size of an end table hit the ground. Falin landed beside it, his blades in his hands, and his gaze already on the two approaching dragons.

"Look out," Holly yelled as she emerged from the woods.

My head snapped in the direction she pointed. The magic circle now had bright red cracks like blood veins snaking through the barrier, and at the point where the disruption charm touched it, the barrier bulged, the thick magic inside pressing against the weak spot. Like a crack in a dam, the magic began trickling out around the charm. The full force of the magic would be next.

I turned, intending to run for the shelter of the trees. I didn't have time.

Arms grabbed me, dragging me down and pressing me flat. Magic roared across my back, tearing at the bit of skin exposed on my shoulders. The smell of singed hair and burned clothing met my nose as the shock of the blast faded. I struggled to push to my knees and discovered that not one but two bodies covered mine.

"Let me up, guys," I said, sliding out from the tangle of arms. "Everyone okay?"

I received an immediate nod from Death. Falin just rolled to his feet and offered me a hand up. *Well, the three of us survived.* I glanced around to assess the rest of the group.

A second copper disk lay on the ground, the dragon apparently having gotten caught in the crush of the magical tide. The other dragon was missing, momentarily at least. The gray man and the raver hadn't bothered taking cover from the blast and they looked fine. I didn't see Holly or PC. My throat cramped. The dog had been inside the circle last I'd seen. The blast wouldn't have caught him from the inside. The dancers all still spun and leapt, so clearly the explosion of magic had affected only those of us outside.

But where is Holly?

Then I saw her red hair as she passed a dancer who had dissolved down to his sternum. With the circle down, the spell on the enchanted panpipes had spread. All the dancers glowed the light yellow color I associated with humans. As the only other human in the clearing, Holly had been called to the dance.

Chapter 38

"Holly!"
Her head swiveled in my direction, her green eyes huge and terrified, but she didn't stop dancing. She couldn't. The circle was gone and the magic dispersed around the clearing, but it wasn't like the magic vanished. The piper continued to play, the spell taking shape behind her.

I dashed forward only to be knocked back by a blast of air. Dirt and leaves swirled around me as the last remaining dragon swooped out of the sky. It landed between me and the broken circle, blocking the way. Falin grabbed my shoulders, pulling me farther from the beast. It opened its mouth and fire filled the air. A wall of heat cut across our path.

Damn it.

"We have to stop the piper." Because regardless of who was under that cloak, she was not going to dissolve my best friend.

The dragon fanned silvery wings and released another ball of fire. I dove to the right, Death and Falin at my side, and the raver and the gray man dove in the opposite direction. The air heated, my lungs burning with each panicked breath. I glanced at the destroyed circle. Holly still danced, and she still looked whole, but . . . *How long will that last?*

"Distract it," I yelled over the wall of flames now separating Death, Falin, and me from the raver and the gray man.

"Distract it how?" the gray man called back as I fought to draw my dagger. "Think it would like a sonnet?"

As if in response, the dragon slashed at the gray man, its wickedly sharp claws slicing through the air. He dove aside, and the construct caught grass.

Now or never. I dashed forward, Falin and Death on my heels.

Falin lifted his dagger as he ran. He changed his grip as if he would hurl the dagger, but as his eyes cut over the dancers, he shook his head. "I can't get a clear shot."

I didn't stop running, but sent my power ahead of me. The dancers were dead. My power recognized that fact. A dead body wasn't a natural place for a soul. I reached through the spell that kept the bodies dancing as if it weren't there, and the souls popped free. Five bodies collapsed, the spell releasing them now that they couldn't fuel the ritual. A clear window to the piper opened.

We'd reached the edge of the broken circle, and Falin threw his dagger without changing stride. The blade gleamed in the moonlight, the fae-wrought steel unmarred in my grave-sight. His aim was good. Perfect. The piper looked up as the blade approached, her cloak flaring with the movement.

Then everything went wrong.

The long-coated reaper appeared. He knocked the piper aside, and the fae blade passed harmlessly through his torso. He turned, a snarl-like smile curling his lips as he focused on us.

The piper hit the ground, and the music stopped. All around us, dancing bodies froze, dead muscles turning stiff. They collapsed, hitting the trampled grass with fleshy thumps. Only one dancer remained standing, her red hair wild around her face and her cheeks glistening.

Holly's hands flew to her head, her fingers digging along her scalp. "I'm all here, right? I'm not . . . ?"

"You're good." I didn't stop running. The piper was already picking herself off the ground. I shot Holly a desperate glance. "Get out of earshot of that spell."

"What about you?"

I didn't tell her I'd be fine—that might have been a lie. My grip tightened on the dagger and a small dog yipped. PC jumped over a leg twisted unnaturally under a fallen dancer, and I almost stopped, my sprint cut short as a wave of relief washed through me. But I didn't have time to celebrate yet.

"Take PC with you," I yelled to Holly.

"But—"

I wasn't listening anymore. The reaper opened his coat and pulled a looped whip from a strap in his belt. The whip rustled as it uncoiled. He flicked his wrist and a loud crack thundered through the clearing. I faltered, my hands covering my ears without conscious thought on my part. Then a new sound competed with the ringing in my ears.

Pipe music filled the night, and my body responded to the sound. *No. No. I wouldn't dance.*

I couldn't help but move, my feet leading me in a turn, a leap. And I wasn't the only one. Falin, his teeth gritted and his hand clenched around his remaining blade, also danced. *She's playing for fae souls now.* Only she wasn't playing. The pipes played themselves, the magic coalescing in the air streaming through them.

"Rianna, why?" I cried as my legs carried me in the dance.

The piper turned, her cloak moving as she tilted her head. Then she pushed the hood back and I wasn't staring at Rianna's sunken green eyes and lank red hair but at the face of a stranger. Relief coursed through me, though it didn't last.

"You should have helped me. Told me how you touched the dead. Opened realities for me," she said, frowning at me, and I realized with a sick sense of shock that I recognized her more handsome than pretty features.

"You're the woman from the Bloom. The one who thanked me for releasing you from the endless dance."

"Yes." She smiled, but it was a smile cut with sadness and darkened with hate. "Trapping me in the Eternal Dance was some fool's idea of an ironic punishment, but you freed me and soon nothing and no one will keep me from my love."

Her love. *The reaper.*

Another crack cut through the air from the reaper's whip, but I didn't have enough control over my body to cringe, let alone twist to see what was happening. The piper—Edana, that was what she had called herself—closed her eyes, her head tilting back as magic coursed through her and the pipes. No, not just magic. An unstable gap opened behind her, the edges wavering, flickering through planes of existence.

No. She couldn't merge realities.

But she was.

I struggled against the spell, fought to stop dancing. To still myself. My body continued twisting and jumping.

Beyond the circle, the gray man and the raver fought the dragon, jerking souls free one after the other, but the construct didn't shrink. A leap and swirl in the dance turned me away from Edana so I couldn't see the spreading rift. But I could see the reaper. His whip snaked outward, wrapping around Death's neck. Death winced, but grabbed the length of the whip, holding it immobile as the reaper tried to jerk him forward. Death held his ground, not budging.

Then magic slammed into his back.

Death toppled forward, falling to his knees. A woman's laugh twined with the pipe music. I couldn't see Edana, but I could see the thick black lines of the spell she'd hurled. A spell with lines not only slamming magic into Death but pulling something out of him as well.

His essence.

"You're exactly what we need," she said, and the dance turned me, bringing her into view again.

"Stop. Leave him alone!"

She glanced at me. "You'll have your own time to fuel the spell. Be patient."

I swallowed. Falin and I were both part of the spell now. I could see him in my peripheral vision, still whole and alive. The spell holding us was killing us slowly. Whatever she was doing to Death was draining him fast.

I have to stop her.

Grave essence leached off the fallen dancers' bodies, the magic their souls had generated filled the air, and Aetheric energy shot through all of it. The gap had spread, the bodies closest to the center of the circle rotting away as the land of the dead touched them. Aetheric energy swirled in the air, dark tendrils wrapping around Edana as if she'd plugged herself into the very fabric of the magic realm.

I forced my shields wider, opening myself to everything, blocking nothing. The chill of the grave rushed into my body, but there was more magic to be had than just grave essence. I drew it in indiscriminately, pulling power until my skin felt ready to burst. Then I let it explode out of me, hurtling toward Edana.

She wasn't a corpse, so my power couldn't sink into her, or jerk her soul free of her body. It slid over her skin, her life and her shields protecting her. *No.* I had to do something. I *had* to.

Fred had told me that when the world decayed I'd have to do what was against my nature. According to Kyran, my nature was to weave reality together, but I could also shove it apart. So that's what I did.

I shoved.

With everything I had inside me, I shoved at the realities converging around Edana. I started at her skin, pushing outward. As it had when I'd been in the shadow court, reality buckled and then moved under my magic's touch. I poured more power into the effort, thrusting with my magic. The enchanted pipes slipped out of Edana's hands as though she could no longer hold them, and the music stopped.

I tumbled to the ground, my legs collapsing under me. My whole body shook, a darkening light-headedness threatening behind my eyes. Still I pushed with my power. Layers of reality peeled away from Edana, leaving an area like a giant bubble around her clear of everything but mortal reality.

The spell draining Death fizzled out of existence. He slumped forward, and I released the power channeling through me. I tried to climb to my feet, but all my limbs were numb, too heavy, too slow. A scream interrupted the sound of my teeth chattering.

Edana backed through the gap she'd opened, and the bubble I'd created moved with her. Layers of reality pushed aside, bunching around the tear. As they fell back into place, the already tenuous gap snapped closed, reality righting itself everywhere except the bubble I'd created around her.

Edana screamed again, still backing away. "No! What have you done? What have you done?"

The reaper dropped the whip, letting it fall to the grass as he ran toward her. "Love, what is it?" he asked and then stopped short three feet away. Right on the edge of the bubble.

He couldn't pass. His reality didn't exist around her.

He pounded on the empty air. "No! What's happening?"

As Edana lifted hands suddenly withered and liver-spotted to her rapidly wrinkling face, I wondered the same thing. Before my eyes, she aged until her back bent and her skin turned paper thin around a skeletal frame. Then she crumbled, turning to dust.

I swallowed. I'd cut her off from all realities, all magics. Even Faerie. And changelings relied on Faerie's magic to keep their years from catching up with them. Soon all that was left of Edana was a dim, sickly yellow ghost standing in the middle of a dead spot. But the land of the dead didn't exist in the bubble, and her energy dissipated as she tried to retain a sense of herself.

Then she faded from sight.

"No!" the reaper yelled, still pushing on the bubble of reality. Then he spun around to face me. "You." His eyes were hard, fierce, and if I could have backed away, I would have. But my body still wasn't working.

The reaper stormed toward me, the air crackling around him. "You did this. You took her away from me." He lunged for me, his fist slamming into—and through—my chest wall.

"Alex!" Death jumped to his unsteady feet.

He wouldn't be fast enough. We both knew it. The other two collectors had finished off the dragon, but they were still too far away to get to me in time.

I stared at where the reaper's wrists disappeared into my sternum, knowing what would come next. He would pull my soul free and it would be over.

Then something flickered in the moonlight as it soared over my head. A fae-wrought blade buried itself in the reaper's chest. He blinked at it, as if he couldn't believe it, and his hand fell from me. Falin's dagger fell free as soon as the reaper released me and I stopped acting as a bridge between him and reality. But the damage was already done. Dark blood seeped from the chest wound, and the raver grabbed him from behind.

She wrapped her long fingers around his upper arms. "End of the line," she said, and they vanished.

Falin pulled me to my feet, and held me there when I would have fallen. "I've got you," he whispered. "Are you okay? Is he gone?"

I nodded, leaning into Falin. My soul might be a bit jarred, but I would make it. Death finally reached me, but the gray man grabbed his arm, pulling him back.

"She's fine," the gray man said. "I'll make certain of that, but in the meantime, you need to go." When Death would have protested, he shook his head. "Go."

Death frowned, his gaze moving to me again. Then he vanished.

The gray man strolled across the grass, collecting the half-dissolved souls of the late dancers. His roundabout route brought him directly in front of me, and he stared at me, whether studying or assessing, I wasn't sure.

"Remember this day. Remember this place," he said, sweeping a hand out to encompass the remains of the ritual. "This is why the two of you can never be." He stared at me for another long moment. Then he vanished.

The two of us? Death and me.

I frowned at the empty space where he'd been for a long time until a rustling in the trees behind us caused Falin to turn, taking me with him. Kyran walked into the clearing, still carrying his hourglass, all the sand now in the bottom half.

"Brava, brava," he said, leaning the staff in the crook of his arm so he could offer an exaggerated clap. "I must say, I was a bit worried about the dragons at one point, but splendid job."

"You were watching the whole time?" I asked around my chattering teeth.

"But of course. I said I wouldn't miss it. Well, my dear, I believe we are about to get more company." He gave me a small bow. "Until you dream again."

He disappeared into the woods just as Holly stepped

into the clearing. She carried PC under one arm and in her wake stormed several ABMU officers in full tactical gear.

I glanced around. Falin and I were the only ones left standing in a field of dark magic and bodies. *How come when I end up in these situations, the bad guys have always disintegrated?*

Chapter 39

❖❖❖ ❖❖❖

I sat in the middle of my bed, huddled under blankets. I hadn't spent a night in jail this time, which had shocked the hell out of me considering that most of the witnesses to what had happened were soul collectors and not inclined to speak to the police. While I'd walked the detectives through a heavily edited version of the events surrounding Edana's ritual, I'd remembered Edana had owed me a debt. *I might not have had to destroy her.* Not that I'd meant to completely remove her from all planes—I'd needed to stop her. And I'd done that. But now I had more blood on my hands.

The explanation of what had happened had stretched my newfound inability to lie, so the police knew more than Faerie was likely to appreciate. Of course, the fae weren't the only ones with things they would rather that mortals did not know tied up in this mess—the collectors had more than a few of their own secrets precariously close to the surface of the tale. And, speaking of soul collectors, I hadn't seen Death since he disappeared. It had been only a day, and it wasn't like he showed up daily, but I was worried about him. I was also worried about what the gray man had said.

Though I hadn't seen Death, I couldn't keep Falin from hovering. I'd lost even my psychic sight by the time we were released from the crime scene, and my vision hadn't improved with sleep. So now I sat on the bed, listening to the news because I couldn't see it.

". . . Still no explanation for the bizarre dreams that attacked the city two nights ago." Lusa's broadcast voice mixed with the sound of static before clearing. "While nightmares are a common occurrence often brought on by stress and other life events, the sheer number of people who called police in the early morning hours because they thought their dreams were real has led some experts to speculate that outside forces might be involved. Despite the number of emergency calls, no one was hurt, but the OMIH continues to investigate. In other news . . ."

I tuned out the TV as the bed shifted under Falin's weight. He pressed a steaming mug into my hands, and the scent of rich coffee met my nose. Then he lifted the comforter from my shoulders so he could slide closer before wrapping us both in the covers again. My skin reacted to more than just his body heat, and I focused on the mug of coffee I couldn't see.

I didn't know whether to enjoy the giddiness that erupted in my body with every stray touch of Falin's body, or to run and deny the emotion. How could I very much want to be here, right now, with Falin and still be worried about Death? I ached to see Death and know he was okay, to see that easy smile that hid so many secrets, and to know what might have happened if there hadn't been a hydra at that bridge. *I feel like I'm trying to run in opposite directions at the same time.*

Not that anything too serious could happen between Falin and me. Not at the moment, at least. Holly had taken PC for a walk and was due back any second.

Poor Holly. She had attempted to eat mortal food after we returned home, but it turned to ash on her tongue. She could never again eat any food but Faerie food—if we figured out how to get her some.

Falin had left a message at the Bloom for Rianna. I hoped that she'd be able to send Ms. B or Desmond with food for Holly, but if that wouldn't work, we'd have to think of something else. Which might mean sending Holly to my castle to live. She'd moped around my apartment for most of the last day, the three of us taking comfort in each other's company and avoiding discussion of any important topics like changelings, planeweavers, or the queen's bloodied hands.

"So if fae can't say 'thank you,' how do they express appreciation?" I asked, thinking about the fact that I couldn't thank Falin for saving my life. Of course, I guess I'd also saved his, so we were probably even.

He brushed my hair away from my neck and leaned closer. "Gifts or gestures. Actions that say more than words ever could." He brushed a kiss on the spot where my neck met my shoulder and a shiver traveled through my body, nearly making me spill my coffee.

He scooted closer, his heat sliding over my back. Then a loud knock sounded on the front door, and I jumped. That time I *did* spill the coffee.

Holly let herself in, PC scampering around her, his nails clicking on the hardwood. As soon as she released him from his leash, he pitched himself onto the bed and planted himself in my lap. Holly sat on the bed a moment later, the mattress shifting slightly under her weight, but she couldn't have settled herself before another knock sounded on the door.

It opened, and I felt Falin stiffen. "My queen," he whispered, sliding to his feet.

Oh, crap. What was the Winter Queen doing at my house? I tugged the comforter tighter and cracked open my shields.

Nothing happened.

I'd burned out both my physical and my psychic sight. I could hear the click of her heels as she swept into my small apartment, but I couldn't see a thing.

"Hello, knight, planeweaver." She paused. "Mortal." I could imagine her unimpressed gaze assessing the mismatched furniture and the broken TV.

I considered trying to scramble off the bed, but what would I do then? Stumble around blindly? I remained in the middle of the bed, PC in my lap and a cup of coffee in my hands.

"Planeweaver, I believe our acquaintance suffered in our first meeting."

You think? Might have been something to do with her threatening to have me tortured. "Alex," I said.

"Excuse me?"

"My name is Alex. Not planeweaver."

"Al-ex." She drew the syllables out, and judging by her

tone she wasn't impressed. "What a dreadfully masculine name. I believe I will call you Lexi."

Great.

"As I was saying, Lexi, our first meeting could have gone better. As a gesture of goodwill, I have brought you your friend."

The door opened again, and I recognized the touch of familiar magic that zipped through the air.

"Caleb!" Holly yelled.

Thank goodness. I'd hoped he'd escaped when the Shadow King had helped me out of the winter court, but when we'd returned home we discovered that he was still missing. Of course, just because she'd returned Caleb didn't mean she'd freed the rest of the independents.

"What about the others?" I asked.   •

I could almost hear the stillness in the room. Then the queen's heel clicked on the floorboard, one quick *clack*, as if she'd tapped her foot.

"I will consider the idea. Now, I have heard that you have family in the shadow court and have a friendship with the upstart in the nightmare realm. Do not forget, dear Lexi, that there is something—or at least someone—who interests you in my court. While I do hate sharing my toys, I'm always willing to trade up, and having a planeweaver in my court would please me." Her skirts rustled as she turned, and the door opened. "Come along, knight. I've heard that you'll require a new abode, so you might as well show me around this dreadful city."

With that, she left, the door banging shut behind her. I thought Falin had followed, but then his hand traced the edge of my cheek, his fingers trailing into my hair as he leaned his forehead against mine.

"Don't you have to follow her?" My question was a whisper because I wanted the answer to be "no" even though I knew it wasn't. I blinked, wishing more than anything to be able to see.

"Alexis," he whispered. Then he kissed me, his lips taking possession of mine as if everything that hadn't been said could be passed through our lips, tongues, breath.

"Wow," Holly whispered behind me, and I heard Caleb clear his throat.

I didn't care. I returned that kiss. Savoring the press of his mouth, the taste of him. And knowing that this kiss was good-bye.

"Knight," the queen called from beyond the door, and Falin broke off the kiss.

But he didn't pull back. Not yet. His lips pressed a smile against mine, and he said, "Don't you dare throw out my toothbrush."

Then he was gone.